Sacrifice of Love

Grey Wolves Series, Book 7

By Quinn Loftis

Published by
Quinn Loftis at Smashwords

© 2013 Quinn Loftis Books LLC

All rights reserved. No part of this publication may be reproduced, distributed, or transmitted in any form or by any means, including photocopying, recording, or other electronic or mechanical methods, without the prior written permission of the publisher

This ebook is licensed for your personal enjoyment only. This ebook may not be re-sold or given away to other people. If you would like to share this book with another person, please purchase an additional copy for each recipient. If you're reading this book and did not purchase it, or it was not purchased for your use only, then please return it, and purchase your own copy. Thank you for respecting the hard work of this author.

Dedication

For Bo, my true mate, my best friend, my love.

ACKNOWLEDGMENTS

First and foremost, I give thanks to God for loving me in all of my un-loveliness and for blessing me and my family beyond measure.

Thank you to Bo, my best friend, my love. You are simply amazing and I am in awe of you, and humbled that you chose me.

Thank you to the Wolf Pack. You girls are amazing and I appreciate all of your support and encouragement.

Thank you to Candace Selph, all of your help and words of wisdom are invaluable and I thank God for your friendship.

Thank you to the Hell Cats for the laughs, the shout outs of encouragement, and off the wall humor that is more than likely totally inappropriate, which somehow makes it appropriate for me.

Special thanks to Tiffany King for all the texts that hollered out random bits of affection. I totally get you and I'm so blessed to know you.

Special thanks to Megan Bagley; your friendship is invaluable to me. Thank you for listening to me tell you repeatedly how funny I am…because seriously I'm freaking hilarious.

Special thanks to Susan and Leigh Ann, two ladies who have prayed for me, taken care of my son, fed my family, and listened to my endless droning about my latest book, all with smiles on their faces. Both of you are such blessings to me and I praise God for bringing you into my life

My sincerest thanks to the readers, for the long nights you have stayed up reading and embarking on adventures with these characters, for all the tears, swear words, shouts of joy, and laughter, for every friend made, for every foe defeated, for every love found. Thank you so much for sticking it out with the girls and their wolves. I am so humbled that you have loved them as much as I do. God bless you all!

Books by Quinn Loftis

Grey Wolves Series
Prince of Wolves
Blood Rites
Just One Drop
Out of the Dark
Beyond the Veil
Fate and Fury
Sacrifice of Love

Elfin Series
Elfin, Book 1
Rapture, Book 2 (Coming Winter 2013)

Stand Alone Works
Call Me Crazy

Prologue

"When I look in the mirror I see my face, my blue eyes, black hair, and strong jaw. But I don't recognize the figure staring back at me. Something inside me has changed, grown darker, and colder. My wolf rages inside, constantly fighting me for control. I know I mustn't give in. For if I do, chaos will come crashing down around us, along with lifeless bodies."

~Fane

Fane felt sweat dripping from his brow as he ran. His lungs burned with effort as he tried to suck in more air. He could see her just up ahead. She was crying and screaming for him to help her.

"I'm coming!" he yelled.

His footfalls pounded against the earth, seeming to fall in time with the beating of his heart. Every time he got close to catching up, she would be ripped from his grasp. He was losing her. He felt his wolf clawing to get out, raging, howling inside of him. Yet no matter how he tried, he couldn't phase. He felt helpless, and that feeling only fueled the burning anger deep inside of him. She was his. His to protect and over and over he failed her.

Fane sat up suddenly, gasping for breath. He blinked several times and looked around in the darkness of the room he shared with his mate. *Another dream,* he thought. Sleep continued to elude him. Along with it, the peace he so desperately wanted. He glanced over to where Jacquelyn lay, *or should be laying,* he thought with a frown. He closed his eyes and reached out to her through their bond. He found her sitting with Jen and Sally by the large stone fireplace in one of the sitting rooms in the Romanian mansion, a place at which she seemed to take refuge more and more lately. No fire burned. The hearth, like his heart, was cold.

Fane bit back the anger he felt at her for leaving him alone in their bed—again. But he knew he couldn't blame her. He knew he had been distant from her, knew that she ached for him to talk to her, to touch her, and yet still he held himself back.

Utter fury boiled inside of him; he needed to destroy an enemy that was not flesh and blood. But he feared that she would see this and he didn't know how he could explain that to her. How did he fight a memory? How did he defeat something that was no longer happening, but wouldn't let go of him? He was at a loss and so he kept her at arm's length to protect her from what he had become.

It had been two weeks since they had defeated Desdemona and yet it felt as though it was only yesterday. Vasile and the other Alphas were doing their best to work together in a peaceful manner attempting to formulate a course of action. A new enemy had a risen just as the old one had fallen and the supernatural world now waited with bated breath to see what this new evil would bring.

Fane knew he should be helping his father and the others. He knew that it was his duty to lead and to set an example for others, but knowing and doing are two very different things. The cold truth was that his control was gone. Something in his wolf had snapped after seeing their mate trapped in her own mind. She had been experiencing the worst kinds of violation and abuse and he had only been able to stand by and watch. Now it took every ounce of strength he had just to let her out of his sight. For the first few days after the battle he hadn't left her side. It was only after she threatened to have Peri put a binding curse on him that he relented to her demand to have time with her two best friends. But he was always in her mind, always attune to her whereabouts and safety. It angered her more that, though he demanded she stay near him, he would not let her in. The bond was open, but not where she could see into his heart. He remembered her exact words when he had finally relented to her pleas.

"I'm tired of being in this room, Fane," she had told him. She had been standing by the window gazing out longingly. She kept her back to him as she spoke. "I love you, you know this, but I need more than just this."

"I just want you safe," Fane had told her through gritted teeth.

She had laughed bitterly, "Safe and caged are two very different things. You have got to get over whatever obsession it is you have with protecting me. We are in your father's freaking house; I couldn't be safer."

"Too many wolves."

She laughed again and turned to face him. "I'm done. I've tried to be patient and understanding. I've tried to talk to you, to get you to help me understand what's going on with you, but you won't let me in. I'm your damn mate, your wife, and you won't talk to me. You can either get your crap together and respect me the way I deserve to be respected…or I will drag Peri into this mess and bind you. You won't be able to touch me, not like you normally do anyway," she spat out and Fane had felt as if she had slapped him.

"Jacquelyn," his chest ached as he spoke her name and he took a step towards her.

"Don't," she snarled as she held up her hand. "You are going to fix this, Fane Lupei, and it better be sooner than later because I'm this close," she'd held up her hand pinching her fingers together with no space in-between, "to packing my crap and finding a different room."

Fane would like to say that he didn't lose his cool. He'd like to say he didn't shred the sheets on the bed or throw the TV across the room, but he'd be lying. Her declaration brought out his wolf. The idea of her leaving him, of not being in their room where she belonged, was more than his wolf or he could take. Jacquelyn's eyes had widened, but there was more anger than fear in them when she had stormed from the room. That had been two days ago.

He hadn't known if she would come back that night or not. She had briefly spoken to him through their bond to let him know where she was but then she had shut him out cold. She barely spoke to him when she chose to be around him and what little she did was short and to the point.

Coming back to the present, Fane climbed out of bed and staggered a bit. His limbs felt stiff and tight from the intensity of the dream and it took a few steps before he felt them loosen. He went into the bathroom and splashed cold water on his face but avoided looking in the mirror. He didn't want to see what stared back at him.

When he came back into the bedroom, he stopped abruptly in mid–step when he saw Sally sitting in one of the chairs that was in the small sitting area.

"Does your mate know you are in another man's room?" he asked dryly as he altered his course to the closet and grabbed a shirt. He slipped it over his head and then rejoined Sally though he did not take a seat.

"He does, though he is not happy that I did not allow him to come with me." Sally stared at him as if he were a new species of bug that needed examining. He stared right back. He felt his wolf stir and had to push him down. Sally stood and walked over to him. He tensed but didn't move. She slowly lifted her hand and placed it on his chest and he watched as she closed her eyes. He wanted to push her away and growl at her for thinking she had a right to touch him, but then, she was a healer and it was, therefore, her right.

He tried to keep the walls in his mind up but Sally was strong and she pushed through with little effort. He waited for her to see what he had become and then run screaming from the room. He felt her presence, but it wasn't the same as the mate bond. There was no intimacy involved, and yet, at the same time, he felt very vulnerable. She stepped back as her hand dropped and her eyes opened. She met his gaze and her face became stern.

"She could help," she told him firmly, but her words were gentle.

"At what cost to herself?" he asked.

"It is her right to sacrifice for you. Just as much as it is your right," she continued before he could speak. "It's spreading inside of you like a disease and eventually your wolf will take over. The wolf taking over, all instinct, without any of the reasoning of the man would be a very, very bad thing. Though, the fact that you are not in control might actually be worse. You know this and still you hold back. She is aching and empty because of your refusal to allow her to be what you need."

"You saw what happened?" he asked, knowing she would understand that he was asking her about his memories.

She nodded.

"You saw who touched her, who she willingly allowed, and yet that doesn't anger you?" his voice dropped to a growl.

"It wasn't real, Fane. It was a curse that fed our deepest fears. She has suffered enough and you are causing her more pain than the curse did. You have to find a way to let it go. You need her and she needs you. If you can't talk to her right now, then talk to someone because you are on a war path to self-destruction, and if you lose this battle, it won't only be Jacque who suffers."

He watched as Sally walked from his room closing the door gently behind her. He knew what she said was true. He had to fix this mess he had created. He needed his mate, needed her like a drowning man needed air. Sally spoke of Jacquelyn aching and his gut plunged to the ground. He knew that ache. It was his constant companion as well. His arms longed to hold her. His wolf needed to possess her, and he needed to love her—to show her how desperately he loved her.

He didn't know if he had pushed her too far or if she would forgive him. He didn't know how to tell her about the madness inside of him. He didn't know how to bear his weaknesses and shame to her, but he knew that if he didn't he would destroy them both.

"Love, we need to talk," he sent through their bond and pushed so that it penetrated the wall she was keeping between them. He felt her shock, and then the utter despair that filled her, rush through to him. *"Please, Jacquelyn, come back so we can talk."*

He held his breath waiting for her answer, praying it wasn't too late.

"It's about damn time," she growled at him.

He nearly fell to his knees and wept as she reminded him of who she was. She was his and she wasn't giving up on him.

"No I'm not giving up on you, but I just might kill you." She was coming to him; he could feel her getting closer.

"If dying by your hand means I can feel your touch, then you can kill me a thousand times," he knew his words sounded as fraught as he felt.

"Don't tempt me."

Fane growled as he felt the pain inside of her at the mention of touch. It had been so long since they'd touched and it was his fault.

"I'm going to fix this, Luna, though I fear how you will look at me once you know everything. But I'm so empty without you and the darkness is beginning to drive my wolf mad. He growls for you and I can barely hold him back from snatching you and begging you not to leave. I need you but more than that, I want you."

He knew that is what she needed to hear. She had felt like he didn't want her anymore and that she was no longer worthy to be his mate. The door slammed open as she rushed inside and threw herself into his arms. Fane buried his face in her neck and breathed deep.

Her scent rushed into his lungs and for the first time in weeks he felt as though he could breath. He held her close and shuddered when her fingers twined in his hair.

"I'm sorry," he whispered against her hair, "I'm so, so sorry."

Jacque bit her lip as she tried to hold back the tears. She knew they were a long way from okay, but they were a step in the right direction. She knew there were going to be many fights ahead, but she also knew that meant lots of making up as well.

"I heard that," Fane told her as he nipped her neck.

Jacque let out a weary laugh, "We have much to discuss before we get there wolf-man."

Chapter 1

"I hate reality television. That's not something I can change. I do, however, wish that in reality, we had life lines. You know, phone a friend, street shout out, hit man hotline. Any of those would work for me." ~ Jacque

"How did it go with Fane?" Vasile asked Sally as she entered his office with Costin's hand at the small of her back. Though Sally was technically the Serbian pack's healer, she knew Fane better than Rachel. Vasile felt it would be better for a friendly face to confront his son.

"It wasn't pretty," Sally answered. She leaned back against Costin when he let out a low growl. "Relax bartender, he was no threat to me," she told him gently.

"That isn't the point," Costin responded curtly. Sally glanced over her shoulder at her mate and gave him a pointed look. Costin did not appear intimidated.

Vasile stood-up from his desk and let out a slow, deep breath.

"You mated males are aging me before my time." Vasile met Costin's eyes briefly and then returned to Sally. "What is wrong with him?"

"You know the darkness that rules inside of the males before they are mated. It almost enslaves them. We mates bring that darkness to heel, freeing the wolf to be what he needs to be for his mate and pack. But Fane is making the choice to keep his mate's light from him. He is allowing the darkness free reign inside of him because of the rage that is building," Sally explained.

Vasile began to pace slowly around the office, his eyes on the floor as he considered her words.

"Am I going to have to step in?" he asked.

Sally shook her head. "I don't think so. I saw Jacque running to their room only minutes after I had left. I think he realizes what he has been doing to both of them."

"Healer," Vasile stopped directly in front of Sally and held her gaze. He heard something in her voice, something she wasn't telling him. "Be straight with me. Will I need to step in?" he asked her again more slowly this time.

Sally bit the inside of her lip as she considered the Alpha's question. She knew what she had seen inside of Fane, knew the extent of the darkness, but she didn't want to give up on him just yet, even if it did mean that her mate might have to take on the Prince of the Romanian Greys.

"Not right now," she finally answered as honestly as she could. "But I think at some point he is going to need to talk to Costin."

Vasile frowned at her while Costin continued to let out low rumbles from his chest unable to completely leash his wolf.

"Why Costin?" Vasile asked.

Sally felt her face begin to heat with the flood of embarrassment at having to discuss such intimate details with Vasile, whether false or not, especially with her mate right at her back.

"When Jacque was under Desdemona's spell, one of the things she experienced was being intimate with another male," Sally explained hesitantly and hoped that Vasile would not ask for details.

"What do you mean?"

She groaned inwardly. *Of course he would ask. Why on earth would he make this easy for me?*

"Answer him, Sally mine." She heard Costin's voice in her mind and the irritation and anger behind it. She didn't think he was angry with her, not exactly anyways.

"Okay," she began, "as a male, one of your biggest fears is not being able to save your mate from something horrible like torture or rape, right?"

Vasile nodded as he watched the healer closely.

"Other than having her taken unwillingly, in various ways, how else would you fear her being taken?" Sally's jaw tensed as she waited for realization to hit Vasile. She saw the moment he understood as his eyes widened. "Every man, be he wolf or human, fears his woman turning to another man willingly." Vasile's eyes jumped back to Costin.

"Under the curse, Jacque allowed you to have her," he said as he watched Costin's eyes begin to glow. Costin was holding onto his temper by a thread. He couldn't stand the idea of Sally thinking he had been with Fane's mate, even though he hadn't. He also didn't like the idea of Fane thinking that Costin would ever consider looking at Jacque, even though Fane knew it wasn't real. It hadn't really happened. But Fane was young, and with youth came insecurities.

"Fane saw what happened through Jacque's eyes—he saw her enjoy being with another male. That is very hard for any male. Of course Jacque was sick with disgust and despair once the curse was lifted. She wants to be touched by another male like she wants to be boiled alive in acid." Sally was trying to be as frank as possible because she could feel her mate growing more and more furious. "For now Costin and Fane need to steer clear of one another, at least until Fane can come to terms with his emotions. If you interfere right now, he will feel like you are protecting Jacque from him. That would make him feel like you were going to take her, and we all know how well Fane handles his mate being taken from him."

Vasile waited several heartbeats before he finally nodded.

"Alright," he whispered softly, "you protect your wolves."

"As is my right, Alpha," Sally reminded him.

"Yes, yes it is. But it is my right to discipline them when needed. Do not wait to tell me until it's too late, Sally. Do not wait until your mate is in a fight for something that never happened."

The warning in Vasile's voice made the hairs on the back of Costin's neck rise and he bit back the growl that rose in his chest. He wrapped a protective arm around his mate and pulled her close to him.

"Relax, Costin. I am not threatening your mate; I am warning her. But I *am* threatening my son." Vasile shook his head wearily and retreated back to his desk. "You both are dismissed. Sally, thank you," he paused, "for speaking with him."

Sally gave a slight bow of her head before following Costin from the room.

Vasile sat in the chair behind his desk. The aged leather wrinkled and groaned beneath his weight. His heart was heavy with the burdens their pack had so recently endured, but he knew that there were more to come. A new threat had risen, just as an old one had fallen. Now in the midst of that threat, Vasile also had to worry about his only son. He had known that Fane wasn't coping well in the aftermath of Mona's spell, but there had been too much going on for him to address it. Now that he considered it, he wondered if he had fallen short as an Alpha and father for not making the time.

"As usual, you take on blame that is not yours to bear." He heard Alina's words in his mind. He smiled to himself as he reached out to her.

"Isn't it? I am his Alpha, his father. Is it not my place to make sure that he is well?" he asked her.

"He is a grown man and he is mated. It is her place to care for him first. Should she not be able to handle it, then it is her job to come to you. Do not add to your already heavy load my love. For even you, as strong as you may be, can be crushed."

He chuckled out loud at her chastisement and took pleasure in knowing that she was the only one who could ever get away with it.

"How did I ever deserve to have you as my mate, Mina?" he asked her gently.

He felt her hand brush the back of his neck and her lips against his own.

"When I figure it out, I'll let you know," she teased.

Vasile growled at her cheekiness. "I swear I'm going to have to limit her time with those girls and that damn fae as well."

"Were you ever going to tell me what you saw?" Costin asked Sally as they headed to the pack healer's room. She had been working with Rachel on different herbal remedies, going through the archives of their people, and relearning all that the gypsy healers once used to tend the wolves.

"I think there is some sort of healer/wolf confidentiality that Fane is entitled to," Sally told him with thinned lips.

"Did you really have to go see him alone? I don't like you being with a male by yourself, especially an unpredictable one."

Sally huffed. "Fane would never hurt me, Costin, and he's mated. You are going to have to curb your possessive instincts in order for me to do my job."

"No, you are going to have to learn to let me in. We are a team. It's my job to protect the healer and I can't protect you if you don't let me near you." Costin's voice was becoming more and more gravelly with each word.

"Why are you so cranky?" Sally asked as she pushed open the door to the healer's study. Shelves filled with plants, herbs, and odd looking stones lined the walls. Books were scattered across the two tables that ran the length of the room.

"How do you feel about it?" Costin asked quietly.

Sally knew what he was asking. He wanted to know if she was angry about what Jacque experienced. But how could she be angry when she had experienced something very similar?

"How are you not losing it like Fane over what I experienced?" she countered. "Why aren't any of the other males killing each other over what their mates felt while under the curse? You have to know that all of you males fear us going to other men. So we all went through that same thing." She walked over to him and looked up into his hazel eyes—eyes that shown with such love that when they gazed upon her, it took her breath away.

"I know you want no other than me. I know that you would never touch another male and because I know that, deep in my soul, I have let go of what happened under the curse. You showed me the night we were bonded that there is nothing that could ever take your love from me. So what do I have to be upset about?"

Costin reached up and tucked her hair behind her ear and Sally leaned into his touch. He leaned down until their foreheads touched and inhaled her scent through slow deep breaths.

"Thank you," he whispered softly. He wrapped his arms around her waist and pulled her close to him. It was his favorite place to be—wrapped around his mate, protecting her, loving her, and reminding her that she was his.

"I love you," she told him gently.

He grinned at her flashing his dimple. "What's not to love?"

Sally rolled her eyes as she pulled back from him and he reluctantly let her slip away.

"I swear you and Jen were separated at birth," she grumbled as she turned to open up one of the healing books.

"So what are we doing today?" he asked as he rubbed his hands together like an eager child.

"A tonic," she told him as she flipped the pages.

"A tonic for what?"

"Overbearing, jealous, obnoxious, yet hot, werewolves."

Costin let out a laugh that filled the room and flooded Sally's heart with joy.

"Will it affect my good looks?" he asked her playfully.

"Oh, yes perfect," she muttered to herself ignoring his question.

"What's perfect?" he asked as he leaned over her shoulder to see what she was doing.

"You just reminded me that I forgot to add something to shrink your ego."

He put his hands on her hips and leaned down to her ear.

"As long as we aren't shrinking body parts, love, then it's all good."

Sally leaned her head back against him and closed her eyes with a huff. "I can't win."

Costin chuckled low and she felt his warm breath against her neck.

She finally leaned forward and pushed him away. "Alright, Romeo, back up. I've got work to do."

"Work away, gypsy lady. I'll just sit over here and supervise."

Sally blushed but refused to comment, knowing she would only encourage his teasing, which would only lead to her becoming a pile of goo at his feet begging for his attention. *Yeah Sal, that would be so dignifying,* she thought to herself.

Chapter 2

"Waiting sucks. I can't think of a time where waiting is fun. Wait, I take that back, but if I get into that Dec will have an aneurysm. But those of you grinning, and you know who you are, know what I'm talking about. But I digress. Right now we're sitting here twiddling our thumbs while we wait for this psycho warlock to go all crazy on us. I mean, seriously people, there is only so much hot chocolate I can drink. All I'm saying is I'm pregnant, bored, and ready to kick some warlock ass. Can I get an amen?" ~Jen

"Jacque, it's been two months. If this dude doesn't make a move soon, I'll be too big to kick him in his baby making parts and that just won't be cool," Jen grumbled as she slumped down on the couch in the library of the Romanian mansion. She had been travelling back and forth between the Serbian and Romanian packs, mainly because she hated being away from Jacque and Sally. Since Sally was working with Rachel and Peri, Jen was stuck by herself at the Serbian pack mansion. Of course, there were pack members in and out all of the time talking to Decebel, but it wasn't the same as having her girls with her. Not to mention, she was so emotional these days that most people could hardly stand her. She alternated between gushing about how glad she was to know her friends or raging because she couldn't control her emotions. Each passing hour was a toss-up.

"This is one of those rare instances when you say *making a move* and you don't mean a guy going for the bases," Jacque told her best friend with a quick glance and then turned back to the book she had been reading.

"We all know that I don't have to complain about Dec not making a move. My man has plenty of moves. But if I tried to kick him in his baby making parts, he would just get more excited."

Sally laughed. "When you first told me you were interested in Decebel, I honestly thought that there was no way you two would ever work. But man, you are both such freaks, I honestly don't think anyone else could put up with either of you."

"Or keep up with us." Jen winked.

"Ugh," Jacque groaned, "Jen please. The more your little baby bump shows, the weirder it is for you to talk about your sex life with your mate. I mean, seriously, we just don't need the mental image."

"Speaking of sex lives," Jen pointed at Jacque, "how are you and your fur ball?"

Jacque's head fell back against the chair as she closed her eyes. She blocked her thoughts from Fane, despite the fact that she would hear about it from him later. But she didn't need him listening in right now, and she knew he would be.

"He talked to me after Sally went and spoke with him."

"That was all your father-in-law," Sally interrupted quickly.

"I told you I was cool with it, Sally, and I meant it. Fane knew I was at my breaking point."

"Sooo," Jen prompted her to answer her previous question.

"He's still distant, but he's trying. I'm just at a loss as to what to do to help him." She looked down at her hands and bit her lip to keep from crying. She hated crying.

"It's just going to take time, Jacque," Sally told her gently.

"How much more time? He still won't go anywhere near Costin." Jacque's eyes narrowed as she felt the familiar spark of anger ignite in her. She and Fane hadn't even known each other a full year yet and so she had never seen him like this, so angry and almost out of control.

"Vasile is going to step in before too much longer," Sally warned but tried to soften the harsh-sounding words.

"Maybe he and Costin just need to have a go at it and get it out of their systems," Jen suggested.

Jacque's eyes snapped over to Jen and fear flashed in the emerald orbs quickly and was gone just as fast. "They would kill each other, Jen."

"Naw, not if there were Alphas there to keep things in check. You know how guys are, Jac. Sometimes they just need to get it beat out of them." Jen threw her head back and laughed. "There I go again. I swear I need a notebook for all the awesome innuendos I come up with."

Sally coughed and Jacque shook her head at her nympho friend.

"Okay," Jen continued, "I'm serious. They need to just beat the living crap out of each other and then they will be able to move past this."

"I'm not about to suggest that to Fane," Jacque shook her head. "I honestly don't know if he could stop himself from doing something he would later regret, when he…," she paused and took in a shaky breath, "if he ever gets back to normal."

Like an indolent cat stretched out for an afternoon nap, Reyaz sat lazily on a large tree branch. He leaned back against the trunk of the ancient tree with his legs stretched out in front of him and his hands behind his head. Though his body gave the appearance of being languid, his eyes were ever watchful and vigilant.

For two months he had roamed the Balkan Mountains, observing his brother's kingdom and listening for any information of what the supernatural world was planning now that he had revealed himself. But that was not all he observed. He also had paid special attention to the human woman his brother had taken a shine to, and, if he wasn't mistaken, planned on taking for his mate.

His upper lip lifted in a snarl as he thought about his brother having something that he did not, something that had been ripped from his hands so very long ago. Yet the wound left behind was as raw and bloody as it had been the day she died. Thea, his love, his reason for living, was gone and it was Cypher's fault that she was no longer by his side. In truth, he should be glad that his brother had found a mate, because now he had something to take from him. Something that would be equal what Reyaz had lost.

The leaves rustled in the trees and the entire forest shuttered with awareness of his malice, but he ignored it and continued his waiting and watching. His time was coming, and when it finally did, he would rain down his fury in an eruption of destruction unlike anything the supernaturals had ever seen. And he would destroy anyone who got in his way.

Lilly Pierce stood in what was known as the throne room of the warlock castle. The castle itself was built into the mountains, hidden from any who didn't know exactly where to seek it. She watched as Cypher paced around the large chair that sat at the front of the great room. He had been restless for weeks, and though they were still getting to know one another, she was beginning to understand the responsibility he had to his people and the passion he felt for them. He wanted what was best for them. He wanted them safe. But most of all, he wanted to know that they had a future in this world. That wasn't the only thing bothering him, however. Lilly could tell he struggling with something else, but she didn't feel as if she had a right to ask him about it. They hadn't discussed moving forward in their relationship, and even though he claimed that she was his mate, he had yet to pursue anything more with her. They spent time together. He was affection towards her and she could tell that he cared deeply for her, but something was holding him back and now she was unsure as to where she stood with him.

She hadn't decided how long she would stay at Cypher's mansion. Jacque and the girls had wanted her to stay with them and she had for a few days after Desdemona's death. But Cypher had needed to get back to his people, and she had felt at the time that she needed to be with him. It was weird to think of her daughter as a grown woman with a husband and no longer needing Lilly's constant guidance. Her first instinct had been to stay at the Romanian mansion, but she knew deep inside it wasn't where she belonged.

Now she didn't really know where she belonged. After everything that had happened, after everything she had experienced with Cypher, she couldn't imagine going back to her life as a bookstore owner and single middle-aged female with a grown daughter and a broken past. She wanted more. She needed more and she thought that *more* had been here with Cypher.

"Lilly." The deep voice made her stomach clench in anticipation just as it had been doing for the past few months. Cypher held his hand out to her, beckoning her to come to him.

She walked slowly across the room towards him and nearly melted under his heated gaze. *Good grief, Lilly, what are you seventeen? He's a man, not a freaking Greek god.* She silently chastised herself, even as she thought that Cypher probably resembled exactly what a Greek god might look like. The closer she got to him, the shakier her breathing became. Once again she wanted to kick herself for acting like an infatuated adolescent, but then, why shouldn't she be affected by him? He was incredibly handsome, strong, caring, and surprisingly gentle for such a large man. There would have to be something seriously wrong with her if she wasn't affected by him at least in some way. *Well, at least I'm not defective,* she shrugged inwardly, deciding it was okay for her to swoon like a school girl...sort of.

"I'm sending you back to your home."

Lilly's stomach dropped to the floor and her heart clenched painfully in her chest. *Damn, didn't see that one coming.*

"Have you heard any news?" Decebel asked Peri.

"Nothing definitive," she told him through clenched teeth. "The forests are restless; nature knows when evil is among us. He's out there. He's not hiding out behind another veil in another land or hunkered down in a hole somewhere."

"Did you just say hunkered?" Jen asked with a sly smile.

Peri's eyes snapped over to the female alpha. "I find that being around you humans is expanding my vocabulary. And unfortunately, it's not in ways that make me sound intelligent."

"We aim to please, Peri fairy."

Peri snorted. "Judging from the look of your expanding belly, I would say you must be succeeding."

Jacque spewed the water she had been drinking out of her mouth as laughter bubbled up.

Jen patted her rounding stomach and grinned over at her mate. "What do you think B? How's my aim?"

"Jen," Jacque was still laughing as she tried to talk, "*your* aim is not the one you should be worried about."

Jen paused as she thought about Jacque's words and then a wicked, wicked grin spread across her face. "Good call, Jacque.

Alright, I'll revise my question," she looked back over to Decebel. "B, how's your aim?"

The room erupted into laughter. Decebel bared his teeth at his mate. *"I would say it's spot on, Jennifer,"* he growled through their bond.

"Dec says it's...,"

"Jennifer," Decebel interrupted her and she was laughing too hard to continue.

"Can we please get back to the matter at hand?" Vasile asked as he rubbed his forehead. The group gathered around Vasile had been chosen months ago, chosen to lead, and chosen to stand as examples to each of the races. Vasile had called this meeting to discuss what could be done about their mutual enemy. The only ones not present were Sally and Costin. Decebel had told his second that he thought it best that he stay away for now. Costin had not been happy about it, but then he could not defy his alpha.

"Well, in this case, no news is not good news," Peri said as her eyes met Vasile's.

"I've been trying to go through the archives to see if we have any information on this Reyaz character," Wadim spoke up from where he sat on the floor.

"Have you come up with anything useful?" Decebel asked.

"Not much, just that he's the warlock king's brother and that they had a falling out. But the records don't go into the history as to why."

"It's obvious what we need to do then," Peri glanced around the room.

"Please tell me it has something to do with eating," Jen muttered.

Decebel placed his hand on the back of Jen's neck from where he stood behind her.

"I'm not going to let you starve, Jennifer," he teased her.

"You know I get cranky when I'm hungry."

"When are you not cranky, baby?"

"Not the point, B." She reached back and smacked his hand away, but he just chuckled and put it right back where it had been.

"As important as your appetite being satisfied is to all of us, Jen; it's not quite the top priority," Peri's voice was gentle as if she was talking to a child.

"It should be. That's all I'm saying."

"Noted," Peri nodded. "What I was going to say before the pregnant woman enlightened us with her needs, and surprisingly enough they were not carnal in nature, is that we need to get Cypher over here to explain just why his brother is…,"

"Mad cow disease crazy?" Jacque interrupted.

Peri grinned. "That's one way to put it."

"MCDC," Jen piped in, "awesome acronym, sounds like a band."

The room let out a collective groan as they all looked at Jen.

"Jen, get a clue and read Wadim's shirt." Jacque told her dryly.

Jen glanced over at Wadim who, oh so helpfully, pulled his shirt out so that she could read it.

In black bold letters it said, "No really, I'm a werewolf and you're a human, which essentially translates into a steak with legs."

"Are you implying that Wadim's going to eat me, cause I don't know how Dec would feel about that."

Decebel rubbed his face as he let out an exasperated breath. "Jen, Jacque, hush. Wadim, quit encouraging them with your stupid grin."

"I will get in touch with the warlock," Vasile continued as if the banter between Jen and Jacque hadn't taken place.

"I think I should go, Alpha," Peri spoke up. "It will be quicker and I want to check out what's going on in his forest. From what I'm hearing from some of the warlocks I've spoken with, there seems to be a lot of turbulence in the air."

"Fine, do it quickly. Tell him I'll expect him tomorrow."

Peri nodded at him and then was gone.

"I so wish I could do that," Jacque said looking longingly at the spot Peri had just occupied.

"As for the rest of you," Vasile stood as he addressed the group, "I know it's easy to get complacent as we wait to see what our enemy has planned, but you must not let this happen. Females, you need to be training for combat, except Jen,"

Jen snarled at him, but Vasile just kept going. "The healers need to continue to learn and do whatever it is they can to prepare to help the injured, wolves and fae alike. Decebel, it would be helpful if you would stay in touch with the Alphas that have returned to their packs. We need to continue to build the relationships that we have started; we must stay united. Males, I have asked Thalion, prince of the elves, and Adam to train with you. We are strong and fast, but they are faster. It may well be that we need to learn a few new fighting techniques ourselves. They will also be teaching you archery. We need to be prepared to fight back in whatever form the attack comes."

All of the males nodded and murmured their agreement.

"Alright, we will meet again tomorrow when Cypher gets here."

"This means I get to eat now right?" Jen smiled as she stood up.

"Oh my goodness, someone get the girl some food so she'll shut up."

"I heard that, Jacque."

"I meant for you to hear it, you dork," Jacque told her.

Jen looked over at Fane who was standing just behind Jacque. His eyes seemed dull, no longer the bright blue they had once been and his lips were tight.

"Fane, you need to control your woman."

Jacque's head snapped up as her eyes collided with her friends. They were wide and were giving Jen the *what the hell* glare.

Jen shrugged. "It's time he got his head out of his butt and joined the rest of us back here in the living."

Fane didn't growl; he didn't even acknowledge Jen's words. He just placed his hand on the back of Jacque's back and began to guide her from the room. Jacque continued to glare at Jen until she stomped past her.

Jen looked over at Decebel. "I don't get it B. Our baby is scheduled to die on the day she's born and you don't see me walking around with a perpetual scowl, looking ready to kill everyone in my path. Don't you think it's time for Fane to snap out of it?"

Decebel met Jen's gaze and reached out to caress her cheek. "Not everyone is as resilient as you, baby."

Jen's eyebrows creased together as she watched her mate. He was hiding something from her; she knew it without a doubt. But she couldn't find out what it was because he was keeping his mind shut from her. He kept their bond open just enough for them to feel each other, but he didn't give her the open access as he once had. As he stared at her now, the look in his eyes confused her, but she knew that if she asked, he would just deflect the question.

Jen finally turned away from him, knowing he would follow her. She paused and glanced back over her shoulder at him and raised a single brow. "You can't hide from me forever, Dec. At some point, you will let your guard down. And when you do, I won't be kind and give you your privacy. I will take what is my right to have, your complete trust and openness with me. So you can continue to delude yourself that you can keep things from me, but I always get what I want. And I'm not just talking about information. Don't think I haven't noticed that you seem too distracted at night to take care of your husbandly duties and it's pissing me off. A girl has needs, B. Put that in your beef jerky and chew on it."

Decebel followed behind his ticked off mate and tried not to smile at that last comment. *"Did you just say husbandly duties?"*

"Shut up Dec."

Chapter 3

"It never ceases to amaze me how the males of the supernatural races think that they are protecting their females when they try to put them in a bubble. You would think that after seeing this strategy backfire many times, they might learn better. But apparently dogs aren't the only ones to which you can't teach new tricks. Wolves and warlocks seem to have the same problem. And I don't think all the kibble n' bits in the world could condition them to change. Although Jen might be onto something with her type of conditioning, and her poor wolf doesn't even realize it." ~Peri

Peri stood just on the outskirts of the forest that Cypher's magic encompassed. She was leery about entering the warlock's territory. She could feel the wrongness in the air and see it in the way the plants and trees appeared to be cringing. She narrowed her eyes as she tried to look past the human realm and into the magic that she knew was lingering among the trees.

There, she thought as she watched the black swirls that were moving and shifting, intertwining themselves with the green swirls that she knew to be Cypher's magic. His was incredibly strong, but the black swirling wisps were having no trouble interposing themselves and adding their own pungent evil.

Peri huffed in irritation. "Just once could we please have a foe that wasn't versed in the dark arts and psycho crazy with black magic? Would that be too much to ask? Couldn't we just have some pixies hell bent on stealing all the lime popsicles in the world?" she muttered softly. As she stood there, her unease growing, she made the decision to call Cypher to her. She didn't want that taint on her and didn't want to draw attention to herself.

"Cypher, King of the Warlocks, I request an audience," she didn't speak loudly, for she knew that his magic would carry the message to him on the wind.

After several minutes of waiting, she finally saw him emerge as if walking from trees themselves. He wore his signature green cloak and she noticed that his face was tight with worry and anger.

"Peri," he nodded in greeting.

"Cypher," Peri responded. "Do you feel the darkness in your kingdom?" she decided to just lead with that because there was no better way to chat up a king than to tell him he needed to get his ass in gear and protect what was his—right, smart move Peri.

"It comes and goes," Cypher acknowledged. "I know it is the work of my brother."

"Are you going to do anything to stop it or are you just going to hang out in your mountain drinking warlock schnapps and wooing that new mate of yours?"

Cypher snarled at her and she was rather impressed with it, but she didn't back down.

"I am king here, Perizada of the Fae. I decide what's best for my people and you should not be spouting off about things you do not understand."

Peri let out a bark of laughter. "Things *I* don't understand? I think you forget with whom you speak. I'm older and more wise than your finite mind can fathom. I have watched evil rise and fall for thousands of years and I know what happens when we turn a blind eye to what is going on around us. You have to do something before he has a hold on your forest, on your people, and on your mate."

Cypher looked away from Peri, but not before she saw the flash of guilt and pain in his yellow eyes.

"I am taking steps to protect all that I can. I have those who are strongest in magic working on spells to protect the mountain and land. I have my smiths forging weapons and I am sending Lilly back to her home."

Peri's mouth dropped open at his last declaration and then a smirk danced across her face. "And pray tell, just how well did your female take that?"

"I think she was angry." He still would not meet Peri's eyes.

"What would give you that idea?"

"She used lots of words that would ordinarily make her blush, and…" he paused.

"And…" Peri prompted.

"Then she started throwing things at me."

Peri laughed even louder this time. "How's her aim?"

Cypher finally met her gaze and glowered at her. "Is that really important?"

"Oh, it will be if she decides to pick up something a little more deadly than a hairbrush or book or most other things females grab in fits of rage."

Cypher stood in silence as he remembered his fight with Lilly. She was angry, but more than that, she was hurt. But he couldn't worry about her feelings; he had to worry about her safety, about her life. He could handle her rage as long as she was *alive* to direct it at him.

"Peri, what did you come for?" he finally asked.

"Well, aside from the juicy gossip, Vasile is requesting your presence tomorrow."

"I will be there. What time?"

Peri shrugged. "You males never pay attention to detail. Show up when you're good and ready. Will you bring Lilly?"

He shook his head. "I'm sending her home tonight."

"Alone?" she asked as her voice rose in surprise.

"She will be safe in the states. My brother has never left our homeland. Sending someone with her would just alert him that she's gone," he explained.

"And what makes you think that he won't follow her?"

"He wants me dead. If I'm here, he will stay here."

Peri let out a laugh that sounded less than amused as her brow rose at him.

"You just keep telling yourself that, warlock, if it helps you sleep at night."

Cypher was quiet as he continued to stare at Peri. He didn't want to think she was right. He didn't want to believe that his brother would follow after his mate, but he was beginning to think that what he wanted didn't change what simply is.

"Will you go to the airport with her?" he suddenly asked.

Peri was taken slightly by surprise by the request, but her curiosity got the better of her. She definitely wanted to see how Lilly Pierce was handling being shipped off like a fragile piece of china.

"I suppose so," she said attempting to sound disinterested, "what time?"

"Her flight leaves at eight o'clock."

"I will be here at seven fifteen."

Cypher shook his head. "That won't give you time to get to the airport."

Peri rolled her eyes. "I'm not planning on taking a car."

"Oh, right," Cypher said absentmindedly.

Peri was about to leave when a slightly wicked idea emerged. She tilted her head to the side as her eyes narrowed at the king. "Have you thought about what might happen if you send her back?"

Cypher didn't respond.

"Lilly is a beautiful woman. Her daughter is grown and gone, leaving her at home by herself every night, every weekend. At some point a man will pursue her. At some point she will let her heart heal and move on and let somebody else give her what she needs. She's done it before."

Peri watched as her words began to sink in. Apparently he had not thought about this scenario at all. His eyes began to glow an eerie shade of yellow and his skin flushed with anger. By the time Peri had said that Lilly would move on, Cypher's large hand was wrapped around one of the smaller trees, and he was squeezing it so hard that he left indentions in the trunk.

"Alright," Peri said cheerfully not bothering to acknowledge his anger, "my work is done here. I'll be back to get her in a little while." Before the king could respond she was gone.

Cypher did not make any move to leave—not yet. He needed to calm down before he went back into the mountain. Peri's words had ignited a feral rage inside of him and he feared that the slightest annoyance might set him off and some poor innocent warlock would get killed. He had not considered that Lilly would move on. He thought that he would eventually get her back once it was safe. He had no idea how long that could take, but he just assumed she would wait for him. But he couldn't entertain that idea, or he would keep her here, and if she was here, then she was in danger. He pushed the idea of her with another male as far from his mind as he could and brought his thoughts to the matter at hand, his brother and the threat he posed. Everything would have to wait, even his desire to have his mate by his side.

Jacque sat quietly on the bed in her room. After Vasile had dismissed them from the meeting, Fane had taken her back to their room and then gotten her something to eat. He hadn't said much, but he did ask her how she was and if she had spoken with her mom recently. Afterwards, at the request of Vasile, he had gone to do some training with Adam. Now she sat in solitude, lost in her thoughts. She could go hang out with her friends, but right now she just wanted to be alone.

After Sally had spoken with Fane, he had been genuinely apologetic about his actions. They had talked for hours and had even done more than talk, which was a vast improvement over the short kiss good night he had been giving her. He had once again been keeping their bond open, and she could feel the torment and anger that still raged inside of him. He had told her he was angry with Costin, but he knew in his mind that he had no right to be. Costin had not done anything to deserve Fane's wrath. She could see that he was afraid: first, that she would no longer desire him, and second, that he had pushed her too far.

Jacque had gone to talk to Cynthia about the situation because she wanted to know if werewolves ever needed antidepressants. Jacque thought it nearly laughable, except for the fact that her mate needed something and she was desperate to help him. Cynthia had explained that the males feel emotions extremely intensely about their mates, and she didn't know if we could even begin to understand the depth of those emotions. Because of that, everything was magnified—their joy, love, anger, pain, fear. All of it was multiplied by a number greater than could be counted. Jacque asked if there was anything Cynthia could do, and Cynthia had surprised her with her answer.

"He needs to get the rage out," she had said. "If your presence, your touch, is not helping, then he needs to somehow exonerate it.

For a male wolf, that would be fighting or something less violent, if you get my drift."

Jacque had blushed furiously even though she commented, "Yes, well that's not doing a damn bit of good for either of us, so let's talk about fighting."

"You said he is angry with Costin because he is the male who was in your mind from the curse, right?"

"Yes," she had answered.

"Then he needs to fight Costin."

"Excuse me?" Jacque had been completely dumbfounded, more so, because it was Jen's suggestion and now the good doctor was on the same page.

"I know it sounds crazy, but if Fane can fight the object of his pain then it may be enough to bring him closure, to heal a wound that just continues to fester."

The sound of the door opening brought Jacque back to the present. She watched as a battered looking Fane walked in, shutting the door quietly behind him. He looked at her from across the room and his lips lifted in a small smile. Her heart flipped and her stomach tightened from something so small but so needed.

"Feeling better?" she asked hesitantly.

"I don't know if better is the term I would use, but being able to release some of the pent up energy has brought me a sliver of peace." His voice was slightly more emotional than the monotone he had exhibited as of late and that too gave her hope. Maybe he could just fight *anyone* and begin to heal; maybe it didn't have to be Costin.

She felt the growl from across the room before she heard it. And when her eyes met Fane's, they werewolf blue.

"Why is his name in your thoughts, Jacquelyn?" Fane's voice was now laced with a totally different kind of emotion. She hadn't realized he was listening in. She would need to be careful to keep her mind separate from his when she was talking about his problems to others, but the small amount of joy she had experienced at seeing her mate's smile had caused her to let her guard down.

"Fane," she said as she stood slowly from the bed. She took cautious steps toward him and kept her eyes from meeting his own. "I was not thinking of him in a romantic way. You know better. You feel what I feel and see what I see. There is no room for doubt in our relationship."

She continued forward until she was standing mere inches from him. Her hand reached up and, just as it would have made contact, she began to drop it.

"Don't stop."

Her hand froze in midair at his desperate plea.

She finally met his eyes and sucked in a sharp breath at the change she saw. They still glowed but no longer with anger. Now it was something much more intimate. She felt his hands on her waist as he pulled her closer until her body was flush with his. He leaned his head to the side until her hand was cupping his cheek and he let out a shaky breath.

"I need you like I need my next breath. The way I want you is like a dying man in a desert wanting even the smallest drop of water," he whispered and she felt his warm breath against her face.

"I have felt like you needed space from me, Fane." Jacque tried not to sound upset or hurt, but when she saw his jaw clench, she knew she had not succeeded.

"That is my fault. I have been too proud to ask you and too arrogant to think that I could handle this alone. Even after we talked I still tried to keep it from you."

Jacque reached up with both arms and wrapped them around his neck. Her fingers wove into his dark hair as she pulled his head down until their foreheads were touching.

"Are you ready to let me help? Are you ready to deal with your anger at Costin?" she asked gently.

He growled again. "Please don't say his name, not right now. The only name I want coming from your lips is mine. For the rest of the night, it is just you and me."

Jacque trembled under his possessive tone, and as his hands slipped under the hem of her shirt and moved tenderly up her back, all thoughts of anything but Fane fled.

"Jacquelyn," his lips grazed her skin as he lowered his head to her neck and breathed deeply. A soft moan slipped through her lips and she heard him chuckle. It had been so long since she had heard that sound and her desire for him soared.

She pulled him towards their bed and as she laid back, she tugged on his hand until his body blanketed her.

"So all it takes is my laugh to get you in bed?" He smiled at her and nipped at her lips with his teeth.

"All it takes is you," she told him with a sincerity that took Fane's breath away. When she pulled his head down for his mouth to merge with hers, he gave no resistance.

Fane felt his mate's relief at having him touch her. He felt her complete and total trust that he would show her only love and care with that touch. With every graze of his fingers, each touch of his lips, she seemed to glow brighter and brighter. He watched in awe as she gave herself to him absolutely without reservation and it humbled him.

She whispered to him as he loved her and her words began to mend the brokenness inside.

"I love you Fane," and then she kissed his shoulder.

"I need you," a kiss to his chest.

"I'm yours alone," he kissed her deeply at that last declaration and he took everything she gave him, soaking her up greedily.

"Mine," The word rumbled from his chest as he watched his wife, his mate, bask in their shared passion.

"Vasile," Adam bowed his head slightly to the alpha as he grabbed his shirt from a chair in the gym.

"Adam, how did things go with my son this evening?"

Adam could tell there was something very different about Fane. He had become very distant and the easy demeanor that he once carried had been replaced with a stony wall.

"He did well. He is very powerful and worked very hard," Adam answered.

Vasile's eyes narrowed. "What was his temperament?"

"He remained detached throughout the training, but as we sparred his focus increased, and he seemed to let go of whatever burden is weighing him down. He would be a dangerous wolf to fight. He is extremely powerful, but it is not a desire to learn or gain skill that is motivating him."

"His wolf is out of control," Vasile said calmly.

Adam shook his head. "No, not his wolf, Vasile. It's the man that is out of control."

Vasile had no words for Adam's statement. He just stood there watching as the fae left the gym.

If Adam was right and it was the man who was out of control, then things were worse than Vasile had realized. When the wolf was in control, it was pure instinct. The wolf would be dangerous until his mate was safe. Once the threat was neutralized, he would once again be able to be calmed by his mate's light and goodness. When the man was out of control, it wasn't only instinct that was driving him; it was also emotion. Emotions could make people do irrational things. When the man was out of control, it made the wolf in him restless because he would be trying to figure out where the threat is that is causing the man to have such rage sweltering inside of him. Fane's emotions were keeping him from acting rational, from seeing true reality. He won't allow his mate or his wolf to help him gain control. Fane was a ticking time bomb and Vasile was going to have to step in if he wanted to protect the pack and Jacque.

Chapter 4

"People seem to believe that when you find your soul mate, the one person who completes you, that things will just be lollipops and sunshine. I hate to stomp on your tootsie rolls, but being the right person for your mate does not suddenly turn you into this giving, selfless, loving, gentle, and all that other crap person. You are still the person you were without them; the difference is now when you aren't any of those good things, you have someone who will love you anyway." ~Jen

"Where are Fane and Jacque on this nice quiet evening?" Jen asked as she, Decebel, Sally, and Costin sat in the library. Jen's feet were propped up in Decebel's lap and he was absentmindedly rubbing them. Sally and Costin were on the couch across from them and Costin lay with his head in Sally's lap while she ran her fingers through his hair. Both couples had inadvertently wound up in the library together. Now seemed like the perfect time to plan an intervention for their best friend and her wolf.

"I think they decided to go to bed early after the meeting," Sally answered.

Jen let out a hard breath as she pulled her feet from Decebel's lap and sat up on the couch. Her baby bump was still small enough that she could lean forward and put her elbows on her knees.

"I would love to take that statement and turn it in to some graphic sex talk that would make Sally blush, but the reality is, they probably just went to sleep."

"What's wrong with that?" Decebel's deep voice rumbled from beside her.

Jen's head turned slowly to look at her mate. The look she gave him could have burned a hole through a brick building. "Did you seriously just ask me that?"

Decebel didn't say anything. He just sat there meeting her stare.

"When have we ever just gone to…," she was cut off by a growl from her mate.

"Jennifer, stop," Decebel's voice was tight with irritation.

A smile spread across Jen's face and nothing in that smile was friendly.

"You're right, Dec, I should stop. That's a dumb question for me to ask, since the answer is every night for the past two weeks."

Decebel stood up abruptly and his power radiated throughout the room. "Why are you always discussing the details of our sex life in front of every person we know? Have you ever thought that maybe I don't want you to discuss it? Have you ever once considered how I might feel about it?" His voice was so deep that it vibrated in Jen's chest.

Jen stood from the couch slowly. Though she wasn't huge, she still was getting used to having weight protruding from her stomach and she lost her balance a lot. She swayed slightly once on her feet and when Decebel reached out to steady her, she snarled at him and slapped his hand away. "Keep your damn hands off of me. That shouldn't be too hard for you since it seems to be what you want anyway."

After several heartbeats she looked up at his face. She mentally prepared herself to stay calm. *Just keep it together, Jen*, she told herself.

"You forget that I am in your mind B. I am a constant shadow and I know how you feel and what you think," she paused and gritted her teeth to keep from crying. *Damn pregnancy hormones.* "That is until now. So now that I can't see what's going on inside of you, I have to draw my own conclusion as to what has suddenly made you act like a pissed-off four year old whose ice cream has just splattered to the ground. And I've come to the conclusion that I must not be doing it for you anymore."

She took a step closer to him and reached up to poke him in the chest. "How I figure it, *Decebel*, is that as long as I'm raving about how amazing you are so you can puff up like a proud peacock…, wholly crap that's a good one," she said with a tone of regret in her voice, but then shook it off and jumped right back in to her tirade. "As long as you look like a freaking sex god, a mind blowing fantasy for women everywhere, then you don't mind me spouting off to everyone who will listen. But as soon as you start to lag in that area, as soon as your ability is put to question, then you are suddenly uncomfortable with your hot mate discussing the now sore issue."

The room was wrapped in silence but the residue of Jen's words rung out loud and clear. Jen stood there waiting for her mate's response—waiting to see if he would contradict her, yell at her, or decide to throw her over his shoulder and prove her wrong. She was hoping for that last outcome. She might as well have been hoping for the Fates to suddenly appear and say *you got punked; you can keep your kid*.

"You should go to bed, Jennifer. I imagine you're tired after your fit." His jaw was so tense that it sounded as if the words had to be pulled from his throat.

Sally's mouth dropped open as she stared up at Decebel and then looked at Jen. She pushed on Costin to sit up and then stood, about to take a step towards her friend, but Costin's arm snaked around her waist and pulled her back to his chest.

"Not a good idea," he whispered in her ear. She nodded, though it frustrated her that they had to tiptoe around the males when they went into possessive, butthead mode.

Jen closed her eyes and counted to ten. That didn't help so she tried counting to fifteen. Nope, that didn't help either so she just gave up and gave into her fury.

"You're right, Dec. I need to go lie down." Her voice was deceptively sweet as she stepped around him giving him a wide berth so as not to touch him.

"I will be there shortly," he told her gruffly.

Jen stopped and turned slightly so she could see him, but it was more for his benefit, so that he could see her. She wanted to make this very clear for him.

"I don't know how they did things back when you were not over a hundred years old, but I know how we do things now. After the way you have just treated me, the chances of you getting near me, let alone while I'm in our bed, are about as likely as Peri putting on a tutu and pretending to be a fairy god mother. And if that doesn't make it clear then this should. If you value any of your body parts you will stay away."

Decebel didn't try to stop her when she turned and walked briskly from the room. He didn't know what to say to fix what he had royally screwed up, so he decided to let her go so she could cool off. She would be more reasonable after she had calmed down.

"Decebel, what aren't you telling her?" Sally spoke up breaking the silence that had descended once Jen left.

He looked over at the healer and he knew she saw past his walls, past the façade that he had put in place to make it appear that everything was okay.

"Some things are better left in the dark," he told her gently.

Sally shook her head. "You know that isn't true. We can't see in the dark. There is nothing to light the way, so we stumble. We grope around hoping to find our way safe and sound. But there is nothing to grasp onto, and in the dark we can't see those who could help us." Sally stepped out of Costin's hold and walked directly in front of Decebel. Her eyes were filled with compassion and the need to help the wolves that were in her pack. But she could tell that Decebel was beyond help. "Nothing is ever better in the dark, Alpha. Darkness is for those who have lost their way. They have traveled off the road that they should take and the darkness wraps around them, pulling them in with false promises." She paused again maintaining eye contact which for all others, except a select few, would be impossible. Sally took a deep breath before she continued. "Now you listen to me, Decebel, Alpha of the Serbian pack, mate to Jennifer. You are pack, and because of that, the darkness cannot have you. You belong to us, and you know better than anyone that we do not give up what is ours."

Decebel watched in stunned silence as Costin took Sally's hand and lead her from the room. He gave Decebel a brief show of his neck and then left.

"Well, that's a first," Decebel said into the now empty room. "I've been put in my place by a gypsy healer." He let out a low, weary chuckle that quickly faded away when he thought about the darkness that he was indeed walking into. He couldn't tell Sally that his darkness was unavoidable because his daughter's life was on the line. For that precious life, the life that his beautiful wife now carried, he would run with everything he had into the darkness without hesitation.

Lilly stood just inside the entrance to the mountain. She still wasn't used to the magic. From her vantage point, she saw only a normal foyer and front door. But anyone passing by on the outside would only see a mountain, rocks, earth, and shrubs. She refused to admit to herself that she was actually going to miss this place, though she had only spent a short time here. But in truth, it felt like home, or maybe it was just because Cypher was here and that made it her home. She ran a hand across her face as she fought against the tears that had been relentlessly trying to escape her eyes. Crying wouldn't do any good. It wouldn't change anything and it would only make her look like a weak ninny. So instead, she stood rigid, trying to appear nonchalant while she waited for Peri to arrive.

She had actually been relieved when Cypher had told her that Peri would be escorting her to the airport. But the relief was overshadowed by the fact that Cypher didn't plan on going with her himself. But then again, what had she expected? The man was kicking her out. Why on earth would she want him to wave to her as she boarded the plane? *Oh I don't know, Lilly, maybe because you love him and want him to see you at the airport and realize he is making the biggest mistake of his life. Then, in the last moment, he would run to make the plane stop and board it to beg you not to go.* Lilly groaned at her inner dialogue and pathetic scenario, which she must actually be from some sappy romantic comedy she had watched. She had to get a grip, and what better way to do that than by being distracted by an eccentric, ancient, and quite dramatic, fae?

"All right," Peri nearly yelled as she suddenly appeared out of thin air beside Lilly who, for her part, yelped and jumped into the air.

"I hear you have been evicted and must vacate the premises immediately." Peri didn't acknowledge Lilly's jumpiness. Instead the fae just looked at her as if she hadn't just nearly given Lilly a heart attack while simultaneously reminding her that she was being kicked out of her man's house, or in this case, mountain castle, which she loved.

"Thanks for that, Perizada. I'm glad that you reminded me that Cypher has decided to send me home, because I sort of forgot, even though I'm standing her in the freaking foyer with my packed bags."

"Okay, note to self, human is touchy about eviction topic," Peri said absently as she picked up Lilly's bags. "Alright, have you said your goodbyes? Have you done all the ranting you require? Have you shredded all his sheets and burned the curtains? I saw that in a movie once and it seemed therapeutic."

"Can we just go?" Lilly said as her shoulders slumped forward, her eyes devoid of their usual spunk.

"Grab my sleeve please, and try not to puke."

Lilly closed her eyes, expecting there to be some sort of flash or rush of air. But instead there was nothing and then when she opened her eyes she was no longer in the foyer of Cypher's home.

"Uh, Peri, I thought Cypher told you to take me to the airport," Lilly said slowly as she looked around.

"You must not know me very well if you think that I always do what those bossy, arrogant supernatural men tell me to do. I mean, where would the fun in that be?"

"That sounds like something Jen would say," Lilly smiled.

"Well if she does, it's because she learned it from me." Peri's voice was full of her usual haughtiness.

"Whatever you say, Peri fairy."

"I'm going to let that slide since your boyfriend just gave you the boot. Now, come on, let's go find your offspring and her cronies."

Decebel knocked on Dr. Cynthia Steele's door. He had debated for half an hour whether or not he should speak with her about his dilemma and finally decided that it was the best option he had. He wasn't sure how Cynthia was going to respond to his admission, but he knew that as her Alpha he could command her to keep her silence if need be.

The door opened and Cynthia's eyes widened in surprise.

"Decebel," she said carefully, "is Jen alright? Do you need me to come and check on her?"

Decebel shook his head. "She is fine. I've come here to speak to you about something that has to do with me," he paused and then amended. "Well, it has to do with both myself and my mate, but I do not want her to know that I have come to see you. I also must insist that everything that is said in this room tonight stays between you and me. Is that clear?"

Cynthia nodded as she stepped aside so that he could enter.

"What can I do for you," she asked as she motioned him to a chair, which he did not take.

Decebel rubbed the back of his neck and Cynthia noticed then that his face was lined with worry and his eyes a little brighter than she liked. She waited patiently, not wanting to provoke an already agitated Alpha.

"I need something to keep Jennifer from being able to enter my mind while I sleep."

Out of all the things that she thought he would say, that was definitely not one of them.

"I don't know of any sort of human medicine that would do that, Alpha. Why haven't you sought out Rachel or Sally?" Cynthia attempted to keep her voice as calm and clinical as possible.

"This is something that I cannot trust them with. Their loyalty to my mate will overrule their loyalty to me."

"What about Peri?" she asked.

Decebel's jaw clenched. As he breathed out, the air forced through his gritted teeth made an eerie snake-like sound. "Do you really think I can trust a fae who would rather skin us males than look at us?"

Cynthia nodded. "Good point."

They were both quiet for several minutes. Cynthia wracked her brain for some way to help Decebel. He was obviously very distressed about something and if it had to do with Jen then he would be relentless until he found a solution. Then it hit her. She grabbed her cell phone and began texting quickly. She thanked the Great Luna that all of the females in their group had exchanged numbers.

"What are you doing?" he growled.

Cynthia held up a finger and hoped that he wouldn't bite it off. She pressed the send button and then looked up at him.

"I realize that whatever it is that you are dealing with is sensitive and private. The person I just asked to come can be trusted. Please trust me."

Decebel could see the sincerity in the doctor's eyes. Though he didn't really want to trust her, what other choice did he have?

"Fine."

Just as the word was out of his lips, Elle appeared next to Cynthia. She glanced from Cynthia to Decebel and huffed. "This is going to be bad isn't it?" she asked.

Decebel looked at Cynthia with tight lips and a raised brow. It was very much a look that said *what the hell, Doc?*

"You say I can trust her?"

Cynthia nodded and then looked at Elle.

"Elle, now would be the time to reassure the obviously upset Alpha that he can trust you so that he doesn't make you a snack before dinner."

Elle let out a quick breath. "Right, um, you can trust me, Decebel."

"No matter what I tell you? You cannot share it with Sorin." He narrowed his eyes at her and took a step forward.

To Elle's credit she did not back away.

"Yes, no matter what you tell me. And I won't tell Sorin anything that you do not want me to. I'm capable of keeping my thoughts guarded."

He told Elle the same thing he had told Cynthia and then waited for the fae's response.

"I can put a block in your mind that will be triggered as you relax into sleep. Unfortunately, Jen will be able to tell that it's there. There is nothing I can do to prevent that."

Decebel would have preferred she make it appears as if his mind was just blank as he slept so that Jennifer wouldn't think there was anything wrong, but at this point she knew something was up and as much as he hated it, this was his only option.

"Fine," he told her gruffly. "Do what you must."

Elle stepped towards him slowly as if approaching a beast that could rip her to pieces in a matter of seconds. She cringed inwardly as she realized that was exactly what she was doing; only the beast was an alpha Canis lupus.

"I have to touch your head," she told him as she raised her arms.

Decebel knelt down so that she could reach him. She placed her hands on either side of his head and began to speak in a language that he didn't understand. He felt warmth radiating from her skin and his scalp tingled. Then she took her hands away and the warmth was gone.

"That's it?" he asked.

Elle nodded.

"Why does everything with the fae seem so anticlimactic?" Cynthia asked absently.

Elle smiled. "Peri likes to make a show of it, but the theatrics are more for intimidation rather than necessity."

"For some reason, that doesn't surprise me," Decebel said dryly.

Elle smirked. "Well can you blame her? She's older than the seventh layer of the earth. She has to get her kicks somehow."

After reiterating several times to Elle and Cynthia that they were to keep silent, he left them and headed toward the indoor garden. It was the only place he knew to go to find solitude and privacy. He walked all the way to the back and took a small amount of something akin to peace from the rippling of the indoor creek and trickling sound the water made as it flowed over the rocks. Life seemed simple in here surrounded by nature, no matter that it was created by man rather than out in the open somewhere. His wolf longed for the forest, the smells of the earth, trees, and water. He longed to run with his mate alongside him, playing with him as they had done so many times. He forced himself to push those memories aside and to focus on the present.

He knelt when he reached the farthest corner of the garden and closed his eyes. His mind reached out to their Creator and he prayed she would hear him.

"Why is it that you insist on worrying that I will not come when you call?" The Great Luna sat before him on the steps that led up to the gazebo where a swing hung silently.

"I suppose that I feel very insignificant in this large world and imagine that you must have more important things to do," Decebel admitted.

She smiled gently at him. "Well, there is nothing more important than one of my own seeking me out. It takes great strength to kneel and ask another for help, to know that you cannot do it on your own, and I never intended for you to."

"Thank you," Decebel told her and the words felt dry in his mouth as he knew they did not convey the gratefulness that he felt.

"I have some questions," he paused and waited.

She nodded for him to go on.

"When will the bond be broken?"

He noticed that her eyes grew sad as she watched him. "It cannot be undone all at once. If I were to take the bond away immediately it could kill you both as you are of one soul. It must be done slowly, gradually, and even then it will be painful for you both."

"Is there anything that will make it easier on her?" Decebel felt his wolf fighting him; the wolf did not agree with what the man was doing. His wolf was convinced that they could find another way to save their pup.

"Physical distance between you would help. As you know, you crave each other's presence and touch. It makes the bond stronger."

Decebel's head fell forward as her words wrapped his heart in an icy cold embrace. The idea of not being with his mate, especially if these were his last months with her, made him sick and angry at the same time. He didn't know how he would leave her. How could he? She would more than likely kill him if he told her he would need to be away from her. And what excuse could he possibly give her?

"Alpha, are you sure this is what you want?" The Great Luna met his eyes and the care and empathy he saw there comforted him briefly.

"Can't you do something?" he asked and the words came out through a deep growl that he could not control.

"I have given you all free will. I do not force my own desires and will upon you, making you mindless robots. It is because of that free will that you sometimes choose things with consequences that are difficult to bear. Jennifer was offered a way out of death, a death that was meant to happen. And because of that there are consequences. She will face the consequences of her choice in one form or another. Don't mistake my words for uncaring. It breaks my heart to see my children hurt. It pulls from me the deepest of grief and I mourn with you." She stood up and walked over to him and placed a hand on his shoulder. He felt peace rush through him, and he let out a slow breath.

"Death is a part of life, child. I did not create you to be immortal, even though I gave you long lives. Jennifer was to come home to be with me, and she chose not to. She went against the laws of nature. The Fates are the ones who watch over all supernaturals, not just my wolves. They keep the balance and even I cannot interfere with that balance. If you are still sure that this is what you want, then it will begin tonight. She is in her second trimester of the pregnancy. It will take the rest of that time to fully eliminate the bond between you. And do not worry about how you will put distance between you. There is an opportunity coming."

Decebel's stomach tightened at this information. When he started to ask her what she meant, she was already gone.

As he started to stand, he felt as though the weight of the world was now draped across his shoulders and he saw no way to be rid of it. He turned to leave the quiet peace of the garden, and just as he reached the door, he grabbed onto the frame as he stumbled. He felt a sharp pain rip through him and then it was gone. But left in its place was what felt like a small tear in whatever seam held him together. He closed his eyes, searching for Jennifer, needing to know if she was okay. He found her in their bedroom. Her face was pale and Sally was helping her sit down. He clinched his jaw as he thought about how it should be him helping her. It should be his arms around her, checking on her and comforting her. She looked so confused and scared.

It had begun, just as the Great Luna had promised, their bond was being broken—the bond that had saved him from darkness was now being taken from him and it was of his own doing.

Chapter 5
"Whoever came up with the saying *when it rains it pours* was a bloody optimist. In my experience, when it rains, it doesn't just pour. More likely, it is a tsunami. I mean the wind blows so hard that houses fly around like Dorothy's shack and Toto can just kiss his hairy butt goodbye. Rain comes down in sheets so thick that you might just drown out on the street. And while all this is going on, we have werewolf males doing the complete opposite of what is in their nature to do. They are running in the wrong freaking direction. I mean, seriously guys, what the hell is up with that? When it rains it pours, HA, that's a good one." ~Jacque

Sally was sitting next to Jen on the bed when the door came flying open. Jacque came running in with a frown on her face. Behind her, Peri and Lilly followed.

"Lilly!" Sally smiled and jumped to her feet to give her a hug.

"Hey Ms. P," Jen said from the spot where she sat. She didn't get up because she was nervous that the sudden pain would come back. Sally had called Cynthia to come check on her, and they had been waiting when Jacque and the two others had come barging in.

Jacque had yet to say anything but stood off to the side with her arms folded across her chest with her face pinched into a tight frown.

"Um, Jacque aren't you glad to see your mom?" Jen asked.

"She would be, if the reason she was seeing her wasn't because her king is giving her the boot," Peri interjected.

"Thank you for that, Peri," Jacque snapped.

"What?" Sally's eyes widened as she took a step back so she could see everyone in the room.

"What do you mean giving her the boot?" Jen nearly snarled as she started to stand.

The door flew open again before anyone could answer and Cynthia came rushing in.

"Are you alright...any blood, nausea, vomiting?" The questions flew from her mouth like rapid fire gun shots as she continued towards Jen. She ignored the others as she took Jen's pulse and listened to her respirations and then listened for the heartbeat of the baby.

"Calm down, Dr. Quinn, medicine woman. It was a false alarm. I had a brief moment of pain and then it was gone. Sally was just being over cautious."

Cynthia looked around and noticed for the first time that the room was full of women.

"Where the heck is your mate?"

Yet again the door flew open, only much harder since it was a large, upset wolf who came through it.

"Jennifer," Decebel maneuvered quite gracefully for his large size around the women until he stood in front of his mate.

"Are you alright?" he asked gently as he brushed his fingers against her cheek.

Jen felt the familiar butterflies that Decebel always triggered in her as if they lie dormant until he touched her or even simply looked at her as he was doing right now.

She nodded. "It was nothing, just a sharp pain and then gone."

Decebel stared into her eyes. As she tried to search in his mind to find out what he was thinking, she felt him gently push her out. She was still angry about their earlier discussion, but now there were other things to think about.

"Not now, okay. Later, we'll talk." He leaned down and kissed her on the forehead and the act was so gentle, so unlike her mate, that once again she felt the unease of knowing that something was wrong.

"What's going on?" Decebel asked as he turned to face the group of women.

Peri let out an exasperated huff. "Can we please just get anyone necessary for this little meeting of the not-so-stable minds in here so we don't have to repeat it fifteen bloody times?"

"Vasile wants us to meet in the great hall," Costin said from the doorway. All the eyes in the room swept over to look at him.

"Finally, someone who doesn't nearly rip my door off to get in," Jen grumbled. Decebel slipped his hand into hers and gave it a small squeeze, which just sent those damn butterflies soaring up her throat and nearly out of her eyes in the form of tears.

Everyone in the room was still looking at Costin like he was a funny growth on the wall.

He huffed when nobody moved. "My mate informed me of what was going on so I took it upon myself to share it with Vasile. That's how I have a freaking clue. Can we all please go to the great hall now?"

Everyone nodded in unison with small 'oh' and 'right' coming from them. By the time everyone had filed out of the room, Fane was there waiting to take Jacque's hand. They stayed at the back of the group with Lilly walking next to them.

No one spoke, as if there was an unwritten law that kept them from discussing the matter until they were all gathered, just as Peri had suggested.

Vasile, Alina, Wadim, Cyn, Sorin, Elle, Adam and Crina all sat waiting for them in the large room.

"The gang's all here Vasile," Peri announced, "gathered again. It's sort of like one of those *where are they now* specials on Oprah."

Jen let out a snort as she took a seat with Decebel by her side. "Do you do anything besides watch daytime television and perform dramatic special effects?"

Peri raised a brow at Jen. "I keep your *not so tiny anymore* ass out of trouble."

"Hey," Jen nearly shouted, "not cool Peri, no talking about the pregnant chick's backside. Once it's back in its former glory, you can make jokes about it all you want. Until then, you will learn to like big butts."

"And I cannot lie," Sally whispered bringing a snort of laughter from everyone except Vasile and Alina who looked bewildered.

As usual, Vasile cleared his throat to bring everyone's attention back to the matter at hand.

"From what I understand, we did not come down here to discuss Decebel's mate's posterior. So would someone please enlighten me as to what is going on and why we have the pleasure of Lilly's company?"

Lilly stepped forward before anyone could speak and nodded to Alina and Vasile in greeting. Her smile was tight and it was obvious she was upset.

"I'm sorry to have barged in on you," she started but was interrupted by Jacque.

"First off, you are welcome here anytime. Second, it was the fairy who barged in."

Peri rolled her eyes but didn't comment.

"Cypher has decided it is not safe for me to stay," Lilly continued as if her daughter had not spoken, "because of his brother. So he has asked me to return to my home in Texas."

Vasile did not speak right away. His eyes were narrowed, but not in anger. He seemed to be carefully considering what he would say.

"Did Cypher consult you on the matter before he asked you to leave?" he finally asked.

"No."

"Surprise, surprise," Jen muttered.

"Peri, what part do you play in all of this?" he asked as he turned to look at the fae.

"I went to talk with Cypher like I told you I would. It turned out to be a very informative conversation. First, we discussed the disgusting evil that is permeating his forest, and then we discussed the eviction of his supposed mate. Then I told him you requested his presence. Just as I was getting ready to leave, he asked me if I would accompany Lilly to the airport. Being the kind hearted person that I am, I agreed."

There was a collective snort from the females in the room.

"If by kind hearted you mean meddlesome, then yes, you are indeed kindhearted." The words came from Elle who sat across the room and surprised glances shot her way. She simply stared back, waiting for Peri to continue.

"Why did you bring Lilly here and not the airport?" Alina asked.

"I thought she had a right to tell her daughter what was going on and say her goodbyes."

"So you do plan to go back to the U.S.?" Vasile asked.

Lilly glanced over at Jacque who stood rigidly with tight fists at her sides and narrowed eyes. Fane stood behind her with a hand resting on her hip. After several heartbeats, Lilly looked back to Vasile.

"Yes."

"I'm going with her," Jacque said as soon as the word was out of her mother's mouth. She stepped away from Fane. He let out an audible growl and reached for his mate, but Jacque swatted his hand away. She walked over to stand next to her mom and took her hand.

"I know that Cypher thinks that he is making her safe by sending her home, but if his brother is as whacked as he says he is and he wants my mom, then an ocean is not going to keep him from her."

Vasile looked from Jacque to his son and felt the weight of his position settle over him. Fane was in no state to travel, to be out of his territory, and out of Vasile's control. And Vasile could not order Jacque to stay here. If he did, she would probably end up resenting Fane because of it. Next to him, Alina patted his leg and then stood up.

"I will go with Lilly and Jacque," she announced. Vasile did not look up. He was not surprised that his mate would offer such a thing, and he would be a very dumb man to think he could stop her. He knew what she was doing, trying to appease their son and help keep Lilly and their daughter-in-law safe at the same time. Fane just might be okay with Jacque going if his mother was with her—maybe.

"I'm going too." Sally suddenly jumped up and hurried over to Jacque's side. Costin's face resembled Fane's as he took several steps after his mate. The looks on the ladies' faces had him stopping in his tracks. He had no doubts that they would claw his eyes out if he tried to get Sally; females could be protective like that.

"And me." Jen was up as quickly as her pregnant self could move and standing next to the group. She looked back over her shoulder, expecting Decebel to be right behind her snarling and objecting. But instead, he was rooted to his spot. His jaw was so tense she thought he just might break it from clenching and his eyes were bright, bright, amber. For the first time in their relationship, he wasn't stopping her from leaving his side, and with her being pregnant no less. The shock of it nearly drove her to her knees. She felt a warm hand slide in hers and looked over to see Sally giving her a gentle smile. Sally, the glue to the trio's friendship, always knew what to do and when to do it. Jen turned her attention back to the group, effectively putting her mate at her back.

"If Jen goes, then I go." Cynthia stepped forward with a resigned sigh.

Rachel, Crina, Elle, and Cyn stepped forward next and the growls in the room were beginning to drown out the voices.

"This is really a tough choice," Peri grumbled. "I can either live in estrogen city or testosterone valley." She looked from the men to the women and then stepped towards the females. "But at least in estrogen city there will be chocolate and Jen to keep me entertained."

Jen grinned. "We aim to please, Peri fairy."

Alina turned to her mate questioningly. "What would you say to this, Alpha?"

Vasile stood and looked around the room at the very tense, very angry mated males and then back at the determined females. "*You are asking the impossible my love,*" he told her.

"*Lilly is pack by way of Jacque and it is our job to protect her. The males need to stay here and figure out a plan to deal with this new threat. I would think you all would be happy to have us out of harm's way.*"

He chuckled out loud. "You would play that card."

Alina tilted her head to the side and waited for his decision.

"It is within my right to speak for the females of my pack. Decebel will need to speak for the females in his pack." He paused and glanced one more time at the males. He wouldn't be surprised if they tried to strangle him in his sleep. "The females who have requested," he laughed at that, "to go with Lilly will do so except Rachel." Rachel looked at Vasile, waiting for his explanation and knowing the Alpha always had an agenda. "Rachel, we cannot have both healers away. One must remain here to tend to the needs of the pack and since you are in my pack, you stay."

Gavril let out a satisfied rumble and walked over, tugging Rachel away from the group. He pulled her into his arms which seemed to soften the frustration that had been written across her tight lips.

Sorin stepped forward and Adam was right behind him. "Don't you think some males should go with them?"

"And who would I send?" Vasile snapped, "If I send a couple of the mated males, the others will feel slighted. If I send any of the unmated males, they will die by the teeth of one of the mated males. So tell me, Sorin, who can I send?"

Sorin did not have an answer and he knew Vasile was right. He stepped back, but his eyes continued to glow as he turned his eyes on his mate.

"Decebel, you must decide if you will allow your mate and Sally to go." Vasile took a step back, giving the other alpha the floor.

Decebel's eyes bore into Jennifer's back. She refused to look at him and he knew it was because he hadn't refused her request. How ironic was it that the one time he did not object to her, she gets angry about it.

"They may go." his words rung out through the hall and he swore that everyone stopped breathing. Was he really so unreasonable that they would be so shocked over his decision? He thought back over the course of the past few months and decided, yes, he definitely was unreasonable when it came to Jennifer because the idea of losing her was enough to drive him to the most irrational choices sometimes.

"We leave tonight," Peri announced. Growls and chairs being shoved out of the way began to fill the room as angry mates tried to keep their anger under control. Costin lost the battle and phased right there—clothes tearing, eyes glowing, saliva dripping from his fangs. He gave Sally one last look before turning and running from the great hall.

"Oh dear." Sally blew out an exhausted breath.

"I think that's going to top the understatements of all understatements," Jacque told them as she pointed them in the direction of her own mate who was standing so still he didn't even look like he was breathing, but his clawed hand gripping the door frame was the damning evidence that his own control was nearly gone.

"So where are we meeting and what time?" Jen spoke up and drew all the females' attention away from the ticked-off males.

"Vasile said we can take the pack jet and it will be ready to go in two hours," Alina told them.

Cynthia rubbed her hands together and was suddenly in *all business* mode. "Alright then, we have two hours to pack and calm the guys down enough so that they might not tear the mansion apart while we are gone."

They each again glanced over their shoulders and Jen let out a snort. "Yeah, I don't think anything we say or do is going to calm this bunch down. Look," she pointed, "Vasile has Sorin up against the wall by his throat."

Elle's eyes widened and she took a step in her mate's direction, but Alina stopped her with a gentle hand on her arm.

"That is between Alpha and pack member. Do not interfere; you will only make it worse."

Elle's lips pursed and it was obvious that she didn't want to listen to Alina. But after one last glance, she turned away.

The girls all agreed to meet at the front doors of the mansion in two hours whether their males were calmed down or not. Jen pointed out that maybe there should be some sort of signal if they were detained, "by ropes or something equally as fun," she told them. They all shook their heads at her. With audible groans, they headed towards their rooms.

Jen turned to look at Decebel who hadn't appeared to have moved from the spot where he had announced his decision. She narrowed her eyes at him and a snarl worthy of an alpha female ground out through her lips.

"Our room. Now."

Decebel flinched under his mate's stare and the words that she pushed through their bond, the one he was trying to close off, tore at his heart. That pain would be nothing compared to the anguish he was about to endure because he was doing something that went against everything in his nature. His wolf was in an absolute rage, and Decebel knew that if he let his wolf have any amount of control, he would grab Jennifer and never let her out of his sight. The idea of their mate and their child so far away was like a knife ripping through his organs, twisting this way and that, destroying any function they might have had. And this was only the beginning.

Chapter 6
"Sometimes, no matter how hard you try, there is no right choice in a situation. You can go over it and over it in your mind, looking at every angle, and there is simply nothing you can change. I would rather have her by my side, but then she would be in perilous danger. So I will send her home, but then she is out of my reach if something does go wrong. I must choose the lesser of two evils, but I'm beginning to wonder if even that will be too much a price to pay." ~Cypher

"Enter," Cypher called over his shoulder at the sound of the knock. He was attempting to sound civil but there was nothing in him at the moment that felt civil. Lilly was gone. He had sent her away. And so now here he stood on the brink of some sort of war with his brother and no mate to tell him all would be well. Whether a man knew it or not, he needed a woman at his back—someone to remind him that all is not lost, someone to show him the sliver of light that is creeping its way through the dark, someone to hold him, even when he didn't realized he needed to be held.

"She is gone," Gerick, the general of his army, spoke softly behind him.

Cypher bit back the snide comment that was on the tip of his tongue. It wasn't Gerick's fault that Lilly was gone. It was nobody's fault but his own.

"I know, but thank you for telling me."

He knew that Gerick wanted to say more but was not sure if it was his place to do so.

"What is it, Gerick?" Cypher finally asked as a loud sigh gusted from his lungs.

"Was it really necessary to send her away?" Gerick was attempting to keep the accusation out of his voice, but he wanted his king to be fully aware of the disapproval. "It isn't just you who feels her absence."

Cypher closed his eyes as he thought about the past couple of months that Lilly had been with him and his people. They had grown to love her nearly as much as he did. She was kind and understanding, willing to just listen when someone needed to talk. She had definitely brought something back to their kind that had been missing, compassion and hope. Cypher never thought that he would find a mate, and his people were convinced that they would eventually fade away as the magic continued to fade from the human realm. Cypher wasn't sure if that was what would happen, but he understood what they meant. They felt insignificant, without purpose and unsure of what to do while they watched their king flounder his way through his existence, trying to make sense of what he needed to do next.

Humans simply did not understand the importance of a mate in the supernatural community. A mate was more than a spouse, more than someone you just spent your life with or procreated with. A mate in the supernatural world was the completion of something that was not whole. A mate filled a space that no one else could.

Lilly was that person for Cypher. She was his, and through him, she was his people's as well.

"Gerick," his voice was soft as his head fell forward and a rush of air left his lungs, "I would not have sent her away if I had thought there was another option."

"I know that. But by sending her away you have brought fear into the hearts of our people."

"They should be afraid!" Cypher snarled as he whipped around and his eyes bore into Gerick's. "My brother has nothing good left in him. Anything worthy in him died with his woman, and all that is left is an empty shell, yearning to be filled with the blood, sorrow, and grief of others. They should be afraid," his last words come out in a near whisper.

Cypher knew that his words were cruel and that his anger was misplaced, but that did not help him keep it under control.

"I will be leaving in a little while to go to the Romanian pack. I'm going alone. You will need to keep an eye on the perimeter. The blackness in the air hasn't grown any thicker, but it has not abated at all either," Cypher's voice had lost some of the edge and he was beginning to lock up the emotions that were threatening to consume him. He didn't have time to pine over his mate. He had an enemy to defeat and he could not defeat him by standing in this throne room whining about things he could not change.

Lilly was gone, at least for now. Once the threat of his brother had been neutralized he would go and get her back. He only hoped that her heart did not move on while he fought to keep her safe and alive.

Decebel closed the door quietly behind him as he walked into the room Jennifer and him shared at the Romanian pack mansion. He watched quietly as Jennifer went into the closet and began bringing out clothes and laying them on the bed. She didn't look at him or even acknowledge that he was in the room, so he waited. He didn't have any idea what he was going to say to her, but he was terrified that as soon as he opened his mouth it was going to be to beg her to stay and plead for her forgiveness. He had hurt her so much in the past month, and he knew that she would only continue to hurt. *What choice do I have?* he growled to himself. He wanted to save the life of their child, and he didn't want to put Jennifer in a place where she had to choose between him or their baby. This was the only solution he could come up with, and he knew Jennifer would tell him it sucked and to come up with something new, but he was fresh out of *new*.

"Are you going to tell me why you are okay with letting your pregnant wife fly halfway around the world with a woman who is being hunted by a crazy warlock?" her voice was calm and even.

Decebel took a step towards her but she held up her hand to stop him.

"Answer me, B," she told him firmly.

"I love you, Jennifer. I love you more than any man has a right to love. That is all you need to know." He tried to implore her with his eyes to just trust him. But could he really ask that of her when he knew he was planning on ending his life without telling her.

"As romantic and fuzzy as that sounds, it's a crap answer Dec and you know it." Jen grabbed her suitcase from the closet and started putting the clothes she had laid on her bed into it. She let out a dry laugh that said she was anything but humored. "I mean seriously, after all we've been through together? After all we've done together, you honestly believe I will just take what you're telling me and act like I have my head shoved so far up my butt that I can't smell the shit you have spewing from your lips?"

His eyes widened at her language. He was use to her being crass, but even for her this was intense.

"Yeah, I said it," she threw her arms out wide, "what are you going to do about it, *Alpha*? Tell me another sweet nothing and hope that I choke on it so I can ignore the fact that my mate is shutting me out and shipping me and his unborn child off to another country without so much as a *'bye babe, hope our baby lives through delivery.'* Come on, Dec. What the hell is that?!"

Decebel turned abruptly and slammed his fists into the wall tearing through the plaster even as her words tore through his heart.

"HOW COULD YOU EVEN THINK SUCH A THING?" he snarled but kept his back to her. "You have no concept of the pain that I am going through right now, mate." He turned slowly to face her as his breathing increased and he fought for control to keep from phasing. "The thought of you gone, where I can't touch you, can't hold you, can't be there if you need me, is like a hot skewer being shoved into my gut."

"How am I supposed to know, Decebel?" she snarled right back. "You won't let me in. You hide your thoughts from me. You keep your touch from me. It's like you can't stand to be with me. WHAT AM I SUPPOSED TO THINK?" Tears were sliding down her cheeks and she had abandoned the half packed suitcase.

Their eyes met and the pain they both felt radiated between them. Decebel stumbled forward and fell to his knees in front of her.

"Please, I know I don't deserve it, but please trust me," he whispered against her stomach as he leaned against her.

Jen closed her eyes and soaked up the contact as she ran her fingers through his dark hair. It had grown enough in the past couple of months that it dropped in front of his eyes, adding to his off-limits allure.

She felt more tears slide down her cheeks and drop onto his face as he looked up at her. Decebel stood and wrapped his arms around her, pulling her in as tightly as he could without hurting her.

"Baby," he whispered against her hair. He breathed in her scent and could taste her on his tongue and he longed for the nights of shared laughter, whispers, and love. "I'm so sorry I've hurt you. But you have to believe me, I love you, I love our baby, and I'm not abandoning you."

Jen shuddered as she felt his breath against her neck and his hands run up her back, firm and confident in his touch. She loved that about him. He saw what he wanted and he just took it. He had wanted her, and he had taken her, and she had gone willingly with a big fat grin on her face. That felt like ages ago, but it hadn't even been a year. She never thought she would need anyone, not the way she needed Decebel. As he held her asking her to trust him, even though he wouldn't tell her what he was keeping from her, she knew she would. She would give Decebel anything he asked for, even if it broke her heart to do so.

"Promise me you will be alright," she told him as she pulled back far enough to be able to look up into his amber eyes, "promise me that you will come for me and your child. Promise me that," her words were cut off with a choke as she tried to keep from falling apart.

"Shh, Jennifer," he told her gently. He kissed her forehead, her cheeks, her chin, and then her lips. Decebel's hand slipped up into Jennifer's hair on either side of her face, holding her still as he took her mouth in his. He kissed her deeply imprinting his taste in her mind, his love in her heart, and, as usual, she gave as good as she got. He nipped at her lips and smiled when she moaned and pressed her swollen body against his. He continued to kiss her but let one of his hands slid down until it rested on her stomach. She gasped as she pulled back from the kiss and pressed her forehead to his. Her eyes met his as she covered his hand with her own.

"I love you," her whisper reached into the dark places that were beginning to form as their bond began to weaken. He pushed the thought from his mind and focused on the woman in his arms—his woman.

"Sometimes *I love you* seems inadequate for what I feel for you," he whispered back.

"Please tell me to stay," Jennifer pleaded with him and it brought a fresh wave of anguish.

"I want you to baby, more than you know. But you need to go. You will be safe there."

Decebel's wolf snarled at him. *We make her safe,* he told the man. *We protect her; she is ours.* He couldn't argue with his wolf because all of those things were true, but the man knew that sometimes protecting meant letting go of the one needing protection, no matter how badly you want to hold on.

Jen waited, but he didn't say anything more. She pulled him tighter against her, trying to memorize the feel of his body.

"I'll go," she told him finally, "but I'm still pissed at you."

A small smile curved the side of his lips and she reached up to kiss him.

"It is noted that you are still pissed," he told her in between kisses.

Their kiss grew more and more intense as words seemed incapable of describing the love and need that had been growing in both of them. Jen grabbed on to him like he was a life raft in a turbulent storm. Her hands roamed over him and he didn't stop her the way he had so many times before.

"I'm sorry, baby. I'm so sorry," he murmured over and over and his own hands caressed and loved her as he had not allowed himself to do in so long.

He knew he should just kiss her, help her pack, and then walk her out to go, but he couldn't. This might be the last time he would be with his mate, the last time to kiss her, touch her, and love her, and so he would take what was his, what he had denied himself and her for too long.

"I love you Jennifer," he told her as he laid her on their bed and covered her body with his own.

"Show me," she was breathless as the words left her mouth.

"I plan to," he whispered against her ear. His wolf howled triumphantly and Decebel was powerless to stop himself as he sunk his teeth into his mark on her neck that branded her as his.

"Yours," she agreed.

"Mine."

"I understand why you want to go." Fane was standing with his back against the wall and his arms were folded across his chest. He just barely kept the growl out of his voice, but he couldn't stop his eyes from glowing. He was angry - angry with Cypher for sending Lilly away, angry at Jacquelyn for deciding to go without speaking with him first, angry at his father for agreeing to it, and angry at himself because he couldn't do a damn thing about any of it.

"If you understand, then what is the problem?" Jacque asked as she threw her clothes haphazardly in her suitcase not bothering to check what was in her hands.

"The problem is I'm not going to be there to keep you safe."

Jacque stopped what she was doing and looked over at her mate. "Have I not proven that I'm capable of protecting myself?"

"That's not the point," Fane snapped, "You're my mate. You belong by my side."

Jacque groaned and threw her head back. "Are you kidding me? Look, I understand that you males have this weird complex that makes you all possessive and whatnot, but this is my mom, Fane. She's hurting and I'm not going to stand back while she goes back to the states after the man she loves has sent her away."

"It's for her own good. He's just trying to keep her safe." Fane pushed off of the wall and walked towards his mate. "It's not like he doesn't love her."

"And you think that makes it less painful?" Jacque slammed her suitcase closed and zipped it shut with much more force than was needed. *Poor suitcase*, she thought, *it's not your fault all the males on this blasted continent are clueless buttheads.*

"I can hear you, you know?"

Jacque raised her eyes to look at Fane. "Yes, I'm well aware of the fact that you frequently listen in when you are not invited."

She jerked the suitcase from the bed and set it on the floor, pulling up the handle so that she could roll it behind her. She made another pass through the bathroom, but then decided that whatever she'd forgotten her mom would have at her house. If not, then Walmart was a hop, skip, and a jump away.

Fane watched in brooding silence as his mate flitted around the room. He couldn't make her stay. He had argued all the things he could think to argue and it just wasn't enough. As she headed towards their bedroom door, dragging the suitcase behind her, she looked back over her shoulder.

"Walk me out?" she asked him in a voice that was much softer than the one she had been using with him. It was the voice she used when she wanted something, the voice he could rarely deny.

He growled but walked to her and took the suitcase from her.

"I'm not happy about this, Jacquelyn," he told her as his blue eyes bore into hers.

"Noted."

"Do you care?"

She huffed, "You know I do."

"But you're still going?"

"Yes."

He leaned forward and kissed her forehead, surprisingly gentle considering the scowl plastered on his face. He grabbed her then and pulled her from their room, suitcase in one hand, Jacque in the other. There was nothing more to say. Now he just had to hope that he could hold it together until they were together again.

Sally was extremely surprised at Costin's volatile response to her decision to go to the States with Lilly and the others. Of all the male wolves, Costin was the most relaxed and easygoing. But his relaxed nature was gone as he paced around their room, having just hastily shoved on a pair of pants, which was necessitated by his rage induced run.

She stood silently next to her packed things and waited for him to speak. She had packed everything while he was gone and now had an hour to spare or argue with her unreasonable mate, whatever the case may be.

"I'm not unreasonable," he snarled. "My mate wants to fly across the globe without me. I'm sorry if I find that a little upsetting."

"Costin," Sally's voice was gentle but firm, "come here please."

She waited patiently as he made a couple more laps across the room and then finally walked over to her. She looked up into his hazel eyes and saw turmoil dancing frantically in them. She reached up and brushed the hair that perpetually fell across his forehead to the side. His eyes closed and a low rumble emitted from his chest at the contact.

"I love you, and I need you to let me do this," she told him as she stepped closer to him. She moved until she was pressed against him and his scent swirled around her. She opened her mind and their bond as wide as she could so that he could see this wasn't easy for her. She didn't want to be away from him. Surely, he had to know that leaving him was not the ideal choice, but it was the only choice there was.

"No," he whispered as their foreheads touched, "you could choose to stay."

"Lilly needs Jacque, and Jacque needs Jen and me. That is the way it works with family, Costin. You know this. Don't ask me to choose between you and my friends because you know that I will choose you. How can I not choose you, the other half of my soul? But you know it would kill me to do so."

He squeezed his eyes closed tight. She was right. If he asked her, then she would stay and it would destroy her if anything happened to her friends and she hadn't been there. But then if something happened to her while she was gone, it would destroy him. Where was the compromise in that? How is a man to send his mate off without protection and be okay with it? He let out a slow breath and then reached up with one of his hands, gripping the back of her neck. His other hand rested on her hip and tugged her closer. He tilted her head back and looked down into her eyes before he pressed his lips to hers.

It wasn't a gentle kiss. Costin was feeling anything but gentle and he couldn't even feign it. He kissed her deeply, attempting to drown in her taste and hoping that when they came up for air all of it would just be a bad dream. Sally responded passionately as she always did when he touched her. She leaned into him and reached up, wrapping both arms around his neck. The small noises she made drove him crazy and he was beginning to think kissing her was a bad idea because it was only reminding him of what he wouldn't be able to have the entire time she was gone.

"It won't be that long," she told him as they continued to kiss.
"How do you know?" he asked as he nipped her lip roughly.

She pulled back and looked up at him. Her cheeks were flushed and her breathing was rapid. She was beautiful.

"Because if you think it's going to be easy for me to be away from you then you have been sniffing too many of the herbs I've been working with. I don't want to be away from you any longer than I absolutely have to be."

His hands slid to her back and then began sliding lower.

"Could I convince you to stay? Show you what you will be missing?"

Sally nearly groaned as she watched the playfulness return to her mate. It was this flirty, teasing manner that drove her wild and he knew it. He wielded it ruthlessly against her and she nearly always caved.

"Believe me. I know what I will be missing."

Costin smacked her backside, something he seemed fond of doing, and growled at her.

"As long as you know, then you should know I will be reminding you frequently." He tapped her head indicating their mental bond.

She felt her skin heat as blood rushed to her cheeks.

He chuckled. "I see you're remembering just how good I am at using our bond to drive you crazy."

Sally stepped back from his hold and narrowed her eyes at him, though there was a note of playfulness in her tone. "You just remember that payback's a bitch, dimple boy."

Costin grumbled as he wrapped an arm around her. "Name calling, Sally mine? Do you really think now is the time to start that. You know that I like it when you play rough."

Sally elbowed him in the side as they left their room, and though she appreciated the playfulness he was showing her, she could still feel the underlying anger that he had chosen to bury. She could feel his wolf fighting with the man for dominance. She tried to take a deep breath and not worry about how and when that anger might come bursting free and whether or not she would be there to help him regain control.

Chapter 7
"How does a man protect his heart from a lust for power, greed, and self-indulgence? How does a man remain humble and able to recognize that the world is not his to create and command? I truly believe that the only way to protect myself from becoming one such as this is to give sacrificially of myself, my love, my time, and my possessions. If I am not doing these things, then how am I any different from the tyrant we now pursue? How can I say I am on the side of good, if evil reigns within?" ~Vasile

"You don't have to do this," Lilly told her daughter as they walked towards the chartered jet owned by the Romanian pack.

"Life is not about things we do or do not have to do; it's about doing what we should do, about doing the right thing. There's no reason for you to go home by yourself, especially after everything we've all been through." Jacque didn't break stride as she walked beside Lilly. She knew that her mom would try to talk her out of going, but that wasn't an option and she wanted her to know that.

"Thank you." Lilly reached over and squeezed Jacque's hand and fought back tears that had been on the verge of falling since she had arrived at the Romanian mansion. It didn't feel right to break down in front of her daughter. She was the mom, the mature grown-up, and so she pushed away the hurt and disappointment and plastered on her *things are fine* face.

The mates of each of the females were the only ones allowed to accompany them to the airport and so Vasile, Decebel, Fane, Costin, Sorin, and Adam each stood with their mates while Peri and Cynthia stood off a little to the side, giving the pairs some space.

Jacque had no intention of dragging out the goodbye with her mate. They had said all they needed to say and if she stayed too long he would just start his assault of reasons on why she should not be going without him.

"I love you," she told him as she stood on her tiptoes and took his face in her hands. She gave him a firm kiss on his lips and when she pulled back she saw that his eyes glowed wolf blue. She got the distinct feeling that if she did not get her butt on the plane now he just might throw her over his shoulder and run.

"Be safe," his words were a growl, but the hand that reached out and caressed her face was as gentle as if he were handling a delicate treasure. "You are priceless to me," he told her softly.

Jacque took another step back and met her mate's eyes one last time before turning and hurrying towards the jet. She didn't look back for fear that she would run back into his arms and tell him to take her home. She needed to be strong for her mom. She needed Fane to know she was capable of taking care of herself, and more than anything, she needed Fane to pull himself together. Having her with him didn't seem to help. Maybe with her out of the picture, he would be able to figure out what he needed to do to move past the anger and hurt that was consuming him.

"I can't talk you out of this, can I?" Costin asked Sally.

She wrapped her arms around him and pressed her face to his chest. His scent wrapped around her and though she didn't have the sense of smell that the wolves did, she still knew his scent and would know it anywhere. She never knew that the way someone smelled could stir such emotion and longing. She wished that she could bottle it and take it with her so she could have it when she needed his nearness.

"No," she whispered softly knowing he would be able to hear her.

He let out an exhausted sigh and she hated that she was causing him such distress.

"I'll be fine," she told him as she pulled back and looked up at his all-too-handsome face. "I love you."

He gave her one of his heart stopping grins, dimples and all, and she felt her pulse quicken. She wondered if that grin would still cause such a reaction in her twenty or even fifty years from now. As she stared into his hazel eyes where mischief danced, she knew it would.

"I love you too, Sally mine." He wrapped a hand around the back of her neck and pulled her to him pressing his firm lips to her soft ones. He kissed her deeply, devouring the feel and taste of her. It was more than a kiss. It was a claiming. His heart was hers, just as her heart was his. He pushed every ounce of need, want, and love for her into that kiss and Sally felt it deep in her soul.

When he finally let her up for air, he gave her one last kiss on her forehead then gently pushed her in the direction of the plane.

"Go now before I chain you to my side."

Sally took him at his word and turned and walked briskly to the plane, following the same path Jacque had just taken.

Jen watched as Crina said her goodbyes to Adam and Elle to Sorin. Neither of the males looked any happier than her mate did. The difference was that their tortured looks were because they didn't want their mates to leave. Decebel's tortured look, however, was for a reason unknown to her, which thoroughly pissed her off.

"Please try and stay out of trouble." His voice pulled her eyes from the other two couples and she turned to face him.

"I don't think many men like to see a pregnant chick strip, no matter how beautiful she is, so I don't think you need to worry about that—for now." Jen was trying her best to keep the snarkiness out of her voice. No matter how upset she was with her mate, she didn't want to leave on a bad note.

"Stripping is not your only talent when it comes to trouble, mate." His eyes were narrowed at her but she heard the playfulness in his tone and that small thing loosened something inside her, if only for a minute.

"Don't you just take comfort in knowing that you have a very long life to try and keep me out of trouble?" she teased back. And just like that, his guard was back up and it was like the past two hours hadn't happened.

"Let me know when you land. I love you, Jennifer." He leaned forward and held her face in both of his hands. His eyes held hers for several heartbeats and then he pressed a firm kiss to her lips. She nearly fell forward when he released her, and had his hands not steadied her, she might have landed on her face. She glowered at him.

"I love you too, Decebel," she said just as stiffly as he had. "Let me know when you decide to act like the mate who claimed me without reservation. Because this," she motioned to him from head to toe, "is not working for me. I seriously liked you better when you refused to let me out of your sight. What happened to that, B? After I died, you told me you wouldn't let me be away from you. So what happened?"

"Things change, Jennifer. Circumstances change. I love you. We've already been over this. I will come for you soon." Decebel took a step back away from his mate and the look of rejection on her face ripped at his already shredded heart.

Jen made a motion to step towards her mate, but arms came around her to stop her. "Let it go for now Jen," Cynthia's soft voice penetrated the haze of anger and pain that had rushed over Jen when Decebel backed away from her. She nodded, met Decebel's eyes, and then turned to walk away from him.

Decebel watched as his mate walked to the pack jet, her shoulders pulled back proudly, and her head held high. She wouldn't cower, not his woman. No matter how her heart ached, she wouldn't allow the outside world to know it. His hands clenched into fists at his side and the swirl of fear and regret churned in his gut. He should just let her go. There was no need to draw this out, but the further she got from him, the more desperate his wolf fought to be free, to run to their mate. *To hell with it,* he thought as he walked quickly to her.

"Jennifer," his voice was rough with emotion and he knew that his eyes were glowing. She whipped around, surprised by him. He took advantage of catching her unaware and grabbed her face, pulling her to him. Her mouth parted instinctively as his tongue pushed in. Her flavor flooded his taste buds and he savored it swallowing her down and reveling in the response she gave him. Her arms wrapped around his neck and she pulled him closer. He held her for a few seconds longer before finally pulling away and stepping back.

"I love you and I am still the man who claimed you. Never doubt that again." Before she could respond he turned and walked away.

Jen looked over at Cynthia who looked as shocked as she felt.

"If anything, he's still as bossy as ever," Cynthia told her.

Jen grinned and they started towards the plane again. "And too sexy for his own good. If he were ugly I totally wouldn't put up with it."

"Shallow much?" Cynthia snorted.

"Oh no doc, not shallow, just painfully honest."

They were all quiet as they found seats on the jet, each lost in their own thoughts. It wasn't until Jacque jumped out of her seat and smashed her face against the window looking out with a terrified expression that they all were pulled from their stupors.

"FANE!" she yelled as she slapped her hand against the plastic window.

"What's going on?" Jen asked as she made her way to a window to see what Jacque was so freaked about.

Sally's breath caught in her throat as she looked out her own window. She felt as though her heart was going to beat straight out of her chest.

"They're going to kill each other," Cynthia murmured as they all stared in sick fascination at the fight going on between the two males, now in wolf form.

Firm arms wrapped around Jacque as she started toward the door.

"GO!" Alina's voice rang loudly against Jacque's ear and she cringed under the volume and command behind it. Jacque knew Alina was addressing the pilot, and as the plane began to move, she knew that Alina wasn't going to let her go.

"I have to go to him, Alina," Jacque told her Alpha as she struggled with her.

"No. You need to let Vasile handle it. They will not kill each other. They just need to get it out in the open and deal with it. They can't do that with you and Sally there because they don't feel they could protect you and face one another at the same time. This is a good thing, Jacquelyn."

The plane continued to move, gradually gaining speed just as Jen shouted, "Oh! Wow that was a good shot, Fane."

"Jen!" Sally growled.

Jen held her hands up. "Hey don't get all pissy with me. As soon as Costin gets a good lick in, I'll cheer for him; no need to worry that I'll play favorites."

Jacque finally let her shoulders relax and gave up her fight to get out of Alina's arms. After several seconds, Alina let her go. She headed back to the window, knowing that what she was going to see would be painful. Though she wasn't receiving the blows, there was nothing she could do to help her mate. And that was just as painful as any physical agony.

As the plane gained speed, the girls had to crane their necks to watch the wolves. Jacque reached out for Fane's mind, but he had blocked her completely.

"He won't let you in either?" Sally asked noticing the grimace on Jacque's face.

Jacque shook her head. "They will be alright, Sal," she told her, unsure if she was trying to convince herself or the healer.

Sally nodded but looked no more convinced than Jacque felt. So apparently her attempt had failed on both accounts.

They felt the plane lurch as the wheels left the ground and the jet rose into the air, taking them further from the fight and further from the males who so desperately wanted them to stay.

"I will say one thing about those males, there is never a dull moment." Peri suddenly appeared causing everyone to jump.

"Blood hell," Jen barked.

"Couldn't you send out some sort of signal that you're about to appear out of thin air?" Lilly asked.

"What do you want me to do...fart just before I appear so the smell alerts you?" Peri took a seat next to Alina and crossed her legs, appearing regal despite her crude words.

"Why do you say we would be alerted by the smell, rather than the sound?" Sally asked.

Peri smiled. "I think you humans call them *silent but deadly*."

"That's just gross. Could you please tell us something useful?" Jacque snapped, apparently not enjoying the banter.

"What would you like to know?" Peri asked her.

Jacque's jaw tensed as she tried to maintain her composure. Her mind just kept jumping back to the vision of her mate lunging at Costin, claws and fangs extended, eyes glowing, and frothy saliva dripping from his muzzle like a rabid beast.

"Apparently the altercation was started because of a comment from Vasile," Peri told them.

Alina let out a huff, "I told him to stay out of it. Tell me it was at least subtle."

Peri grinned in delight. "Oh you should know better, Alina. Your mate is about as subtle as Jen is prudish." That earned Peri a snort from everyone and a *you're just jealous* from Jen. Ignoring them she continued, "He told Costin to kick Fane's ass." Everyone's mouths dropped open and eyes widened, "and then he told Fane to quit running from his fear and anger and to deal with it. He told him that if he didn't deal with it, then Vasile would deal with him. And then it was on."

Jen let out a sharp burst of laughter that filled the cabin of the plane. "Alina, please tell me you tap that regularly because you have to admit, your man is hot."

"Okay, first off, EWW!" Jacque pointed at Jen. "And second, why on earth would Vasile do that?"

Alina slid forward to the edge of her seat and placed her elbows on her knees. She took in a deep breath of air and then met her daughter-in-law's eyes.

"Because it's the only thing that will help Fane get over this rage and fear inside of him. He is more dominant than Costin, though perhaps not by a great measure. Other than when we were in America, he has never felt the need to establish that dominance. As the son of the most powerful Alpha in generations, he has never been challenged on his home turf. But now he feels that Costin has wronged him. He needs to establish that dominance to help prove to himself that he can protect Jacque. The other reason is a simpler one. He's a male, and he's ticked off at another male. They resolve their differences with a physical fight. It's that way with human males as well, is it not?"

Sally blew out a big breath of air, causing her cheeks to puff out. "This just sucks."

"Seriously," Jen agreed, then added, "if Vasile is going to start fights between hot, bossy, possessive werewolves, he should at least do it when we get front row seats, cause let me tell you my kicks are few and far between these days. I could use all the help I can get." Jen's voice was lighthearted and playful, but Jacque and Sally saw the pain in their friend's eyes.

"Jen," Sally said as she reached for her hand.

"Not ready to talk about it," Jen said quickly and then looked at Lilly. "So your oaf of a man is the reason we're on this little journey. Fill us in on what he did." Jen's statement effectively got the attention off of her and distracted her two best friends from fretting over their feuding mates. Two birds, one stone.

Peri rubbed her hands together as she nodded. "This is going to be so good."

Lilly frowned. "You already know what happened," she told the fae.

"Maybe, but the point is, one never tires of hearing about a king running like a scared rabbit while his mate throws things at him and berates him with a sailor's mouth."

"Get the popcorn," Jen called out, "we are in for some wicked entertainment ladies. If their fight started out with that much foreplay, then the finish is bound to leave us all breathless, and maybe even satisfied."

The group groaned collectively.

"What?" Jen asked innocently.

"Not everyone's fights end with sex," Jacque informed her.

"Oh well, then you guys are missing out. I mean seriously. That's like saying Santa doesn't need Rudolph and his shiny nose, or that the fourth of July doesn't need fireworks, or that Harry Potter doesn't need Ron and that bushy headed girl. I mean, it's like…,"

"Jen," Jacque cut her off, "we get it."

Jen's head shook vehemently. "Nope, sorry wolf-princess, you can't possibly get it until you've gotten it, if you know what I mean, after having a knock down drag out with your mate. Then and only then, will you get it."

"Was that clear as mud to anyone else?" Sally asked.

"I think she's saying we need to have relations with our mates as often as possible, including after fights," Crina said calmly.

Jen clapped her hands together with a loud yell, "FINALLY! Somebody gets it."

"How long are you going to let this go on?" Decebel asked Vasile as they watched the two wolves battle it out. Thankfully, the pack had its own private hanger to house the jet, so there was no one to witness the snarling beasts tearing into one another.

"As long as it takes," Vasile responded. "They won't kill each other. They know that it would kill the other's mate as well." Vasile was calm and unwavering while the males around him growled or cringed in response to the fight before them. Vasile had thought it would be his job to step in and deal with Fane's struggles, but the moment he saw the two wolves together, he knew what needed to be done. Fane needed to let go of his anger, and Costin needed to prove that he was capable of taking Fane on and that he could still be Fane's pack mate and still care for him once this was over.

Vasile and Decebel both had to use their power to keep the other males from joining in. All of them were itching for a fight after having just watched their mates fly off to another continent without them. Decebel himself was fighting his own wolf, which longed to tear into any flesh that was available, but he wouldn't give in to the desire. He didn't need Vasile knowing what he had planned. He knew the Alpha would not approve.

Fane's mind was covered in a haze of rage as he lunged at the wolf who had dared to touch his mate. His claws dug into flesh and it satisfied something in him to see the rich, red blood spill forth, matting the grey fur. He jumped back quickly, but not fast enough as he felt Costin's teeth sink into his side. Even the pain from the assault was like a balm to the internal wounds that had been plaguing him for so long. Over and over they circled each other, and over and over they ripped into flesh, but neither of them ever made a mortal wound. This wasn't about death; it was about righting a wrong, healing the brokenness. Brokenness had reached so far into Fane that he felt like he would never be whole again. Fane nearly stumbled when he heard a voice in his mind and it didn't belong to his mate.

"You can only heal if you forgive, Fane Lupei, child of mine."

The smooth voice wrapped around him and stopped his progress immediately. Fane closed his eyes and waited for the Great Luna to speak. When she didn't, he acknowledged her.

"I'm listening," he responded.

"Costin is your brother. He has not wronged you in any way. Dark magic has twisted your reality. Reach past the darkness, Fane. Grab hold of the light that your bonded mate gives to you and see the truth in the situation. No amount of blood shed will heal this wound. You have to choose *to be healed."*

Fane opened his eyes and saw that Costin was standing across from him, still in his wolf form, staring at him warily. He had stopped his attack as soon as Fane froze and he was waiting for his next move. He noticed that there was no condemnation in Costin's eyes, no hate or disgust. He simply stared and waited.

"I'm tired," he admitted.

"I know you are. You are not alone. Let go of your anger and let those who care for you, those who love you, help you move past this." He felt the warmth of an embrace and then she was gone.

Fane phased back into his human form and Costin quickly followed suit. All of the males were still, their breaths barely perceptible as they watched the two males.

"I know that it wasn't real," Fane finally spoke, "but even knowing that, I felt something inside of me break when I saw it."

Costin took a step closer heedless of their nudity. "We all experienced it, Fane. Our mates each went through the same thing but with different males."

"How could you stand it?" Fane asked desperately.

"It hasn't been easy if that's what you're thinking. But I realized that it would do more harm than good to dwell on it. Sally had hurt enough and I wasn't about to add to her pain."

Fane flinched at his words, knowing that he had caused his mate so much pain. He was supposed to protect her and instead he had pushed his fear and anger onto her.

Fane bowed his head to Costin and tilted it slightly, bearing his neck. "I ask for your forgiveness, packmate. I have wronged you. I have disrespected you and I have disrespected your mate."

Costin instinctively let out a low growl at the submission Fane was showing. "There is nothing to forgive, but even if there was, you are forgiven."

Fane let out a deep breath as he felt some of the darkness recede. The heaviness that had been weighing on his chest eased and he finally felt as though he could get air into his lungs. He turned to his father then and again gave his neck in submission. "Alpha, I apologize for losing control and not seeking out the help I needed."

Vasile walked up to his son and patted his cheek affectionately. "It is not my forgiveness you should worry about." Fane nearly fell to his knees as he thought about Jacquelyn. He had hurt her and now she was going back to Coldspring, so far from him. How could he make things right between them when he couldn't hold her? How would she see the sincerity in his eyes if she wasn't there with him?

"She will forgive you," Costin told him as he took the sweats Decebel handed him, which he had retrieved from a storage locker along the wall. Like most of the places the pack visited frequently, it was stocked with spare clothes for just such an emergency. "Maybe not today, or tomorrow, or in ten years, but eventually she will." All of the males chuckled goodnaturedly and Fane couldn't help the smile that curved his lips. His mate was hotheaded, but she didn't hold a grudge. He might have to do some serious groveling, but he would prove to her once again that she was the most precious gift he had ever been given and he would treat her that way again.

Vasile turned to address the group and as soon as he spoke the humor fled from their faces.

"I know that you are all angry with me and Decebel. I know you think we've made the wrong decision. Only time will tell. But until then, we are not going to sit and wallow in anger, or pity, or even the pain that will accompany the separation. Once again, evil has reared its ugly head and we must be the ones to defeat it. For if we do not do it, who will?" He met each of their gazes and one by one they dropped their eyes. "You were created for a greater purpose, not just to love your mate, but to take care of the world we live in so that our mates will have a safe place to live and our children will have a safe place to grow up. So you have until we arrive back at the mansion to wipe the scowls off your faces and I think Jen would say, *'put on your game faces.'* Our women will return to us, and when they do, we had better have good news for them or the Great Luna help us all."

"Do you think the Great Luna could help us against the wrath of your American mates?" Sorin asked with a smirk.

"Knowing our luck, they would probably convince her to join in their cause to kick our posteriors," Vasile retorted.

"Posteriors?" Costin asked as amusement danced in his eyes.

"My daughter in-law is Jacque."

"Enough said."

Chapter 8
"Evil comes in all forms, shapes, and sizes. That is the beauty of it. Because it is dark, you do not see it coming. It remains quiet until it has snuck right up behind you. It is often appealing, so you do not even realize that it is evil until it has caught you in its web and you cannot move. It is the manifestation of the worst parts of us and like calls to like. So as your evil rises to the surface because of wrongs and pain that you can't let go of, I will find you and latch onto you. Together our evil will devour any good left in each of you." ~Reyaz

Alston, highest member of the council of the fae, paced the room restlessly. He had summoned the other council members to discuss the treachery of Lorelle, one of their own and Perizada's sister. They didn't know where she had gone after the witch had been destroyed. Alston had sent out his best trackers to find her so they could bring her to justice, but they hadn't heard even a whisper of her whereabouts. When he had asked Peri for her help, her response had been quite candid. *"If I find her, I will cast her to the pits of hell where she belongs, and that is after I gut her with a spoon."* He would like to say that Peri was bluffing, but Peri never bluffed so he was sure she would follow through on her threat.

"What is so urgent?" Gwen asked as she entered the council room followed immediately by Disir, Nissa, and Dain.

Alston stopped his pacing and faced the council members. "We agreed to make our presence known in the human realm. We gave our word to Perizada that we would no longer sit back and watch as evil overtook them. A new evil resides in the forest near the Warlock King's stronghold."

"We know this," Dain answered. "But he has made no move yet. How are we to fight him if we can't find him?"

Alston nodded. "I completely agree with your sentiment. However, Peri dropped in to let me know that Vasile was having a meeting with Cypher tomorrow and thought it might be a good idea for me to make an appearance. She says that they are deciding not to wait for Cypher's brother to make a move but to act on the offensive instead."

"Do you think this wise?" Nissa asked.

"It does not matter what I think. It only matters that whatever we do, we do it as a united front."

"Do you want us to accompany you?" Dain asked.

"No, I would like for two of you to go investigate the forest yourselves. Find out if the disturbance there is indeed Reyaz."

"And if it is?"

"Do not engage him. You are simply there to observe. Stay as long as you can without detection."

"What if he discovers us?" Nissa's voice would, at one time, have trembled over such a question. Now she had been battled tested and it would take more to rattle her nerves.

"Do not get caught."

"Easier said than done Alston," Disir grumbled.

"If, in all these centuries, Perizada has kept her nosy, trouble-seeking self from being captured, then I assure you it can be done."

"Mother of pearl and father of wine, it is good to be home," Jacque groaned as she fell back on the couch in her mother's house. She couldn't help but take comfort in the familiar cushions, the way they sunk down from years of use, and the smells that unlocked memories of a childhood filled with love. For just a few minutes as she absorbed the familiarity and normalcy of the moment, she pushed away her worries. She pushed away her worries about Fane, her fear for Jen's unborn child, the anxiousness caused by the strife between Jen and Decebel, and the pain that her mother was feeling. She was choosing to live in the now, because all too soon, the past and future would come crashing down on her.

"Bloody hell," Jen yelped. "I just realized something; I'm going to have to see my parents. And though they might not always be the sharpest tools in the shed, there is no way they could miss this," she said as she rubbed her growing stomach.

And just like that, Jacque was pulled from her brief vacation back into the chaos that had become her life.

"That means I'm going to have to see my parents as well," Sally nearly whispered as her eyes widened, "They don't know I'm married, or mated or…,"

"Relax Sally, it's not like you have ex-virgin tattooed on your forehead. You don't have to tell them you're married; there's no harm in it. You still look as innocent as you did the second before you and your man did the…,"

"Do not finish that sentence," Jacque growled.

"Fine, but you get my drift."

After the luggage had been drug into the foyer, each of the women went to the living room and collapsed on whatever surface was available. A haze of exhaustion permeated the air and even Alina seemed caught in its web. But it wasn't long until the necessity of food roused them.

"I'll order pizza," Lilly told them as she pulled her cell phone out of her pocket. "There is no food in the house and if there is I would advise against eating it. Unless it's a nonperishable," she added.

By the time the pizza arrived, bathroom times had been established, sleeping arrangements had been made, and threats of bodily harm declared by the not-so morning people. Through all of this, they had somehow managed to keep from talking about anything that had happened. It was almost as if they thought that by not talking about it, then it couldn't possibly be real. But they couldn't ignore it forever, and if they had been planning on trying, Cynthia squashed that idea.

"Jacque, Sally, have either of you heard from you mates?" Cynthia asked just as she held a piece of pizza up to her mouth. It was covered in layers of cheese but a little sparse on the pepperoni she noticed with a small frown.

Both girls shook their heads but said nothing.

"Has anyone heard anything from any of your mates?" Cynthia had abandoned her pizza as she waited to hear their answers. Just when she was about to get worried, Crina spoke up.

"Adam says everyone's alive."

"Sorin concurs with Adam," Elle offered.

They all looked at Jen expectantly and waited to hear what her mate had said.

Jen reached out to Dec but found that not only was their bond shut tight, but it was also weaker than it had ever been. He had a wall up blocking her from even the smallest hint of his emotions. Her wolf felt panicky at the loss of the connection but Jen refused to allow hysteria to rule.

"I got nothing," Jen finally said.

Her words seemed to bounce off the walls and reverberate in the small living room. Nobody moved and most of them were doing their best not to even breathe. The silence was broken by the chirp of a cell phone. Without a word they all fished for their phones, trying to identify the culprit. Suddenly a burst of laughter rang out through the room, but there was no humor or joy in it.

"Sit on a brick!" Jen snarled as her laughter died down. "He sent me a text! My freaking mate sent *me* a text!" Ok, so maybe she was going to let hysteria reign. Hell, it could have a freaking field day for all she cared. Jen read the text for the tenth time.

Dec: U made it

A part of her wanted to smile at the memory of the first and only time they had ever texted before. It was at the Gathering, but the other part of her wanted to reach through the phone and beat the living crap out of him. She knew she should wait until she calmed down before responding, but global warming will have finally melted the ice caps and everyone would be flailing around in life boats trying to survive by the time that happened, so she decided against waiting.

Jen: R u telling me or asking me?

She hated the feeling of anticipation that stirred in her stomach as she waited for his response. Hated that he had so much power over her, and at one time she thought that they were on equal ground, that she too had the power to drive him crazy. Now she wasn't so sure. The chirp of her phone drew her attention back.

Dec: Just want confirmation.

Jen growled. *Way to make me feel like a piece of luggage that you are making sure made it to your next connection B*, she thought to herself.

"What does the text say?" Sally asked.

Jen looked up and found herself staring at eight sets of eyes. Her attention had been so focused on her phone that she had forgotten there were other people in the room.

"You made it," Jen said dryly.

"Is he asking or telling?" Crina asked.

"Exactly what I said."

"So what did you tell him?"

"I told him if he was referring to the poopy I did on the plane, then yes, *I* indeed made it." Jen couldn't hold back the grin as she watched her friends choke on their pizza and drinks because of her outlandish statement. It was a much needed comic relief. But it didn't take away the hurt of having her own mate text her when they had a bond that gave him direct access to her mind. Her phone chirped again as the laughter began to subside.

Dec: U r there

Jen realized that she had never responded to his earlier text and as she read his latest text she let out a cackle of laughter worthy of a witch.

"Shut the front door!" Jen guffawed.

"What?" Jacque's smile dropped as she watched her friend. The others gathered closer around her.

"This text says *you are there*. Where else would I be? I mean can he be any more Tarzan-like with the monosyllabic words?" Jen grumbled as she replied.

Jen: I don't know y u insist on telling me things I already know.

Dec: I just wanted 2 know u arrived safely.

Jen: U didn't have 2 text me 2 find that out.

Dec: I love u baby.

Jen's breath caught at his latest text message, and she had to bite her lip to hold back her tears. She didn't doubt his love. She knew to the very core of her being that Decebel loved her completely. What she did doubt was his truthfulness with her. Since the day she had met Decebel, he had always been very up front about his feelings. He was painfully honest and hilariously blunt and those were things she adored about him. Now he was nearly the complete opposite and she was at a loss as to how to get him to open up to her, to trust her, and it was killing her.

Jen: Good 2 know. Any other headlines u want to share?

Dec: About 2 go n meeting with Vasile, Cypher, and the other males. So I will b out of touch 4 a little while.

Jen: Whatev

As soon as the message was sent Jen hit the power button on her phone and watched with sick satisfaction as the screen went black. She tossed it onto the coffee table and let out a deep breath.

"I don't know about y'all, but I need a drink." Jen started to stand but Sally pulled her back down to the couch.

"Jen, you don't drink, and you're pregnant," Jacque reminded her.

"Well, my sweet wolf-princess, in the words of the profound band Little Texas, there's a first time for everything."

"How about instead of drowning our problems, we talk about them?" Cynthia piped.

"Bloody hell, you aren't trying an intervention are you?" Jen's eyes narrowed.

"Jen, I think she's just trying to help take some of the pressure off. You haven't exactly been discreet about things between you and Decebel. We love you and hate to see you hurting, either of you."

"It is an intervention," she whined and slumped back into the couch, "of all the things I could possibly have needed an intervention for, it had to be Werewolves Anonymous."

"I take it that you have no loyalties." Reyaz walked leisurely around the forest that surrounded his lair. He had decided to take a much needed break from spying on his brother, but on his way home, he was interrupted.

"I am loyal to myself," Lorelle told him boldly, though she felt anything but bold. She hadn't planned on approaching him this way, but the opportunity presented itself and she had to take it while it was there. Reyaz was not an easy man to find.

"How do I know you will not betray me?"

"I have no reason to betray you. I simply want my sister out of the picture. I can't kill her. If I did, I would be banished from my realm forever. But in your line of work, and specifically your latest endeavor, you will more than likely run into her. I was just hoping you could give her a little zap."

Reyaz's brow rose and his mouth twitched as if to smile. "A little zap?"

Lorelle nodded. "Like you did to Vasile."

He laughed at this and she tried not to cringe at the sound. The air coming out of him sounded as if it was grating against lungs that had not been used for this purpose in a very long time. Like the creaking and moaning of an old wooden staircase that had not been walked on in years. His raspy laughter assaulted her ears.

"You are calling that a little zap?" he asked as his skin-crawling laughter died.

Lorelle decided that it was a rhetorical question and did not answer.

"What do I gain if I give your sister this *little zap* you are asking for?"

She had known that he would ask for some sort of payment. It's not like evil people do anything for free. There was no such thing as evil charity. Lorelle had wracked her brain endlessly trying to come up with something that he would consider valuable. But she had come up empty-handed.

"I can grant you a request to redeem at your liking." She had finally decided on the granting of a favor. Though she hated to give him such power over her, there was nothing that she could give Reyaz that he couldn't simply take for himself.

He didn't respond right away. She watched as he took slow measured steps, his feet crunching on the dead leaves that littered the ground. He was considering it, no doubt thinking of all the possibilities such a payment would give him.

"Any request?" he qualified.

"Yes."

"I accept. And I already know what you must do," he finally told her.

Lorelle gave a short nod and tried not to look as nervous as she felt. "What will it be?"

"You are going to deliver a message for me, but not from me," he told her. "It seems that my brother has finally realized that the trolls need to pay for their part in the death of one of his females. He has attempted to keep the peace with them, but he has come to see that in order for justice to be served and real peace to reign, then they must pay. So you will take Thead, the Troll King, a declaration of war on behalf of the King of the Warlocks."

Lorelle's mouth dropped open and she knew her eyes were as wide as saucers. She couldn't believe what he was saying.

"Why? Why would you do this if all you want is your brother's woman?" she stumbled over her words as she spoke. "You want to destroy two races over the life of your mate?"

"They won't destroy each other," he scoffe. "The trolls don't stand a chance against my brother. As much as I hate to admit it, he is extremely powerful."

"Do you honestly believe that the wolves will just stand by and let the trolls be slaughtered?"

"What do you care, Lorelle, faithless and one without loyalty?" He snarled at her.

"One person is very different from an entire species!" She felt nauseous as she thought about the part she would play in this, but there was no getting around it. She had cast her role in his game and she would have to play her part or it would be her life on the line instead of her sisters.

"Fine," she said and the word tasted like bile in her mouth. "I'll do it."

"I had no doubt that you would," Reyaz told her smugly.

"Some free advice, woman," she heard his voice just as she started to go, "if you betray me, I will kill you in the same manner that I take your sister, only much slower and much more painfully."

He was gone before she could even swallow down the lump in her throat. She had come to him wanting his help in destroying her sister, the one thorn in her side who wouldn't go away. Now she would help him destroy at least one entire species, and quite possibly even more.

Chapter 9
"None of us are exempt from the difficult choices in life. They are written in the fine print on the day we are brought forth into this cold world. And though they are set in stone, what is not set in stone is how we respond when those difficult choices are put before us. That is when we discover if the pain and suffering brought on through our birth was worth all the trouble—when we stand before those difficult things and say, I can do this, and I will do it for the right reasons." ~Decebel

Vasile stood in the library of the pack mansion listening to the steady drone of murmuring from the gathered males. He was lost in thought after having spoken to Alina through their bond. Alina had informed him that Jen was having a rough time. He assumed it was the pregnancy and the worry about the baby's birth, but then Alina had told him that Decebel was texting his mate instead of using their bond. He understood then that Jen was probably having more than a rough time. For her mate to withhold the intimacy of the bond would be painful on the best of days. For him to do it while they are so far apart and she with child was akin to torture. He couldn't imagine what would cause Decebel to behave in such a manner. It was completely out of character for him. Frankly, failure to use the bond would be out of character for any wolf.

His eye's drifted over to his former Beta and he watched as Decebel too studied the room. His usually focused eyes seemed to be restless and flighty, darting over the other males and to the doors. It didn't appear to be as much vigilance as it was looking for a way to escape. He looked tense as he clenched and unclenched his jaw and shifted from foot to foot. Decebel was naturally a very still creature; his every movement deliberate and calculated. Just in the few seconds of watching the Alpha, Vasile could see that something was definitely off. Why hadn't he seen it before? How could he have missed such big behavioral changes in a male he had known for over a century?

Vasile let out a tired sigh as he thought about the problems and stresses plaguing their combined packs. Fane, Costin, and now Decebel, three males he loved dearly, were all struggling with things that they desperately needed their mates to help them cope with, and he, like a good Alpha, had sent them all away. Even though Decebel was technically responsible for Jen and Sally, he certainly would have relented if Vasile had opposed the idea. It was again one of those situations where Vasile had to ask himself, *was there really any right answer?*

Decebel felt his muscles twitching as he stood waiting for Cypher to join them. He hadn't slept since before Jennifer had left and he barely had an appetite. His insides were a constant knot and anything he put in his stomach seemed to want to crawl right back up his throat again. He could feel her, just barely, but she was still there. He missed her with such fierceness that his bones ached with it. Every minute was a relentless battle with his wolf and he knew that he was walking a very fine line when it came to keeping it under control. The hardest part for Decebel wasn't that Jennifer was not by his side. The hardest part was knowing that she was in pain, just as he was, and he was the cause of that pain. Their bond had been so very strong, and as it grew weaker with every passing hour, he could feel the life being leeched out of them both.

The Great Luna assured him that their child would be safe, but as he bit his tongue to keep from snarling out in anger at the pain he felt pulsating through his veins, he wondered if the goddess knew just how excruciating this process was truly going to be. Jennifer was tough, he didn't doubt that, but even the toughest of them had limits. Jennifer had a limit and he was terrified that he was very close to pushing her past hers, and that once he had, it would be too late for her to come back.

The door to the library opened slowly and the room began to quiet. Cypher stepped through and calmly looked around, giving slow nods to each male. Based on the tense and nearly painful looks on the faces of the wolves, he knew something bad had happened.

"I've come in peace, Vasile, to honor our agreement as allies and to help in any way that I can," Cypher told the Romanian pack Alpha calmly. His voice was strong and carried out to the walls. It almost seemed to push away the angst and worry. He took in a deep breath, attempting to use all of his senses to see if he could understand what had happened to make the usually very forward wolves hold their tongues.

"We welcome you, Cypher, King of the Warlocks. You are accepted as our guest and under our protection," Vasile responded formally. "Have you come alone, King, or did you bring your mate?" Vasile knew he should probably leave it alone, but he found himself to be in a mood and decided to start the meeting with a little prodding. His lips twitched as he watched the usually calm and confident Warlock King squirm under his scrutiny.

"I have come alone." Cypher said no more and he continued into the room and took one of the empty seats.

Vasile motioned to the other wolves in the room and, one by one, they took seats, all except Decebel. Vasile made eye contact with him briefly, an unspoken message that he was aware something was off with him. Vasile was about to speak when the library door was once again pushed open.

"I realize I wasn't invited to this meeting," Alston said as he stepped into the room, "but I was told by a little fairy that I should be present."

"Did this little fairy happen to have a big mouth?" Decebel asked coolly as chuckles vibrated across the room.

Alston tipped his head briefly to Decebel before straightening back up. "Perizada often sticks her nose where it isn't welcome, though often it is needed."

"Please join us, Alston," Vasile spoke up. "Perizada was right to contact you. I would have thought to do it myself had I not been distracted by pack issues."

"I suppose it is good that we have nosy females who step in when we are distracted," Alston said as he took a seat next to Sorin.

"A very good thing," Vasile agreed. He turned back to look at Cypher and his face grew serious. "Peri brings us news that your brother has been meddling in your forest."

Cypher nodded as his lips tightened in a grim scowl. "I have not seen him with my eyes, but his evil permeates the air."

"What does he want?" Sorin asked.

"To punish me," Cypher answered without pause. Cypher didn't know what he expected from the males when he answered. Perhaps they would tell him to hand himself over so that his brother's wrath would be satisfied and then maybe he would leave everyone else alone. But he knew they were too smart to believe that his brother would stop with only him. He had, after all, already killed Vasile, or at least attempted to, simply to display his power. Therefore, he wasn't at all surprised by the patient looks they gave him as they waited for him to elaborate.

"His mate died many, many years ago and he blames me for her death," Cypher continued.

Decebel's eyes narrowed as he watched the king. "Blames you? Or your actions?"

"The lack thereof," Cypher told him. "His mate made a decision to act as an ambassador to another supernatural race and I warned her not to, but she was determined to do what she wanted."

"Aren't they all?" Fane growled under his breath. Grumbles of agreement floated across the room and Cypher gave them questioning looks.

"Ignore their grumbling, Cypher," Vasile interrupted the noise. "Their women have deserted them." Dirty looks were shot his way but he ignored them and concentrated on Cypher.

"She went anyways and was killed," Cypher continued. "It is my brother's belief that I could have stopped her, and I am inclined to agree with him."

"Were you willing to tie her to a tree and put her under constant guard?" Decebel asked. "Because unless that was the action you were prepared to take, then your brother is a bigger fool than I have already determined him to be. Surely you know, now that you have a mate, there is no forcing our women to do anything they do not want to do, nor is there any stopping them once they have made up their minds."

"I understand what you are saying, Decebel," Cypher told him, "and Lilly has argued the same point, but it is hard for me not to take some of the blame."

"It is in our nature to feel responsible for the lives under our care," Vasile said, "but if we are to be effective leaders, then we must learn from the past and then let it go. Why is your brother not acting on his threats from the night of the battle with the witch?"

"I'm not sure," Cypher admitted. "My first thought would be that he wants us to become complacent. I think he figures that as more and more time passes without him taking any action then we will become lackadaisical in our watchfulness."

"And your second thought?" Sorin prompted.

"That he doesn't even know what he wants to do."

Costin frowned as he leaned forward in his chair. "You think that after all these years of brooding over the death of his mate, he doesn't have a plan?"

Cypher thought about it for a minute before he answered. "No, I think that maybe circumstances have changed and now he has to revise whatever plan he had originally devised."

"What circumstances changed?" Fane asked.

"Lilly," Vasile answered before Cypher could speak.

Cypher nodded. "Exactly."

"That's not all that has changed," Wadim spoke up. "We are united. The supernatural races are working together. That's a pretty big freaking change."

"Freaking?" Cypher's brow rose at the historian.

"Hey, you're mated to an American. Just wait. She'll have you saying all kinds of weird sh—,"

"Wadim," Vasile's voice was sharp as he interrupted him.

Cypher chuckled, but his eyes were sad. "Yes, they do say some of the strangest things."

"I asked you here because I want to talk about how we move forward *now*," Vasile told him. "I don't feel it is wise of us to just wait for our enemy to attack. I think that if we want to end this quickly, then we will have to be the ones to make the first move."

"You realize that if you pursue him, he will retaliate swiftly? He is very versed in dark magic and he basically has no morals."

Costin laughed. "So basically he is Mona with a…,"

"Bloody hell, what is with you males?" Vasile growled. "You're mates haven't been gone a full day and all of the sudden you can't keep from saying something foul?"

Cyphers eyes snapped up to Vasile. "Where have their mates gone?"

Vasile glanced down at his shirt and brushed away invisible lint, cleared his throat, shifted in his chair, and crossed one leg over the other before finally folding his hands in his lap and then meeting Cypher's gaze once again. "Our mates have gone with yours, of course."

Cypher's gaze traveled over the room. His eyes took in the tense shoulders, clenched teeth, and semi glowing eyes. He had known something was wrong the moment he walked into the library. Now that he knew what that something was, he had to hand it to the wolves, they were handling it rather well.

"Lilly was here?" he finally asked.

"Courtesy of our nosy fairy," Decebel told him.

Alston shook his head with a small smile on his lips.

"Perizada brought Lilly here?" Cypher didn't know whether to be angry that the fae had disobeyed him or happy that she had thought to bring her to see Jacque.

"She felt like Jacque had a right to say goodbye to her mother," Vasile explained.

Of course she had a right to say goodbye to her child, Cypher thought. He hadn't even thought to ask her if she wanted to see Jacque before she left. "So you all know why I sent her away?" Cypher stood from the chair and walked slowly toward one of the windows on the far side of the library.

"We know that you made a difficult choice, and you will make more before this whole thing is over."

Cypher turned slowly and saw that all of the males were now standing. Their faces were grim, but the looks in their eyes told him that they understood the choice he had made.

"So why did you send your mates with Lilly?"

Growls rumbled through the air and Vasile let out a toothy grin. "We did not send them, king; they sent themselves."

Cypher chuckled. "Of course they did." His face sobered then. "She is well?"

"She was ticked off when we saw her last," Costin told him with a smile. "But she wasn't in the clutches of a psycho dark warlock, so I guess you have to pick your poison."

"Well he's picked his poison alright." Peri hitched herself up on one of the tables in the library and smiled at the group of stunned males. She wiggled her finger at them. "Toodles."

"Peri," Vasile said dryly.

"Alston!" Peri's smile widened. "I'm so glad that you made it. I see that Vasile had no objection to you being here?"

Alston shook his head. "No, he was quiet pleasant about the whole matter."

"I knew he would be. I told you that he would even mention that he should have thought to call on you himself."

"He did."

"I'm standing right here," Vasile growled at the two fae.

Peri waved him off. "Don't mind him; he's just cranky because he isn't getting any."

Vasile growled a warning at the fae, which she promptly ignored.

Alston looked at her questioningly. "Getting any what?"

Costin started laughing so hard he was choking and Fane was beating him on the back, trying not to laugh himself.

"You've caused enough mischief Perizada of the Fae," Cypher spoke up, "surely you have more of a purpose here than to torment these wolves."

Peri's brow rose as she looked at the warlock king. "Surely you do not know me very well if you think there is anything more important to me than tormenting these very wolves before us." She waited for his response as she unfolded herself from the table and stepped down to the floor. He watched her but did not speak. Peri gave him a slight tilt of her head and then turned to face the two Alphas. "Have you come up with a plan?" she asked her playful tone replaced by the snappy, business-like voice.

"We hadn't made it that far yet," Decebel told her.

"What the crap have you been doing? Giving each other facials and reading self-help books to help your bruised egos?"

"We were getting everyone caught up to speed," Decebel snapped back. "It would be stupid to rush off with some half-assed plan without making sure we have everything straight."

"So now that you have everything straight, you can rush off with your half-assed plan?" her voice was syrupy sweet as she smiled at the Alpha.

Decebel growled low as he bit back a snarl.

"Relax, Independence Day, don't get your panties in a wad." Peri winked at Decebel as she watched his eyes widen. She saw the recognition of the reference in his glowing amber orbs and knew she would pay for that comment later—if he could catch her.

Vasile stepped forward to stand between the two. "I've decided to go to Reyaz myself and see if there are any terms that can be negotiated for peace."

A collective "WHAT!" rang out across the library as all eyes turned on Vasile.

"Vasile, you know that there are no terms he will meet," Cypher implored.

Vasile nodded. "Yes, and there are no terms that I will accept or meet either. I simply want him to think that I'm…an idiot."

Peri cleared her throat. "That shouldn't be too hard. You all just sent your mates across a flipping ocean without any male protection. I think the idiot part is pretty much a given."

"Peri," Costin said softly, "let's not poke the already angry Alpha wolf, no matter how fun it seems at the time. It's all fun and games until a little fairy gets eaten."

Peri threw her hands in the air. "Fine, have it your way! You," she pointed at Vasile, "go to the crazy warlock and prove again what an idiot you are, and you," she pointed at Cypher, "get in line behind Vasile because you're just as big an idiot as he is, and the rest of you," she motioned to all the other males, "put your tutus on and blindly dance behind them like the little idiots you are. Well," she paused and then looked at Decebel, "except for you. You might as well put on a tutu, a tiara, and carry a scepter because you're the queen of the idiot procession!" And then she was gone.

"Is she always so respectful towards you all?" Alston asked.

"Yes, Dad, we're back in the states," Jacque told her father. Though it was nearly midnight and they had only been back in the states for eleven hours, she had decided she had better go ahead and call him and give him a heads up. She thought that Vasile might have already talked to him since they had been gone nearly twenty-two hours, but based on his reaction he hadn't heard anything from anyone.

"Is Fane with you?" Dillon asked.

"No, none of the males came with us," Jacque pulled the phone away from her ear as her father's raised voice came blaring through. "Dad, Dad," she said loudly, "you can't come here and you can't just try to jump in anytime Vasile or Fane do something you don't agree with. Dad, no."

Just as she was about to put the phone back to her ear it was snatched from her hand. "Hey," she hollered but then stopped herself when she saw who had her phone.

"Why didn't they send any of the males you ask, Dillon, Alpha of the Denver pack? Why don't you call those idiots and find out? Have a nice night." Peri hit the end key and tossed the phone back to Jacque.

"Uh, Peri, I was sort of talking to my dad," Jacque said.

Peri snorted. "You were sort of talking, but I can guarantee he was sort of not listening."

"Why do you say that?" Sally asked as she came into the living room and joined Jacque on the couch.

"Because he has a penis," Peri said matter-of-fact like.

Jen's foot hit the bottom step just about the time Peri finished talking and she had a wicked grin on her face. "Peri busted out the P word! Ok." She hurried her pregnant self around to the love seat and sat down. "Now, what's with all the penis talk? Are we comparing notes, learning new techniques?"

"As truly interesting as any of those conversations would be, that is not why I busted out, as you put it, with the P word." Peri fold her arms across her chest and glared down at the three girls.

"Okay," Jacque prompted, "so can you tell us why you felt the need to use a man's body part as a way to make a point?"

"Which, by the way, you picked the perfect part if you indeed were trying to make a point," Jen added.

Peri's lips twitched and Jen reached over and held her fist out to her two best friends. "I made the fae twitch with her own penis point."

Jacque and Sally's heads whipped around at Jen's words and they busted out laughing. Jen shrugged. "I know, I know, I'm freaking hilarious." She looked up at Peri and grinned when she saw the fae smothering her own laugh with her hand.

"Okay, pull it together you perverts," Peri finally told them as she collected herself. "I went and saw your males during their meeting with Cypher."

"What happened?"

"Are they alright?"

Sally and Jacque asked at the same time.

"Pipe down you two. Your men are fine. Although, after I told them they were all idiots, they might have been less than happy with me."

"You told Decebel he was an idiot?" Jen asked in awe.

"Sort of, I actually told him he was the queen of the idiots."

"Nice," Jen grinned.

"Um Peri, I'm totally in agreement with penises and idiots, but if Costin is alright then why has he not used our bond to contact me and why is he not responding to me when I try to contact him?" Sally asked.

"Yeah," Jacque agreed, "what she said, only with Fane's name in his place."

Peri gave both girls a dry look. "You both know that I love you, right? But do I look like a couples' counselor to you? I don't know why they won't get their heads out of their asses and talk to you. What I do know is they're idiots."

"And they have penises," Jen added.

"Thanks for the clarification, Jennifer," Peri rolled her eyes.

"Just want to make sure we stay on the same penis, I mean page."

Jacque and Sally were laughing again as Peri glared at Jen who shrugged. "I told you. I'm freaking hilarious."

"Actually," Jacque said as she wiped the tears from her eyes, "I think we are just so tired that you could add the word penis to anything and we would laugh."

"But don't," Peri said quickly, "we don't need a verbal vomit of your favorite P word."

Jacque and Sally groaned as Jen's smile widened.

"Oh fairy Peri, who told you penis was my favorite P word? They were mistaken. My favorite P word is by far p—,"

"Fire!" Sally yelled interrupting Jen.

Jacque jerked around and looked at her. "What?"

Sally shrugged. "I was just trying to keep Jen from saying her favorite P word. You know how I hate that word."

Jen laughed. "It's just a word, Sal."

"Not the way you use it," Sally said with a pointed look.

"You are correct, Sally dear. It ceases to be just a word when I use it." Jen laughed at her blushing friend. "Married, mated, no longer a virgin... and she still blushes."

"Okay, I realize that the change in time, location, altitude, longitude or whatever has messed with your little brains, but could we please focus?" Peri nearly snarled.

The three girls stared up at Peri in shock. Peri looked down at herself and noticed she was floating off of the ground. She took a deep breath and released it and then her feet were planted firmly on the ground again.

"Now, as I was saying," she started, "I saw the males. They were making no progress in putting together a plan and when I pushed them on it, Vasile had the brilliant idea that he is going to go see Reyaz face-to-face."

"What?" The three gasped at the same time.

Peri nodded. "I know right." She shook her head and began to pace. "I don't know why they think Reyaz is going to play nice, or why they thing he is going to leave Lilly alone."

"If you didn't think he was going to leave her alone, then why didn't you speak up before we all left?" Jacque asked her.

Jen let out an exasperated sigh. "Because they have penises. Haven't you been listening?"

"Thank you, Jen." Peri nodded her approval. "I didn't say anything because I was hoping they were right."

"And in the nearly twenty-four hours that have passed since we left, what has changed that made you see that they were wrong?" Sally asked.

"I saw Reyaz," she said too nonchalantly.

"What do you mean you saw Reyaz? Where?" Jacque asked as she slowly stood from the couch.

Peri shrugged. "In your front yard."

"Well crap," Sally retorted.

"You're sure it was Reyaz?" Alina asked Peri.

Jacque called a house meeting after Peri had made her little announcement. Now, after midnight, nine tired and worried females sat in Lilly's living room waiting to hear about the crazy warlock who might have been in the front yard.

"It was Reyaz, but it wasn't Reyaz," said the fae.

"Explain." Alina crossed her legs and leaned forward on the edge of the couch where she was perched.

"It was a projection of himself," Peri told them. "That part I understand. It's dark magic. What I don't understand is how he accomplished it."

"What do you mean?" Elle asked.

"In order for something like that to work so specifically he would have to have something personal of Lilly's or Jacque's. He knew exactly whose house he was in front of, so it wasn't a blind projection of himself, or a vague projection. It was very specific."

"Okay, so this is new to us," Sally spoke up. "Is this something he can do simply because he uses dark magic?"

Peri nodded. "Yes, like many who crave power but don't have it, they seek it out and care not how they obtain it or who it hurts or kills in the process. Black magic is fueled by blood and death. So whatever he had to conjure to make that little trick work, something had to die."

"Life just gets cheerier and cheerier," Jen muttered as she rubbed her swollen stomach.

"Did he say anything?" Cynthia asked.

Peri snorted. "He said he'd see us soon."

"Oh snap," Jacque muttered.

"I think we're beyond being snapped, Jac. We have moved on to being well and truly screwed," Jen said as she stood and yawned. "I know that we basically just found out that a crazy warlock dude is planning a visit, but I'm tired so wake me when he gets here." She waved at the group as she turned and headed back up the stairs to Jacque's room.

"Don't tell Vasile for now," Alina told Peri.

Peri smiled. "Keeping secrets from the wolves. I like your style, Alpha."

Alina chuckled. "Yes well, I don't feel there is a need to alarm him until absolutely necessary."

Everyone nodded their agreements and then began making their way back to their designated sleeping quarters. Peri spoke up before everyone could leave.

"Elle and Cynthia, could you two please wait a second. I would like to speak with you."

Elle shot Cynthia a worried look but sat back down. Cynthia took a seat next to her and they waited as everyone else cleared out of the room.

"Oh good grief, Elle, quit stressing out. I'm not going to dissect your mind or anything," Peri huffed as she watched her nervous comrade.

"Wait, could she do that?" Cynthia asked nervously.

Peri quirked a brow at her mischievously.

"Honestly doc, I wouldn't underestimate anything about Perizada. Not anymore."

"Dually noted," Cynthia mumbled.

"So ladies," Peri said dramatically, "my, my haven't we been busy." Both Cynthia and Elle squirmed under her gaze. "I take it the block on Decebel's mind is your handy work?" she directed the question to Elle.

Elle nodded. "He asked me to."

"Why?" Peri asked.

"He made us promise not to talk about it with anyone," Cynthia spoke up quickly hoping to keep Elle from falling under the pressure of someone she obviously considered her boss.

"Doctor Steele, I have the highest respect for you, but I'm going to have to ask you to shut it." Peri looked back at Elle. "Why?" she asked again.

"He wanted to keep Jen from being able to see into his mind while he is sleeping." Elle slumped forward once the words were out, as if a weight had been lifted from her shoulders.

"How are you involved?" she looked back to Cynthia.

"He came to me first to see if I could help him. When I told him I couldn't, I thought of Elle. He seemed very distraught and it's very weird to see Decebel that way."

"I imagine it is. Probably just as weird as seeing him fidgeting like a four year old." Peri sat across from the two women and stared at them, but she wasn't seeing them. She was lost in thought, remembering just how out of character the Alpha had been acting when she had popped in on their meeting. "He's hiding something very important," she finally said, "and if I know anything about our wolves, it's that they will do anything to protect their mates."

"You think he's doing something to protect Jen and the baby?" Cynthia asked.

"I think he's figured out a way to save his child. And he knows his mate would kill him if she knew his plan."

"What?" Elle and Cynthia asked at the same time.

Peri shook her head. "Let's just say that if what I think is happening, is really happening, it's going to get so much worse, and never better."

"Don't you mean it will get much worse before it gets better?" Cynthia asked.

"If he's doing what I think he's doing doc, then there is no getting better."

Chapter 10

"Free will is a gift and a curse. It is a gift to the one to whom it is given. They then have the right to choose their thoughts, actions, and beliefs. It is a curse to the one, like me, who grants it. I have to watch when the ones I have gifted with free will make decisions that I know are harmful and dangerous. And though I can direct and guide, I cannot force, and sometimes when you love someone so completely, you desperately want to force."
~The Great Luna

She was being called again and there was a jolt of joy inside of her that brightened her spirit at knowing her children called upon her. Creator and created working together as it should be.

"I did not expect you," The Great Luna stated not unkindly to her guest.

Perizada bowed low before standing back up. "It is an honor to be in your presence, Luna."

"The honor is mine, Perizada. You have ministered to my wolves so long now, and still you do not grow weary."

Peri laughed. "I wouldn't go that far. Your wolves frequently make me weary."

The Great Luna smiled as she walked slowly around the yard.

"This is the home of Lilly." It was a statement but Peri nodded her agreement anyway. "How is she doing?"

Peri glanced at the house and then back to the goddess. "She's very resilient."

The Great Luna nodded her head. "She will have to continue to be so, for there is much more in store for her that will require not only resilience, but strength and bravery. Now," she turned and faced Peri directly, "what troubles you, High Fae?"

Peri let out a deep breath and rubbed her forehead. "Decebel has to be the most devoted mate I've known in all my centuries. His love for Jen is at times sickening. You know his plan?"

"I do."

"And you approve?"

"There is no greater show of love than to sacrifice oneself."

Peri growled in frustration. "There has to be another way."

"Are you offering your life in place of the child's?" The Great Luna's voice was not condescending or expectant. It was simply a question.

"Is that what you would have of me?" Peri asked, her voice a whisper.

"I would have you do what you were put here to do, Peri. You have always been an ambassador of sorts to the wolves. You offer your wisdom and council when needed. You serve when needed, but the sacrifice in this case is not yours to give."

"Isn't it," Peri asked desperately. "I am the one who snatched Jen from the hands of the Fates. Shouldn't it be my life and not the child's that they take?"

"It is not your time, Perizada."

Peri watched as The Great Luna began to fade. "Wait," she yelled, "what do I do?"

"You be there for her. When the time comes that she needs you most, don't let her down."

"I miss you," Fane whispered into his mate's mind. It had been two weeks since the females had left. Two weeks since his father had decided to go and confront the warlock Reyaz. Two weeks since Costin and he had ripped into one another. Two weeks away from his mate and it felt as though he hadn't touched her in two years.

"I miss you too," her voice was a caress against his wolf's fur. His ache for her was a physical pain, not just because of the bond between them, but because he truly hated to be without her. She was the brightest part of his life, and especially now, during these dark times, he needed her light more than ever.

"You seem better," Jacque told him, *"more in control."*

"I am."

"The fight helped?" he nearly laughed at the skepticism in her voice. How can a man explain to a woman that sometimes you needed to hit something, or in his case someone, for things to be right?

"I wish I understood it myself, Luna, but yes it helped. I'm sorry that I hurt you. I love you more than anything. I want you here with me, where you belong." Fane imagined he probably sounded a little like a petulant child, but he didn't care. He wanted his woman.

"Are you going to stomp your foot?" Her laughter warmed the cold dark places inside of him and he couldn't stop the smile that spread across his face.

"Will it make you get on a plane and get your cute butt back here?"

She laughed again. Oh how he missed seeing the smile that came with that laugh.

"No, but it would be funny to watch. Stop worrying about me and help your father. We are completely safe here. We've been shopping and listening to Jen whine about how big her butt is getting."

"Sounds fun," he told her dryly. *"And both of those things are things you can do here."*

"Fane."

"What?"

"Soon."

Fane growled. *"Not soon enough."* He sent her an image of him kissing her, letting her feel through their bond the need he had for her. He heard her breath catch and smiled to himself.

"You're not playing fair," she told him breathlessly.

"I never said I would, love. I play for keeps."

"Oh boy."

He laughed out loud at her words and couldn't help teasing her just a little more before he told her goodnight.

"Hello?" The question in Costin's voice made Sally smile.

"Hey," she said cheerfully.

"Sally mine, why are you calling me on the phone?"

She felt the heat of her blush work up her cheeks as she realized just how stupid her idea had been. But she wanted to hear his voice, not just in her mind. She wanted to hear it physically too. She didn't even know if that made sense, but regardless she had picked up the phone and dialed his cell, something she had never done before.

"Don't be embarrassed, brown eyes. I know what you mean. It is different to hear someone in your mind than with your ears. I get it," he told her gently.

"You do?"

"Yeah, I do."

She smiled as she leaned back against the couch. It was very late and everyone was asleep. She hadn't been able to sleep. All she had been able to do was think about Costin—his hazel eyes, his dimple, his warm sure hands, and confident swagger—her mate, her husband; she missed him like crazy.

"Is it supposed to hurt?" she asked him.

"Our bond, our wolves, demand that we stay close. We are one soul with two halves, and they don't want to be a part. I'm sorry you're hurting. I don't want that for you." She could feel his fingers on her face and she closed her eyes and enjoyed the sensation she knew was only there because he was sharing it with her through their bond.

"Why did it take you so long to contact me after your fight with Fane?" she finally asked the question that had been bothering her for the past two weeks. They had talked through their bond daily since the fight, but she hadn't brought it up. Something in her had told her it wasn't the right time. But for some reason, now felt right.

"I needed to deal with my emotions before I opened up to you. Violence is not something I want to share with you, and sometimes after a fight, our control can be a little testy."

Sally leaned forward. "What aren't you telling me, Costin?" she paused and thought about it for a second. "Wait, if I had been there, would you have felt out of control?" She waited for his answer and when it didn't come she snarled, "Answer me."

"Yes, if you had been here things would have been different."

"Then why did you let me leave?" Sally's heart hurt knowing now. From what Costin was sharing through their bond, he had been engulfed in rage after his fight with Fane.

"I'm sorry," she whispered.

"Don't be, Sally mine. It wasn't your fault. We knew the risks we were taking when we sent you ladies off."

"Stupid," she grumbled.

"Probably," he laughed. "I miss you, brown eyes."

Sally's skin heated as she heard the simmer of passion in his deep voice. She knew that tone. She knew before he even sent her the thought that he was planning on turning her skin fifteen shades of red.

He chuckled. "My sweet innocent, Sally," he murmured to her.

"Not so innocent," she told him boldly.

Costin purred to her through the phone, "Come home and prove it."

"How are you feeling?" Decebel asked as he listened to Jennifer breath through the phone.

"I'm going on four and a half months pregnant, Dec. I'm feeling fat. How are you feeling?" She didn't hide the frustration or hurt in her voice.

"I feel lonely, baby," he told her honestly. Every day was becoming more and more painful. Breathing was becoming more of a burden than a necessity and he'd considered giving it up more than once.

"Does that mean you miss me?" she asked.

"More than anything."

"Good."

He chuckled at her tone and fought the urge to reach through the phone and pull her to him, if such a thing were possible.

"I'm tired, B," she told him gently. "I love you."

"Okay baby, I'll let you get some sleep."

She snickered, "I don't think you've ever said those words to me."

Decebel grinned to himself. She was right. "And you like that I haven't," he flirted. He shouldn't be flirting, he shouldn't be doing anything to strengthen the bond, but he missed her and the pain from it was beginning to drive him mad.

"You are correct, my hot mate; I love that you have never let me sleep. But you're way over there and I'm way over here, so your incredible hands can't keep me awake tonight."

"Wanna bet," *SHUT UP!* he thought to himself. *What on earth am I doing? I'm flirting with my woman that's what,* he snarled to himself, *and I'm freaking talking to myself.* Decebel let out an exasperated sigh.

"As soon as you're home, you won't be getting any sleep for a while," he told her suggestively.

She let out an unladylike snort. "That's just because I'll have a crumb catcher keeping me awake."

"Is that my new bedroom nickname?"

This brought a full laugh from her and his wolf wanted to roll around in the joy of hearing their mate so carefree.

"That was a good one, Dec.," she let out a sigh as the laughter died down. "I really do miss you," she told him softly.

"I know, baby, I know."

"Night, B," she finally said after several seconds of silence.

"Night, baby."

"You're going to find Reyaz tomorrow?" Alina asked her mate.

Vasile let out a slow deep breath and she felt his exhaustion through their bond.

"I want to see him face to face one more time."

"You do remember he killed you, right?" She was trying to remain patient with her mate, but she was beginning to feel a little desperate at the idea of him essentially going to see his murderer.

"He has no grudge against me, Mina. I was simply meant to be an example," he reassured her.

"Exactly, you were meant to be, but you didn't die. He might take that as a challenge."

"Mina," he whispered to her, *"you know that I cannot sit around and wait for him to decide to do something. I do not want us or any of our allies having to live looking over their shoulders, wondering when he is going to finally rear his ugly head."*

Alina knew this. She knew that they had to do something, but she also knew that Reyaz had already made a move of sorts when he had shown himself outside of Lilly's house. She had kept that little tidbit from Vasile and would continue to do so until she felt it absolutely necessary that she tell him.

"Just be careful please," she finally said. *"I love you, Vasile."*

"And I'm a better man because of it." He pushed his love through their bond, wrapping her in his scent and warmth. *"I love you, Mina; be safe."*

Lilly jumped when her phone began to vibrate on her night stand. She knew who it would be and she had to rub her palms, which has suddenly developed over active sweat glands, on her thighs before she picked up the phone.

"Hello," she said calmly, though she felt anything but.

"Little one," Cypher's deep voice reached through the phone and she swore she could feel his caress on her face. She hadn't heard from him in over a week and it had taken everything inside her not to pick up the phone and call him. She had spoken with Alina about it and more than once berated herself for acting like a teenager running to her friend to ask advice about a guy she liked, well, more than liked actually. She had told Alina that she didn't want to come across as the needy girlfriend. Alina had pointed out that she was a mate, not a girlfriend, and that carried a lot more weight and rights. She still didn't call him.

"Cypher," she responded.

"How are you doing?"

She sat down on the bed and folded her legs up as she thought about his question. How was she? Tired and somewhat lonely because she missed him, but overall she was alright.

"I'm good," she answered honestly.

"Oh?" She heard disappointment in his voice and it nearly made her laugh. He thought she didn't miss him. Stupid man.

"I'm good under the circumstances, Cypher. I would rather be with you. Does that make you feel better?"

"Much," he told her, his voice dropping to a deep growl. "I miss you like crazy," he admitted. "I want you here with me. I need you to believe that. I only wanted you to go back because I thought you would be safer there."

"I know," she told him. "I get it, but I wish you would have discussed it with me, instead of just telling me what to do. I'm an adult, Cypher. I can decide for myself what danger I want to put myself in."

He laughed. "Female, you are my mate. When it comes to any danger and you, I will always be the one making the decisions."

Lilly rolled her eyes. "You're a Neanderthal."

"Maybe," he agreed, "but I love you and don't want anything to happen to you."

Lilly felt her stomach jump into her throat at his declaration. He had no idea what those words meant to her, and she didn't feel like over the phone was the way to explain it.

"I love you too, Cypher," she told him softly.

"Good, stay safe, and," he paused, "stay away from any males."

She laughed. "No one is going to hurt me here, Cypher."

He growled. "I'm not worried about them hurting you. I'm worried about you moving on."

"Are you going to come for me, when you feel it's safe?" she asked.

"Yes," there was no hesitation in his answer, "and if another man is in the picture, Lilly, I'm not the type to just walk away. You should know that now. You are mine. I will not give you up."

Lilly let out a loud sigh. "My daughter is so right about you Alpha males—bossy and possessive. Thankfully you don't have fur, so I think I have one less worry than she does."

Cypher chuckled. "I have to admit that I'm happy that I don't have fur. But she is right; we are very, very possessive. I'll let you get some rest. I needed to hear your voice. I love you," he told her again.

"I love you too, night." Lilly hung up and felt her heart lighten just a tad. She refused to give into the urge to jump up and down and squeal. She decided that would be a little too ridiculous. She missed him, but she felt better about where they were in their relationship. He wanted her, and for now that was enough.

Chapter 11
"The wind is shifting brother. Do you feel it? You, who thought you were protecting the one you hold most dear, have opened a door I didn't dream you would put before me. I must give you all the praise for setting this up so nicely for me. So please remember to take a bow when you see the play I have in store for you." ~Reyaz

Reyaz stood just on the edge of his brother's forest. He knew Cypher was gone again visiting the wolves. He chuckled to himself. Cypher thought that the wolves could defeat him. But Reyaz was not a simple witch with a desire for power. His cause was much more specific and much more personal. He wanted revenge, restitution, and recompense. At first, he had planned to be satisfied with taking Lilly, his brother's new found mate. But now..., he grinned. Now he had a whole harem at his disposal.

"I thought you would be more difficult to find." The deep voice from behind him did not startle him. He had known he was coming, knew it, and welcomed it.

"The King of wolves graces me with his presence. Not the King I was expecting, but you will do nonetheless," he told Vasile as he turned to face him.

"What is it that you want, Reyaz?" Vasile asked bluntly.

"No pleasantries? Well, I must have really offended you."

"I tend to get offended when someone kills me, so I apologize if I'm being a tad abrupt."

Reyaz laughed. "I like you, Alpha. You have pizazz."

"My daughter-in-law would be proud," he said blandly. "Again I ask; what is it that you want?"

"What all men who have lost love want—the one who took it to pay." Reyaz took a step to the left and motioned in the direction of the warlock mountain and stronghold. "My brother has ruled for centuries. He has lived with *my* people following his every command while I have withered away with my sorrows."

"And whose fault is that?" Vasile asked. "You have separated yourself from your kin and from your people. You have made the choice to put the pain from your loss above your good sense."

Reyaz snarled, "IT WAS HIS FAULT!" He took several deep breaths before he spoke again, this time not as loudly, but with every bit the same intensity. "He is the King; he has absolute power and he should have stopped her from her foolish quest."

"You know as well as anyone that you can't control your female. They are every bit as stubborn as we are, especially when it comes to nurturing relationships and creating peace. The death of your mate lies in the hands of her attackers and no one else."

"Oh really? Put yourself in my shoes. What if it was your mate that insisted on coming here today, instead of you? What if your Beta was the last to speak to her? And what if she came and I killed her? Who would you blame? Me? Of course. But who else? Shouldn't he have made absolute certain that she didn't put herself in harm's way?"

Vasile's eyes had begun to glow. "As her mate, ultimately it would be my fault. She is my responsibility. But she is also responsible for her actions. Your mate was an adult, and she made a choice to do something dangerous because she believed in the cause behind it."

Reyaz shook his head. "I think I really could have liked you under different circumstances. But, alas, we have met on a battlefield instead of under times of peace. You may go now, Vasile, Alpha and King of the wolves. But our next meeting will not likely end in such civility."

Vasile watched the warlock for several heartbeats before speaking again. "I too wish things were different, but I can't let you hurt Lilly. She is pack and I protect what is mine."

Reyaz watched in fascination. Vasile turned and, in the blink of an eye, where a man had stood, a wolf leapt off into the forest.

"Well, things just got more interesting," he murmured and then turned back to the mountain. He reached into his pocket and pulled out the vial of blood, unscrewed the lid, and tossed the red fluid towards the stronghold. His arms reached out and he closed his eyes as he called on the words of the spell he had composed.

"Ancient magic, born of black,

Bring your power, bring your will.
Let chaos reign, bring war back,
No peace shall come, none be still.

Anger, pain will rule their hearts,
Sickness, disease will fill their beds,
Strike their souls like poison darts,
Cast strife and worry upon their heads."

Reyaz felt a jolt of power rush through him and knew the magic had done its job. Now all he had to do was wait for a few days and let the spell settle in and begin to do its work.

He closed his eyes as he pictured the house that he had visited, Lilly's house, and all the delectable she-wolves and a gypsy as well. He smiled slowly; his reward for his patience would be great, and Cypher and the wolves won't even realize what has happened until it's far too late.

Gerick stood in the armory of the mountain stronghold checking the number of weapons they had. It had been a very long time since any new weapons had been forged. Because of this, he had been in contact with Prince Thalion of the Elves requesting help to create some new ones. Cypher was hoping to avoid an all-out battle with his brother, but he thought it better to be prepared than just to hope to not need them.

Cypher had been gone, off and on, to talk strategy with the wolves. And apparently, the fae were also involved. It seemed that desperate times continued to unite the supernatural races. Though he wished it were under different circumstances, it was good to see them all working together.

"Have you decided on what you would like my elves to make for you?" Thalion's voice broke through his thoughts.

"Plenty of bows and arrows for a start; I imagine fighting from a distance will probably be a good thing to do with Reyaz."

"But what will you be fighting? Will he have an army?" Thalion asked.

"Honestly, I have no idea."

"Doesn't that worry you?"

Gerick shook his head. "What worries me is that something about this whole thing feels wrong. Cypher is convinced that Reyaz is simply looking to hurt him or Lilly, but I think he has bigger plans than that."

"The forest is full of his darkness." Thalion looked at the rock wall surrounding them as if he could see through it into the forest he spoke of. "It is malevolent and a sickness is in the air."

Gerick took a deep breath, but the air got caught in his lungs. He began to cough until he had to lean against a row of swords to keep from falling over. He felt light headed and the room swam before him.

"General, are you all right?" Thalion asked as he stepped towards him.

Gerick closed his eyes and tried to focus himself. He counted to ten and finally the feeling passed and he could breathe again.

"I'm fine, sorry," he cleared his throat. "I don't know what that was but I'm better now."

Thalion watched him briefly before nodding. "I will get your bows made and some new swords as well. I will return in a week with them."

Gerick nodded. "Thank you, Prince Thalion."

Once the Elvin Prince was gone Gerick sat abruptly down on one of the benches that lined the walls. He didn't know what was going on, but his heart was pounding painfully in his chest, and his head felt as though it might split open. He had been telling the truth when he said he could breathe again, but he didn't add that now his whole body felt as though something was trying to explode out of him, like his skin was being stretched too thin against his frame.

He heard a commotion out in the hall and tried to listen to see what was going on. He didn't have to listen long when the door that Thalion had recently exited burst open.

"Gerick, you must come now." Finbar, the mate of one of their healers, motioned for him to follow.

"What is going on?" he asked as he stood from the bench and stood still until he felt steady enough to move.

"Just hurry please," Finbar said desperately.

He followed quickly and his skin began to crawl as he heard wailing. They entered the great hall of the mountain and Gerick's mouth dropped open.

"What happened?" he asked as his stomach rolled at the smells of sickness that permeated the air.

Gerick watched in horror as male and female warlocks alike doubled over in pain, some grabbing their heads and others clutching around their stomachs. Sounds of retching began to fill the air and then the wails of anguish climbed up the walls of the hall into the high ceiling of the mountain. Gerick moved forward, running to the first person he could reach. It was Indigo, one of his fellow warriors, and his skin was soaked in sweat and flushed with fever. He placed his hand against Indigo's face and felt that he was burning up. When the male turned his face up at Gerick, he watched as his eyes went from green to blazing red. Indigo took several deep breaths and then closed his eyes. Gerick took a step back and waited as he tried to tune out the cries around him. Finally, the warrior stood up straight, opened his eyes which continued to burn bright red, and let out a deep breath.

"Indigo," Gerick said cautiously, "are you alright?"

"I am," Indigo answered.

Gerick watched him for several seconds, but the noise around him ripped through his concern over what was happening with Indigo. He shook his head, attempting to push away the raging headache that had suddenly latched on like a vice grip and was attempting to drive him to his knees. He didn't have time to be ill, not when his King was away and something was terribly wrong with their people.

"Fine," he said in frustration, "help me with the others." Gerick motioned toward the room that continued to fill up with more and more sick warlocks. Indigo nodded and then headed towards the closest sick person.

Gerick started to head to another warrior but changed course when he saw Avrora, one of their healers come rushing in.

"Avrora," Gerick nearly yelled, "what is this madness?"

Avrora looked around slowly and Gerick was reminded of why she was the head healer. She was legendary for her calm and collected demeanor in times of stress and it was very apparent now that she was exactly what was needed.

"It's dark," Avrora finally said coolly. "Dark magic at work, General."

"What do we do?"

"I don't know," she looked over at him and, despite her control, he could still see the undiluted fear in her eyes.

Gerick felt another stab of pain in his stomach and then his vision swam as he fell to his knees. The words 'dark magic' floated through his head as he felt his mind being wrapped in a fog of confusion. He tried to push through the haze and think clearly, but he couldn't grasp onto a single thought. He heard his name being called, but he couldn't respond. He felt completely out of control of his faculties, and just when he was sure he was going to lose his mind, suddenly everything was clear.

He pushed up from the ground as his eyes opened. He rotated his neck, working out the stiffness. When he heard his name being called, this time he responded.

"My King," Gerick turned to see Cypher striding towards him. He fell to one knee as he bowed his head. "When did you return?"

"I've been back for about an hour. Are you feeling better?"

Gerick stood up and nodded. "I'm much better now, and all of our people will be well."

Cypher nodded. "Good. We have a war to plan."

"My thoughts exactly," Gerick agreed.

"Did you speak with Thalion today?"

"Yes, sire, he is making the bows and swords."

Cypher nodded as he looked around the great hall. He watched as one by one the warlocks who had been sick only moments ago now began to stand, shaking off the effects and opening their eyes revealing blood red irises. "Have him double the amount. Trolls can be hard to kill."

"Cypher," a female voice spoke up from across the hall.

Cypher looked over and his eyes narrowed. "Cyn, what are you doing here?"

The female Guardian fae walked slowly toward him. "Thalion mentioned that Gerick seemed to be ill today when he was here." Cyn watched the King she had spent over a month traveling with and noticed that, like the others, his eyes were a brilliant red. Her skin crawled as she felt the sickness in the air try to latch onto her. But it quickly retreated from the goodness she held in her heart.

Cypher chuckled darkly. "It seems that we have all been a little ill today, but as you can see we are healing quite quickly."

Cyn looked around and her lips tightened. Something was terribly wrong and she was beginning to realize that she was the only one who thought so. "Have you noticed anything different about your people, or about yourself, King?"

Cypher smiled, "Other than feeling stronger than I have felt in a long time? Then no, I do not notice anything different."

"How is your mate?" she asked suddenly. His eyes flashed back to their usual yellow briefly but the red was back in a blink.

"She is not my concern right now."

"Why not?" Cyn asked. She was fishing, but for what she didn't know just yet. For the moment, she was content just to keep him talking.

"In times of war there is no room to be worrying over a female." Cypher shifted his weight and she could tell the words almost seemed forced, as if he were actually fighting them from coming out.

"War?" she raised her voice just a tad, effectively grabbing a hold of the attention of the other warlocks in the room. "War with whom?"

Cypher's eyes grew even brighter and a smile that made Cyn's skin crawl flashed across his face. "The trolls. It is time they pay for their treachery."

A roar of agreement came from the others in the room as fists pumped into the air and heads nodded in agreement. She needed to go, and she needed to go now.

"I am on my way to see Vasile and his wolves. Should I send him a message?"

"Tell him he's either with us, or against us."

Cyn moved with purpose as she crossed through the veil. Her mind was so distracted on what she had just seen and heard that she didn't realize where she had taken herself until she heard his voice.

"Twice in one day, Guardian," Thalion spoke up as he watched Cyn move through the forest toward him as if she were a part of it. "I feel honored. What brings you back into my realm so soon, female?" the flirtatious tone in his voice was one that she usually welcomed, but he noticed that she did not respond in kind.

"As much as I enjoy your teasing, Prince, I must ask that we forgo that part of our usual conversation."

Thalion noticed once she was closer that her face was taught with worry and her body rigid with the need to act.

"What has happened?" he asked with urgency brought on by her obvious unease.

"You mentioned that Gerick had seemed off today when you saw him, so I thought perhaps I should check on the Warlock King and make sure all was well," she explained. "It turns out that all is far from well."

"Are they sick?"

"Something has twisted them. The last thing Cypher said to me was that he was going to war with the trolls."

Thalion took a step towards her, setting down the bow he had been holding.

"War?" he asked.

She nodded. "But that wasn't the only thing. Their eyes glowed red."

"Cypher's?"

"Not just his, all of them, every warlock, male and female had glowing red eyes," Cyn shuddered inwardly at the picture in her mind. "Their eyes glowed red," she continued, "and their faces were a mask of anger."

"Did Cypher say anything else?" Thalion asked as he took a step towards her.

"I told him I was going to see Vasile and asked if there was a message he would like me to give to him. I just wanted to see what he would say." Her eyes met his. "He told me to tell Vasile that the wolves were either with them or against them."

"Cypher is willing to risk going to war with the wolves?" Thalion shook his head. "That is not the Cypher that we know Cyn."

"I agree," she told him.

"Have you told Vasile?"

She shook her head. "I thought I was on my way there, but then I ended up here."

Thalion's full lips spread into a smile. "Are you worried for my safety, Guardian? Were you coming to protect me?"

Cyn rolled her eyes. "I was coming to tell you not to make the weapons for them. Cypher plans to use them against the trolls."

"You're right. We definitely do not want the warlocks to have Elvin weapons if they are going to possibly wield them against the trolls." His eyebrows drew together as he looked at her. He seemed to be studying her features as he took yet another step towards her. "I find myself rather frustrated at the moment," he said.

Cyn tilted her head to the side. "Why?" she asked slowly.

"Because I've finally have you in my life again," he paused.

"And that frustrates you?"

He chuckled. "No, love, what frustrates me is that everyone seems hell bent on killing each other when all I want to do is spend time with the woman I love, which I can't do because the woman I love has a kind and generous heart and refuses to leave these species to their own demise."

She smiled warmly and blushed. "You think I'm generous?"

Thalion took another large step towards her and wrapped her in his arms. She gasped at the speed of his movements, but she didn't push him away.

"I just told you I love you, and all you heard was that I think you are generous?"

"I already knew you loved me," she told him matter-of-fact like.

"Really?"

She nodded. "But I had no idea you thought I was kind and generous, and that changes everything," she teased.

Thalion threw his head back and laughed. Cyn rarely played; she was usually very serious, but when she did play, when she did show him her softer side, Thalion found himself wanting to bask in the joy she brought him.

He took one last breath after composing himself and looked into her eyes. "We need to warn the wolves."

"Yes," she told him but didn't attempt to pull away from him. She met his stare with the same intensity he was giving her.

"But before I can do anything else, I have to kiss you."

"Have to or want to?" she whispered.

"Both."

Cyn nodded and licked her lips nervously. Thalion's eyes followed the tip of her tongue as it traveled across her mouth and he groaned as he leaned forward and closed the distance between them. He kissed her deeply with a centuries worth of passion. She wrapped her arms around his neck and pulled herself closer to him, finally giving into the emotions that threatened to consume her. She had wanted him for so long but stayed away because he refused to be a part of any world but his own. She knew she could not be with someone who only thought his own people's needs and safety were important. But all that had changed when she had come to him for help just a few months ago. He had stepped forward and told her that he would no longer keep his people separate from the rest of the supernatural or human world. He agreed that as one of the most powerful supernatural races it was his duty to help and to protect when need be. When he had decided that, *she* had decided that if he wanted her still, she would be his.

When they finally pulled back from each other, their breathing was rapid and their lips glistened with the passion of their kiss. She reached up and traced his lips with her fingertips and the warmth of his breath on her skin made her shiver.

"Is that a yes?" he finally spoke once his breathing was again even.

"Yes?" she asked.

"To the question I posed so long ago. Will you be mine and mine alone?"

Cyn smiled one of her rare smiles that showed just how beautiful she was, not only on the outside but on the inside as well. "It is," she answered.

Thalion leaned down and kissed her again, but this time it was gentle.

"Finally," he whispered against her lips.

"Can we go tell the wolves now?" she asked.

"Yes, but when this is all said and done, I will not forget what has happened here today, Cyn."

She pulled back and grinned mischievously. "If you do forget it, then I apparently did not do it right and perhaps will have to ask Lilly what I am doing wrong, since Cypher seems to like to come back for seconds so often."

"There will be plenty of times for seconds, and thirds for that matter once the warlocks are dealt with."

"And Reyaz," she added.

"Okay," he agreed, "and Reyaz."

"Oh, and we get the females back from the United States. Oh, and Jen and Decebel's baby is saved."

Thalion grabbed her hand and started to pull her quickly behind him.

"Thalion?" she called out nearly laughing. "In a hurry?"

"Yes, at the rate you are throwing names out there for us to save I shall never get seconds."

"Or thirds for that matter," she added and then laughed when she heard him growl.

"I can get us there quicker, Prince," she told him as she continued to laugh at his obvious frustration. She pulled him to a stop and then in a flash they were standing before the Romanian pack mansion.

She turned and looked at him. "Better?"

"I'll keep you posted," but softened his words with a wink as he ushered her towards the front door.

Chapter 12

"Attention all clueless beings out there. Be on the lookout for crap hitting the fan in the form of a psycho warlock tossing out dark magic like it's freaking candy on Halloween and a warlock king who suddenly got an itch up his butt to roast some trolls. These are dangerous times people and we all know what we should do during dangerous times...yes, exactly, drink more hot chocolate, use profanity when completely inappropriate and for the love of all things carnal, make babies people, or at least practice." ~Jen

"The book store looks like it's been doing well," Jacque told her mom as she walked around the familiar space. They had been back in the states for over a month now and though Lilly had been going to the book store nearly daily, the others hadn't ventured out of the house much thanks to Peri's interlude with Reyaz. But everyone was getting cabin fever and Sally really wanted to see her parents. Jen knew she was going to have to see her parents as well, but she wasn't really sure how they were going to react when they saw that their 18 year old daughter was well and truly pregnant. So they made plans to join Lilly at the book store that night to help her with inventory. They ordered pizza, pulled the shades to the windows, turned on music, and tried to forget the outside world.

"It has been doing well, and I'm glad because hopefully that means it will be easier to sell." Lilly's back was to the room when she made the statement so she didn't see the shock on Jacque, Jen, and Sally's faces.

"What?" Jen finally blurted out. "You're selling your store?"

"Well it's going to be kind of hard to take care of a store when I live on another continent," Lilly said as she continued to unpack the box of books on the floor next to her. It was one of many that would need to be unpacked that night.

"When did you decide this mom?" Jacque asked.

"After I talked to Cypher a week or so ago," she admitted. "Beside him is where I'm supposed to be, Jacque. I know you get that."

Jacque did get that, as weird as it was to hear her mother say it. She couldn't argue with her because she knew exactly what she meant. Beside Fane was where she was supposed to be, and instead she was in Coldstone, TX, in a book store. Yeah, life sucked sometimes.

"Well, it's your store, so if that's what you want to do, then go for it." Sally smiled as she looked at Lilly.

"Thank you, Sally." Lilly grinned.

Sally's smile faltered when her phone began belting out the ringtone Jen had set for her, *My Maria*, simply because it had the words *gypsy lady* in it. She pulled it from her back pocket and swallowed hard when she saw her mom's name pop up.

"It's the 'rents isn't it?" Jen asked.

Sally nodded wordlessly.

"Well, time to face the firing squad." Jen patted Sally's shoulder as she walked past her. "Get it over with quick Sal, like ripping off finger nails."

"Don't you mean band aides?" Crina asked.

Jen shook her head. "Uh, no. Any time you're dealing with parents, it's never like ripping off a band aide. It is always much, much, more painful."

Crina chuckled. "I am so glad I've been a werewolf all this time."

Sally finally hit the key to answer the phone and put it to her ear. "Hello," she said tentatively.

"Sally!" her mother's voice came shrieking through and Sally had to pull the phone away from her ear.

"Yes, it's me," she answered. "How are you?"

"How am I? I'm wondering how long my child has been back without coming to see me? And did you bring that young man of yours? How is school going? Do you like Romania? How are Jacque and Jen?"

"Mom, mom," Sally's voice rose as she tried to get her mom to slow down. "Hold on, okay. I can't answer all your questions at once."

"Oh, sorry, I've just missed you."

"I know. I've missed you too." Sally was surprised to feel her eyes begin to water but she quickly wiped them before any tears could escape. "Can you and Dad come to Lilly's book store?"

"Oh, honey," her mom cooed, "your dad is out of town. He won't be back for a week or more."

Sally felt her chest tighten at the guilt of not contacting her parents sooner. If she had, she would have gotten to see her dad, but she had waited and now he was gone. Maybe he would be back before she left. But that thought was a double-edged sword because though she wanted to see her dad, she was so very ready to get back to Costin.

"But I can come," her mom finished pulling her out of her thoughts.

"Okay, well we're all here now."

"We who?"

"Um, well, Lilly, Jen, Jacque and the others," Sally said vaguely.

"Oh, so you brought your young man?"

"No mom. It's just the females," Sally cringed as she realized that she had used the word females, which was not something humans said in reference to women very often in everyday conversation. "Oh, mom, can you stop by and pick up Jen's parents? They don't know Jen's here so let's make it a surprise."

"Oh! That's a wonderful idea; see you in a few."

Sally hit the end key and was already moving before she heard Jen's voice behind her.

"I'm going to kick your ever loving gypsy ass, Sally Miklos!" Nervous laughter flitted around the store as the others watched Jen attempt to go after Sally.

Peri reached out and snatched Jen's arm before she could grab Sally's pony tail. "Calm down Jen or you're going to go into labor and get Lilly's pretty floor all bloody with your pregnant body fluids."

Jen looked at Peri and smirked. "Did you seriously just say pregnant body fluids?"

Peri rolled her eyes. "Yes, I did, and why do you three always insist on asking if someone seriously said something? Do you think that they didn't seriously say it and therefore feel the need to double check your hearing by asking?"

"Did you seriously just ask that?" Jen asked and the room erupted into laughter.

Peri huffed as she pushed past Jen, "Why the hell did I decide to come with the girls?"

"Because we are entertaining," Elle told her.

"Yes and so is a cage of chimpanzees. I'm just waiting for you all to start crapping on the floor and then throwing it at each other, all the while squealing and pointing."

The laughing jumped up a notch and when the knock on the front door of the store finally came, Jen was doubled over holding her stomach as she giggled. She wiped the laugh induced tears from her eyes as she prepared herself for all hell to break loose in a completely different way than she was used to. Put her before a psycho witch, a bossy possessive werewolf, or a deranged warlock and she smirked. But put her before her parents who didn't know that she was married, let alone pregnant, and she wanted to crawl into the deepest hole she could find.

Lilly unlocked the door and pushed it open. Sally's mom walked in and squealed when she saw Sally. Jen's mom was next and then her dad. Her mom's eyes lit up as they landed on her and then dropped to her stomach.

"Surprise," Jen said lamely and let out a deep breath when Alina walked up next to her and put an arm around her and then smiled at her parents. Alina's charms were legendary, but they were about to be put to the test.

"Jennifer." Her mom smiled and moved towards her wrapping her in her arms, effectively pulling her from Alina's.

"Hi mom," Jen said and it came out muffled as her mom tucked her head into her shoulder.

"Oh, I've missed you!"

"You too," Jen said as she pulled back and attempted to untangle herself from her mom. Her dad came up next and gave her one of those one arm hugs that were equally awkward and annoying.

"Hey Dad," she said as she quickly hugged him back and then pulled away.

The room was completely silent after the brief reunions and all eyes were on Jen and her parents.

"Jen's pregnant," Sally suddenly blurted out. Heads swung around and eyes landed on her and she slapped her hand over her mouth as if it had acted without her consent.

"Thank you for that," Jen muttered as she glared at Sally and then looked back at her parents. It was obvious by the looks on their faces that they had really just been hoping that Jen had suddenly developed a love for Pork Rinds and had been eating enough of them to support North American sales all by herself.

"Surprise again!" Jen said in a sing song voice and a shoulder shrug.

Jen's mother's mouth dropped open and then closed, only to do it again, making Jen think of a fish that had been taken from water and was desperately gasping.

"How," she finally sputtered.

"Well, mom," Jen's voice took on the patronizing tone that seemed to always tick her parents off, "when two people love each other, they want to show it. And sometimes they show that love by taking their clothes off and going at it like rabbits."

Jen looked past her now shocked mother to the forms of Jacque and Sally, who were making cutting motions across their necks and mouthing for her to shut up. She simply shook her head. She was eighteen. Her parents could look at her like she had lost her mind, but they couldn't punish her, not any more.

"You're really pregnant?" her dad finally asked.

"Yes dad, I'm really pregnant. I'm pretty sure there is no such thing as sort of pregnant, but I could be wrong. It's been known to happen once or twice a year—me being wrong, not being sort of pregnant."

"Is it this Decebel guy?" her mom asked.

"Yes it is Decebel's baby." Jen couldn't help the huge smile that spread across her face at the mention of her mate. Regardless of all their crap, she was carrying his child, made out of love and that was definitely something to smile about. And she had just shocked the hell out of her parents and that was just a bonus, like when you find a couple fries thrown in with your order of tots from Sonic. Bonus fries were the best.

"Where is he?" her dad asked with a frown.

"He didn't come," Jen told him.

"He let you travel by yourself in that state?" her dad growled and pointed at her stomach.

Alina stepped forward, and though she had a smile on her face, her eyes told a different story. "Jen is perfectly safe with me, with us," she amended as she motioned to all the women in the room. "Decebel and the other males had business that required them to stay in Romania, and the girls wanted to take a little break. We have a doctor with us," she motioned to Cynthia who waved and smiled. "Dr. Steele keeps a close eye on her."

Jen's parents continued to stare at her. Their eyes darted every now and then to Lilly, giving her looks that clearly said they blamed her for their knocked-up daughter. The tension in the room was palpable.

"I think Peri's suggestion earlier of crap throwing and squealing is sounding really appealing right now," remarked Jen. "So who's going first, Mom? No, okay Jacque, come on we all know your bowels are irregular. You should have something ready to go."

A snort erupted from Sally and she turned away as Elle patted her on the back while she and the others snickered at Jen.

Peri coughed as she tried to cover her laugh. "Jen it wasn't a suggestion, you twit, I was being sarcastic."

Jen smiled at Peri as a single brow rose. "Oh come now, fairy Peri, you know you love a good crap throw as much as the next person."

"So," Lilly suddenly jumped in, "who wants hot chocolate?"

At least three hands shot into the air.

"Bloody hell, that was torture," Jen whined as she climbed into Jacque's bed.

"I have to agree," Sally said as she took the sleeping bag on the floor.

"But hilarious as hell," Jacque laughed.

"Please, pray tell wolf princess, which part was hilarious?" Jen growled. "Was it the part where my dad asked if Decebel had any other children or a wife or was it when my mom asked if we had been using protection?"

"No, it was when you told your mom that yes you had been using protection and not to invest stock in the flavored condoms because they just weren't as strong as the box claimed."

All three of the girls shook with laughter. "And then hot chocolate came out of your dad's nose!" Sally added breathlessly.

"That was a MasterCard moment," Jen sighed. "Flight home- $300, cup of hot chocolate- $1.50, Dad snorting up cocoa because of discussing daughters sex life…,"

"Priceless!" they all said in unison and erupted into laughter all over again.

As their laughter died down, another feeling began to pool in their stomachs.

"Is anyone else sick of hurting?" Jen asked.

"Totally."

"Entirely."

Sally and Jacque said at the same time.

"Then why are we still here?"

"Because this is where they obviously want us," Jacque said.

"What do you mean?" Sally asked as she leaned up on her elbows.

"If our men really didn't want us to be here, you know there is nothing-no amount of screaming, whining, or threatening - we could have done to make them let us. They may have thrown their little tantrums, but some part of them wanted us away and that is why we are here."

"Ugh," Jen groaned, "we so got played."

"Jen, babe, are you okay?" Sally asked softly. "You seem to be a lot worse off than Jacque or I and don't tell me it's because of your pregnancy."

"You know, ever since you got this whole gypsy title, you've become very bossy," Jen told her and Sally could hear the smile on her friend's face.

"Quit avoiding the question."

"He's shut me out completely, even from his sleep," Jen finally admitted and when the words finally emerged she felt the flood gates give way. She rolled onto her side as the tears began to slide down her cheeks and she bit her bottom lip to keep them from trembling. "I feel like he's slipping away from me. Like every day, every hour, the thread between us gets thinner and thinner."

Sally's breath caught at the pain she heard in Jen's voice. She crawled up into the bed on the other side of Jen as Jacque took the opposite side so that they had sandwiched her in. Both girls wrapped their arms around her and just held her as she cried. There were no words spoken, no false promises that everything would be fine. The reality was that more than likely nothing was going to be fine. So instead they simply took comfort in knowing that in everything they had been through, they had always had each other. Their friendship had stood the tests of life, death, bloodshed, war, and love, and it would continue to do so.

Sally pressed her hand to Jen's head, brushing her fingers through the blonde locks. She slipped silently into Jen's mind, trying to keep her friend from realizing what she was doing. As she closed her eyes and opened her spirit to Jen's, she had to bite her tongue to keep from gasping. Jen's bond, the thin chord that linked her to Decebel, was stripped, like a rope that had been shredded until there were only a few strands holding it together, so was Jen and Decebel's mate bond. She could see the emptiness in Jen where Decebel's soul should be, the other half of hers now nearly gone. Sally was surprised that Jen didn't simply lie around groaning in pain. It was a miracle that her wolf hadn't taken over in a desperate attempt to get back to her mate. Sally took her hand away from Jen and rolled onto her back and listened to the slow even breathing of her two best friends.

What did it mean? What could be doing this to their bond and was that why Decebel had been acting so out of character? She didn't know, but she had an idea of who might. She slid out of the bed, careful not to wake Jacque or Jen and then hurried quietly from the room.

She knocked on the spare bedroom door and was surprised when she heard a muffled, *come in*. She wasn't expecting anyone to be awake. She pushed the door open to find Cynthia sitting up in the bed with a book in her lap. She glanced up at Sally before looking back at the book and slipping a piece of paper in the pages to save her spot.

"Sally, is Jen alright?" she asked quietly. Of course she would assume that something must be wrong with Jen because of her state, but she didn't answer right away.

Sally walked over to the end of the bed and sat down without saying anything. She tried to gather her thoughts but then decided there really wasn't any easy way to break this.

"Jen and Decebel's bond is dying." She watched the doctors face for any sign of outrage, surprise, or shock, but there was none. "You knew?" Sally asked with a frown. "And still you let her come?"

Cynthia laughed bitterly. "Like anyone can keep Jen from doing something she wants to do. And no, I didn't know, but I had my suspicions."

"What's going on doc? What's wrong with Decebel?"

Cynthia pulled her legs up and wrapped her arms around them as her eyes met Sally's. "I don't really know any more than you."

"How is Decebel keeping Jen out of his mind while he sleeps?"

"That is a question you should be asking me." Sally turned at the sound of Elle's voice and saw that Peri was right behind her.

"Sorry to bust up this little sleepover, but if you want answers, Healer, then you need to go to those in the know." Peri leaned against the wall, looking more awake than anyone at that hour should and definitely looking like she was in the know.

"So what happened to Decebel?" she asked again, this time directed at Elle.

"He asked for me to make it so that when he slept Jen could not get past his barriers."

"Why?"

"Do we really have to go through this again?" Peri groaned. "Because he has…,"

Sally held her hand up stopping the fae from going on. "I know, I know, he has man parts. I get it, but that doesn't fully answer my question."

"He has a secret and he doesn't want her to be able to go snooping and find it," Peri told her and appeared very put out at having been interrupted.

"Decebel isn't the type to keep things from Jen," Sally argued.

"People will often become very different from who they really are when life and death matters are at hand," said Cynthia.

"I thought that people showed who they truly are when they are in life and death situations." Sally's eyes narrowed at the doctor.

Peri waved her hand as if batting away a fly. "Sally, really, do you think we can possibly unravel the workings of the alpha male Canis lupus, especially starting with Decebel?"

Sally didn't answer; she simply stared at Peri as if everything she wanted to know was going to explode out of her head at any moment. Then the words hit her again.

"You said life and death," Sally pointed at Cynthia. "This has to do with their baby, wait," Sally gasped and covered her mouth. "He wouldn't," she muttered around her hand, not speaking to anyone but simply staring at the ground as her mind tried to grasp what she was realizing. "Oh," she whispered slowly, "but he would. They all would."

"He's going to sacrifice himself. But he can't do that if their bond is intact," Sally finally spoke up loud enough for everyone to hear.

Peri smiled like a proud parent. "I knew she was the smart one in the bunch. Didn't I tell you Elle," she nudge the other fae. "Didn't I say that the quiet, innocent one is the smart one?"

Elle nodded. "Yes Peri, you did," she said dryly.

"Jen's going to kill him." Sally's eyes locked with Peri's.

"You can't tell her, Healer," Peri's face suddenly went very serious. "It is not the place of any of us to meddle in the Alpha's business."

"She's my best friend, Peri. That makes it my business," Sally argued.

"No," Cynthia spoke up. "If she were only your best friend, then yes, it would be your business. But she isn't only your best friend. She's Decebel's mate, Sally, his wife. There are some things that are between husband and wife that the friend card no longer holds any sway over."

Sally glared at Cynthia while hearing her words, hearing their truth, and hating them. She knew that there were some things that weren't her business because Decebel wasn't just Jen's boyfriend, he was her husband and that did make it different.

"But he's making the wrong choice," she whined. *Way to be real mature Sally,* she thought to herself.

"That is not for you to decide," Peri told her, the words of the Great Luna echoing in her mind. "The Fates will ultimately decide whose life they will accept. There is so little we control in this life, and as much as we would like to think life and death is one of those things, it just isn't."

Sally let out a deep, resigned sigh. She couldn't tell Jen. In fact, she couldn't tell anyone.

"This freaking sucks," she grumbled.

"So goes the story of our paranormal lives," Peri agreed.

"I've been waiting for you," the Great Luna said softly to the wolf in human form before her. The warm night air blew through her shimmering hair and the moonlight made her skin glow.

"You knew I was coming?"

"Yes, and they have agreed to hear you." She motioned for the wolf to follow her. She walked into the forest. As the trees swallowed her, the wolf paused just for a second before following the goddess inside.

They wound through the trees until there was a canopy of limbs that hung over an opening to a cave. Light flickered at the entrance as if a fire burned inside and the flames danced, tempting them to enter and seek its warmth. The Great Luna stepped aside and motioned for the wolf to go into the cave. "This is as far as I go," she told the wolf who continued forward, following the beckoning light.

The wolf walked deeper into the cave until a voice said to stop.

"We have agreed to hear your petition." The three figures of the Fates suddenly appeared before the wolf. "What is it you ask for?"

"I come to offer my life in the place of one that you have claimed. I ask that you allow the child to live and let me fulfill the debt. Let my blood wipe clean the slate." The wolf's voice was full of sincerity.

"Why would you offer yourself as a sacrifice for this child? It is one thing for the father to do so, but who is this child to you that you would lay down your life?"

"The child is pack. She is family and she is loved. What greater way to show that she is loved than to give my life for hers?"

Silence filled the cave as the Fates watched the wolf, and then they finally spoke again.

"We will consider your sacrifice, but you will not know our decision until the moment it is due. You must tell no one of your choice. For true sacrifice does not seek approval or crave attention.

You will do this and no one will know until you have left this life and passed on to the next."

The wolf left the cave and walked into the arms of the Great Luna.

"Can you restore what has begun to be broken?"

The Great Luna's eyes filled with moisture as she shook her head. "I cannot. They still might choose him. If their bond was restored, then she would die also. I am proud of you, but I hurt for you as well."

"It is what should be," the wolf told her.

The Great Luna nodded. "Just because it is right, does not make it easy."

"No, but it just might atone for my wrongs."

"Oh child, all you need do is ask for forgiveness and the wrongs are wiped clean."

"I want to believe that," the wolf looked into her eyes, "but there is a part of me that feels that I can never be forgiven, that I will never be worthy of it."

The goddess took the wolf's face in her hands and held it gently. "You are not worthy. Not on your own, but *I* have made you worthy. My love for you has made you worthy."

Chapter 13
"Peace is a fragile thing. It is forged on the trust that your enemy will choose respect over pride, selflessness over greed, and mercy over power. It is not won in wars, nor bargained for in treaties, for it can't be won and it can't be negotiated, not real peace. Real peace, peace that lasts, comes when parties who do not agree, set aside their disagreements for a greater purpose. It comes at the price of self. That is why true peace will never last on this earth, because we are not beings who find many things worth the price of our self." ~Skender

"Will you not welcome one of the Fae Council into your midst, Thead?" Lorelle asked the troll king.

Thead's eyes narrowed on the fae and the stirrings of mistrust rolled in his gut.

"Since when has the Fae Council ever shown interest in the trolls, Lorelle?" Thead asked. His deep voice rumbled and he smirked as he watched the female shift nervously.

"Since we have heard rumors of war coming your way."

Thead didn't give her the pleasure of acting fearful, or surprised, though he might be both of those things. He could tell that there was something amiss with this Lorelle of the fae.

"Then tell me your rumors and be on your way."

She drew herself up and pulled her shoulders back. She met his eyes, and though she was taller than he and probably more powerful, he didn't flinch under her gaze. He didn't flinch until she spoke.

"Cypher, King of the Warlocks, has declared war on the trolls for the murder of Thea, mate to Reyaz, the king's brother. He will accept no prisoners; he will extend no mercy, blood for blood, life for life."

Thead continued to hold onto the mask he had donned as soon as Lorelle had appeared, but it took everything in him to keep from lashing out. Cypher had promised him long ago that no retaliation would come after Thea's death. He had told Thead that he would not condemn an entire race for the misdeeds of a few and he had believed him. Now, centuries later, what would bring him to go back on his word? What would change his view on something so very important?

"You do know that Cypher has taken a mate don't you?" Lorelle said as if she had just read the questions in his mind.

"No, I had not heard that," he admitted.

"I suggest that you ready yourself, King. Cypher will not be swayed and war will be at your door before you know it."

Thead stood there staring at the spot that Lorelle had just occupied. He had always hated the disappearing act that the fae could perform; it left him uneasy in the sudden silence. War was coming, she had said, and at the hands of the warlocks. He and his did not stand a chance against them. They were not very powerful to begin with, but with the magic in the human realm waning, their ability to protect themselves had dropped greatly. He honestly had no idea how he could possibly ready himself and his clan, but he knew he wouldn't just lie down and let Cypher destroy them. If he was going to die, he would die fighting.

"Cyn, Prince Thalion, it is good to see you again," Vasile told his unexpected guests as he motioned them to take a seat in his office. "I have a feeling this is not a social call."

"I wish I could say otherwise," Thalion said as he took a seat. Cyn sat next to him on the love seat, her serious face firmly back in place.

"Cyn has come across some very disturbing news," Thalion began. "Let me back up. I went to see Gerick at the warlock stronghold. Cypher has commissioned my elves to make his warriors' weapons. I was there to verify the amount and the types today. While

I was there, Gerick exhibited some very strange behavior. But he said he was fine, and so I took my leave," he paused and looked at Cyn who took it as her cue to continue.

"He mentioned the behavior to me so I went to check on the situation. When I arrived, Cypher was there in the great hall, along with nearly all of the warlocks. They were in various states of illness. Some vomited while others writhed in pain. But still others were standing up appearing perfectly normal, other than their eyes being a blood red. Then I heard Cypher talking about war."

"War?" Vasile had been listening quietly as the two spoke but at the mention of war, his wolf perked up. "With whom?"

"He has declared war on the trolls," Cyn said.

Vasile sat back in his chair as her words sunk in. They reverberated through his mind and crawled into his veins like thousands of tiny ants. War, the word rung ominously in the room. Hadn't there been enough war? Hadn't there been enough blood spilt, enough lives taken to last many lifetimes? And where had this idea come from? Cypher hadn't mentioned any ideas of attacking the trolls when he had met with Vasile. He had seemed completely focused on his brother and dealing with that problem. As his mind wrestled with the questions and thoughts surrounding this new dilemma, he stood and pulled his phone from his pocket. He pressed the number three and then waited.

"Alpha," Skender's voice came through the speaker.

"I need you in my office now." Vasile hung up without waiting for a response.

Cyn and Thalion had also stood and were staring at him, waiting. He didn't like repeating himself so he didn't speak until the door opened and Skender came striding in with Decebel right behind him. *No surprise there,* Vasile thought to himself. Decebel was attempting to find any way to stay busy, to keep from having to be still, and to deal with whatever it was that kept him and his wolf so riled up.

"Skender, I need you to go see the King of the trolls," Vasile said.

Skender nodded once before asking "Is there something…,"

Vasile held his hand up, cutting the wolf off. "I will give you the information you need if you will be patient and let me get it out." A low growl emanated from his chest as he spoke. Skender immediately dropped to one knee and exposed his neck. Vasile's power was radiating through the room and it caused the others to shift uncomfortably.

"Cypher has declared war on the trolls."

"You have got to be kidding me," Decebel grumbled under his breath. Vasile ignored him and continued speaking.

"I need you to find out if Thead is aware of the declaration and if so, what response he is mustering."

"Yes Alpha," Skender said.

"Stand up Skender," Vasile said in exasperation. He pinched the bridge of his nose with his thumb and forefinger and squeezed his eyes shut briefly. "My anger is not at you. It is at the situation," he explained.

Skender simply stood and nodded.

"I will go with him," Decebel spoke up.

"I would prefer you stay here, but as I am not your Alpha you may decide."

Decebel met Vasile's eyes trying to get a read on him, but all he could see was frustration and irritation.

"Fine, I will send Costin with him."

"I am not going to deliver the weapons to Cypher," Thalion told Vasile, "not until this threat he has professed has been retracted."

"I think that is wise," Vasile agreed.

"Decebel, I would like for us to speak with our top males about this. We will need to take action and it will need to be swift and hard. Thalion, you are welcome to stay and listen in. Cyn could you please summon Alston?" Vasile turned then and looked at Skender, "Wait until after we've discussed everything before you leave."

Fifteen minutes later, Vasile's office was filled with wolves, fae, and an elf prince. Decebel had quickly gathered Costin, Fane, Sorin, Gavril, Adam, Wadim, and Drake. He had asked Vasile about Boian, but Vasile had simply said that he had the wolf looking into other things. Cyn had brought Alston, and Thalion had chosen to stay. He stood leaning back against his desk, staring at absolutely nothing.

"I'm beginning to see a pattern here," Wadim spoke up. "Every time we meet like this, you tell us that someone wants to kill us."

There were a few snorts around the room at his joke but it died down quickly when Vasile finally looked up at them all. His eyes glowed with the power of his wolf and frustration was written across his brow.

"Unfortunately, I *have* gathered you because of death, but it is not our death that is being sought after." Vasile informed them of everything Thalion and Cyn had told him. He watched as expressions changed from shock to confusion and anger.

"This doesn't sound like something Cypher would do," Sorin said.

"I agree," Vasile answered. "I have Skender and Costin looking into it. If it's true, then Cypher will need to be dealt with."

Peri's sudden appearance into the room caused several wolves to growl. She looked around until her eyes landed on Vasile. "Can someone please tell me why I have just been informed by Dain that a hoard of angry and quite possibly deranged warlocks, led by none other than our friendly neighborhood Warlock King, are running through the forest straight towards the land of the trolls?"

Immediately everyone was on their feet, but their growls and questions were held back by Vasile and Decebel's authority.

"Are they cloaked?" Vasile asked her.

She nodded. "Yes, Cypher has them completely covered from view, but they are moving fast. What the hell is going on Vasile?"

"Why did Dain come to you?" Alston asked though he didn't sound offended, just curious, since he had been the one to send Dain on the mission.

Peri crossed her arms over her chest and narrowed her eyes at him. "I was in the area and we bumped into each other."

"Why aren't you in the states with the females?" Decebel asked as he took a step towards her.

Peri did not like the look in the Alpha's eyes nor the tone of his voice. "Did I or did I not just inform you that Cypher has lost his damn mind and is about to attempt to make the troll population extinct?"

"You're hiding something, Perizada, and if that something puts my mate in danger we are going to have a problem." Decebel's amber eyes flashed with light and she could see his canines were lengthening.

She held his gaze, knowing that was probably the dumbest thing she could have done, but she had to make him think she was not hiding something, especially since she was. It was a pretty big something, seeing as how she knew that if the wolves in that room knew that Reyaz had shown himself at Lilly's, and Peri hadn't told them the minute after it happened, she was as good as dead. Then again, judging by the fury in Decebel's face, she just might be as good as dead anyways. *Might as well put the final nail in my coffin,* she thought.

"Obviously you don't catch on real quick wolf, but you already have a problem and if my idea of your problem is correct, then I can guaran-damn-tee you do not need *another* problem, especially one as inventive as me. So, back, the heck up," The last few words were bit out one at a time as she motioned for him to step away from her.

With Peri and Decebel's little encounter over, the room began to focus on what Peri had told them.

Vasile looked at Alston. "You and yours are the only ones who can get there quickly enough to at least hold them off until we can get there."

"Say no more," Alston told him. Then he looked at Peri. "Are you in?"

"Puh-lease," she huffed, "like I would miss an opportunity to kick Cypher while he's down." She in turn glanced at Adam.

He smiled his heart stopping smile, one that she knew Crina would have loved to have witnessed. "Let's do this gorgeous; it will be like old times," he said.

"Old times?" she scoffed, "We just did this a few months ago."

Adam shrugged, "Okay, it will be like good times with all the killing and maiming."

"Now we're talking."

"No killing unless necessary, Peri. Just incapacitate until we are sure that Cypher isn't under the influence of dark magic," Vasile warned.

"You wolves take the fun out of everything. No stripping, no flirting, and now we're going to war and we can't even freaking kill anything."

She was gone as the last word hit her lips.

Vasile looked at Adam. The fae gave thumbs up. "No killing, only taking out knee caps and chopping off hands so they can't hold a weapon. We got this." He was gone just as quickly as Peri.

Alston was gone next. Cyn glanced at Thalion. His eyes told her he was worried about her, that he didn't want her there without him, but the resigned nod told her that he knew this was a part of her job and he couldn't stand in the way of that. He gave her a quick wink, which made her blush, and then she was gone.

Vasile was pretty sure Adam had been joking, but then he was still pretty new to the pack and he hadn't quite figured him out just yet. He looked at the remaining males in the room and started moving towards the door. "This is all we're taking," he motioned to include all of them. "I want to move fast and I want to move quiet. You all heard what I said, no killing."

"What if we have no choice?" Sorin asked.

Vasile answered even as he began his phase. "Make it clean; make it quick."

"Hello Thead, I see that magic still protects your home." Peri smiled as she stepped up to the trees that led into the home the trolls had hidden there. They had used magic to create the illusion of a forest so dense that light didn't even penetrate it. Only supernaturals could see the entrance and even then you had to know what you were looking for. There was a time when the trolls had occupied the Balkan Mountains on the furthest Western side close to what is now Serbia, but the mountains were becoming more and more travelled by humans. It was either dig deeper into the mountain or leave and find sanctuary elsewhere. They had voted on it, and the majority of their clan had wanted to flee the mountain.

Thead had known there was no way for them to conceal themselves and so he had sought out the help of the fae, well, one fae in particular. Peri had agreed to help them, and she had attached no strings to her assistance. When Thead had asked why she didn't want any form of payment, Peri had simply said, *"Someone is sure to want to find you one day and it will be amusing to laugh while they wander around like idiots looking for you."*

"If it is working, why are you here?" Thead asked.

"Who has been here recently, Thead?"

He hesitated before finally speaking, "Lorelle was here."

"Bloody, freaking—," Peri let out a stream of profanity worthy of a Jen performance as she paced. It shouldn't have surprised her that her sister was involved. That would explain how Cypher had known where to go. "Cypher is on his way here now. They are moving very fast and there is a bunch of them. Oh, and they have freaky red eyes," she added. Though she wasn't sure why, she thought he should know.

"Peri, you know we are not strong enough to defeat them."

Peri smiled just as Alston, Adam, and Cyn came walking out of the forest around them. "That, my old friend, is why we are here." The other three fae bowed to the king and smiled reassuringly.

"Vasile and his wolves are on their way as well," Adam told him.

Thead looked off into the forest, his eyes searching, his ears listening. "I don't know why he is doing this now," he said without looking at the fae.

Peri let out a deep breath as she thought about it. She had to agree that the Cypher she knew would not suddenly declare war on a race that he had kept peace with for so long.

"Have any of your clan been near his mountain?" she asked him.

"No, we rarely leave and I always know who is leaving and where they are going," Thead told her.

"He's under a lot of stress right now. He sent his mate away for her own safety and he's dealing with all this crap about his brother," she said absently as she thought out loud.

"His brother?" Thead's voice betrayed the nervousness he hid from his face. "What about Reyaz?"

"He's decided to come out and play, only no one wants to play the kinds of games he seems interested in," her words faded off as she thought about them. Games, Reyaz was definitely into games of any variety, including ones that would cause one species to attack another. "Awe crap!" she growled just as the ground began to tremble beneath her feat.

She braced herself, leaning forward on the balls of her feet and watching for the attack that was imminent. The others followed suit. She smiled when she saw Adam did a few standing jumps and then rolled his shoulders like a boxer would just before a match.

"Thead, go back into your forest and do not come out until you hear from me," Peri told him as she continued to watch.

"I will not hide behind you."

"You will or I will turn you into a yard ornament."

Thead's eyes widened as he backed up and then finally turned and fled into the safety of the protected forest.

"Remember, no killing," Adam announced just as running warlocks came into view. They moved through the forest like ghosts, whipping around trees and jumping over foliage. It was hard to believe that beings so large could move with such grace. The red eyes that peered out from each of their faces glowed dangerously and their lips were lifted in threatening snarls. Suddenly a knife flew past Peri's ear so closely that she heard the whistle of it as it spun end over end through the air.

"Screw that," Peri snapped, "I am in no mood to lose any body parts today, so if it comes down to my ear or them, I will not hesitate to save my ear."

Adam laughed as he flung his arm out, his magic deflecting another soaring knife. "Vasile won't be happy."

"Vasile can go jump in a lake," her words were followed by a war cry as she dodged the first warlock to finally reach her. As Peri dodged kicks, flung away knives, and dished out magical bursts meant to harm but not kill, her mind briefly jumped to her earlier realization that Reyaz was behind this. She knew it like she knew the sun would rise in the East tomorrow. The red eyes should have been enough to clue her in. But though she knew it was dark magic, her initial thoughts had not been to blame Reyaz and that idea made her think there must have been more to his spell than just planting the thirst for war in the warlocks' hearts. So why did he do it? she asked herself as she kicked a female warlock in the face. He knew that the trolls couldn't kill his brother, and that was what he was ultimately after, wasn't it? At least it had been at one time. So what changed? What variable had been altered enough to change Reyaz's plans?

When it hit her it was like a punch to the gut, well that and the fact that she was indeed just punched in the gut by the female warlock who refused to stay down. "Lilly," she muttered, and then revised that statement, "the females." She flung her hand to the woman's chest and pushed, sending a jolt into her. The woman collapsed, but she was still breathing. She turned in a circle and saw that Dain and Nissa of the council had joined in the fight. And what a fight it was. Since they were trying not to kill the attackers, they were knocking the warlocks out with jolts of powers, effectively interrupting their nervous system. But warlocks were magical and still pretty powerful, so they weren't staying down long. Her eyes found Cypher and she stood still, briefly, in awe of his power, grace, and control. He stood back just a ways, watching the battle, waiting for a moment when he would need to step in. His face was blank, void of emotion, and it sent a chill down her spine to see a man who was usually so passionate look so complacent.

She didn't know how long they had been fighting when she heard the howls, but she did know it was about bloody time that the fur balls had shown up. She felt the air whip around her as a flash of black flew in front of her and a huge wolf landed on a male warlock battling with Adam. The huge wolf swiped his paw across the man's head and knocked him out cold.

The wolf turned his massive head back to Peri and bared large, sharp teeth. Amber eyes burned into her as a growl rumbled out of him.

"Decebel, get over yourself and go growl at the prey you can actually take on."

With one final snarl for good measure, he turned and jumped back into the fight.

"I swear, Great Luna, if you give me a wolf for a mate I will neuter him and shave him like a poodle," she muttered as she hurried back into the fight. She ran over to Adam who was battling four warlocks at once. She pressed her back to his. "I've got you covered," she yelled over the battle sounds.

"Did you know there were this many warlocks still living?" Adam shouted to her.

Peri grabbed the arm of the warlock who had just attempted to gut her with a sword. She bent his wrist and he dropped it with a yelp of pain. He fell to his knees and Peri once again sent her power into him to knock him out. "Yes and No," she answered.

"What does that mean?"

"It means that sometimes I don't know everything."

He laughed. "Can I get that in writing?"

"Would you shut up and focus on injuring these psychos so that you don't get yourself run through?" Peri turned, just as she heard a deep growl, and had to duck to keep from being knocked down by Vasile in his wolf form. She glanced over her shoulder to see why he had lunged over her only to see him in battle with Cypher.

Apparently, the King had decided that it was time he added his two cents to the fight.

Now that the wolves were present, the battle was more evenly matched, though the warlocks still continued to get up after being knocked out. Peri wasn't sure how long they could keep fighting at this intensity before some of them began to get hurt. Out of the corner of her eye she saw something drop from above the battle. She looked up quickly only taking her eyes off her opponent for a second and saw that Thalion had brought his elves and they were dropping from the trees. It was a sight that Jen would have appreciated and surely would have deemed it worthy of some weird military lingo.

"Welcome to the party, Prince," she told Thalion as he immediately began fighting.

"I see no one has died," he told her.

"No," she agreed, but under her breath she murmured, "not yet."

Chapter 14

"When I close my eyes I see your face, only your face. Fire rains around us, lightning strikes, and the blood of those we love threatens to be spilled at every turn and yet all I can see is you. You are the touch I crave, the scent I want to drown in, and the air that gives me life. There is nothing that can captivate me as you do. No matter the beauty, the violence, or the intrigue, you are the only thing that holds my every thought, my utter devotion, and because of that, you will also hold my life in the palm of your hands." ~Decebel

Sally felt his anger, but before she could feel anything else, Costin closed the bond between them. She stumbled and reached out for the wall at the sudden absence of his presence. She looked up around the bookstore to see if any of the other women had felt anything similar. She noticed Crina leaning against the counter with her head down. Jacque had stopped in mid-step and was squeezing her eyes closed. So she wasn't the only one.

"Sally," Jen's voice came from behind her, "you okay?"

Sally shook her head. "Costin closed the bond." She motioned to the other females.

Jen let out a low growl. "I would know things were going on if my freaking mate would keep our bond open even a little. Do you feel like they are in danger? Did you get any glimpse before he closed it?"

Sally shook her head. "No, it was quick and that's why it hurt so much."

"Let's get everyone home. From the looks of it, none of you are going to be in any shape to be doing inventory or helping annoying customers. Lilly?" Jen yelled.

Lilly's head popped out from around the corner of a book shelf. "Yes," she looked at Jen with brows raised expectantly.

Jen pointed at Sally and then at Jacque. "Something's going down with the males. We need to get the chicks back to your house."

Lilly's eyes filled with concern as she took in the group of women and noticed that all but Cynthia looked to be in pain. She nodded to Jen, "Okay, I can get the manager to take over."

Twenty minutes later everyone was once again gathered in Lilly's living room. Alina was pacing like a caged tiger. Though she continued to reach out to Vasile, she was unable to get through.

"He has never kept me out this long," she growled as she ran her fingers through her hair for what seemed like the hundredth time.

"I just don't understand how none of us can get through to them. That just doesn't seem likely," Sally pointed out.

"She's right," Jen agreed. "There is no way all of our men would just leave us hanging in the dark. One of them should have checked in by now, and not to mention our pesky little neighborhood fairy. Where is she?"

"Peri has been going back and checking in with Vasile," Alina explained. "Not just for the males' peace of mind, but ours as well."

"Okay, so she's gone to check on the men who have suddenly dropped off the planet and Peri hasn't returned. I'm going for *Houston we have a problem for $200 Alex*," Jen said dryly.

"Elle," Alina said suddenly. She turned and looked at the fae, her eyes wide with hope. "Can you go check on them?"

"Crap, that's right." Jacque smacked her forehead. "Elle, you can flash too."

Elle nodded but her face was set in a grim frown.

Jen rolled her eyes with a groan. "Okay just from the look on your face I'm betting that Perizada has done something to make sure your happy little fairy butt didn't go hopping off after her. Am I right?"

Elle nodded again. "Peri is much more powerful than I am. She informed me I was not to leave you all, and like pack magic, there is a magic that can bind my magic to her words. I'm as stuck as you all are."

Alina sat down in a huff with a string of Romanian flying from her lips. Each of them looked at each other helplessly, hoping that an idea or solution would simply pop into one of their minds. An hour later they still sat staring aimlessly off into the room. The tension was growing by the minute and by the time there was a knock at the door, they all nearly came out of their seats as the sound reverberated through the stillness.

Lilly started towards the door but Alina intercepted her and gave a small shake of her head, making it clear that she wanted to open the door. Alina stepped up to the door and tilted her head up to take in a deep breath of air. She frowned and sniffed again. There was nothing. No smell of any kind. She listened and heard two heartbeats but other than that, there was only the noise of the breeze through the trees. Just as she reached for the door it flew open and Alina stumbled back. A pair of arms held her steady as she righted herself. Elle let her go and then stepped up beside the Alpha and her eyes widened.

"What are you doing here?" Elle asked.

"Is that the kind of reception you give to your own kind?" Lorelle asked as she stepped into the house. She sidestepped Alina and Elle and her eyes widened at the room full of females. A wicked smile spread across her lips and her eyes flashed with humor. "This is simply too good to be true." Lorelle turned and looked at Alina. "Why on earth would you bring all of these females to one location without the protection of any males?"

"Uh, excuse me but we don't need protection." Jen stood up and walked towards the fae. Her eyes were narrowed in suspicion. "Who the crap are you and why did you just walk your fairy butt up in my friend's house?"

"Please tell me you're just fat, because I can't imagine why the wolves would let *you* procreate." Lorelle was looking at Jen like she was slime on her shoe that she was trying to figure out how to wipe off.

Jen let out a low threatening laugh as she stood up from her spot on the couch. "Oh honey, I'm more than a step up from your gene pool. Considering your sister issues, and probably mommy and daddy issues, any child of yours would be the poster child for the fae's new psychiatric facility. So throw me a freaking bone and keep your procreation remarks to yourself. Unless of course you would like a facelift, which I would be more than happy to assist you with." Jen gave her a toothy grin as she took a step towards her.

Lorelle raised her hand as if to strike at Jen but Elle and Alina stepped in front of her, blocking her view to the pregnant she-wolf.

"It might be wise not to poke the pregnant werewolf," Cynthia snapped at the fae.

"Lorelle what are you doing here?" Elle asked again wanting the answer as much as she was trying to get the fae's attention off of the wolves. She knew what Lorelle was capable of and if she was here and Peri was not, things could get dangerous very quickly.

"I'm here at the request of my employer, for lack of a better term, to get the merchandise he requires."

"Give me a freaking break," Jacque growled. "Are you telling me we're being kidnapped? Because seriously I've been kidnapped one too many times in my life and I'm really tired of it. Can't we do something else? How about a competition of some sort? That would at least be more interesting."

"Good call, Jac," Jen spoke up, "kidnapping is so old school."

"I have to agree," Sally said. "If your boss wants to be original as a villain in today's market, he really needs to be more inventive than the run-of-the-mill kidnapping."

Lorelle's eyes widened. "Are they for real?" she asked Elle.

"They're just getting started," Elle smirked. "Just wait, it gets worse."

"Are you working for Reyaz?" Alina gently pushed Elle out of the way and met the fae's eyes. The set of her jaw made it clear she expected an answer.

"We have an arrangement. And as it pains me to hear that you think my methods lack originality, there is something to be said for the rate of success. So I'm afraid that I have to say, yes, this is me kidnapping you."

"How exactly are you planning to take all of us?" Cynthia asked.

"Good question, Doc." Jen nodded and gave her a thumbs-up. "But a better question would be: in what world could you possibly take on this many wolves and a fae?"

Lorelle smiled and it was a smile that said she knew something they did not, and it was an important something.

"I spoke too soon didn't I?" Jen asked. "I hate it when I do that."

"Totally takes the bad assness out of it," Jacque told her.

"I'm pregnant, Jacque. I'm pretty much out of bad assness at this point."

Lorelle reached into a pocket in the cloak she wore and pulled out a dark stone. She held it in the palm of her hand and it began to glow red.

"Why do I feel like that rock is more than just her pet rock, Earl?" Jacque muttered as all their eyes locked onto the stone in the fae's hand.

Elle's eyes widened at the sight of it. She turned and held her hands out to the room and shouted something but Lorelle was faster. She pushed Elle back causing her to stumble and whatever protection she was attempting to cast over the females crumbled. Alina lunged for Lorelle but slammed into an invisible barrier, one much like the kind she had seen Peri conjure.

The room around them began to shimmer and shift and then suddenly it was gone and there was only darkness.

Jen attempted to reach out to Decebel as the darkness swallowed her and the others.

"DECEBEL!" she screamed at him tugging on the bond that was so fragile and barely there. She needed him, needed his strength and assurance that he would find her. She waited, hoping against hope that he would feel her even though he had shut down their bond. Maybe if she pushed enough, he would feel her. Maybe if she sought him out with everything inside of her, then even he wouldn't be able to keep her out.

"Please B, hear me!"

"Jennifer?" The sound of his voice in her mind, after so long without it, made her gasp and caused the ache in her chest to intensify. *"What's wrong Jennifer? What's going on?"*

He was angry and his anger spurred hers, pushing away the hurt and sorrow over their breaking bond.

"You would know what was wrong if you hadn't severed our bond. You would have known that Lorelle showed up at Lilly's house and calmly informed us that she was kidnapping us. You would have known that we have been

worried sick about all of you because we haven't heard a damn thing from you. That's what's going on Decebel. Welcome to the party."

"*You've been kidnapped?*" he snarled and she felt a shiver run through her. Here she was being taken by a psycho, and she was getting turned on by her mate's temper. Well she never claimed to be normal, why start now?

"*She certainly isn't inviting us over for a slumber party. So yes B, we've been kidnapped.*"

"*Can you tell me where they're taking you?*"

"*Not so much. She's doing that fae thing where they flash themselves.*"

"*As soon as you can see your surroundings, I need you to tell me as much as you can about where you are.*" He paused and she could barely feel the worry coming off of him in waves. "*Are you alright?*"

Jen bit her lip. She would not cry. She would not show any weakness, not to him, not anymore. "*I'm as good as a pregnant werewolf with a mate bond that's nearly gone and is being kidnapped can be. As soon as I have some helpful information for you I'll let you know.*" She snapped the barrier down between their minds quickly, hoping that he didn't sense how much control it was taking her for her to not break down and cry. She hated crying, and yet lately that seemed to be her answer for everything. She wondered briefly if there was such a thing as a tear ductectomy. Probably not, but it was a thought, a crappy one—yes, but a thought nonetheless.

"*Sally?*" Sally heard Costin's worried voice and latched onto it desperately. The rich deep tone enveloped her like a warm blanket and she wished more than anything that it was his arms that were enveloping her.

"*Sort of have a little problem,*" she told him carefully.

"*Are you fighting warlocks too?*"

"*WHAT?*" Sally nearly hollered out loud, but caught herself before it left her throat. "*Why are you fighting warlocks? Is that why you shut me out?*"

"*The why isn't real important at this point and I didn't shut you out, I thought you shut me out.*" He sounded out of breath and for him to sound that way through the bond told her that he was fighting hard. Worry for him threatened to overwhelm her. She took a slow deep breath and kept her eyes closed. The darkness around her was oppressive and beginning to disorient her from knowing which direction was up and which was down. She focused on feeling him through their bond, feeling his warmth and love.

"Sally, can you please tell me what the problem is that you mentioned?"

"We're sort of going on a trip," she cringed when she felt the swell of alarm in him.

"What sort of trip?"

"The sort that wasn't planned and we weren't exactly willing to go on."

"You're being kidnapped?"

"Afraid so." Sally felt deflated but not scared, at least not yet. *"Please don't worry about us, okay? You focus on fighting the warlocks or whatever it is you're doing so you don't get hurt. We can get ourselves out of this mess."*

"Don't worry? Sally mine, have you been drinking because the only way that you could possibly think that a male would not worry about his kidnapped mate would be if you were so inebriated that you couldn't walk straight."

She huffed and tried not to stomp her foot like a toddler. *"There is no sense in worrying just yet. Please, just try and stay calm okay? I'm sure once Decebel finds out what's going on he will freak out enough for all of you."*

"Are you hurt? Don't lie to me," he growled.

"No, well, not because of being kidnapped. Being separated from you has been painful, but other than that I'm fine."

"We will find you, Sally."

"I know you will," her words came out as a whisper and though she wanted to sound strong and confident for him, she was tired, and she didn't feel all that strong.

"You're very strong love, I have faith in you."

"I love you, Costin. Please be careful."

"I love you more." She felt his lips on hers briefly and then she closed the bond so that he could focus on fighting the warlocks. Her chest tightened at the thought and she kicked herself for not pressing him harder about what was going on, not that he would have told her.

Jacque felt the bond between she and Fane open suddenly and relief flooded her like a dam being opened.

"Fane!" she said his name desperately as if the mere sound of it would save her.

"I'm here, Luna," his voice came through deep and strong into her mind and she wanted to climb into his lap and press her nose to his neck so she could breathe in his familiar scent.

"Reyaz is working with Lorelle and she came to my mom's house."

"Are you alright?" She could feel his fear for her and his desperate need for her to be safe.

"I'm fine. She's flashing us somewhere. Are you alright?" She felt his reluctance to answer. *"Spit it out wolf-man."*

"Cypher has attacked, or attempted to attack, the trolls. So we are sort of fighting the warlocks."

"Sort of fighting? What the crap does that mean sort of fighting? How do you sort of fight, Fane? What are you slapping at each other like girls?" Jacque felt as if she couldn't breathe as the implications of Fane's words hit her. Cypher was attacking the trolls. Why would he do that? Was he alright? Crap, what was she going to tell her mom?

"It's sort of a long story."

"Well gee, I'm being kidnapped so I sort of have all the freaking time in the world," she snapped, not really meaning to be harsh but the worry for him was making her impatient to know how bad things really were.

"I'll explain it to you, Jacquelyn, but not right this minute. I'm literally in battle as we speak," he told her and she realized that she could feel how tired he was.

"Bloody hell man, then stop talking to me and focus," she nearly yelled at him. *"I love you."*

"As soon as you know something about your whereabouts, Jacquelyn, I had better know it as well," he warned her.

"Well snap, I was planning on keeping it all to myself because I love being kidnapped by a crazy, psycho fae and an equally off-balance warlock."

"Jacquelyn," Fane warned.

She started to answer him but suddenly he was gone.

"Fane." She reached for him like she had a hundred times, but there was nothing.

"I've delivered what you asked," Lorelle said as she walked into the cave where Reyaz had built his home. Though he lived in a cave, it looked like anything but. He had afforded himself every creature comfort; he even had a fire place. It was protected by powerful magic, dark magic that caused a chill to crawl up her spine and a whisper in her ear that told her to run as fast and as far as she could.

"They are in the dark forest of my realm, just as you instructed. The magic there is too strong for their bonds to work between mates so they will not be able to contact them."

"What about the fae girl?" Reyaz asked.

"Elle cannot flash; I made sure of it. Although I think my sister might have already bound her powers."

Reyaz stood from the chair he had occupied. He walked slowly around the room as he held his hands steepled together. His mind wandered to the mates of the females Lorelle had captured for him. He nearly laughed at the thought of their reactions once they realized their females had been taken while they fought the warlocks. But he relished even more the thought of his brother's pain when he realized that his mate had been taken because he had sent her away, unprotected. He would have to live with the knowledge that his woman had been taken because of his foolishness.

"That will be all," he told Lorelle absentmindedly.

"Our deal changed when I agreed to this, warlock. I expect you to uphold your end."

He looked up at her and his lip curled. "You will get what is coming to you. But you will be patient because things that get rushed get ruined."

"As long as you follow through."

Reyaz watched as the fae flashed, leaving an empty spot where she had been standing. He stared at the vacant space for several minutes as he considered what his next move should be. So much of his plan had been changed and now he found himself in the possession of not just one mate, but seven, plus an unmated female. One of those mated females just happened to be the mate of the most powerful Alpha in history. For a moment he thought that it was either the stupidest thing he had ever done or the bravest. He figured the answer to that would come if he found himself at the other end of the Alpha's jaws.

Chapter 15

"Once in a lifetime, someone will grab onto your heart, dig in deep, and grasp with all their might. They will have the power to strengthen it, to crush it, or to keep it beating when it threatens to stop. Once in a lifetime, love will seep into you, filling every empty place, warming every cold spot, and illuminating all the dark spaces that threaten to engulf you. Once in a lifetime, one person will have the ability to bring you back from the edge of insanity just by reminding you that they chose you; that they love you." ~Cypher

"Something has got to give," Peri shouted to Alston.

The battle against the warlocks had been going on for nearly two days. Vasile and Peri had organized a rotation between the fae, elves, and wolves, to fight in waves so that everyone would get a chance at rest. The problem was for every ten warlocks they knocked out, five were waking up. They continued to fight without killing as Vasile had instructed, but frustration levels were running high and exhaustion was beginning to take over.

"CYPHER!" Peri yelled across the trampled battle field. Trees had been knocked over and plants crushed and destroyed as feet and bodies pounded into the ground. She called on her power and drew into her the magic of all the supernatural creatures around her. "How much longer will you fight a battle you cannot win?"

Cypher paused from his fight with Decebel and looked over at her. His eyes burned red with madness and rage. His body was tight with the need to destroy. He stared at the fae who was bathed in light. He felt her goodness pulsating off of her and he wondered why she was fighting him. He hadn't come here to fight the fae, or the wolves, or the elves for that matter. He had come to kill the trolls.

"Until my enemy comes out from hiding," he answered calmly. His head whipped back around to Vasile and he pulled the sword back, ready to slash out at the Alpha.

Peri's hand swung out just as Alston and Adam's did and they all pushed power into the Warlock King, staying his sword from completing the arc.

"You have no enemy here Cypher, King of the Warlocks. You have been at peace with the trolls for centuries. You have no cause to declare war on them." The battle around Peri came to a halt as they all began to realize that Cypher was no longer fighting and that there was a powerful, glowing fae in their midst.

"I have every cause! They took the life of one of my own; they murdered her." The words were right, but there was no passion, no conviction behind them in his voice.

"That crime has been dealt with and the debt paid for by the lives of those who committed the crime. You would not condemn a whole race as evil just for the actions of a few. You agreed to this with the troll King. Why would you change your mind now, especially when you have found your mate? Why go to war now with your mate in danger from your brother?" Peri was trying to get him to think about his actions, to push past this intense desire to destroy, and to contemplate why it is he wants to destroy.

Cypher's eyes flashed briefly to their usual yellow color as he spoke. "Mate," the word tasted foreign on his tongue, and yet he knew it to be true in his heart. He had a mate.

"Yes," Peri told him. "Lilly, your mate."

Lilly, he thought, *that's her name. That's my mate's name.* He shook his head as he squeezed his eyes closed. He felt a haze trying to wrap around his mind and push the thoughts of her from him but he latched onto them like a rabid dog latches on to its prey. He had a mate, but now he was going after the trolls. That wasn't right, was it? Did he want to go to war with the trolls? He knew the answer was no, but something inside of him was driving him to attack, to kill.

"Fight it, Cypher," Vasile said as he phased back to his human form. "Fight the spell your brother has put on you."

Peri, Alston, and Adam all lowered their hands as they watched Cypher lower his sword.

One by one, the wolves all phased back and watched as the king's eyes flashed from red to yellow over and over as he struggled to regain control of his own mind.

"You have to fight it, Cypher. Your brother has our mates," Decebel snarled as he stood up from where he had just been standing in his wolf form. His eyes still glowed bright and his canines were still too long to belong in a human mouth, evidence of how close his wolf still was to the surface.

"What?" Cypher snapped, and this time his eyes stayed yellow a little longer and when they flashed back to red, it was much duller.

"Sally told me as well," Costin spoke up.

Vasile nodded as his lips tightened into a straight line. "Alina said the same thing. Lorelle came."

"Lorelle?" Peri's voice carried from her where she stood, still in her fae glory. The light around her brightened and her eyes began to pulse with power. "My sister has taken the girls?" The warlocks that had been standing close to her slowly began to back away, as well as a few of the elves. Peri's eyes snapped over to Cypher. "Okay you have to pull your crap together because your bastard of a brother has my girls and that is not cool. So you can either get a clue and fight the rest of that spell off or I will zap your ass with so much power that you'll walk around asking everyone if they're your mamma."

"I'm with Peri on this," Adam said from behind Cypher. "We don't have time to be goofing off with a bunch of cursed warlocks, not if my mate is in the hands of a deranged psycho."

Sorin stepped from around Vasile and met Peri's eyes. "Why didn't Elle come and tell us? Why didn't she flash?"

Peri felt a small pang of guilt in her gut as she thought about Elle. "I bound her power so that she couldn't flash."

Sorin let out a low growl. "You kept her from me."

Peri took a step towards him, headless of his nude form. "I did not keep her from you. You kept her from you when you stuck her on a plane bound for the Americas. I kept her from getting her butt into trouble. I wanted to know that the females were staying all together when I wasn't around and I didn't want any of those girls talking Elle into doing something stupid, as we all know they are prone to do. I wasn't trying to put her in danger. I was trying to keep her safe. You remember this, Sorin. She was mine before she was yours and I will always consider her mine."

Sorin's glowing eyes held Peri's, neither of them willing to back down.

"ENOUGH!" Vasile barked. "Sorin, your mate is going to be fine, just like all of our mates. Peri, don't challenge my wolves when we are in a crisis. Cypher, have you gotten yourself together?"

Cypher had been listening to the exchange and fighting the curse as he reminded himself over and over of Lilly—her smile, her laughter, her southern accent, and her sharp wit—his mate. He felt the effects of the curse flow off of him like water on a slick roof and suddenly he could think clearly again.

"I'm good," he told the Alpha.

Vasile nodded. "What about your people?" He motioned to the other warlocks.

Cypher drew on the magic that flowed in his blood, his birthright, and pushed it out into the spirit of his people. He helped them fight off the black magic and regain their own power over their minds. Slowly the warlocks began to look around as if being woken from a deep sleep. Their eyes were wide and mouths drooping open at seeing where they were and the state of the forest around them.

Fane stepped up to his father and placed a hand on his shoulder. "I can't feel Jacquelyn," he told him.

"I know. I can't feel your mother either. Somehow the mate bonds have been closed off." Vasile glanced around to meet the eyes of each of his wolves and then Decebel's. "We need to get back to the mansion." He turned to Peri and looked at her as if to say, *your call.*

"I believe a reunion is in order with my dear bat-mess crazy sister," she told him with a sickly sweet tone that dripped with disgust at the mention of her sister.

"Tell her, 'hi', for me," Adam said, "and by '*tell her hi*', I mean slap the crap out of her."

"Consider it done," Peri told him and then flashed.

"Vasile," Cypher's voice broke through the murmuring of the warlocks, "I will meet you at your mansion, if that is alright?"

"He has your mate too, Cypher," Vasile said in answer.

In a matter of minutes the wolves had all phased back and were once again on the run headed back to the Romanian mansion. Cypher ran with them after having told Gerick to take the rest of their people home and have the healers tend to them. The fae agreed to help and told Vasile that they would be there as soon as they had heard from Peri. Thalion had also agreed to help in rescuing the females and offered any aide his people could give.

Vasile ran side by side with his wolves with a desperation driving him that he hadn't felt in a very long time. His mate, along with others that he cared deeply for, had been taken, right from under his nose. And now that the battle with the warlocks had been averted, he felt the full weight of the news falling on him. His mate, his Mina, was beyond his reach, not only physically, but mentally as well, and it was driving his wolf mad.

Decebel pushed himself as hard as he could. His wolf reveled in the burn of his muscles as he ran, the flexing of tendons, and the tightening of ligaments as his paws hit the ground in jarring force. He ran as though the hounds of hell were on his heels. And if he could have ran even faster, he would have. It was his fault. It was his fault she had been taken. If he had just kept her here, by his side, where she belonged, no matter the pain of the bond being broken, she would be safe. But now she was in the hands of a mad man, beyond his aide if she needed him and pregnant with their child. How had he let this happen? He felt his heartbeat pounding in his chest and his lungs burned with exhaustion as he drug air into them. The pain of the separation and the breaking of their bond was a constant reminder of what he had done, a constant thorn in his side of the decision he had made without talking to his mate. Was this his punishment? Was he to be chastised for wanting to protect his daughter and mate? The questions and fears continued to fester like an infected wound inside of him. It refused to heal and with each step his anger grew. He was tired of their women being in danger. He was tired of trying to hold himself together when all he wanted was to crawl into the arms of his female and weep for their loss, whether it was him or their child. He was so very tired and yet he didn't have the luxury of giving into the exhaustion that racked his body.

Fane glanced over at Decebel as they ran and noticed the huge dark wolf was running at a full sprint. They had a very long ways to run, but he understood the Alpha's need to push himself. Jacque had sounded fine when he had been talking to her and she had told him that they had been taken. She was nervous, but she sounded more angry than scared. It was for those reasons that he had not completely lost his cool, but now that the adrenaline from the battle was dropping, a new surge of adrenaline was beginning to pump into his veins and it was fueled by fear and rage. How many times would evil attempt to take their mates from them? How many times would they endure seeing the women they loved hurt? He would like to say that he wasn't at his breaking point, not yet. But he didn't know if he could tell that to himself and still be honest. He had been at his breaking point only days ago and when he had finally given in to the need to sate the wolf and man's rage, he had begun to heal. Now here he stood again, worried for his mate's safety and wellbeing and unable to do a damn thing about it. So, like Decebel, he ran as hard and as fast as he could. He ran as though she stood just out of his reach and if he could just push himself a little harder he would have her in his arms again, safe, where she belonged.

Costin reached for Sally again, and again, and again, as he ran. She had been there in his mind and then even when she had closed the bond he could feel her, like white noise in the background. She was always there, until now. There was nothing. He felt empty, devoid of anything good, as if he had no mate at all. The thought was like a knife to his heart, twisting in the organ, preventing it from beating. The pain radiated out to his limbs and he stumbled briefly before he once again felt his legs regain their rhythm as he ran with his pack. He could never go back to a life without Sally. She was his light, his warmth, his healer, and she had restored all the places inside of him that he hadn't even realized had been broken. He tried again in vain to feel her and again he felt his heart wrench. His wolf was on the verge of taking over at the thought of losing their mate and he had to fight to keep control. He couldn't find her if he lost control. He wouldn't be able to help her and so he latched onto that knowledge and ran as hard as he could. They would get their females back, and they would destroy the one who took them, just as they had destroyed the evil that came before him.

"Come out, come out, wherever you are," Peri sung into the forest close to the veil of the fae realm. She could sense her sister and could feel the anger that radiated off of her and the madness that had begun to ooze into her mind snaking around her thoughts and emotions. She had given evil a foothold and now it wanted the whole freaking mountain. "Come now, Lorelle, since when have you ever been a coward? Face me like the powerful fae you are."

"Not as powerful as you," her voice carried from beyond the trees and Peri waited to see if she would emerge.

"Those are your words, not mine," Peri pointed out.

"Truth, nonetheless." Lorelle stepped from the shelter of the trees and eyed her sister warily.

"What games have you been playing, Lorelle? It seems you have taken up with some new playmates lately and I have to say that I do not approve. They seem to be poster children for 'how to turn into a twisted, evil nit-wit overnight'."

Lorelle laughed and Peri noticed that even her laughter had changed. It was no longer a happy sound, but more of the sound that came just before a crazy witch stabbed you with her fork.

"Perizada, always clever with words, always talking but never saying anything," Lorelle cooed. "I have grown tired of living in your shadow. I want my own power, in my own right, not because we share the same blood."

Peri's brow creased as she stared at the woman who she had grown up with and now hardly recognized. "Do you realize how ridiculous you sound? We all possess the power we have because of where we come from, whether it is great power or a little. You cannot bleed yourself dry to rid yourself of our bloodline and then fill yourself back up again. Whether I live or die, Lorelle, you will always have the same power in you that flows in me."

"NO!" she shrieked. "I will only have the power you allow me to have. You have taken any power that I could have had and kept it as your own. You have always made sure that I was one step behind you and I'm tired of looking at your backside."

Peri was beginning to realize that there would be no reasoning with her sister. She had deluded herself into thinking that Peri had stolen her power or kept her power from her. What Lorelle didn't realize was that she was very powerful, but her power had yet to reach its full potential because of Lorelle's spirit. She desired that power simply for the sake of having it, not for the good that she could use it for. She no longer remembered the things they learned when they joined the council. The rules and laws that came with great power can be given and can be taken away. But no amount of words would bring the truth to light for her sister. She had allowed too much wickedness into her.

"Where are the females, Lorelle?" She decided to go with a direct approach, though Peri had a feeling that it would take a little bit of taunting to get the truth from her proud sister.

"Females? Whatever are you talking about sister?"

Peri rolled her eyes and leaned casually against a tree as if she had all the time in the world, which in fact she definitely did not.

"Okay, I'll jog your memory—six or so she-wolves, one of which is knocked up, a fae, and a human all hanging out in the great state of Texas. Ring any bells yet?"

Lorelle simply stared at her.

"Okay, how about the mates of said females that would pretty much rip your head off of your body, fight over who got the bones, and then spit you out just for thinking about taking their mates? Remembering anything now?"

"Peri, do you really think I would waste my time with some worthless females that belong to the worthless wolves?" Lorelle picked at her nails as if they were more interesting than the conversation at hand.

"I think that you seem to like to waste your time with the likes of Reyaz and if I'm guessing correct, I'd bet you've become his lackey. I thought you wanted power? And yet you would choose to work for him as a beck and call girl, running his errands, collecting his prey instead of sitting on the high council of the fae? Have I summed it up pretty good for you? Maybe you should change your name to Renfield." Peri saw Lorelle's jaw tighten and her hands clenched into fists at her sides. She was fighting it as hard as she could, but she was losing. The need to put Peri in her place was so very strong and so very tempting.

"I've accepted that for now, Reyaz will be more powerful and therefore is calling the shots. But it will not always be so, and though I'm not known for my patience, for this I can wait. I'll see you soon, sister, though I don't know if you will be *seeing* me."

"Dammit all!" Peri yelled as her sister disappeared. She thought she had her and had pushed her far enough that she would tell her where the women were, just to prove to Peri that she had been powerful enough to capture them all by herself. She had underestimated her sister's desire to see Peri in a grave, because no doubt Reyaz had promised just that, if Lorelle cooperated with him.

"I really want to say that things couldn't get worse, but then I'm sure something worse would happen, like me growing a horn out of my butt or all of the males running off getting themselves turned to stone or something. Then I'd have to run off to save them looking like a freaking fairy hornet," Peri laughed under her breath at her description and knew that Jen would appreciate it. Now if only she could get them back so she could tell Jen about her ludicrous thoughts.

"Now all I have to do is face a room full of raging wolves, piece of freaking cake," she muttered as she flashed to the Romanian mansion.

Chapter 16

"At some point in the mess of the supernatural world you really think that you have learned all that there is to know. I'm here to tell you, that's the dumbest thing you could ever possibly think when it pertains to this world. You should be prepared for anything, poised to take in even the most outlandish information, and smile even if you're thinking *this is some crazy, messed up shizzel*. So that said, get ready people because the boat is about to be rocked and if you don't hold on, your butt is going over and I'm not coming in after you." ~Jen

"Bloody hell, thank you for turning the lights on," Jacque said when suddenly she could see everyone and everything around her—though seeing her surroundings didn't really give her much relief.

"Um, does anyone else feel like we've just been dropped into the fire swamp from The Princess Bride?" Sally asked as she looked around at the dark, mangled forest around them. The air smelt of sulfurous fumes that burned her lungs and she fought the urge to gag.

"Probably should be on the lookout for ROUS's," Jen added.

"I'm just going to pretend I know what you're talking about," Crina said as she stood up and brushed off her backside. "But if whatever you're talking about is creepy, then I agree."

"So seriously, where did that crazy fae leave us?" Jacque asked.

Alina walked around the clearing where they found themselves. As soon as she reached out her hand to touch one of the gnarled trees, she felt a jolt of electricity run through her body knocking her back several feet.

"Guess that answers the question of whether or not we can wander in this desolate place," Jen muttered.

Alina looked over to Elle as she attempted to shake off the effects of the jolt. She saw exactly what she expected—utter shock and fear in the fae's eyes. "Elle," Alina spoke her name softly, "please share with us what you know."

Elle continued to stare off into the black woods that seemed to be filled with dancing shadows and eerie eyes that watched their every move. She shook her head as her mouth dropped open and a very un-Elle like squeak emerged. She snapped her mouth closed and took several deep breaths as she attempted to gather herself. Finally she met the gaze of the Alpha. "I'm sorry but I'm trying to figure out how it is possible that we are here. How it is possible that Lorelle was able to bring us here?"

"And where is here?" Cynthia asked.

Elle's eyes never left Alina's as she answered, "The dark forest in the realm of the fae."

Alina stumbled back and nearly touched one of the trees again, but caught herself and pulled back. Her eyes grew wider and she shook her head, attempting to deny the words that penetrated her ears. "That can't be," she whispered. "It's not possible."

"I know," Elle agreed, "but our presence here suggests otherwise."

"I hate to break into this obviously shocking moment, but could you please share with us what you know so that we can properly freak out?" Jen asked matter-of-fact like.

"It's not something that is talked about, ever," Elle told her.

"Well circumstances have changed, so I think it's time to start talking about the fae's dirty little secret."

"I think we better all sit down for this," Alina told the group.

"Crap," Jacque murmured, "it's never a good sign when they tell us we need to sit down."

"Have to agree with you there wolf-princess. It usually means they're about to drop a new supernatural creature in our laps, and I swear if it's a sparkling vampire then I'm going to push someone off the ledge of ridiculousness we are all perched on like morons," Jen huffed as she sat on the ground, attempting at gracefulness, but failing miserably because of her swollen belly.

"Is it a giant centipede that releases slimy secretions as it crushes everything around it?" Sally asked.

The group collectively turned and looked at the healer with furrowed foreheads and raised eyebrows.

"What?" she mumbled. "It could happen."

"Okay, I take it back. Sparkling vampires are a step up from Sally's random slime infested centipede. Where did you come up with that, gypsy? I mean is that your *one* great fear like people who are terrified of spiders? What would fear of giant centipedes be called anyways? Pede-acrophobia?" All the eyes had now swung around to Jen who didn't seem to notice the incredulous looks.

"If you girls are quite done, I can enlighten you as to why Elle and I are so shocked at our appearance here," Alina waited.

"Ignore me," Jen told her. "It's the hormones. Being pregnant has somehow caused me to ramble about completely unimportant things and expect others to care. I'll be crying in a minute."

Lilly patted Jen's leg sympathetically before turning back to Alina.

"A very long time ago, before even I was born, and before the great purge of the witches, there was an evil that was unleashed in the realm of the fae," Alina paused and looked at Elle. "Maybe you should tell it since you lived through it."

Elle nodded, but didn't look pleased with the idea. She pulled her knees up to her chest and glanced down at the ground. Her face glazed over as she allowed herself to be pulled back into the past, a past better left forgotten. "The fae have always been the most powerful of the supernatural beings. I have often questioned the Fates' wisdom of giving one race such supremacy. Power can be very heady. It beguiles the wielder and seduces with the promise of greatness, all the while hiding the truth behind the shiny exterior. Sacrifice is the most important part of being the strongest. Those who refuse to make sacrifices, but instead use the power for selfish gain, begin to rot on the inside. With every act of self-indulgence or with every choice of turning a blind eye to those in need, a piece of that person dies. They become blind to their own egocentricities and so drunk on the authority that all they desire is more, and they will do anything to acquire it. We have seen that first hand with Desdemona, but she was not the first."

"One of our own, the most powerful of our people, abused his power, and he sacrificed many using their blood and spirits to fuel his need for more. There was so much malice in him and so much desire to conquer and rule that his very presence began to kill our land. Not only was his evil killing everything around him, but he also was creating offspring from human children, and they were given the title of witch or wizard."

"Shut! Up!" Jacque's words were echoed by others. "The fae were the creators of the witches?"

Elle frowned. "No, only one fae was responsible—Volcan. I will only say his name once because names are powerful. He is the one who created the witches and wizards. He used his own blood to fill them with his magic, and then he released them back into the human world. Blinded by his need to defeat and control, it never dawned on him that his creation might turn from him and seek out their own desires. Once we realized what he was creating and letting loose, we knew he had to be stopped. He couldn't be allowed to destroy the human world. So we destroyed him. It was a long and bloody fight with many lives lost. But in the end we killed him."

"If he's dead, why is this forest still on lockdown…and so creepy?" Sally asked.

"Sometimes the infiltration of evil is so profound, so abundant, that it cannot be uncontaminated. There was nothing we could do to purge the evil inside so we had to contain it. That way it could not seek out those who might be easily swayed by its lure."

The group was quiet as they digested the information, once more blindsided by the happenings in the supernatural world. It was Jacque who finally broke the silence.

"Why is it a big deal that we not know about this? I mean I can understand that you might be worried another fae would seek out the power, but what do the wolves have to do with it?" Jacque could tell she had asked the one question they had been hoping no one would.

Alina glanced at Elle before she spoke, "I think that is enough speaking about such dark things, for now, especially since we are sitting in the home of those dark things."

Jacque decided to let it be for now, but only because of the haunted look that peered out at her from behind Alina's stoic demeanor.

"So what's the plan?" Lilly asked.

"Stay alive," Crina muttered.

"That's always a good one to start with," Jen agreed.

"Okay, let's think a little broader than stay alive," Lilly amended.

"Are any of you able to use your bonds?" Alina asked as she glanced at each of the mated females.

"I lost contact with Costin at some point when we were surrounded in darkness," Sally answered.

"I got nothing, but then that's not news," Jen said.

"Nothing here," Jacque added.

Crina shook her head at Alina and Elle shrugged.

"This feels different than just the bond being closed," Sally stood and began to pace as she talked. "It's like the bond is nonexistent, like it never was."

Alina nodded. "I agree. We've all been experiencing the usual pain of being separated from the males, but it is important that you pay attention to the intensity of the pain. If it begins to get worse, then that might mean that it is more than just the bonds being closed."

"What do you mean *more*?" Lilly asked as she looked at Jacque nervously.

"It could mean that the bonds are being severed."

"I've decided that I don't want this news. Let's rewind and go back to sparkling vampires," Jen said sarcastically but her words lacked their usual humor.

"For now, we just wait," Alina told them.

"Waiting sucks," Jacque complained.

"Not just waiting, Jac, but waiting in a creepy forest where a sadistic, power hungry fae used to turn children into his little minions." Jen smiled sweetly at her friend when Jacque growled at her.

"You're not helping."

"I'm pregnant. I'm not supposed to be helpful."

"How long are you going to play that pregnant card?" Sally asked her.

"Uh, probably until I am no longer pregnant," Jen answered with a smirk plastered on her face.

"You being pregnant sucks," Crina jumped in and it brought a soft hum of laughter from the exhausted, weary group.

"Where could she have taken them?" Decebel asked for the tenth time. "It must be someplace that suppresses the mate bond."

"What about the In-between?" Costin asked.

Rumbles of growls rippled through the room at the idea of the females in that horrid place.

"Good guess, but no cookie," Peri said as she flashed into the library where everyone was gathered. "I've already checked; they aren't there."

"How did you check?" Fane asked.

"I have my connections," Peri told him but offered no other explanation.

"Perhaps another realm?" Sorin said.

"I don't know of any realms that would keep the bonds between mates from staying open," Vasile answered. "And if there were, they would have to be saturated in dark magic."

"Maybe they are here in the human realm but Lorelle or Reyaz have closed the bond somehow," Adam offered. "It is well within a fae's power to block the bond, for at least a little while if they know what they're doing."

"It would take a lot of power to do that with this many wolves," Peri told him, "and to sustain it would take even more."

"So what do we do?" Fane snarled in frustration. "We have nothing to go on—no leads or ideas, and we have no idea if our females are alright."

"I know you are frustrated, Fane. We all are," Vasile's voice was calm but his glowing eyes showed the truth of his emotions. He was every bit as concerned and angered as the rest of them, but he had to keep a level head for his mate and for the males who were desperate to find their own mates. "Wadim, I want you to do what you do best. Find information on all the realms, even ones that might have been forgotten. Peri, join him if you don't mind." Vasile turned and looked at Costin, Fane, and Adam. "You three head North, go on foot, and move quickly. Night is taking over and there are lots of things that come out to play at night, things that might have heard rumblings of Lorelle and Reyaz. Gather whatever information you can, and then come back here. Gavril, Sorin, Skender, and Drake, you will head South.

Cypher, I imagine if he shows himself it will be to you. So myself, Decebel, Thalion, and Alston will join you. We will head toward your mountain to see if his presence is still discernible. And if Cyn, Dain, and Nissa could stay here and add a little more protection, I would be grateful."

Alston bowed his head to Vasile as a show of respect. "We are here to help, and they will guard it well."

With a renewed sense of purpose, the males made their way out of the mansion and into the coming night.

Reyaz watched from the cover of trees as the males filed out of the mansion. The tension in their shoulders and purpose in their strides told him all he needed to know. They were searching for him. A smile spread across his face as he thought about the wild goose chase he had planned for them. Part of him wanted to tell them not to bother; they wouldn't find him. And they needn't worry about not knowing where their females were; he planned to tell them. They would never be able to rescue them, and he felt it a much more fitting form of torture that they know exactly where their mates were being held captive, yet unable to do a thing about it. He hadn't originally planned on bothering with the wolves, but they were meddlesome, and he figured it was better to deal with them now. That way, in the future when he was ready to remove the species that had his mate's blood on their hands, the wolves would not be there to stand in his way. Now all he needed to do was decide what to do with the females: what order to kill them in, where to kill them, and what method. There were lots of options and tons of possibilities.

As soon as the males had disappeared into the forest, he made his way to the front door of the mansion. He took out a folded piece of paper and slipped it in between the double doors. He mumbled a few words then smiled at the knowledge that they would only find the paper when it was time, when the game was in motion. And then he was gone as if he had never been there.

Peri paced the room restlessly as Wadim rustled through papers and books. The musty smell permeated the air and only served to remind her of the daunting task before them.

"You could stop pacing any time now," Wadim said without looking away from the book on his lap.

Peri's head snapped around to look at the historian. For lack of anything witty to say she snapped, "Why do you wear those stupid shirts?"

Wadim looked up, attempting to look offended but missing it by a mile. "Hey, don't hate on the shirts just because you feel like the girls being taken is your fault."

Peri ignored him and read the shirt out loud. "'When in doubt, pee on it.' What does that even mean and I swear if you hike your leg anywhere is this room, I'll nail your paws to the floor."

"Has anyone told you that you need help? Like serious therapy, years of it with lots of medication thrown in," he chuckled at his own words as he went back to searching through the book.

"What are you looking for?" Peri asked as she resumed her pacing.

"Anything," he paused as he flipped the page, "something, heck I don't know. But there has to be something that might point us in the right direction. There has to be some place that would cause the bonds to break, and that someplace would be saturated in power, dark power. Think, Peri," he implored her. "*You* out of all of us know this world and the other realms better than anyone. Where could he stash them that would guarantee that they wouldn't be able to reach out to their mates?"

Peri rubbed her forehead in frustration as she sifted through her many lifetimes, searching for what Wadim described. The closer she came to figuring it out, the faster her mind seemed to push away whatever it was that might be a possibility.

"I got nothing, dammit!" She slammed her hand down on a stack of papers and a cloud of dust rose into the air.

"Okay, well, pull up a chair and start turning pages. Pacing a hole in the ground isn't going to help us find them." His voice wasn't unkind as he motioned towards a chair across the room. "Start with those books," he pointed to the shelves behind her, "and I honestly don't know what to tell you to look for. I guess just any instance in history when a place might have been used to house evil."

Peri pulled out a stack of books and began flipping through, her eyes moving quickly over the page pulling out words and then discarding them just as quickly. "This is going to take forever," she huffed.

"Well for once in our long lives, forever isn't a luxury we have."

Time ticked by and it seemed the hours past quicker and quicker. Still they were no closer to finding an answer than when they both sat down.

"Wait! Wait!" Wadim suddenly yelled.

Peri jumped up so fast that the stack of books in her lap tumbled to the floor and she tripped over them trying to get to him to see what he was shouting about.

"Did you find something? What is it? What does it say?" her words flew out of her mouth in rapid fire.

"Oh, my bad, never mind."

Peri saw the small smile on the wolf's lips.

"You just jerked my chain didn't you?"

He started laughing and had to wrap his arms around the books in his lap to keep them from falling. "I'm sorry but the tension was just too much; we needed a quick break."

Peri smacked him across the back of the head before heading back over to her chair. "I swear, one of these days I'm going to have wolf pelts adorning my whole house, and I'll make sure yours is the one at the front door so everyone will step on you on their way in."

It was midmorning the next day when, group by group, the males returned back to the Romanian mansion. Vasile told them all to get some sleep, and when they argued, he reminded them that if they were delirious with exhaustion they would be no help to their mates. They saw the truth in his words, though that didn't stop them from grumbling as they went.

Decebel called his pack and spoke with his fourth to see how everyone was doing. He felt like he was neglecting them, but he didn't know how to change that at the moment. His mate would always come first, and he hoped that they would understand and that he would be an example to the other males who had yet to find their mates. He pushed the worry for his pack from his mind and felt the despair of the emptiness inside of him. He fought the overwhelming desire to kill anything and everything. The feeling of helplessness was beginning to suffocate him and he didn't know how he was going to sleep with such agony raging inside of him.

He laid down on their bed and her scent enveloped him. He rolled to his side and pressed his face into her pillow and memories of her flooded his mind. The first time he saw her he had been captivated by her and his wolf had surged forward with the need to claim her. She brought indescribable joy to him, and though she drove him crazy, there wasn't a thing about her that he would change. She filled the empty places inside of him, and she loved him when he knew he was so undeserving of that love. His heart ached in his chest and his muscles burned from the pain that seemed to be constantly radiating throughout him. His body called out for his mate. The bond was nearly gone and yet man and wolf still felt the intense need to be close to her. If she died, mate bond or not, he would follow her. There was nothing in this life for him without her here to share it. As he continued to breathe her scent deep into his lungs, he felt the exhaustion take over and pull him against his will into a deep sleep. Instinctively, he reached out for her, needing to hear her voice before the unconsciousness took him, and still there was nothing but a black void where she belonged.

Two weeks past and every day the men grew more and more restless. More than once Vasile had insisted they go spar with each other to work off the agitation and adrenaline that coursed through them at incredible levels.

Peri and Wadim rarely left the archives. When they did, it was only so Peri could throw massive fits, cursing everyone within her sight for not doing more and for resting when they should be out there killing things for information. Everyone made sure to stand a safe distance from her, but still some of them wound up in her line of fire and found themselves ducking as things within her grasp were flung across the room. If it wasn't for Adam and Alston using their magic to keep things from breaking, Vasile would have found himself having to replace most of the decorations in his home.

One month to the day after the females had been taken, Fane found himself standing on one of the highest peaks of the mountain. His wolf had tried to force his phase, but Fane refused it. He had to take off at a dead sprint in his human form to keep it at bay, pushing himself as he climbed the mountain. It was all he could give the wolf in an attempt to satisfy the pulsing need to hunt. But Fane didn't know where to begin, none of them did. They had been all over the mountains and still found nothing. They had sought out other supernaturals, hoping for some scrap of information, but no one knew anything. It was as if Reyaz and their mates had dropped off the face of the earth. Alston and Dain had been going into other realms and searching, but they had come back just as empty-handed. It was maddening. But worse was the utter feeling of loss that ripped through him, pushing him to his knees. He knew what it was, but he didn't want to admit it. None of the males did. It was like the elephant in the room that they all tiptoed around but refused to acknowledge. The mate bonds were breaking. They weren't just closed off. They were dying, day by day, hour by hour, minute by minute. Slowly their mates slipped further and further from their grasps. Soon they wouldn't know if their mates were alive or not because their fates would no longer be tied to each other.

Fane suddenly threw back his head and howled, pushing all of his anguish, all of his desolation, all of his heart stopping fear, into the sound. Seconds later he heard his pack mates answer his call as their howls joined in, every bit as sorrowful as his own. He didn't know how much longer they could control their wolves. The need for blood was a lust that was demanding to be sated. Fane guessed the only thing stopping them from going feral was the knowledge that once they did, without the mate bond, there would be no coming back.

Chapter 17

"For the first time in a long time, I just want to sleep. As in, I only want to sleep. Because in my sleep, you are there. During the waking hours, I can't feel you, I can't see you, and I can't smell you. And as time passes, I almost feel as though at any second I'm going to forget you ever existed in my life. But you come to me in my dreams. You hold me; you whisper words that knit my broken heart back together. But when I wake, it breaks all over again." ~Sally

"I motion that we play Sex I Spy," Jen said from the spot where she laid on her back. "We can call it Spex, for short" she said with a snort.

"Okay, can I just clarify one thing? Are you saying we are supposed to spy something having sex?" Sally asked. Lilly and Alina both shook their heads as they listened to the girls' outrageous discussions that had become an hourly event.

"Jen, I'm bored out of my mind, but I'm still not *that* bored," Jacque told her.

Jen laughed. "And you guys call me a pervert. What I meant was that if you can't find what the person spies, then you have to give up a detail of your love life."

"Uh," Crina's eyes darted from Jacque to Sally, waiting to see what their reactions would be.

"Why would we do this?" Sally asked.

"Because we never got to before our lives turned into The Young and Furry." She pulled her body up into a sitting position and faced the group. "Teenage girls are supposed to go on dates, kiss, make out, and then report back to the girlfriends. It's in the freaking handbook."

"There's a handbook?" Elle asked.

"Of course, I wrote it," Jen's face broke into one of those faces that said *duh what did you expect?*

"Of course you did," Crina laughed under her breath.

"I have to admit that Jen is right on what teenage girls discuss behind their bedroom doors. However, there are usually not parents present," Lilly pointed out.

"Desperate times, Ms. P, desperate times." Jen looked from person to person, noting their blank faces. Finally she huffed. "Fine, we'll play something else."

"Got anything that does not include sex, sexual innuendos, stripping, and the like?" Cynthia asked.

Jacque and Sally laughed as they looked at Cynthia with smirks.

Jen held up a finger. "Hold on, let me think about it." She bunched her lips up as she tilted her head one way and then the next. Then she scratched her head and tapped her lips with her finger. She sat up straight suddenly. "Oh wait, got it," she paused as she held out her hands as if to make the others stop what they were doing. Just as quickly her shoulders slumped back. "False alarm, I got nothing."

Cynthia shook her head at Jen with a small smile while the others let out quiet chuckles that didn't quite meet their eyes. None of their laughter did, not anymore.

They had no idea how many days or weeks had past. It was so hard to tell time in the dark forest where there was no sunlight. There was no changing of the daylight to indicate how early or late it was. Their watches and phones were useless. They had just stopped working the minute they had entered the fae realm, or rather, the dark forest. So they sat; sometimes they stood, or walked around, or slept. They talked about nothing and everything. Jen continued to use humor as a coping mechanism, though there were nearly as many tears as there were jokes. They had begun to grow very hungry and very thirsty, and just when the pain of it was beginning to grow unbearable, food would appear. The first time it happened, they had all nearly peed themselves at the sudden appearance, but after sniffing it and taking tiny bites, they decided it was safe and they had gorged themselves. There had been bread, fruit, turkey sandwiches, and water to drink. Cynthia had insisted that Jen eat and drink her fill first, and everyone had agreed. After a small amount of protest, she finally gave in. They attempted to judge the passage of time by the appearance of the food, but it was no use; its appearance was sporadic at best.

"Holy crap, I'm nearly as bored as I am in pain," Jen grumbled as she laid on her back, staring up into the dark sky. They had given up any games and resorted to just sitting.

"Do you think Reyaz is ever going to show his face?" Jacque asked no one in particular.

"Eventually," Alina answered. "He is meticulous and seems to steer towards the whole idea of his prey growing complacent. I think he enjoys the shock value."

"While I appreciate your evaluation of our captor, I'm just going to go with he's an asshat with brother issues," Sally said.

Jen laughed and gave Sally a thumbs-up. "Captivity agrees with you, Sally. You get snarkier by the day, or hour, or whatever the amount of time has passed."

"My inner Jen seems to be triggered by being dropped into spooky, evil places where we're fed like animals and forced to dig holes to pee in."

"We aren't going to be here forever," Lilly said confidently. She had been attempting to be as positive as possible and she was as relentless as her plight. "You know your mates are going crazy trying to find you, and I have a feeling that nothing stands a chance against them when it comes to getting their mates back."

"As awesome as they are, mom, they are still human," Jacque paused. "Well, sort of, but you get my drift."

"How are you finding your accommodations?" A masculine voice said from inside the darkness. They all scrambled to their feet as they watched Reyaz materialize from the forest. "I know it's a tad rustic, but then you are wolves, well most of you, so I figured it wouldn't bother you."

Alina stepped forward and her body radiated anger and protectiveness for the women with her. "What do you want with us?" she asked pointedly.

"Come now, Alpha. You are intelligent. Surely you have figured out that I didn't really want anything with the wolves. My brother's lovely human mate has always been my target. But you all just continued to get in my way. I don't like it when people interfere with my plans."

"Are you going to kill us?" Cynthia asked him.

His brow rose in surprise at how calmly she asked about their demise. "Are you so eager to die?"

"Are you really that stupid?" Jen growled. "Oh wait, you have to be because you took the mates of some of the most powerful werewolves in history away from them. In what delusion of yours could you possibly think that would end well for you? Even if we die, our mates will rip you apart and then use your bones as tooth picks."

Reyaz took a step closer towards the clearing where the girls were trapped. "You're the pregnant one." It wasn't a question. "I could potentially have an interest in keeping you alive, or at least until your child is born. Can you imagine how horrific it would be for your mate to know that I was raising your child as my own? Training it in my ways and teaching it my magic?"

Jen wasn't the only one who let out a snarl this time as several of the she-wolves lunged forward. "You will never get your hands on my child."

"Relax, mate to Decebel. You don't need to stress yourself out just yet. You have time to fret over it before the child is born. I think you have about a month and a half."

Jen's mouth dropped open but it was Cynthia who spoke. "That's not possible; she isn't eight months pregnant yet."

A grin spread across the warlock's face. "Didn't your fae tell you? Time passes differently in the dark forest. One month in the human realm equals two months here."

"Bloody hell," Jen muttered.

"You girls must be getting bored by now. I think a game is in order. So you all might want to start saying your goodbyes. I will be back for one of you soon and the hunt will begin." Then he was gone.

"He said I have a month and a half left," Jen started, not bothering to acknowledge that he had left. "Okay, I was five and a half months pregnant when we were taken. So if he's saying I have a month and a half that would make me seven and a half months pregnant, which means we've been missing for a month in the human realm and two months here." She glanced down at her stomach and lifted her shirt. She did look bigger, but she didn't think she had grown that much while they had been there. She looked up at Cynthia. "Is she going to be okay? Do you think she's developing according to the time here or the time in the human realm?"

Cynthia's eyes were wide and filled with worry, which did not instill confidence in Jen. Cynthia walked over to Jen and bent down on one knee and pressed her ear to Jen's abdomen. She strained to listen and then heard it.

"Her heartbeat is strong and solid," Cynthia told her.

Sally cleared her throat, bringing everyone's attention to her. "I could check on her." She paused, waiting to see if her announcement was going to freak Jen out; she was so unpredictable these days. When she didn't say anything but just continued to stare at her, she continued. "I mean I could go in and look at her and see how developed she is. If you want?" she finished quickly.

Alina walked over and put her hand gently on Jen's shoulder, "This is why having a healer is such a gift, Jennifer. She will not hurt you or the baby. This is what she was created for."

There was complete silence as they waited for Jen to speak. Jen trusted Sally. It wasn't a matter of trust that was causing her to hesitate. It was fear. Once Sally did her thing, they would know for sure if the baby was alright. What if she wasn't? There's nothing they could do to help her. Decebel wasn't here to hold Jen's hand or to wrap his arms around her and tell her he would protect them. But she knew if he were here, he would have already grabbed Sally and forced her on Jen. He would be brave and he would want her to be brave.

"Alright," she finally agreed softly.

"Here Jen, come lay your head in my lap and I'll play with your hair like you use to make me do for hours when we watched Buffy." Jacque sat on the ground and motioned for Jen to follow.

Jen closed her eyes as Jacque's fingers ran through her hair. She had always loved it when they would take turns fixing each other's hair and brushing it. She felt the air flutter against her neck as the strands were lifted and then felt the soft brush of the locks against her shoulder and back. Over and over Jacque's fingers worked their way through the blonde strands.

She felt Sally's hand press gently to her stomach and warmth began to radiate from it. It began in her abdomen then traveled outward, down her hips and thighs to her feet and toes, and up to her chest, shoulders, neck, and head. The warmth made her relax even further, and she felt cradled in the arms of something greater than herself. She thought of Decebel and wished desperately that he could be with her, that he could be the one running his fingers through her hair. She longed so desperately for him and her mind tumbled back to a memory that made the warmth grow stronger.

He had been sitting on their bed and she had just come back from spending time with Jacque and Jen.

He turned to look at her and her heart melted all over again.

"Hey," she said in an almost shy manner.

"Hey yourself," he said back. His eyes danced with mischief and she knew he was in one of his playful moods, a mood only she got to see.

"Did you have fun with your friends?"

She nodded. "Yes. Did you have fun beating other wolves up?" she had asked him several times to let her come watch him spar with the others, but he was adamant about not letting her go. She had discovered, through doing a little eavesdropping in his mind, that he didn't want her to see all the half-dressed guys. He had no clue how beautiful he was; how utterly perfect he was. She had told them that those other guys weren't even in the same atmosphere as him, that he was on a totally different universe compared to others. He didn't see it. He didn't see how she saw him.

"Come here," she told him.

He rose and turned to face her as he crossed his arms in front of his chest. "Feeling confident today?"

"Why wouldn't I feel confident? I'm mated to you. That must make me pretty dang special."

He walked towards her with a sly smile; his gait so confident and sure. When he was finally standing in front of her he lifted his hand to brush her hair from her face and then cupped her cheek in his large, rough hand. "I don't think you have any idea how special you are to me, Jennifer. But I will spend my life trying to show you." He leaned down and pressed his lips to hers, slowly, gently, until his hand slid back behind her head and pulled her closer. His other hand slid under her shirt and grazed her side where the marks, that testified that she was his, traveled from her hip to under her arm. He pulled away just briefly to whisper against her lips. "You are indeed mine and nothing will ever take you from me."

Her mind returned to the present when she opened her eyes and saw Sally leaning over her with her eyes closed and her brow scrunched up, concentrating. She tried not to hold her breath as she waited for her gypsy friend to do her thing.

Sally pushed her consciousness into Jen and sought out the fast fluttering heartbeat. She was amazed at the little life growing inside of her friend, how perfect every little part was. Sally honestly didn't have a clue what a baby should look like at seven and half months, but Jen's baby was fully developed. Sally noticed that her lungs looked small, but from what she could remember from health class, those were what took the longest to mature. As she watched the perfect little life moving in the safe little home, she felt honored to get to be a part of it. Her little hands were moving; one had even made it to her mouth. Her toes curled and her foot flexed. Amazing was the only word that Sally could think. Amazing, amazing, amazing, and she knew that if she could cry she would have tears streaming down her face. This perfect, amazing life was set to end the minute she took her first breath. She would have no first moments after that—no first smiles, no first noises, no first roll over, or first crawl. Her life was over before it would even begin. How could that possibly be the payment for Jen's life, to take something so innocent in place of someone else. She wondered if the Fates would consider a different sacrifice, a different life in place of the child's. There had to be another way. As she pushed warmth and hope towards the child, letting her know just how loved she was, she vowed then and there that Jen and Dec's baby would live. She would allow no other outcome. She was the healer of their pack, the one meant to protect and care for the wolves. As such, she could not allow a new life to be taken from them.

"Do you hear me little one," she whispered into her mind, "you are loved, and no one will take you from us."

Sally slipped her consciousness slowly from the child and then back out of Jen, pulling herself back into her own body. As her eyes opened she blinked several times to regain her bearings. Finally, when she felt like she had her wits about her, she looked down at Jen.

"I'm not sure how a baby should look at seven and half months, but from what I could tell she has all her parts; her lungs looked small, but other than that she is absolutely perfect."

Jen's eyes filled with tears as she pulled herself up and flung herself into Jacque's arms. She wept for the news that her child was healthy. She wept for being trapped in a horrific place, away from any form of medical help, and she wept for the loss of her mate. It was just too much. And for once, she didn't have anything smart to say;

she didn't have a joke or sarcastic comment; all she had was a broken heart and an empty place where her mate's spirit should have been. She heard the sniffles behind her and knew that the others were crying right along with her. They felt her pain; they knew her fears and they would stand by her through it all. That realization only made her cry harder. She didn't know how long she sat there holding onto her best friend, but she was so grateful that Jacque just let her get it out. And then finally she took some deep breaths and the tears subsided.

"Um, guys, not to interrupt this difficult moment, but we sort of have company." The waver in Crinas' voice and the fear that caused it had everyone turning to face her. The eyes of every one of them widened and multiple gasps rippled across them.

"Could someone explain why there is a massive white wolf staring at us from about twenty-five feet away? Which I will add is not near far enough for me." Lilly attempted to move in front of Jacque and the others as if she had a chance in hell of protecting them against a wolf that large.

"He's not just a wolf," Alina answered and her voice was filled with what sounded like shock, sadness, and guilt.

"He's a werewolf?" Jen asked as she wiped the last of the tears away.

Alina nodded as she continued to stare at the wolf. He lifted his nose into the air sniffing, and suddenly he froze. His head slowly lowered and his narrowed, glowing eyes landed on Alina. He took a slow step towards them as his lip lifted in a snarl.

"Alina, why is he staring you down like that? And a better question would be... why does he look like he's about to rip your throat out?" Cynthia asked.

"I imagine that after what he's been through, he might want to rip me apart and then some," she answered calmly.

"So I take that to mean that you know who he is?" Jen asked.

"I do."

"Okay," Jen drew the word out as she continued to watch the wolf. "I also take it that by your first reaction of shock you weren't expecting to see him."

"I wasn't."

"Bloody hell, like pulling freaking teeth," Jacque muttered.

"I thought he was dead," Alina elaborated. "We all did. Would you agree, Elle?" Alina did not disconnect the eye contact she had with the wolf, feeling that it was the only thing keeping him from attacking.

"We did not believe there could be anyway he survived," Elle answered.

"Alright, are you going to tell us who *he* is anytime this year?" Jen's impatience and earlier emotions were not helping her keep the sarcasm out of her voice.

"He should not be here; he should not have survived. If they had known, they would have done something. They never would have left him to this fate, they would have…,"

"Alina!" Cynthia interrupted the Alpha, attempting to keep her from getting any more out of control than she was in that moment. "Who is he?"

"He is…he *was* Vasile's brother."

Chapter 18
"I've seen a horsefly; I've seen a dragonfly; I've even seen housefly, but I ain't never seen an elephant fly. For some reason I don't think this possibility is so farfetched, not any more. In fact at this point an elephant flying would be the most uneventful sight in my day." ~Lilly

"Bloody hell," Jacque whispered as her breath caught in her chest.

Jen threw her arm up in the air letting out a loud huff, "Just when you think you've heard it all. Next you're going to tell us you carried his love child and that's why he ran off into a god forsaken forest so that Vasile wouldn't rip the jewels off."

Alina shook her head and said just as serious as ever. "No, no love child."

"Good to know," Cynthia added.

The wolf continued to stare Alina down and just when they had begun to think that he was going to become a permanent fixture to their view of the dark forest, he turned and ran off into the dark until the shadows swallowed him up.

As soon as he was gone Alina visibly wilted as she fell to her knees. Her face was pale and her breathing sporadic. She didn't know how it was possible. She may not have been alive during the battle between the fae and Volcan but she had been told the history behind it. She had read the archives and Vasile had told her of his brother's sacrifice. Vasile had been so very young then but he remembered the pack having a funeral for the ones who didn't return. He remembered what it was like to lose a sibling and it had left a hole inside of him.

"So what does this mean?" Cynthia asked.

"I don't know," Alina admitted.

"Is this the rest of the dirty little secret that you didn't want to talk about when you and Elle were telling us about how the dark forest came to be?" Sally asked.

"It isn't my story to tell, but under the circumstances, it is necessary that I tell you what I know." Alina rolled off her knees to her bottom and folded her legs. She paused briefly and closed her eyes as a stab of pain pierced her stomach. It was getting worse and she knew that soon there would be no bond left. When she finally felt she could speak without her voice shaking, she began.

The restlessness that was a constant hum in the Romanian mansion was beginning to be fire in Vasile's blood, and with the added pain of the loss of the mate bond, his control was slipping. He was at a loss as to what to do. He had no leads to follow, no past to learn from, and no scent to follow. For the first time in his long life, he was beginning to fear that he would never see his mate again. And should the bond be broken between them completely, he would never know if she was alive or not. There was a knock on his office door and he snarled before saying, "Enter."

A very frazzled looking Costin stood in his door. The dark circles under his eyes confirmed that he had not been getting any more rest than anyone else. His clenched teeth and tight jaw were a dead giveaway that he was in pain.

"You need to come." His breathing was heavy as if he had been running and a sheen of sweat had developed on his forehead.

"What's going on?"

"It's Decebel."

Vasile growled but was running before Costin could get anymore words out. He motioned for Costin to show him where his Alpha was and easily kept pace with the younger wolf. As they rounded the corner he realized that Costin was taking him to Decebel's room. Vasile came to a quick halt when he reached it and saw that it was hanging on the hinges by a thread and it swung precariously by them. Vasile looked at Costin, "You should go." He didn't have to tell Costin twice.

As he stepped into the room he took in the damage and imagined that it was what the room would look like if a tornado came in and stayed for a few hours. The curtains had been shredded and hung in sad looking strips in front of the window. Every now and then a breeze would hit and they would flutter, allowing glimpses of the night. The dresser had been knocked on its side and the drawers had come crashing out of it, clothes poured out onto the floor. Like the curtains, the bedspread and sheets had been torn and it was obvious that claws had been the method of choice. He could see through the smashed bathroom door, and he saw the mirror on the wall was shattered and it made him think of Decebel's soul. Was it shattered like the mirror? Vasile didn't know the answer to that question yet.

He heard rustling in the closet. As he stepped into the doorway he was not surprised to see Decebel shredding clothes. He seemed to feel the need to rip and tear. Maybe it was a substitute for the flesh he, no doubt, wanted beneath his claws and fangs.

"Decebel, stop." Vasile was no longer his Alpha, but he was still more powerful, and though he didn't like to use it on his longtime friend, he would if it meant protecting him, even from himself. Decebel's hands froze and his back stiffened at the command. He growled low and the rumble in his chest shook the clothes around him. "I am not your enemy," Vasile spoke calmly but firmly. "Stop this madness and come talk to me."

It was several minutes, growls, snarls, and choice cuss words later that Decebel at last followed Vasile into the room. Neither of them sat nor did they acknowledge the destruction around them.

"Tell me what's going on Decebel; trust me as you once did," Vasile told his former Beta. He watched as Decebel began to pace the room restlessly. His face was laced with the obvious pain that he had been feeling for weeks, if not longer. His eyes flashed back and forth from wolf to human and his lack of control had finally reared its ugly head and came bursting out in a fit of rage he could no longer contain.

"I will never see my mate again," Decebel said with a clenched jaw. "I will never hold her hand, I will never kiss her, I will never make love to her, I will never hear her boss me around ever again." Anger mixed with intense pain filled his voice and Vasile ached deeply for him.

"We will get them back Decebel; you have to believe that. We will get them back and we will destroy the one who took them from us."

Decebel was shaking his head as Vasile spoke. There may have been truth in his statement, but not for Decebel. It did not apply to him.

"I petitioned the Great Luna," he finally bit out.

Vasile tensed as he took in this information. There could be only one reason Decebel would do such a thing.

"I take it Jen doesn't know," he asked calmly.

Decebel shook his head.

"Is this why you sent her away with such ease?"

Decebel snarled and turned to face Vasile. He fell down into a crouch, eyes glowing, canines extended, sharp as knives. "If you think that I did it with such ease then you do not know me at all. Putting her on that plane went against everything, every fiber of my being. There isn't a second that goes by that I don't think about her flying off in that plane and feeling my soul rip apart all over again. Every breath without her is like a knife ripping through my lungs. Every beat of my heart screams to have her back. My wolf has nearly taken control several times and I don't know how much longer I can fight him. If she stayed with me, she would be safe at my side now instead of in the clutches of a mad man. That knowledge eats away at me like the decay of death." Vasile remained standing across the room staring at Decebel, meeting his eyes but not allowing his own wolf to rise to the challenge that presented itself before him now. "Alina had told me, before the bond was lost, that Jen was experiencing severe pain. Pain that is greater than that of being separated from you should be. Why?" He waited patiently as he watched Decebel attempt to gather himself.

Decebel took several deep breaths and closed his eyes. *Not the enemy*, he told himself. He knew that Vasile was not the one who should be enduring his wrath, not when the circumstances were all of his own making. He was the one who made the decision to petition the Great Luna. He was the one who sought out Cynthia to block his mind from his mate. He was the one who pushed her across the globe so that their bond would die. So he could die and she and their daughter could live. This was his fault and no one else's.

"The Great Luna is destroying the bond between us so that when I die, Jennifer will live. The distance was supposed to make it happen more quickly. She said it would be painful, but I don't think either of us realized how tight our bond was."

Vasile let out a derisive snort. "You could have asked me; I would have gladly told you what a fool you were for even thinking of attempting to destroy your bond with your mate— your pregnant mate." The last part was said slowly and firmly letting Decebel know just how stupid Vasile thought his actions were. And they were stupid.

"What would you do Vasile?" Decebel stood up from his crouch and ran his hands through his hair. He had not bothered to cut it since Jennifer had left and it was longer than it had been in a while. He knew she would like it and probably make some crack about being able to grab onto it. He nearly smiled at the thought. "If you didn't have a clue how to save your child, what would you do? And now she has been taken. I won't be there for the birth of my baby girl, and as soon as she is brought into this world I will be taken out. I won't be able to tell my love goodbye. I won't," he had to stop to regain his composure before he broke down. "I won't be there while she is in labor, scared and in pain. I should be there!" He pounded his chest as his words reverberated in the room. "Me, Vasile, her mate, I should be the one who tells her she is doing great. I should be the one who wipes the sweat from her skin and kisses her, even though she is cussing me. I should be there and because of my choices she will do it all alone."

Vasile hated to kick him while he was down, but sometimes you need to hear the truth, even if it hurt. "I understand your reasoning, Decebel, probably even more than you do because I have a child. I know exactly what it means to love truly unconditionally with every fiber of your being. But when you took Jen as your mate, you took her as your partner, your equal. How would you feel if she made such a drastic decision without your knowledge? How betrayed would you feel?"

"I KNOW!" he yelled. "I know how I would feel, but the fact is, if I had told her, she would have tried to stop me."

Vasile nodded. "And she would have been right to try. You belong to her. She expects you to make decisions with her not for her. I'm not saying it would be easy, but there might have been a compromise reached. It's too late to know what could have been. What's done is done. Now we just do everything in our power to get her back before she goes into labor." Vasile walked over to one of the chairs that seemed to have taken the least amount of abuse and sat down. There was none of the grace he usually wore like a second skin. Exhaustion was written in every line on his face and in the slow movements in his limbs. "I know that you think you are doing the right thing, and maybe you are. Honestly, Decebel, I don't know what the right thing is. All I know is that what you are doing is destroying the woman you love, and once she gives birth to your child and realizes that you are dead…that you sacrificed yourself without telling her, she might just kill herself so she can come kick your ass."

Decebel sat down equally as gracelessly across from the Alpha. "I know she won't take it well, but how much more painful will it be to hold our child that has no life? Vasile," Decebel clenched his fists and pounded them into his thighs. "I didn't know what else to do! I'm supposed to protect her. I'm supposed to bring her happiness. I'm supposed to keep out the dark things. And I've failed her, not just once, but many times." He held Vasile's gaze for several breaths and then dropped his head forward. For so long, he had been fighting the tears, fighting the pain, fighting the despair, and he was growing so tired. His wolf was growing stronger with every breath and he feared that once his wolf had control, he would destroy the world to get their mate back. "I don't know what to do." The words stumbled out through ragged breaths and he squeezed his eyes closed as he gave in to the utter truth of his declaration. As his bond with Jennifer weakened, he had been growing more and more agitated and the darkness gained more and more ground every day. He could no longer feel her at all, not even when he reached out as hard as he could. What was left of their bond was fragile, and he knew it could break and be gone at any moment.

"We're going to fix this, Decebel. You aren't alone and I wish that you would have come to me. We will always be pack no matter what. Do not let it happen again." Vasile's words pulsated with power as he reminded Decebel that he had claimed him like a son long ago and he would always belong to him.

Decebel nodded. After several minutes he looked back up. "So what now?"

Just as the question was out, Perizada walked through the door holding a piece of paper. She surveyed the room around her and then looked at Decebel. "If I were you, instead of life insurance, I would invest in counseling. Lots and lots of counseling."

"Peri," Vasile called her name attempting to pull her attention from Decebel and perhaps save her life in the process.

Peri nodded and then held the paper up, "We found this piece of paper at the front doors, on the floor. It is a riddle from dear old Reyaz. And personally I would just like to point out how pissed I am that he got that close to this house and none of us knew it."

Decebel was up so fast and snatching the paper from her hands that she had barely enough time to back up to keep from being knocked on her butt by the massive man.

"How many times do I have to remind them who I am," she mumbled, then took a deep breath and let it out slow. "Think happy thoughts, Peri," she told herself, then added, "If you can't think happy thoughts, then picture wolves with their mouths duck taped closed." She grinned to herself; she felt that idea actually had potential.

Decebel read the piece of paper rapidly ten times before finally reading it out loud.

"You are cordially invited to a hunt in honor of my brother's mating. This is like no other hunt you have ever been a part of, nor will it end the way any other hunt has. You will have timed tasks you must complete in order to capture your prize and move forward. Two prizes will accompany each task, but only one may be claimed. Your first task is to find out where the hunt begins. I will be kind and give you a clue to set you on your way:

I am home to many; they are held deep in my embrace,
I have a history of greatness, treachery, and demise,
For many years my land has seen two faces but only one soul,
To know me is impossible, unless the wall is destroyed.

I'm feeling generous due to my good fortune in my own hunt, so I will give you two days to figure out the location and arrive there. I would advise you to not be late."

~R

The room was completely still when Decebel finished reading, as if a spell had been cast, freezing them in place. Shock, disbelief, frustration, and anger became tangible emotions in the air ready to latch onto the first person who came near enough.

Peri was the first to move. She began rapidly pacing and muttering under her breath, over and over again, the riddle Reyaz had given. There was something about it that made her think she knew exactly where he had the females, but every time she reached for it, the thought vanished like a puff of smoke dissipating. "Vasile," she snapped, "gathering hall, now." She left the destroyed room at an inhuman pace not worried about having just given an Alpha an order and not wondering if he would follow it. As she entered the gathering room she wasn't surprised to see that it was full of their allies. Wadim had been with her when she found the paper and he had taken it upon himself to get everyone into one place. *Smart wolf,* she thought as she hurried into the room with a grace that only a high fae could manage.

Once at the front of the room she turned and faced the group. The murmuring that had been steady when she walked in had now stopped as all eyes were on her. She met many of their eyes, holding them only for a few seconds before moving on to the next. She didn't speak; she wouldn't until Vasile and Decebel arrived.

A couple of minutes later the two Alpha's came through the door and the power radiating off of them caused the wolves in the room to stumble, while the others seemed to shrink back from the two men. Normally Peri would have considered it a power play, but not now. Now they were just both that close to losing it and their power was coming out of them like a leaking fuel tank. Heaven help the ones caught standing too close when a flame finally meets the fuel. She noticed Decebel's blank face and tense shoulders, and she was reminded of the Decebel she knew before he had mated with Jen. The sight sent a chill up her spine.

"Have you told them?" Vasile asked Peri as he reached the front of the room.

"No," she answered curtly. He nodded and then turned around.

"Reyaz has made contact with us. He left a note and instead of explaining it, Decebel will read it so you can hear it for yourselves." Vasile nodded to Decebel. In a voice as emotionless as the man who used it, he read the contents of the piece of paper. Just like before, after Decebel was done, the room was in complete silence.

Cypher stepped forward and looked at Vasile and then Decebel. "I must apologize that you are involved in this and that your females are in danger. It is my fault and I will do anything I can to get them back."

"Don't be an idiot," Peri's voice rang out into the silence, "did you put a gun to your brother's head and tell him to be a psycho? Did you threaten to cut off appendages unless he chose to allow his bitterness to eat him until all that was left was a decaying soul wrapped in malice?" she didn't give him time to respond before she continued, "No, you didn't. You just had the misfortune of being related to him and that is not a crime. If you feel the need to apologize, then apologize for wasting your breath and making me waste mine in order to tell you to make yourself useful and figure out what this bloody riddle means."

"Well, when you put it like that," Cypher said with a slight smile as he gave her a small bow and then stepped back to his original place.

Peri crossed her arms in front of her chest and looked out at the males daring any of them to say something stupid so she could tear into them.

"As you've heard we have a very limited window to figure out where this so called hunt will be and get there. I'm asking for each of us here to look into your respective race's history. The tiniest detail could be the break we need," Vasile said. He turned then and caught Alston's eyes. "I would ask something of you."

"We are at your service."

"Could you please transport those who need to travel so that we aren't wasting time moving from place to place?"

Alston nodded. "You didn't have to ask, that was a given."

Vasile gave the fae a look that told him just how much that meant to him.

"Okay, enough with all the 'we're united; hear us roar' crap. We've got stuff to do. History boy, you're with me," she pointed to the right of Wadim, "you too dimple boy," she told Costin.

The room began to fill with the noises of feet shuffling, murmurs, and the door opening and closing as people made their way out, until all that was left were the wolves and Cypher.

"Do you have a plan?" Decebel asked Peri.

"Not really, but I figure if I act like I do, then one will suddenly appear."

"Well what's the not really part?" Fane asked.

"I'm going to find the pixie king. Perhaps he can remember something from our long past that I've missed. I have a feeling that wherever this place is, it is very old. I suggest you go back and find the troll king as well and share the riddle with Thead. He can be trusted and he will want Reyaz destroyed just as much as we do." She pointed at Adam as she continued to speak in her brisk manner.

"Skender, Fane, Sorin, you three will go to the troll king," Vasile interrupted, pointing to each of them and receiving nods in return.

"Adam can find the entrance to their land for you," Peri told them.

"The rest can come with me," Cypher spoke up, "we have extensive archives and some very long memories."

Adam motioned to Cypher, "I can take them first and then we will go to the trolls."

"We will meet back here in twelve hours to find out what progress has been made," Vasile told them.

"Can I ask why you chose us?" Costin asked as he regained his bearings from being flashed.

Peri rolled her eyes. "Don't get all giddy wolf. I chose you two because I tolerate you better than the others. In other words, I'm least likely to make a rug out of you."

"Comforting," Wadim said dryly.

"All right, less chit chat and more walking." Peri took off in a run.

Costin watched after her. "She calls that walking?"

Wadim chuckled. "She calls us walking handbags."

"They don't make handbags out of wolf pelts," Costin pointed out.

"Yeah, I said the same thing. She said there's a first time for everything."

They both shrugged and then followed after the fae, putting on as much speed as they could. After half an hour they finally stopped. Wadim and Costin both were slightly winded which was evidence of just how fast they had been running, since wolves rarely got winded.

"Can I just ask why you aren't doing your flashy thing?" Wadim asked.

"Good grief, were you too just let out of the puppy pen yesterday?" Peri huffed, "Magic, we aren't the only ones with it. The pixie king is powerful and he doesn't want fae flashing willy nilly around his land."

"Okay, wait," Costin held up his hand, "this is the same pixie that turned us over to Desdemona and put us in the In-Between? Why exactly are we seeking out his help instead of having him as an appetizer to the rabbit I'm going to catch for dinner?"

"Ainsel made a poor decision, but he made it out of a need to protect his people. That doesn't make it right, but it doesn't make him evil either. Vasile chose to spare him, and by doing so, gained a powerful ally. You have to realize that there will always be war, and it is a wise leader who picks his battles, and if he can, his enemy as well."

Costin looked at her thoughtfully and though he understood what she was saying, it did not endear him to the pixie.

"Ainsel, we need to speak with you. Please do not waste my time; I am in no mood to play your games," Peri yelled out into the forest.

Slowly one by one pixies began to emerge from the surrounding trees and foliage. Costin couldn't help the way his muscles tensed when he saw the king. He watched silently as Peri knelt down in front of the small being.

"Dark times have fallen over us again, and we need your help," she told them in a voice that Costin had rarely heard her use.

Ainsel glanced from Wadim to Costin and then back to Peri. "This request comes from Vasile?"

Peri nodded. "His females, as well as the Warlock King's mate, have been captured by Reyaz."

Ainsel's eyes widened. He knew all about Cypher's brother and had heard the whispers of the evil that had begun to gather around the mountain he had called home for so long.

"What could we possibly do against one such as him? We may have magic, but we would be no match for him."

"We aren't asking for you to fight," Peri explained. "We need you to think," Ainsel's head tilted to the side at the odd request. Peri explained to him all about the riddle and then waited silently for his response.

"And you only have two days to figure this out?" he asked her.

"The clock is ticking," Costin said and tried to keep the growl out of his voice. He must not have succeeded because Peri turned and gave him a look that said she would cause him bodily harm if he didn't shut up.

"I will do what I can to help, Perizada. I owe the wolves that much if not more."

Peri clapped her hands together. "Great! Okay, so do we need to go to your archives?"

"Would we even fit?" Wadim asked from behind Peri.

Ainsel didn't seem to be offended by the question and answered, "We don't keep our history on paper. Some of our kind are blessed with the ability to hold great amounts of information and they bare the history of our people."

"They remember all of it?" Wadim's tone said he was impressed.

Ainsel nodded. "I will bring them here. Because no, you wouldn't fit in my kingdom," he told Wadim with a small smile.

The pixies disappeared into the forest silently leaving Peri and the two wolves.

"So I've been running the riddle through my head over and over and the first line I think is actually pretty simple," Wadim said as he sat down leaning his back against a large tree trunk. "'Home to many', I would think that would mean people, since he uses the reference of home."

Peri nodded, "I'm listening,"

"Then the second part, 'held deep in my embrace', makes me think, they are in the ground."

"A cemetery?" Costin asked.

Peri thought about it, "A cemetery might work for the second line, but the third and fourth line don't make sense if that's the answer."

"I was thinking a battlefield," Wadim said.

Peri snapped her fingers, "'Dead bodies in the ground, many of them.' Wadim you're brilliant!"

"You aren't going to hug me are you?" he asked her.

Peri's eyes narrowed, "Do I look like a hugger?"

Wadim shook his head quickly.

"So it's a battlefield or someplace where lots of people died and their bodies stayed there until the land took them. But why would the second line say greatness, along with treachery and demise?"

"Greatness does not always equate to good," Ainsel said as he once again came walking out of the woods. Only two other pixies were with him this time. "This is Sully and Dorri. They are the holders of the memories of our history."

"How do we get the memories out of them?" Costin asked looking at the two female pixies curiously.

"You don't shake them if that's what you're thinking," Peri snapped.

Costin blushed slightly, revealing that it had indeed crossed his mind.

"They must choose to give them to you, and you have to ask the right question to get the memory. They don't just give out memories like fae bread."

Costin frowned, "Is that supposed to be significant?"

Peri groaned, "Bloody hell man, fae bread to pixies is like beer to humans. It makes them very happy little people."

Costin nodded as he made an 'ah' sound in understanding.

Peri took a seat on the ground and looked at Ainsel waiting for him to give the okay to the two girls.

"It's important that you ask specific questions. That will make it easier on them to narrow it down," Ainsel explained.

Peri nodded, "Got it, specific. Great, I only have thousands of years to sift through." She closed her eyes and thought about the first two lines of the riddle and how they had decided that they felt it was a battleground of some sort.

Her eyes opened and she looked at Sully. "What battlegrounds in supernatural history bore the most death?"

"Good one," Wadim muttered his approval.

Sully walked over to Peri, her small stature barely reaching the fae's knee. She placed her tiny hand on the skin of Peri's hand and looked directly into the fae's eyes.

Peri's breath caught as images swam in her mind, first they moved so fast she could barely make any sense of them and then gradually they began to slow down until they were moving at a pace that she was able to discern what she saw. *So much blood shed, so many battles and all for what*, she thought to herself as the images continued to run through her mind like a movie. Gradually they slowed again until there were two that seemed to repeat themselves over and over. Then suddenly a third image showed up but it was distorted so much that she could not make out what it was. The three images repeated over and over and she repeated in her mind, *the most death*, hoping it would cause one of them to finally be singled out among them. And then they stopped and the only image left in her mind was of a picture that looked as though the lens of the camera had been severely out of focus when it was taken.

"Dammit!" She blew out a breath and the pixie stepped back. "Thank you," Peri told Sully gently.

"I take it that to the fae the word dammit also means that something severely sucks." Costin said.

Peri looked up at him with a single brow raised. "If you mean severely sucks as in the one image that seems to hold the most deaths is so blurry that all I can tell is that there might have been something resembling a place at one time, then yes the dammit holds true."

"Why would something in your history look like that in their minds?" Wadim asked Ainsel.

"Usually, it is when there is some sort of tampering with a memory. It's either something someone has done to one of the holders, or there has been some sort of spell cast over that specific memory so that though you might have been there when it happened, but you would not remember that it even occurred."

"Why would someone try to wipe out an entire battle?" Costin thought out loud. "Part of surviving as long as we do is from learning from our past, our mistakes."

Peri stood up and brushed off her clothes and gathered herself. "Haven't you ever heard the saying that some things are better left forgotten?"

"Yeah, and the idiot who said it died because he forgot not to walk through the forest of his enemy where some of his friends were killed," Wadim told her.

Peri paused and looked back at the historian. "That's not true," she challenged him.

He grinned. "No, but you have to admit it would be a fitting end for someone who would say something so very ignorant."

Peri gave a noncommittal shrug but didn't disagree, for once.

"Can you lift your magic just long enough for me to flash back, so I don't have to wait for nerd boy and sex toy to keep up with me?"

The two wolves behind her coughed on their surprised laughter at her description of them.

Ainsel waved his hand absently. "Done," he took a step forward when he spoke his next words, "I wish I could help more Peri," Ainsel told her.

"Ouch," Wadim muttered.

"Yeah, that was not a wise thing for him to say to this fae." Costin agreed.

Peri gave the king a curious look and then a slow smile spread across her too beautiful face, "I think you can king. What would you say to action, intrigue, sword fights, pirates, betrayal, and true love?" She nodded at him as if it were the best idea she had ever come up with. "Come on, it will be just like The Princess Bride only better because I'll be there."

The last thing Costin and Wadim heard as Peri and the king flashed was Ainsel's voice. "What's The Princess Bride?"

Costin and Wadim laughed, but their laughter was cut short when suddenly Peri appeared, grabbed both their hands, and then they were gone.

Chapter 19

"If I never see you again, at least I can say that you were mine. At one time, you belonged only to me. I hold onto that as I feel the link between us slipping away. I hold onto the knowledge that there was a time when the bond between us completed our souls, leaving no space between us. There was a time when I did not question how long our lives together would be, because where you went, I went. And now, somehow, we went different directions, and I am so much weaker without you." ~Alina

"Do you think we will ever have children?" Jacque asked Fane as they lay on their backs on a blanket in the floor of their room. Fane had surprised her with a midnight picnic, complete with chocolate covered strawberries and the little finger sandwiches that she always thought were ridiculous. It had made her laugh, and that had been his goal.

"Most definitely," he told her.

"How can you be so sure?"

"I don't believe you could have been brought into this world and not be given the chance to pass on your love, compassion, intelligence, and loyalty to a child who could then be a light in this dark world. How will good remain in the world if those who are good do not raise up the next generation?"

Jacque smiled at him. "Thought about this much?"

Fane chuckled. "If you mean about procreating with you, well, what man doesn't think about that with his wife?"

She smacked his arm and then broke into uncontrollable giggles as he tickled her. Though he never tickled her long, because there was only one thing he liked more than her laughter, at least that is what he had told her, and that was kissing her.

He braced himself above her on his arms and looked down into her flushed face. Her chest rose and fell rapidly as she tried to catch her breath. Jacque looked up into those amazing blue eyes and thought that if she could go to bed every night staring into those eyes, then she would be happy.

"One day, my love, we will have a child and that child will be more loved than any child in history." He leaned down and kissed her gently but had to stop because of her laughter. "What is funny?"

"Fane, every parent feels that way about their child."

"Maybe so, but then those parents aren't Canis lupus. We love on a whole different level."

"Don't I know it," she said breathlessly at the mischievous flash in his eyes.

He leaned down to kiss her again and as Jacque waited for their lips to touch, she felt his weight growing lighter on her, the heat of his body was leaving hers. She opened her eyes and saw that he was fading. "Fane," she called his name, reaching for him desperately. His eyes were sad; as his lips moved, she read the words, "I love you."

Jacque woke with a start as she sat up. Dirt was stuck to her sweaty cheek from where her face had been pressed to the hard ground. She looked around her and remembered where she was—the dark forest-not in her bedroom, not with chocolate strawberries, and not with her mate. Her heart pounded painfully in her chest and she pressed her hand to her chest as if that could take the pain away.

"How are you?" she heard Alina's soft voice a few feet from her. Her mother-in-law looked utterly exhausted. She had been trying not to sleep, worried that the white wolf would return. Jacque hadn't decided if Alina was worried she would miss seeing him because she wanted to see him, or if she was afraid she wouldn't be awake to protect them. Most likely the Alpha was torn between the two emotions.

"The pain is getting worse," Jacque admitted.

Alina's lips tightened into a grim line. "And it will only continue to do so."

Jacque let out a huff of laughter and grimaced from the pain it inflicted. "That's what I love about you; you don't sugar coat it. You simply tell it like it is."

Alina smiled. "I could lie, but then I think you will handle the pain better if you are prepared for it."

"Are you scared of him?" Jacque asked not bothering to point out the *him* she was talking about.

"Yes and no. Seeing him was such a shock, but then there was hope only to be quickly followed by despair. He has been trapped in this place for so very long, Jacque. For him to have been surrounded in this, breathing in the black magic every day, without light in his life, breaks my heart. I don't know how much of him is left."

"You mean how much is salvageable," Jacque said for her. "You think he will have to be killed."

"Yes."

They sat quietly, staring off into the dark woods, watching shadows move that shouldn't be moving, and hearing noises that caused goose bumps to rise on their skin. Gradually, the other women began to wake up and the groans and whimpers from the mated females was just another reminder of their dire situation.

"Any more visitations by Vasile's long lost brother who is probably completely evil and wants to eat us?" Jen asked.

"Jen, really?" Sally said as she cut her eyes to Alina.

"I am not offended, Sally," Alina said. "Jen's evaluation of the situation is correct and I won't delude myself into thinking anything else."

"See," Jen motioned to the Alpha, "at least one of us isn't trying to dance around like some bat sniz crazy woman singing *I Will Survive*, when we all know that the last thing we are going to do is survive."

"Bloody hell, who crapped in your dream?" Jacque growled.

Everyone stopped moving and looked at Jacque who shrugged. "What?"

Jen laughed and then grabbed her stomach as cramps doubled her over. "I like that one wolf-princess," her voice came out strained as she held her stomach. Cynthia knelt down beside her, instructing her to take slow deep breaths. Slowly, the cramps subsided, like they had before, only now they were happening more often.

"To answer your question, Jen," Alina said. "He has not shown himself, but he is watching."

"Okay that sort of creeps me out," Crina said.

"I have to go with the Romanian on this one," Jen agreed, "wolf form or not, I really don't like an audience when I pee, having you all in my bathroom is bad enough."

"I don't know how much of the human is left, if any," Alina told them. "If he has been in his wolf skin all this time, there is little chance that anything human in him remains."

"So, anyone have any good news for the day, or night, or whatever the hell time it is?" Lilly asked. Surprised looks were cast her way as Lilly had been their perpetual positive force. "Hey, don't look at me like that. I still have hope; I'm just going to be pissy while still having hope."

"Pissy hopefulness," Sally said. "I can see that catching on."

"You Americans are so weird," Crina told them as she stood and stretched out her limbs, groaning just as much as the others as the pain pulsed in her muscles.

"So what's the plan?" Jacque asked. "Are we going to sit and stare at the forest on the left side, or are we going to stare at the right side?"

"Well, Jacque, it's a difficult decision because they look so different," Elle joked.

"Yes well, being a captive is hard work, but someone's got to do it."

"Yeah, well could we bloody hell get someone else to volunteer next time?" Jen quipped.

"Shh," Cynthia suddenly said as she waved the others to be quiet. She pointed off to her left and they all turned in slow motion to find the white wolf lying very still, watching them.

Alina stood and walked to the furthest edge of the clearing as she dared. She knelt down and bared her neck to the wolf. When she heard a low rumbled, she sat down and then looked at him.

"Do you remember who you are Lucian?" Alina asked.

"I take it that's his name," Jen whispered.

Sally shushed her as she pulled Jen down to sit next to her. The others followed suit and listened as Alina spoke to the wolf.

"You are a man, not just a wolf. You have family, a brother who has mourned for you. Lucian, blink if you understand me."

They waited with baited breath. When he blinked, there was a collective sigh and then gasps passed through the group.

"Okay, that's a start," she said. "Do you remember who you are?" Blink. "Do you remember your brother, Vasile?" Nothing. "Can you still take your human form?" Blink. Another round of gasps.

"Okay that's a whole 'nother freaking ball game Alina," Cynthia spoke up. Alina held up a finger to silence them.

"Do you mean us harm?" Nothing. "Okay, that's good," she said as relief flooded her voice and body. "Will you talk to us?" Nothing.

Then, as quietly as he had appeared, he got up and left.

Alina stared in the direction he had gone and tears filled her eyes. She had never known Vasile's brother, and yet she felt a strong sense of loss because she knew how it had hurt her mate to lose him. And now he was back, but he didn't remember Vasile.

"Is anyone else just a little freaked out that the wolf just told us he can still phase?" Jacque asked.

"A tad," Sally agreed.

"Maybe a little," Cynthia added.

"Frankly, I'm just glad he doesn't want to snack on us," Jen said.

They didn't know how much time passed before they saw the white wolf again, or Lucian as Alina called him. They were guessing that it had been three or four days, maybe more. They were trying to judge time off their sleeping patterns, but they had determined that the pain from the bonds breaking was making them sleep more. Cynthia said it was a way for the body to deal with the pain, to run away from it. Food kept showing up, but they hadn't seen Reyaz since the first time he had come.

"Maybe he forgot about us," Crina said.

"As much as I don't want to be in the clutches of Reyaz the crazy, if he forgot about us we'd be even more screwed than we are now. Jen don't even think about it," Jacque cut Jen off before she could get a word out. "We would be stuck here with no food and no way to escape." she finished.

Sally looked over at Jen who was rocking back and forth with her lips pressed together. "It's killing you, isn't it?" Jen nodded.

Jacque groaned. "Fine, spit it out you nympho."

"Ugh, thank you! You said *screwed*." Jen pointed at Jacque and giggled.

Jacque's eyes widened as she looked at Jen, then she turned to Sally. "Things are much worse than we realized if that is her only sex remark."

Sally nodded. "I think it's a lack of you know what. She's losing her touch because she doesn't have anything to draw her ideas from."

"Oh, good call, that's a great psychoanalyst of her." Jacque agreed.

Jen frowned. "Okay, so what I'm hearing you two say is that I need to get some."

"Pretty much," Sally nodded.

"This is what you guys are subjected to all the time isn't it?" Lilly asked Alina, Elle, and Crina.

Alina laughed. "It's never boring when they are around."

"When did females begin talking so openly of bedding?" A deep voice shattered the calm moment. The words were choppy as if the owner hadn't spoken in a very long time and he had just had to relearn how to use his lips.

"Lucian," Alina's voice held so many emotions it was hard to tell which one was dominant. She walked towards him, but Elle grabbed her arm, keeping her back when she would have gone closer.

"How do you know me?" he asked. His head cocked to the side in a very wolf like gesture but the furrow of his brow held all the intelligence of a man trying to remember.

Elle stared at the man before them and tried to remember if this is what he had looked like so many years ago. His hair was blonde, which was rare for someone of his descent, although not totally unheard of. He was every bit as tall as Vasile but he was leaner. She imagined that could be attributed to the fact that he had been living in a land that was essentially was dead. His facial structure was very similar to his brothers, but instead of blue eyes, Lucian had silver eyes with a rim of black around the iris. It looked as if someone had taken eye liner and drawn a circle around the silver, capturing it and causing it to jump out at the one who bore the weight of their gaze.

She didn't know what she had been expecting him to wear, nothing at all if she had actually thought about it. He did, however, have on a pair of loose fitting cotton pants. Her head tilted as her mind processed this. If he was wearing a pair of pants that were obviously from this time, someone else was aware of his presence here as well. Elle was still trying to figure out how Lorelle and Reyaz knew about the dark forest. It was not something that anyone was supposed to have been able to remember, and the fact that two supernaturals had, did not bode well for everyone else. Alina's voice drew her attention back to the scene before her.

"I am your brother's mate," she answered.

He stared at her blankly. No emotion crossed his features at the mention of a brother. He seemed to be trying to figure them out, as if they were an complex equation with which he was struggling.

"What does the dark wizard want with you?" he asked her.

Alina blinked several times, confused by his question. "Dark wizard?"

"Yes, the one who brought the fae with him."

"Oh, you mean Reyaz. He isn't a wizard, he's a warlock," she told him. "He wants to kill us."

"Why?"

"Revenge. He wants to kill Cypher's mate because his own mate died and he blames his brother," Cynthia answered.

"Okay, so is anyone else wondering why we're just spilling our guts to this Neanderthal?" Jacque whispered.

"Dude, shut it. This is the most interesting thing to happen since Sally had her dirty dream." Jen said.

"It wasn't a dirty dream," Sally muttered defensively.

"Just keep telling yourself that Sally, whatever makes you feel pure and innocent, but we know the truth."

"Is there anyone searching for you? Do they know you are missing?" Lucien asked.

"Our mates know," Alina answered. "They are probably frantic by now."

"Why did they let you out of their sights?"

"And there it is, the butthead gene that they all share," Jen said without trying to keep her voice down.

"At least they're consistent," Sally commented.

Jen started to reply but once again felt her stomach cramp and nearly fell to the ground. Cynthia caught her and eased her down and the other girls gathered around her protectively. Cynthia pressed on her abdomen to feel which direction the baby was turned and kept the frown to herself when she felt that she was dropping into the birth canal, preparing for delivery.

"What is wrong with her?" Lucian's urgent voice broke through the murmurs and Lilly turned to answer him.

"She is pregnant and getting very close to her due date, and the bond between her and her mate is nearly broken, so she is in a lot of pain. In fact, every mated female here is losing the bond with their mates and are in a lot of pain, though they hide it well."

Lucian continued to look at Jen and the women hovering around her, but he still spoke to Lilly. "Why are you telling me this? Why are you not worried that I will somehow use it against you?"

Lilly looked at him thoughtfully. She took in his bedraggled appearance, and the obvious neglect of his health. His body was so lean, unlike the werewolves she knew. She watched as he looked on at Jen. Worry was written on his brow and the need to do something showed in the way he bounced lightly on the balls of his feet. "You are not a bad man," she finally told him. "You may have been in a bad situation for a very long time, but if you were evil, it would have overtaken you long, long ago."

"I may not be evil, but there is darkness inside of me and where there is no darkness, it is empty, just waiting for the darkness to fill it up."

Lilly was caught off guard by his candidness and a swell of compassion rose in her heart for this man who had been alone for so long in such a desolate place.

When Jen was finally able to sit up and breathe without crying out in pain, they all gathered in a semicircle facing Lucian who sat ten feet away from them. He was still very leery of them, but at the same time it was apparent that he was starved for companionship.

"What happened to you, Lucian," Lilly asked, getting right down to it.

"I volunteered to fight the witches and Volcan, along with some other warrior wolves."

"Why did you survive and no one else?"

"I don't know." He ran his hand through his shaggy hair. The motion looked so unpracticed and new. Many of his movements were that way, like he was relearning how to use his body in his human form.

"Okay," Lilly said calmly, "How have you survived? What have you been eating?"

This time his eyes widened in shock as he looked at the females. "I don't know that either."

"Have you been alone the whole time," Elle asked.

He nodded. "Yes, until Reyaz and the fae showed up, it was only me."

Elle sensed there was something he wasn't telling them. She didn't feel as though he had ill intent towards them, more like he didn't quite trust them yet to bare his soul.

Alina was about to ask him another question but he jumped to his feet, moving so fast they barely saw him. "He's coming," he told them with wide eyes, "he must not know about me." He turned and, just as he had done before, he became one with the darkness of the forest.

"Hello ladies," Reyaz smiled at them, but it was not a happy smile. It was a smile that a child gave to the piece of cake sitting before him covered in thick, rich icing. Needless to say, it was creepy.

"Hello Clarice," Jen whispered in her best Hannibal Lector voice. Sally elbowed her but then whispered. "Silence of the Lambs."

"The hunt will begin soon so I need to get you all in your places. I have set up a nice little game for your males and they are trying to figure out where you are as we speak so that they can begin the hunt. So, Lorelle will do the honors of taking you each to your resting place, no pun intended." He chuckled at himself and it made Sally want to stab him with something very sharp over and over again. The violent thought should have bothered her—*should have*, she thought, *but didn't*.

"Don't worry, you won't be alone. You will go in pairs. That way you will have someone to talk to while you wait."

Lorelle appeared out of nowhere and grabbed Elle and Lilly and then was gone so quickly that it took the others a second to realize what had just happened.

"Mom!" Jacque screamed just as all the others joined her in calling out after Elle and Lilly. She turned to scream at Reyaz, but he too was gone. More quickly than they could have imagined, Lorelle was back and grabbed two more, this time Cynthia and Jen. Next, it was Sally and Crina and last Jacque and Alina. No matter how they tried to hang on to each other, Lorelle pulled them apart and flashed with them before the others could retaliate.

When the clearing where the females had once been was empty, the white wolf stepped out from the forest and stared at the spot. He let out a low growl, then threw his head back and howled like he had done so many times, only this time there was someone to hear.

Chapter 20

"I know that the saying goes that life isn't fair. It's a complete and total given that life isn't fair. I'm just hoping that death is fair; that my *death will be fair. Because for anyone else to die in this place, for this reason, would be less than fair, it would be tragic, and these people have had enough tragedy for one lifetime." ~Unknown*

"Read it again," Cypher said for what seemed like the fiftieth time. As if hearing it *one* more time would suddenly cause an epiphany.

"We all agree that it's a battlefield, right?" Adam spoke up.

"We agreed that sixteen hours ago; quit beating a dead horse," Peri barked. Her fuse was growing shorter and shorter with every hour. "We only have eight hours until this *hunt* starts."

After everyone had returned from their separate fact-finding missions, they had reconvened only to discover that they had all come to the same conclusion about the type of place of which the riddle spoke. They had yet to figure out where exactly that place was located or how they would get there.

Fane, Skender, and Sorin had returned with the troll king, though it was not by their choice. He had demanded to see Perizada and insisted that he help in any way he could. Peri had been surprised and touched by the troll's out-of-character offer. The pixie king had also joined them, though that was because he couldn't get away from Peri fast enough. He did seem to be a little calmer when she explained that there were no pirates involved. Why pirates were what scared the pixie, she had no idea, and she didn't care to ask because she had way more important things to wonder about.

Sorin ignored the two fae and did as Cypher requested and read the riddle again. They all listened as if it were the first time they had heard it and then went to murmuring and guessing all over again.

"What does the reference to 'two faces yet one soul' mean?" Alston asked out loud, though he spoke to no one in particular.

"A werewolf," Vasile said as he growled, "how did I not see that. It's a wolf; two faces - the man's and the wolf's - but one soul."

Murmurs of agreement and growls of irritation of not seeing it sooner cascaded across the group.

"Okay, so we have a battlefield that has only seen a werewolf for many years. We are really breaking it down people," Fane said dryly. "I think we just might have this thing figured out by next year." Fane slammed his hand down on one of the tables and bit back a snarl.

"Fane!" Vasile shouted. "Enough! We are all just as frustrated as you are, but this," he motioned up and down to his son, "is not helping."

Fane met his father's gaze for a count of three heartbeats but then dropped it. He bowed his head as he leaned back against the wall. His shoulders were tense and his fists were clenched at his sides, but he managed to pull himself under control, barely. Vasile gave him a stern look before looking at Alston.

"Did that help at all?" he asked the fae in regards to his questions about the two faces and one soul.

Alston rubbed his chin absently as he considered Vasile's words. "Maybe," he answered. He looked at Peri and then said, "I need you to come with me."

"Where?" "Why?" Peri and Vasile asked at the same time.

"I have a hunch, but before I say it out loud I need to verify it," he explained.

Peri shook her head. "Wait a minute. You think this place is something that is so evil you aren't even willing to speak of it out loud?"

"I don't know, Perizada. That is why I need you to come with me." He turned back to Vasile. "We will be quick."

Vasile's jaw tensed but he nodded as he watched the two fae disappeared.

"What do you know that you don't want the wolves to know?" Peri asked as soon as she and Alston arrived in the room of the high fae council. "Not to mention the fact that you don't want to speak with the other members of the council about it."

"You know as well as I do, Peri, that some things should not be spoken about. And when they must, it should be with as few ears listening as possible."

Peri waited as he walked over to a large door, one that wasn't opened very often. Her eyes widened as he pressed his palm to the door and muttered words only the high fae knew. The door vanished. Alston turned back to look at her; his eyes were wide with fear. Peri had only seen Alston fearful a handful of times in their long lives, and she had to say, it wasn't a good look on him.

"We need to remember," he told her.

Peri frowned. "Remember what?"

"To know me is impossible, unless the wall is destroyed." The words of the riddle flowed from his lips and seemed to reverberate off the walls.

"You think the wall being destroyed is figurative?" Peri asked.

Alston nodded. "The words have been haunting me since I heard them, chipping away at my mind, almost like trying to scratch an itch I can't reach."

"And you decided the appropriate back scratcher is in our records?" she asked him only half joking.

Alston frowned. "You've gotten cranky in your old age."

"First off, I'm not old. And second, I have always been cranky. Now what wall is it that you think needs to be figuratively destroyed?"

He tapped his head. "A wall we ourselves devised and built."

"No way," Peri's voice lowered as though someone might hear, though they were the only ones in the room. "You think the riddle is referring to a block we put up?"

"Yes. I'm actually pretty positive."

"How?"

"I wrote the spell that those exact words are in, the spell that we all cast and weren't ever supposed to remember."

"I told you that memory spells are never a good idea," she scolded. "They always come back to bite you on the ass. This time it just happens to be in the form of an unhinged warlock."

"What do you think he knows?" Fane asked Decebel.

"Who knows? The fae are as notorious for their secrets as they are for their power. All I care about is that, whatever it is, it will get us where we need to be. He had better decide to share."

Fane's eyes narrowed. "Peri wouldn't allow him to keep anything from us that would help us find our mates."

Decebel shrugged. "I would like to think not. But right now all I can really think about is Jennifer and how she needs me and…," Decebel bit back a snarl of frustration.

"And you need her," Fane finished for him. "We will get them back Decebel. If we have to tear every realm apart in order to do so, we will get them back."

"I agree with young blood," Costin said as he walked over to the corner that Fane and Decebel occupied. "The world may wind up being drenched in blood, but we will find our females, and anyone in our way will die."

"Who are we killing?" Adam asked as he tossed one of his knives over and over in the air.

"No one," Vasile growled and at the same time Decebel snarled, "everyone."

Adam looked between the two Alphas. "Does that mean I get to kill half as many as planned, or twice as many?"

"Anything?" Peri asked Alston again.

"I told you that as soon as I found it I would tell you."

"Well time is growing short," she huffed. "The hunt begins in two hours. How will you know you have found it if you don't remember what it is you're looking for?"

"I'm not certain, but I think that there was sort of a key in the spell itself so that once a person started remembering bits and pieces of what it is they were supposed to forget, all of it would come back to them, given the correct trigger."

"I'm guessing you're not talking about the kind of trigger I could pull," she said dryly.

"You know exactly what kind of trigger I'm talking about." Alston looked up from the book in his hands and peered at Peri thoughtfully. "You really do care about these girls, don't you?"

She shrugged non-committedly. "They're like a fungus; they grow on you."

"Yes, but a fungus is something you try to get rid of, not something you rescue when it's been taken."

"If it's a mushroom and you really like mushrooms, then it most certainly is something you would try to get back."

"Whatever you say, Peri," he told her as he started flipping through the book again.

Several minutes passed in relative silence as Alston searched books and Peri stood wondering what it could have been that they had blocked from everyone's memories, including their own. What could have been so horrible that they didn't want anyone in any species to remember?

"The dark forest." Alston's words couldn't have struck any deeper if they had been attached to a harpoon and shot straight into Peri's soul.

"What did you say?" she asked. Though her voice sounded calm, she was anything but.

"The dark forest: Volcan, witches, wolves, death." Alston's words seemed to ring loudly in the quiet, still room.

Peri stumbled and caught herself on the wall. "Holy hell," she muttered.

"We need to hurry," Alston stood up, not bothering to put any of the books back on the shelves. He started to push past Peri and when he noticed that she wasn't following, he turned and looked back at her. "Peri, we need to hurry; we need to get Vasile and the wolves to the dark forest."

Peri's eyes had grown large and held the haunted look in them of someone who had seen too many shadows in their life. "When he remembers, he is, he will..." When her eyes met Alston's they were wet with unshed tears.

Alston nodded. "He will hurt, and the wound will feel brand new."

"Why does this seem too easy?" Jacque asked Alina as she walked slowly around the forest where Lorelle had dropped them, literally, on their asses. Alina had let an uncharacteristic cuss word slip, causing Jacque to laugh, which earned her yet another cuss word.

"Because it is," Alina answered. "Lorelle is fae; she will have something up her sleeve."

"Magic?" Jacque asked.

"Exactly. Vasile will not underestimate her," Alina spoke confidently of her mate.

Jacque wished she shared that confidence, but all she could think was that by the time the males found them, they would be frantic and probably not thinking very clearly. But instead of pointing that out she asked a question, "Do you think the others are in similar situations?"

"Probably," she answered. "He's set this up as a hunt, so he isn't going to want them giving away their location by crying out in pain," she paused thoughtfully then finished. "Then again, he could have some spell keeping any noise from escaping."

"That's not helping, Alina," Jacque growled.

"Then let's just go with their situations are probably the same."

"Sally," Crina's voice broke through the fog covered air, "are you okay?"

"I'm good," Sally answered as she stood from the ground and brushed the dirt from her palms where she had caught herself after being tossed by Lorelle. "How about you?" Sally asked.

"Say something again."

"Something again?" Sally's words came out as a question as she waited for Crina's response. She nearly jumped out of her skin when she felt a hand close around her shoulder. "Bloody hell, Crina." Sally grasped at her chest and swallowed down the scream that had nearly clawed its way out of her throat. "Give a girl warning before you just reach out of the fog and grab her, okay?"

Crina's face emerged from the haze and frowned. "I told you to say something so that I would know where you were since I couldn't see you."

"But you didn't say, 'hey Sally, I'm going to grab your arm and scare the crap out of you'," Sally pointed out.

"Okay, next time I will make sure to tell you that I am going to scare the crap out of you." Crina smiled a toothy wolf smile.

Sally rolled her eyes. "My inner Jen wants me to call you a smartass."

"What does your outer Sally want to call me?"

"A bitch," the word slipped from Sally as easy as butter slips from the hand and Crina laughed out loud.

"Then you'd both be right." Crina winked at the now blushing Sally then looked around. Fog surrounded them on all sides and kept them from seeing further than a foot in front of them. There were no other sounds than that of their own breathing.

"Do you think she meant to just leave us free like this?" Sally asked.

"I definitely think she meant to leave us like this, but I think we are anything but free."

🐾 🐾

"Elle, give it to me straight, on a scale of one to screwed, how bad is it?" Lilly asked the fae as they stood as far from the ledge of the cliff as they could.

"Considering that there isn't a cliff in the dark forest, and we are standing on a very obvious cliff, then I'd say we're pretty screwed," Elle told her as she stuck her head far enough out to see down. It was a very long way down.

"Well, I'll be honest, that's not what I was hoping to hear. But at least you were honest with me."

"It could be worse," Elle admitted.

Lilly looked hopeful. "It could?"

Elle nodded. "We could be in the hands of a revenge crazed warlock, hell bent on killing his brother's mate, and you could be his brother's mate, oh wait…" she paused and looked at Lilly with a sly smile.

"Ha, ha," Lilly said dryly.

"You have to make your mind believe that what you're seeing isn't real," Elle said suddenly serious. "That's how we are going to survive this."

Lilly nodded, now every bit as sober as the fae. "Okay, it isn't real, it isn't real," she began repeating over and over.

"Lilly?"

"Huh, what?" Lilly asked absently as she continued to repeat her mantra.

"Does it help to tell yourself out loud that it isn't real?" Elle looked at her quizzically.

Lilly let out a huff of laughter. "Yeah, don't you know that trick? Tell yourself something enough times and it makes it true."

"If it gets us off this cliff then I'm all for it."

Lilly frowned. "What do you mean if it gets us off here? You know it isn't real."

"Yes, but Lorelle is smart, and the only way we are going to get off this cliff alive is for anyone seeing it to believe it to be false."

"Son of a… Crap!"

"Exactly."

"Did she seriously just drop us in a cave?" Jen asked as she stood at the mouth of the cave.

"Looks that way," Cynthia's words faded off and Jen turned to look at her to see what had caught her attention.

"What is all of that?" Jen asked.

Cynthia began opening the boxes. The first contained blankets, the next water, and the next surgical instruments. There was one box left and it was smaller than the others. Cynthia's hand hovered over it and something inside her did not want to open it. In fact, it was screaming at her to run the other direction, but there was nowhere to run. Cynthia knew with a certainty that she couldn't explain that they could not leave. The opening of the cave may look like they could walk away at any second but she knew better. They were stuck in this cave until someone came for them. She just hoped they made it until the *right* someone came.

She finally lifted the lid on the final box and found a birth announcement. The paper shook in her hand as she held it and her mouth suddenly felt as dry as a barren desert.

"Doc?" Jen's voice was in the back of her mind, but all she could focus on was that folded piece of paper. She gingerly unfolded it and stared at the print on the inside. She read it several times, hoping that it would change and that the words on it would suddenly be wiped clean.

"The date, Jen, what's the date?" Cynthia asked.

"Crap, I don't know. If we're talking dark kingdom of fae then I'm thinking late August or early September, but human realm, it's like June. Why?"

Cynthia swore under her breath as she read the paper again. *Congratulations, Jennifer and Decebel, on the birth of your baby girl on this 30th day of August.*

"Um, Cynthia what the hell?" Jen said from over her shoulder. She plucked the paper from her hand and stood up, reading it with eyes that were as wide and worried as the doctor's. "What does this mean?"

Jen looked over at Cynthia only to see that she was holding another piece of paper. "Crap, what does that one say, that he's throwing me a baby shower?"

Cynthia's eyes rose slowly from the paper to meet Jens. She shook her head. "No, it...," she stopped and tried to look away from Jen.

"No," Jen snapped her fingers, "You look at me when you tell me horrific news; now spit it out."

"It says that, it..."

"Read it, Doc," Jen growled.

Cynthia cleared her throat before starting, dread building in her stomach over the words she was about to force out. *"Dr. Cynthia*

Steele, Once you see the hunting party in your line of site out of the mouth of the cave, you are to perform a Cesarean section on Jennifer, mate to Decebel. I have given you all of the necessary medical supplies to perform this safely, though perhaps not painlessly. You are to have Jennifer lie on the X marked on the ground. Once the child is born, you are to turn sixty degrees and take two steps with the child held out in front of you. You are to make sure your body is parallel with the wall so that Decebel has a clear view of his child."

Jen stood speechless staring at Cynthia, unsure of what to say. She had just been told she was going to be gutted like a fish and have her child handed over to a mad man while she and Decebel watch helplessly.

"Can't we try to escape?" Jen asked, suddenly very desperate. She pointed to the opening of the cave.

Cynthia shook her head, "If I were a betting doctor, I would say it's spelled to look as though we can walk out or anyone can walk in. I'll double check though, just so that we aren't the idiots who trapped themselves because they didn't bother to attempt to run away."

"Please do, because of all the blonde idiots on T.V., I don't want to be the one in the horror shows who gets killed first because she's too stupid to run," Jen told her as she tried to shake off the terror that was threatening to suffocate her. She wasn't ready for her child to be born. It was too soon. They hadn't found a way to save her and now she was going to be brought cruelly into the world only to be taken out of it before Decebel could even hold her.

"ARRRRRRGGGGHHH!" Jen screamed. "She's just a baby! I just need to kill something! But there's only you," Jen pointed wildly at Cynthia, "and dammit I need you to deliver Cosmina."

"Glad to know that I'm unavailable for your hit list based on my credentials," Cynthia said as she returned back from her unsuccessful attempt to leave the cave.

"Yeah, well just be glad that I'm, for all intents and purposes, a nice person who usually doesn't just kill people because she's ticked off."

"Oh believe me, I'm glad," Cynthia pointed to her face. "See, this is me being glad."

Jen flipped her off as she pulled up a box to sit on, lowering her aching pregnant body to it slowly. "I'm just saying."

"I know Jen. I don't like this any more than you do."

"What if we don't do what he says?" Jen asked.

"I don't have a clue. He might start killing the males while we have to helplessly watch."

"Damn this sucks."

"Understatement."

Chapter 21
"To be powerful and yet utterly helpless to save the one person in your life that you would do anything to protect is the worst kind of hell." ~Fane

"We have bad news and we have worse news," Peri said as she and Alston appeared back in the Romanian pack mansion.

"We only have thirty minutes left. At this point, the only bad news is no news," Fane said.

"Good point," Peri conceded. "We know where he is keeping the girls."

"Where?" Decebel snapped as he stepped away from the wall where he had been silently brooding.

Peri's eyes cut to where Vasile stood. Her heart broke for the Alpha knowing that what she was about to tell him would not mean anything for at least a few seconds and then the memories would all come rushing back and so would the guilt. She especially was to blame and she dreaded seeing the accusations and betrayal that she knew would stare out at her from his piercing blue eyes.

"The dark forest in the fae realm," she blurted out not taking her eyes from Vasile's.

"Where?" Costin asked obviously as confused as the rest of them.

Adam was the first to remember. "No," he whispered in utter horror. "How does he even know if it? How did he remember it?" Adam realized then that Peri and Alston shouldn't have remembered it either.

"Archives," Alston answered Adam's unasked question. "We made sure it was documented before we set the spell for everyone to forget. We should always be able to remember our past. We must learn from it or be doomed to repeat it."

"Why on earth would you think it was your right to take away a memory from the rest of us?" Vasile asked as his own memories resurfaced along with anger. "Those memories, those painful times that happened to each of us, are ours. You aren't God to have the right to play with our free will."

"We didn't want anyone to be able to return to the dark forest, Vasile. That land is tainted with so much evil; the power left over is enough to cause some serious danger." Alston said as he tried to justify what they had done.

"And how did that work out for you?" Fane asked. "Did taking away the memory of that place make it cease to exist? Did it protect it from evil people using it?"

"For centuries, yes, it did," Peri snarled.

"Stop!" Cypher yelled, "We don't have time for your anger and explanations. We have twenty minutes to get to this dark forest and time is ticking. Peri, can you flash us there?"

"Yes."

"Now, who is with me?" Cypher glanced from person to person waiting.

"I will stand with you," Vasile said immediately.

"I will also." Decebel stepped forward.

"You know I'm in." Costin smiled wickedly.

"It goes without saying, I will stand with you," Fane said.

"I will stand with you," Ainsel squeaked. He looked at their surprised faces. "I've been stupid in the past, choosing the wrong side, I won't make that mistake again."

"I will go," Thead said next.

"I will stand with you and be honored to fight alongside you," Thalion spoke up and Cyn stood next to him.

"I will always stand on the side of good," Sorin spoke up.

"I go where my Alpha and pack mates go," Skender said.

"The council will always stand with the wolves," Alston looked at Cypher. "And now also with the warlocks."

"You know I'm going because you fools wouldn't last a minute without me," Peri told them.

Cypher faced the group willing to stand up to his corrupt brother and felt pride and loyalty swell in his chest. "No matter how many enemies we fight, no matter how many times we prevail, evil will always exist in this world and our own worlds, because there will always be some who choose to put themselves before everyone and anyone. But just like evil, there will always be good, as well. There will always be some who will seek justice and desire to see all beings free to live in a world not corrupted by malice. We will always be a part of those who stand on the side of righteousness. We must because we hold too much power to ever let it be used to harm others. When darkness falls as it has today, we must stand. We must stand for those who cannot and for those who would stand with us if they knew the battle before us. Not too long ago we fought for the packs. We fought for unity and for healing. We fought to protect the world from an ancient evil. Today we fight to bring back the ones who bring light to our dark lives. Today we will prevail. There is no other acceptable outcome. Stand with me and together we will bring back the females who have given us life when we were all so close to death."

Vasile reached forward and clasped forearms with Cypher. "We will prevail."

"I completely appreciate the Braveheart moment, and utterly hate that we do not have blue war paint to put on our faces, but we must go, NOW." Peri reached out both of her arms. "All those who can, hold onto my arms; the rest of you grab Alston, Adam, or Cyn."

One by one, the fae left with members of their party attached to their arms. Now that the dark forest was once again clear in their minds, the fae would have no problems flashing there. Whether they flashed anywhere close to where Reyaz wanted them was a different story.

"Do you sense them anywhere?" Reyaz asked Lorelle as the stood in the forest waiting for Cypher and the wolves to show up. They had less than five minutes before the hunt was to begin and he was anxious for them to get started.

Lorelle turned her head to the right and tilted it as if listening for something. "Gotchya," she murmured. Without another word, she grabbed Reyazs' arm, though she loathed touching him, and flashed to where she had felt her sister just arrive.

They appeared directly in the center of the group. Reyaz smiled as he looked around at the grim faces. "So glad you were able to make it on time."

Decebel's head snapped up at the sound of the voice and he lunged forward with a growl that promised death.

"Save your energy, Alpha," Reyaz huffed as he flicked his hand at Decebel and pushed him to the ground. "You will have your time to throw a fit and act like the furry beast that you are."

"We're here, brother. Get on with your games," Cypher spoke up.

"How long has it been, brother?" Reyaz asked regally. "How long since you betrayed me?"

Cypher shook his head. "I did nothing of the sort and we have been over this a hundred times, so unless you have a new argument let's not rehash. Let us just get on with this hunt so that we can save our females."

Reyaz frowned, unhappy about Cypher's unwillingness to engage in the argument. "Fine. It is good that you brought the wolves; their noses will come in handy. You will not hear your mates because of the spell that I have put on them. Once you have found the first two females you will not be able to move on until you have rescued one of them. You needn't wonder when the hunt will be concluded. I have a wonderful grand finale planned." His eyes landed on Decebel and the Alpha visibly tensed.

Peri looked at her sister and for an instant her heart ached for her, but then she remembered all the terrible things she had done. "How did you remember the forest?"

"Reyaz needed a place for his hunt, so I did some searching in the archives. You can only imagine my surprise when I ran across this little tidbit. I couldn't believe how well that spell had worked. None of us remembered in the slightest about this place." She turned to Vasile then and a knowing smile appeared. "There is a surprise here that I think you most of all will appreciate."

"Happy hunting," Reyaz said and then he and Lorelle were gone.

"Am I the only one who wants to see that mofo's head on a spike?" Peri grumbled.

"I'll cut it off, if you'll hold him down," Adam said.

Peri smiled at him and then turned to Vasile, "Do your wolf thing and sniff out our girls."

"Keep your eyes open and pay attention. There is no telling what Reyaz might have planned for us," Vasile told the group.

"I suggest we stay in our human forms if at all possible," Decebel added.

Vasile nodded his agreement. Then without another word, he headed off into the forest. It was Fane who picked up the first scent. He let out a low growl and his eyes began to glow wolf blue. "Jacquelyn," his voice rumbled as he spoke her name.

"Which way Fane," Vasile asked.

Fane pointed and then took off at a dead sprint.

"Crap," Peri yelled. "Didn't someone warn the crazy wolf about running off halfcocked into a freaking dark forest?"

They all took off after Fane. Decebel motioned for them to spread out.

Fane felt his gut tighten as he ran. He could smell her and it broke something inside of him. It had been so long since he'd seen her and so long since he'd held her, and he was desperate for the sight of her. His legs pushed hard and his arms pumped at his side. He felt the warm wind on his face and the sting of branches as they whipped at his skin as he flew past. He welcomed the pain of the slapping branches because it proved to him that he was alive. When he saw her standing there surrounded by trees, hair wild, and skin flushed, he could have sworn that he had died. She was alive and in one piece!

"Jacquelyn!" He bellowed and felt his chest tighten with emotions so strong they threatened to crush him under their weight. He watched as her head turned and her eyes met his. Her face lit into a smile and it was so beautiful, so heart stoppingly beautiful that he just wanted to bask in its glory. She started towards him but then something caught her eye because she turned her head and he saw her eyes widen with fear. When she looked back at him she started shaking her head frantically. She flung her arms at him telling him to go back but there was no way in hell he was leaving now that he'd found her.

Jacque couldn't believe what she was seeing. First she had been shocked to see Fane, and then she saw the others running with him and knowing they were rescued had been enough to nearly have her jumping up and down doing some wild, crazy, soul bearing dance, but then she had seen something that made her heart stop.

She didn't know how to describe them, but *zombies* was the first word to come to mind. Their skin was pale and bluish, tinged as if they had been deprived of oxygen, for like, ever. Their eyes were glassy and lined with red blood vessels. The only thing that differed from their T.V. counterparts was that these zombies were not stiff and sluggish. These zombies were swift and precise in their attack, which Jacque took to mean that they were definitely being controlled and that dark magic was involved. They looked like the dead brought to life, and as stupid as that sounded, she was a freaking werewolf so, really, how far of a stretch was it for zombies to be real? There were hundreds of them, maybe even more. Her eyes flew to the group of men running towards them hell bent on saving them and she didn't see how they could defeat such a huge army. She started waving at them to turn back but it just made them run faster: damn stubborn werewolves, and fae, and warlocks, and *what the crap* she thought as she saw the pixie king jumping from tree to tree like Tarzan. She also saw another male that she recognized as a troll, though she didn't know who he was since she'd only met one troll so far in her, what appeared to be, short life.

She turned to tell Alina to help her and her eyes widened as she saw Lorelle standing off to the side with Alina. Lorelle was speaking calmly to Alina and no matter how hard Jacque tried to listen, she couldn't hear a thing. She watched as Alina's eyes went cold and her jaw tensed as Lorelle handed her something wrapped up in a cloth. Alina slipped it into the back of her pants under her shirt. She gave Lorelle one last look before she turned to Jacque and started walking towards her.

"What was that about?" Jacque asked her. She started to ask her about whatever it was that Lorelle had handed her but then decided if Alina wanted her to know then she would tell her.

Alina's eyes locked onto the scene beyond Jacque as she answered, "Just Lorelle being Lorelle."

"A bitch?" Jacque growled.

"Jacque, *we're* female wolves; let's not give her such a compliment."

Jacque felt the grin spread across her face. Man, she had the coolest mother-in-law.

"Now, shall we go help our men?" Alina motioned towards the males who were now in battle with the zombies.

"I've been itching for a good fight," Jacque said as she popped her knuckles.

"Looks like we've got one."

They both took off at a run. Just when they had nearly reached the battle and were about to phase, they both bounced off an invisible barrier with a thud. Jacque fell back and landed hard on her butt. Her teeth jarred together as she stiffened her neck to keep her head from slinging back and crashing into the hard ground.

"DAMMIT!" she screamed as she slammed her hand onto the ground. Anger flooded her veins as she saw her mate fight off the zombie looking creatures and all she could do was watch.

Vasile saw Alina running towards him and then hit a barrier like the one he had seen Peri use. She fell back, but then quickly stood to her feet so he knew she was alright. He turned his head away just in time to duck as one of the creatures swung out an arm. In its grasp, a wicked dagger suddenly appeared. Vasile could smell the black magic rolling off of the creatures and he had to fight back the nausea. In his long life he had never seen creatures such as these, but much was possible when dealing with ancient dark magic, such as that found in this forest. And all of it was destructive and evil. He and the others continued to fight the creatures. One after another realizing that severing their spinal columns seemed to be the quickest way to keep them down.

Jacque stood next to Alina, rocking from side to side on the balls of her feet. She was itching to get in there and hit a few of those nasty looking zombies, but instead she settled for yelling instructions at the males, as if they needed it.

"Costin, behind you, turn around, turn around now!" she yelled at the top of her lungs. She watched in awe as he spun around with the grace of a dancer ducking at the same time and landing a blow to the being's stomach. When it doubled over, Costin grabbed its head and twisted, snapping it with no effort at all. The zombie fell to the ground. Costin turned and looked at her, giving her one of his dimple grins and a thumbs up. He jumped back into the fray and Jacque turned her attention back to Fane. He was in battle with two of the zombies, both wielding wicked looking knives. She noticed that Fane's claws had lengthened and looked every bit as deadly as the knives. He swung around and his claws ripped across the face of one of the creatures. Then he whipped back around the other direction, making the same slashes across the second of his enemies. He danced back from their blades and then closed in again. Instead of blood running down from the wounds, the zombies oozed a black liquid that reminded Jacque of old motor oil. She cringed as some of the liquid splashed onto Fane as he got in another quick slash. She had a feeling he was toying with the things, expelling some pent up aggression. "Finish them Fane and move on!" she hollered at him. She saw a quirk of his lips that told her he found her amusing. *Butthead* she thought and then felt a pang of frustration over the fact that he couldn't hear her thoughts. She watched as he deftly relieved one of the zombies of its weapon and then used it to behead them both.

Jacque threw a fist in the air with a whoop, "That's my man!" Fane moved on to the next opponent and, one after another, he slaughtered them. But where one fell, another took its place.

Out of the corner of her eye she saw a flash of light. When she turned, she saw Peri flinging out her power, one shot after another, taking out creature after creature. Alston, Adam, and Cyn were all doing the same thing. She looked up and saw Thalion, the elf prince, shoot arrows so quickly that she didn't even see when he reached for the next one. He hit the zombies one after another with such precision that one creature fell for each arrow he loosed. Jacque just knew that at any second they would get the upper hand. At any second, they would defeat the evil beings and she and Alina would be rescued and free to move forward with the males to find the other girls. But she was a fool to think it because out of the forest more and more zombies arrived.

"What the hell! Someone throw them a bone, jeez," she snarled. She looked over at Alina who looked every bit as concerned as she felt.

Alina's eyes never left the man who held her heart, her mate who was fighting with everything he had to save her, and yet she knew it was in vain. Reyaz had made sure of it. She wanted to run into his arms to tell him how much she loved him, how amazing he was, and how she treasured every single moment of their time together. As if he heard her, he turned and looked at her. His eyes pierced her heart just as they had the first time he had ever looked at her all those decades ago. She pleaded with her eyes for him to understand and begged him to not be angry with her because she didn't know what other option she had. She wouldn't stand there and let her mate, or the others she considered hers, die. She wouldn't let the life Jacque and Fane deserved be taken from them at so young an age, not when she had the power to stop it.

She reached behind her and pulled the wrapped object from under her shirt. Her hands trembled as she held it and began unwrapping it. When the fabric fell to the ground, all that was left in her hand was a long, deadly dagger. She looked up and again her eyes met her mate's. His eyes widened as they glanced down to what she held and then back up to her face. He saw it then, and saw the determination in her to do what was necessary. She heard Jacque's voice from beside her but didn't look away from Vasile.

"I love you," she whispered. She watched her name form on his lips and thought of all the times he had said her name, and of all the times he had caressed her face and stared into her eyes and made her feel like the most beautiful woman on earth. He began running towards her, pushing past anything that got in his way. She heard his roar and felt his power and it gave her the strength to do what she had to. Lorelle's words ran through her mind as she grasped the dagger firmly in her hands and held it above her heart.

"A sacrifice must be made. One of you must willingly give yourself for the life of the other. A life for a life, it is your choice. But the battle will continue until the last of your hunting party falls or until the sacrifice is given."

With one final look at her mate she raised the dagger higher and then plunged it into her heart. She felt the dark magic dissipate and the barrier drop. She felt his arms around her as she fell to the ground and heard his voice in her ear as he begged her not to leave him. He loved her, he said over and over, and he needed her. He was so strong and he didn't even know it. She tried to move her lips to tell him, but she couldn't. Her long life was over and she hoped that those she loved would be safe now. With that thought she let go and let the darkness of death take her.

Chapter 22

"From the night I took her as my mate, marked her and made her mine, I believed that when she left this world, I would go with her. I found peace in that because I knew that I didn't want to live a life without her, didn't want to experience anything life had to offer without her by my side. And yet here she is in my arms, no breath in her body, and still my heart beats." ~Vasile

Vasile held his mate's lifeless body. He clutched her to him desperately as he tried to come to terms with what he had just watched. She was gone. She had been standing there looking at him with such longing it had hurt, and then he had seen in her eyes the need to protect, and he had known what she was going to do. He had tried to get to her first, intent on begging her to stop, but he knew there would have been nothing he could have said. He was too wrapped up in his grief to notice that it was silent around him. The battle was over and had been over the second Alina had taken her own life. He leaned down and gently kissed her still warm lips and her scent wrapped around him like a loving embrace, and though his heart still beat, he swore he felt it shatter into a million pieces. He threw his head back and howled. He poured his grief and pain into it and fought to keep it from swallowing him whole. He knew he still had to fight, the other females needed him, though all he wanted to do was curl up around his mate and join her in death, and he would, soon.

Fane ran to Jacque and grabbed her, pulling her to his chest. He was sure he was crushing her, but he needed to feel her, needed to know she was still alive. He pulled back and kissed her roughly and then backed up, grabbing her hand and pulling her over to where his father held his mother. He knelt down next to them and leaned down to kiss Alina on the forehead. The heartache in his father's howl broke his own heart, and seeing his mother lying there, pale with death, made him throw his own head back, and one by one the other wolves joined him and his father's cry for justice.

As the howls subsided, Fane gave his mother a final kiss and then stood. He turned to look at Jacque. "I love you; I love you," he told her over and over again as he pressed his forehead to hers.

Tears filled her eyes as she glanced down to his mother and then back to him. It broke his heart all over again. He pulled her tight against him. "It will be alright," he murmured. He felt her shake her head against him.

"No, Fane it won't. Not this time. I love you, and I am so freaking glad to see you, and I'm so, so sorry." He felt her body shudder against his as her tears began to fall and she pulled tighter against him.

"Vasile, we must move," Decebel told his friend gently.

Vasile let out a warning growl.

"We will come back for her. We will not leave her, but we have to get the others," he told him.

Vasile looked down at his mate. He knew she would want him to go and would expect him to go help, but he didn't want to leave her. He felt someone watching him and looked out into the forest. Twenty feet away sat a white wolf, a wolf he knew. His mouth felt dry as he stared into the eyes of his brother, a brother who was supposed to have died in this very forest centuries ago. Vasile realized that seeing his Mina die must have shattered his hold on reality. He knew it must be some sort of delusion, a need to know that someone would be watching over his mate while he was away, until he could come back for her for the final time. "You will keep her safe," he told the wolf. "You will protect her for me, brother, until I can come back for her." The wolf bowed his head to him and Vasile knew he would do as he asked; he would protect the body of his beloved, and he would be forever grateful to this ghost of his brother.

He gave Alina a final kiss on the lips and pulled her close. "I will be back for you, and then I will join with you, as it should be." He laid her down gently and watched as the white wolf walked slowly towards him. The others watched the wolf warily and, had Vasile been in his right mind, it might have seemed odd to him that they could see his delusion, but as it was, he couldn't care less. The wolf, which looked just like his brother's wolf, lay down next to Alina and placed his huge head gently down next to her own. He let out a small whine and scooted his large body closer to hers and Vasile felt something ease inside of him.

"Let's go," he growled. He looked into the forest and saw that Peri, Sorin, and Skender were already running, obviously already having picked up on a scent. With a last look at his mate's body, he too turned and took off into the forest.

Costin looked over at Sorin. "Smell them?"

Sorin nodded then looked at Adam. "Your mate and Sally," he told the fae who didn't have the nose of a wolf.

Adam's shoulders tensed and his eyes began to scan the distance. "Which way?" he asked.

Costin pointed to the right of them and then took off again. Suddenly Peri screamed. "STOP!" Everyone came to a jarring halt just at the edge of a dark fog that weaved its way into the forest ahead of them.

"What is that?" Jacque asked.

"Evil," Skender said in answer.

"Whatever it is, Sally is on the other side of it, so I'm getting through it one way or another," Costin said as he paced back and forth in front of the line of fog.

"Okay, before we go into this freaky fog, can I please address the elephant in the forest?" Peri spoke up. "Did anyone else notice how the zombies back there all collapsed after Alina made the sacrifice?"

"Sacrifice?" Vasile snarled.

"Stand down wolf," Peri warned. "I mean no disrespect to your grief but I believe this is important. As soon as Alina took her life, the battle ended."

"Reyaz said that we would only be able to save one of them," Thalion said.

"Bloody hell," Jacque whispered, "he expects them to sacrifice themselves."

Costin cursed and took off into the fog.

"Dammit, what is with you damn wolves running off after I've specifically said to stop!" Peri snapped as she too took off into the fog. Without thought, everyone else ran right behind them.

Sally stood, staring off into the fog. She could feel something was coming and her stomach felt as if it was going to climb up out of her throat. Her hands shook at her side and her palms were damp with sweat. She wanted to be brave; she needed to be brave, and if she had to call on her inner Jen to do so, then that's what she would do.

"Sally, are you alright?" Crina asked quietly.

Sally nodded. "Do you feel it?"

"Yes, they're coming," Crina agreed.

"What do you think is going to happen?"

Crina shrugged. "I don't know, but whatever it is we will get out of it together. Our mates and Peri can kick some major ass. It's going to be okay."

Sally smiled. "I'm supposed to be the encouraging one, being the gypsy healer and all."

Crina laughed. "It's okay to let other people encourage you every now and then."

They both looked back out into the fog and watched as it gradually began to recede and slowly reveal the forest, and their pack, as well as a few extras.

"Sally!" Costin's voice broke through her surprise and her eyes filled with tears at the sight of him. He ran towards her and was a mere two feet from her when he was brought up short, frozen in place.

"Costin!" Sally tried to move towards him but she couldn't get any closer. She could walk side to side, but no matter how hard she tried to walk forward she was met with resistance that she couldn't fight.

Suddenly laughter filled the air around them as each member of the hunting party suddenly began grasping at their throats. Wheezing and gasping filled the air as Sally and Crina looked on in horror.

"STOP! Please STOP!" Sally sobbed.

"You know what must be done," the voice that had been laughing told her.

And just as quickly as the group had started choking, they stopped. Costin bent forward trying to pull air into his lungs, as did the others.

Peri looked at Sally sternly. "Don't even think about it."

The tears in Sally's eyes began to fall as she reached into her pocket and pulled out a little blue pill. She looked up at everyone and then back at the pill.

"SALLY!" Peri snarled. "Don't you dare! We will figure this out."

Sally's head shook back and forth as she looked at Costin. "He will kill you all and make us stand here and watch. The things he said he would do, they're horrible."

"Sally, you have to trust me," Costin pleaded.

"Healer, listen to your wolf," Peri told her as she finally stood up, able to breathe again. "We can totally kick this guy's—," before she could get out the words, Peri was on the ground, screaming in pain. Sally let out a squeak of horror as she watched the fae grip her head. Blood began to pour from her nose and ears, and even from her mouth. Sally knew he was killing her. He would draw it out and make it as horrible as possible while she stood watching. Peri's body flipped and flopped as her breathing gurgled around the blood. She glanced back at Costin. "I can't let her die," she told him. "I can't; it wouldn't be right; it's not right."

"Sally," Costin's voice came out in a desperate plea, but what could he say? Could he tell her to stand there while a friend that she loved died a horrible death? Could he really ask her to live with that?

"He will take you all one by one until one of us gives in," she told him. She looked over at Crina and gave her a small smile. "It is my duty as your healer. I don't expect you to sacrifice yourself."

Peri's screams became louder and then Sally heard the fae's words. "Sally! Don't!" she screamed. But she was too late. Sally had already put the pill in her mouth and swallowed. She waited and let out a deep breath when Peri's screams of pain stopped but then were replaced by her cussing.

"Dammit, Sally! I told you not to! Do you know how long I've been alive? Do you have any idea how many centuries I've lived on this earth?" Peri tried to walk closer to the healer but just like Costin, she was stuck. "ARGH!" she screamed in utter frustration and rage.

Sally felt herself getting sleepy as her breathing became shallow. She swayed on her feet and tried to lower herself slowly to the ground as her legs weakened. Her eyes met Costin's as he lowered himself to the ground across from her. He reached out to her, unable to touch her, unable to save her, and she cried for him.

"Sally," his deep voice cut into her heart and the desperation in it touched her soul. She didn't want to die; she wasn't ready to die, but Reyaz had left her no option. She wouldn't watch her friends die.

"I'm sorry, Costin," she told him breathlessly. Her lungs were on fire and her brain was becoming fuzzy from the lack of oxygen.

"Shh, baby, don't talk...it's okay...it's okay," he told her gently. "I know why you did it; I do. I'm just not ready to give you up. I can't give you up."

Sally smiled, or tried to. "Stubborn," she wheezed.

Costin couldn't smile. He couldn't do anything other than breathe and that was becoming increasingly difficult. It was as if his own body was responding to what her body was experiencing and, he wished with everything inside of him that he was, that he too was dying. But he knew the bond had been broken, and as her life slipped away, he would be left here without her.

Sally felt herself growing even weaker. "I'm tired, Costin," she whispered to him.

"Lay down, Sally mine, I'm here with you."

She did as he told her and lay on her side so she could see him. Her breaths were so shallow now; she knew at any second she would take her last. "I love you," she told him and the words were slurred but she hoped he understood. "I. am. S-s—so glad. You. Were. Mine." her words were choppy and so soft she wondered if he heard her.

"*Am* yours, Sally mine, not were. I *am* yours in life and in death and you are mine," he told her, "And I will join you very soon, my love."

Sally wanted to tell him no; she wanted to tell him to live and to find love again but she was out of time. She saw his incredibly handsome face move closer and caught his scent just as death took her.

Costin gathered her into his arms as the force that had been holding him in place let go. He wanted to scream, to maim, and kill. Most of all, he wanted his mate back. He buried his face in her neck and breathed deeply, taking her scent deep in his lungs. His chest ached as he tried to hold himself together and when he heard Jacque's hysterical screams he nearly lost it. He knew she would want to see her friend and would want to hold her, but he wasn't ready to let her go, couldn't let her go, not yet, and maybe not ever. His time with her had been so very short. There was still so much they hadn't experienced together and so many things left to do and say, and yet one little pill and the evil heart of one man had ripped her from him.

Jacque couldn't believe what had just happened. In fact, she was waiting for herself to wake up and for all of this to be some horrific dream that she could tell the girls about over hot chocolate. But there would be no more hot chocolate, not without Sally, not ever again. She watched as Costin rocked her best friend in his arms and her heart broke right along with his. She felt Fane's arms come around her, and even without the bond she felt his love engulf her and knew that he ached for her and would take all of her pain if he could. Her mind flashed to Jen and she felt tears well up in her eyes. This would break Jen. Sally may have meant the world to her, but Jen had a different sort of bond with Sally. Jacque didn't even know if Jen was aware of it, but Sally was what kept Jen grounded. Sally was to Jen what a tornado shelter was to those who needed a safe place to run to in the storms of life and now she was gone. Jacque felt her knees go weak and knew that if Fane's arms hadn't been around her, she would have crumbled to the ground like a house of cards. She heard Fane's voice in her ear, but she couldn't discern what he was saying. Her mind was too much of a mess. Her heart hurt for the death of her mother-in-law, but something inside of her died right along with Sally and she didn't know if it would ever live again.

"We must continue," Decebel finally spoke up. "I mourn the death of our little healer, but there are the others who still need us and we must find the strength to go on."

"I can't leave her," Costin's voice was hoarse and he sounded completely defeated.

"She won't be alone," Jacque spoke up, "I will stay with her."

"Jacquelyn," Fane began, but he was cut off when she pushed away from him whipping around at the same time to face him.

"I'm staying, Fane. I won't leave her here in this forsaken place alone. You all go on and finish this and kill that bastard who took from me what is mine! Then you come back for us." Jacque's jaw was set and it was obvious that it would take an army to get her away from Sally. She walked over to Costin and placed a hand on his shoulder. "Costin, I've got her, honey. I'll watch her. You go and do what you know she would want you to." She waited silently for him to respond to her.

He nodded his head and kissed Sally one more time. Jacque sat down and opened her arms for him to lay Sally's head in her lap. He did so gently and then looked into Jacque's eyes with his glowing ones. "Thank you," he told her simply. Jacque bit the inside of her cheek to keep from sobbing. She gave him a short nod. As he stepped away Fane replaced him and knelt down in front of her.

"I love you," he told her, "you have no idea how hard it is for me to leave you here."

"Yes I do," she said, "but part of loving each other is letting go when we have to. I'll be here waiting for you. I love you, Fane Lupei."

He leaned forward and kissed her being careful of Sally's still form, and then he stood. Jacque watched as they began to move back into the forest. Peri was still standing there after everyone else had already moved on. Jacque looked up at the fae and saw that Peri had tears running down her cheeks. She didn't know if she could remember a time Peri had ever cried, at least not in front of her.

"She shouldn't have done it," Peri said. "Not for me."

"You know her well enough to know that she wouldn't let a fly die for her, not if she could stop it," Jacque said.

"I should have been able to stop him. I should have been able to stop this."

"Peri," Jacque nearly growled, "you are not all powerful. You can't prevent the death of every person you love, no matter how badly you want to."

"Perhaps not, but I can sure as hell die trying."

She was gone before Jacque could reply.

※

"Houston, we have a problem," Jen said breathlessly.

Cynthia stood up from where she had been sitting at the entrance to the cave. She walked back to where Jen was pacing. "What's wrong?" she asked while taking in Jen's flushed skin and rapid breathing. "Crap, you're in labor," she answered her own question.

"What gave it away? The, *I'm in terrible pain,* look, or the, *I'm scared as hell and don't think I'm ready for this,* look?" Jen asked dryly as she tried to breathe through the next contraction. She gritted her teeth and braced herself on the cave wall as her stomach cramped down. She swore that her child was trying to claw her way out instead of going the traditional route. "I guess we don't have to worry about that C-section, huh, Doc?" Jen growled.

"How far apart are the contractions?" Cynthia asked as she went over to the box that contained the blankets. She began making a pallet for Jen to lie on.

"Not freaking far enough," Jen growled.

Cynthia watched her for a little while as she helped her walk slowly around the cave with Jen cussing her all the while. She determined that the contractions were around six to seven minutes apart; so they still had some time.

"Well, look on the bright side," Jen said after a particularly difficult contraction, "at least you don't have to filet me."

Cynthia didn't smile. "We aren't out of the woods yet."

"Pun intended?" Jen tried to smile but it came out more of a grimace.

"I'd like to say that I'm feeling that clever right now, but honestly Jen, I'm just hoping I remember everything I need to about delivering a baby. I haven't done it since med school."

"Uh, Doc, you aren't inspiring a whole lot of confidence here."

"I'm going for honesty."

Jen let out a huff of laughter. "Of all the times, you go for honesty. Remind me to teach you when it's appropriate to lie which is in nearly all stressful situations, by the way."

"I'll remember you said that."

"Tombstone," Jen grinned at the doctor.

"Is there any movie you *haven't* seen?" Cynthia asked.

"Doc, we're from Coldspring, TX," Jen said just as another contraction began.

"Point made."

Chapter 23
"Have we been foolish to believe that we could win? Have we been so vain to think that we were powerful enough to defeat evil and walk away with no casualties? We have been fools. We have walked into the lions' den. Instead of respecting the danger the beast possessed, we believed ourselves to be invincible." ~Peri

"Do you remember the first time we shaved our legs?" Jacque asked Sally, though she knew she wouldn't, couldn't answer. "We were eleven and Jen had told us that she refused to be seen with hairy beasts and if we wanted to remain her friends then we would have to become Schic chicks. You had asked her what the crap a Schic chick was and she had tossed a pack of disposable razors at us and then refused to let us out of the bathroom until we had shaved. I don't think I had ever seen you that mad. You were as pissed as a wet cat." Jacque laughed out loud. "Jen had asked you what the big deal was and you had told her that it should be your decision when you were ready to shave your legs and then Jen had told you that anything related to beauty was always to be deferred to her. I swear I thought she was going to shave your legs for you." She ran her fingers through Sally's brown hair as she looked out into the dark forest. Her mind wandered back to happier times.

Jacque felt the tears as they slowly slipped down her cheeks. She wondered if she would ever be able to smile again, and if so, how? She thought about the other girls and about her mom. *Oh crap, my mom. Please don't let my mom die*, she told the Great Luna. *Please, I don't think I can handle losing her.* Jacque squeezed her eyes closed and leaned her head down until her forehead touched Sally's. She was still warm, though not as warm as someone whose heart still beats, but warm enough to know that her life had only just been taken.

"I'm so sorry, Sal. I'm so sorry this happened to you," she wept. She wept for her friend; she wept for Alina and for Vasile and Costin. She wept for Jen who didn't know about the deaths. And she wept for the loss she knew was yet to come. She wondered if it was possible to die of pain, to die from too much loss, and as the sobs wracked her body, she decided that it just might be a possibility.

"So we know that Reyaz has rigged this so that one of the females will sacrifice themselves for us," Sorin growled, "and there isn't a damn thing we can do to stop it."

The group paused as the wolves took in deep breaths, trying to catch the scent of any of the four females still hidden.

"There has to be a way to stop him. There has to be a way to protect ourselves so the females don't feel they have to make the sacrifice," Adam spoke up as he pulled Crina close to his side. She had tears glistening in her eyes and he rubbed circles on her back, attempting to comfort her.

Peri flashed to where they had stopped and pulled the fae stones from her pocket. "We might have a way to do just that."

Alston stepped next to her. "They show up now? Why not two deaths ago," he nearly yelled. Peri saw that it hurt him nearly as much as it hurt her to lose those under their protection.

"You know I don't know the answer to that," she snapped back, "and asking questions like that isn't going to bring them back."

"Elle and Lilly are that way," Sorin said and his eyes narrowed in the direction he pointed. Part of him wanted to take off in a dead sprint, to get to his mate as quickly as possible, but a part of him was terrified of getting too close and having her put in a position where she felt she had to sacrifice herself for him or anyone else.

"Thank goodness one of you has come to his senses and isn't running off after his mate without a freaking thought in the world," Peri grumbled as she handed out the fae stones; one to Cyn, one to Alston, one to Adam, one for herself, and the fifth she gave to Thalion. She would have preferred to have a healer to give it to, but

Vasile hadn't wanted Rachel to come, and well, the other healer wasn't available either, but she didn't want to think about that.

"Okay, so here's the plan. We're going to cast a protection spell with the stones, one that causes us to be invisible. Even Elle and Lilly won't be able to see us. So once we see them, well, we'll figure that part out once we get there. Everyone with a stone get in a circle and everyone else get inside of the circle. We have to move as one." Peri looked at Sorin and then at Cypher. "You two Neanderthals do not go charging in after your women. I swear I will zap your asses if you do."

Once everyone was in position, Peri looked at Alston and gave a slight nod. They both began chanting softly until the stones began glowing. Eventually, they shimmered and their outlines grew fuzzy, though they could still see each other.

"Okay, we're good. No one else should be able to see us. Sorin, point the way," Peri told him.

They moved quickly and silently through the heavily wooded area. Soon they saw the two women when they were half a mile away. They also saw the cliff that they precariously stood on.

"What the hell?" Cypher said with wide eyes. "How is there a cliff in the middle of a forest that has been well-nigh without a hill?"

Peri narrowed her eyes and sought out the truth of the forest, the truth of what she knew. There had never been a cliff in the dark forest. There wasn't so much as a mole hill. When she believed that with everything inside of her, she saw the truth. Lilly and Elle weren't on a cliff at all; they were just on the forest ground with trees around them, just as the group was.

"It's an illusion," she told them. "You have to believe, really believe that it's an illusion."

"We all have to," Alston said. "It's not enough for a few of us to realize that it's fake. In order for them to no longer appear to be on a cliff's edge then we must all see the truth that they are indeed just standing in the forest."

They all stared silently at the women and the cliff that wasn't there, all attempting to get their brains to reject what their eyes saw. It was easier said than done.

As Peri stood staring at the girls, she saw Lorelle appear beside them. Her eyes narrowed as she watched her sister talk to them and then point in their direction. That piece of crap she called a sister was telling Lilly and Elle that they were here, hiding under the protection spell. Both of them looked in the direction Lorelle pointed and she could tell they were trying to see the invisible figures. She didn't know what Lorelle was up to, but she knew without a doubt it wouldn't end well for them.

"They have a protection spell over them," Lorelle told Lilly and Elle.

"How do we know you aren't just screwing with us?" Lilly asked.

"No, she's right, I can see them," Elle said. Once Lorelle had pointed them out, Elle was able to see past the fae magic. She saw all of them and it wasn't a pretty sight. Peri looked like she was going to murder someone. Costin and Vasile both looked utterly defeated. Crina was silently crying and Fane seemed distracted. Sorin has staring at her with narrowed eyes and a look of determination. She knew for certain that he knew of the sacrifice. He knew that Reyaz had planned it so that both she and Lilly could not survive. One of them would have to die.

"You can see them?" Lilly asked Elle anxiously.

Elle nodded and her jaw tightened when she realized that Jacque was not with them, nor was Alina, or Sally.

"Is Jacque there?" Lilly asked, "Or Sally, or Jen?"

Elle didn't want to answer her; she knew what Lilly would do if she did. When she looked at her, she knew that her face had not hidden the truth. Tears welled up in Lilly's eyes.

"What about Fane and Costin, or Decebel?"

Elle nodded and Lilly broke. She covered her face as the tears fell. She knew that if Jacque was still alive Fane would either be with her, or Jacque would be there with him. The same was true of Costin and Sally and Decebel and Jen. When Reyaz had told them of the hunt, the rules, and how each of them would have to make the ultimate choice, she had immediately thought of Jacque and the other two girls, and she knew that any of them would give their lives for those they love. Lilly's shoulders shook with the force of her tears. She took in huge gulps of air as she tried to get herself under control and tried to think clearly, but her mind just kept going back to the thought that her daughter just might be gone.

"Lilly, we don't know anything for sure," Elle told her gently, then she looked at Lorelle. "Do you know?" she snarled at the fae.

Lorelle shrugged. "Maybe."

"If you aren't going to do anything but stand there and taunt us then get out of here before I rip your cold heart from your chest."

Lorelle clucked her tongue at Elle. "Being the mate of a wolf has made you bloodthirsty, Elle. That's not like our kind."

"And being a selfish bitch has made you a moron, Lorelle, and I would say that makes you even less like our kind." Elle took a menacing step towards her. "Why are you doing this? All because you hate your sister? Can't you see that you will have nothing. You are nothing whether Peri lives or dies? You have brought that on yourself. You had everything, Lorelle. You had a sister who loved you, a council who respected you, and a species that looked up to you, and you threw it all away because of pride."

"You don't know anything about me and I suggest you worry about the lives of your friends, of your mate, and not about me." Lorelle gave them a wave with her finger and then was gone.

Elle looked back at Lilly who was standing there staring at the edge of the cliff. Tears still ran down her cheeks and she had the appearance of someone who had lost everything.

"Lilly, please step away from the edge."

"If my daughter is gone..." her words were cut off by a sob and she brought her hand up to cover her mouth. She shook her head and seemed to gather herself. "A child should not go before the parent, Elle. That is not the way it should work; it isn't right."

"You dying isn't going to make it right," Elle argued.

"But it will save the others," Lilly pointed out. "It will protect you and your mate. I can't imagine a world without Jacque in it, and I know you may not understand, but there is no greater love than that of a parent's love for their child. I couldn't save Jacque, but I can save someone." She started to move closer to the edge and Elle ran forward.

"PERI!" Cypher bellowed, "Lift the protection now!" He watched as Lilly wept and moved closer to the edge. He knew, just like the others she was willing to give her life, but he didn't know why. There was no one dying. There wasn't an immediate threat that she knew of; so why was she standing on the edge of cliff ready to throw herself off?

"LILLY STOP!" he yelled as loud as he could and knew Peri had lifted the spell when Lilly turned at the sound of his voice. Her eyes widened and she turned and took a step in his direction. Her eyes left his then as she searched the group, and when they landed back on him he could see utter grief. He realized then that she was looking for her daughter and by the tears welling up in her eyes anew, she believed the worse.

"SHE'S ALIVE!" he told her and then started moving towards her. He didn't run, but instead moved quickly but cautiously attempting to ready himself for the assault he was sure would come. "Jacque is alive, Lilly," he told her again as he got closer to her.

"Where is she?" she asked when he was ten feet away.

"She's with Sally," Fane answered.

Lilly looked at Fane and then her eyes landed on Costin. She took in the broken look on his face and Cypher could tell she knew.

"She's gone," she said. Her eyes filled with tears again and he wanted to wrap her in his arms and keep her safe forever. He wanted to take her pain and tell her everything would be okay, but that would be a lie. Nothing was ever okay once someone you loved was taken from you, especially if it was before their time and it was so very far before Sally's time.

"I'm sorry, Lilly," he said softly as he took another step towards her. He took another step and another and was nearly to her when Elle yelled out. "STOP!"

Elle held out her hand to Sorin telling him with both her words and motion not to come any closer. She looked over at Lilly. "You can't let him touch you," she reminded her. She saw the panic in Lilly's eyes as she turned to Cypher.

"You can't touch me," Lilly told him.

"Why?" Cypher asked.

"Elle," Sorin's deep voice rumbled as he took another step toward his mate.

"Sorin," Elle nearly snarled, "I said stop, please."

"Tell me why and then maybe I will, but you cannot expect me to see you after so long, after having the bond broken between us, and not want to wrap you in my arms."

"Reyaz has set a trap. If any of you touch us, this cliff is going down, with all of us on it," she told him and pleaded with her eyes for him to listen to her.

"The cliff is not real," Sorin told her.

"Does everyone believe that? To the extent that they can see past the glamour of it for at least a second?" she asked and looked around the group. "Can Costin and, from the looks of it, Vasile as well, see past their grief right now?" she was answered with silence. "That's what I thought. So until all of you, every single one of you, believes that this cliff isn't real, you cannot touch us."

"I'm trying," Lilly said. "But I can see it. I can see the drop and I can feel the wind on my face. I'm getting vertigo for crying out loud."

"You're not the only one, Lilly," Crina spoke up. "I can't get my mind around it either."

Lilly backed up until she was against the cliff wall and sunk to the ground. Elle sat down next to her and the others found seats as well.

"I guess we wait," Thalion said.

Lorelle appeared suddenly, just at the edge. Peri's eyes landed on her and, in a second, she was standing less than a foot from her sister.

"Why are you doing this, Lorelle?" she asked. "When did you become so cruel?"

"I've told you my reasons and I won't justify myself to you any longer." Lorelle tried to side step her sister but Peri reached out her hand and slammed it into Lorelle's chest. The fae flew back into the cliff wall just to the left of where Elle and Lilly sat.

"Tell me why I shouldn't kill you right here?" Peri snarled into her sister's face.

"Because I will kill every single being on this cliff."

"THERE IS NO CLIFF!" Peri screamed.

"Then tell one of them to walk off the side," Lorelle taunted. "If there is no cliff, then they will just be walking into the forest."

Skender stood and made his way over to the edge.

"Skender don't," Peri ordered.

"I have no mate, Perizada. If I perish, it will be no great loss," he told her simply.

"Every single one of you is of great importance, Skender. Mateless or not, you are no less valuable. Do not take another step."

"Skender, do not," Vasile's eyes glowed as he gave the command. Skender stepped back, unable to disobey his Alpha's orders.

"If you are quite finished, Perizada, I came to tell you something rather important." Lorelle gave her sister a pointed look.

Peri slammed her sister into the wall one more time before releasing her. "Deliver your news and then go."

"You might not want to wait too long for this whole *it isn't really a cliff* bit. Jen has gone into labor and I'm not real sure just how long until the baby is born." She turned her eyes on Decebel. "I would think you would want to see your child before she's taken."

Decebel began to lunge for the fae but was stopped by Alston's magic. The fae held out his arm holding the enraged Alpha in place.

"I'll kill you for this, Lorelle. I don't care how long it takes; I will rip your head from you neck and feed it to the wolves." Peri's body shook with her fury and the air around her grew electric.

Lorelle gave her sister one last look before she vanished.

The group was silent as they took in the news Lorelle had delivered. No one moved, as if by doing so they would somehow seal their fate.

Decebel's mind was working overtime and his wolf was raging inside of him, fighting to get free, and needing to get to Jennifer. This wasn't supposed to happen. He was supposed to be with her when she went into labor. He was supposed to hold her hand and support her. Yet he was here, stuck on a cliff that wasn't a cliff. And the moment his baby girl was born, his life would be over and he would never have the chance to touch either of his girls again.

Decebel felt the ground beneath his feet begin to shift and rumble. He quickly drew himself from his thoughts and looked around to see if everyone else was feeling the same thing. Sure enough, they were all looking at the ground curiously and attempting to balance themselves as it shook beneath them.

"Awe crap," Peri huffed. "He's going to bring down the cliff that doesn't even bloody hell exist except in our minds."

Lilly gripped the rock wall trying to balance herself as the trembling grew stronger. "He's going to bring this thing down and kill us all unless Elle or I give in."

"NO!" Cypher thundered. "Neither of you is sacrificing yourself. I've had enough death for one day. We are getting out of this, all of us." He looked over at Peri who had her arms out as she tried to balance herself. "Whatever it is that makes you so powerful that the wolves tremble before you, now would be the time to whip it out."

Peri raised an eyebrow at him. "Damn, I wish Jen was here to take that one; she would totally run with it. Whip it out, that's classic." She shook her head with a smirk still plastered on her lips and then looked over to Alston. "This is going to take blood magic," she told him.

His face was solemn as he answered. "It will be overlooked this one time, for this one instance. There is no other option that I can see, unless we allow one of the females to give her life."

"Not an option," Peri said firmly. She pulled a dagger from seemingly nowhere and then looked at Cypher. "My blood is powerful, and to shed it willingly for a sacrifice is honorable, but it is also something that the fae never do lightly. I do not know if it will work, and if it does, I do not know what the consequences will be, but I have to try."

Cypher and the others stared at Peri, waiting for her to continue.

She took the blade and ran it along her palm, slashing deep into her flesh. The blood welled up from the wound and began to drip to the ground. With the earth around them attempting to crumble beneath them, Peri knelt down and touched the ground with the slashed palm and pressed it to the dirt. She closed her eyes and called on the magic that lived inside her as she spoke. "Ancient power that flows through my veins, I willingly shed my blood to spare the life required by the black magic that fills this place. Let my blood cleanse this place and open our eyes to the truth behind the lies. Break the binding, rip through the ties, and cast out the evil that has taken root."

The ground continued to tremble and the wind began to whip around them. Peri's hair was like a wild mane dancing around her as she let her blood flow into the dirt. She willed it to delve deep into the earth and to seek out the black magic that held their minds captive.

"Peri, it's still a cliff," Adam yelled through the roar of the storm brewing in the air. Dark clouds gathered above them and lightning flashed across the sky.

Peri heard the rumble of laughter that began to grow louder as the storm grew more and more vicious. "You cannot win, Perizada," the voice that was Reyaz told her. "The magic calls for a sacrifice and it will demand the price be paid."

Peri's eyes narrowed. She felt her wrath building and willed even more blood to flow from her vein. She would not lose another to this evil, twisted warlock. She refused to accept defeat, refused to believe that she, as old and powerful as she was, could not break the spell. Her body began to shake with the effort to stay upright, her vision began to blur, and she felt weak from blood loss, but she would not give in.

"You cannot have them," Peri answered the voice. She knew none of the others would be able to hear her over the storm. Rain now pelted them painfully and the temperature dropped, making the drops even more excruciating as they sliced against their flesh. She could feel the magic Reyaz spoke of, could feel the darkness in it, and the intent behind it. And she realized that there was no way around it, not this kind of magic. It demanded a sacrifice and it would not relent its hold until it got it. "So be it," she whispered into the raging storm. She stood slowly, careful to steady her weak legs and turned to look at Vasile. The rain made it difficult to see him clearly and she hoped that he could hear her with his wolf ears. "This is my sacrifice to make. It has been an honor, Vasile, Alpha, friend." She flashed herself to the edge of the cliff and with one final glance back at the wolves she had grown to love so deeply, she leapt.

Chapter 24

"There's a song that I listen to when I need to know that it's okay to fall apart. The chorus says to let it hurt, let it bleed, let it take you right down to your knees. I'm there. I'm on my knees hurting, bleeding, burning, from the inside out. What if it doesn't stop? What if it's just too much? How long do I let it hurt? How long do I let it bleed and what if I can never get up off my knees?" ~Jacque

Decebel looked around at the others and saw that they were all as shocked as he was. The rain stopped, and the wind died down. The ground around them was just a forest floor. Peri's sacrifice had broken the magic. Peri's death had saved their lives. Decebel gritted his teeth together as the anguish continued to build inside of him. He wanted to grieve for Peri. He wanted to show her the respect she deserved and he would, whether it be in this life or the next. But first he had to get to his mate.

He heard the sobs of the females and the murmuring voices of the males attempting to comfort them, but they would find no comfort, not here in a place that continued to take from them and to rip lives that completed their family from them.

"Where did she go?" Elle asked as she looked around the forest for any sign of Peri's body. "Why isn't her body here?" Tears stained her face and her hair, wild from the storm, fell loosely around her shoulders.

"I don't know," Vasile answered. "What she has done for us will not be forgotten, and we will give her the burial she deserves once this is finished."

The others nodded and mumbled agreements as they attempted to pull themselves together.

Lilly buried her face in Cypher's chest as he enveloped her in his large arms. He whispered to her gently, "I'm sorry little one; we will make it out of this."

Lilly wanted to believe him, but then part of her wanted to curl into a ball and let the sorrow swallow her.

"Vasile, we must hurry," Decebel told him. He turned in the direction where the cliff edge had appeared to be and walked a few steps, taking a deep breath. *There*, he thought, *there is my Jennifer.* He took off at a dead run, not caring if anyone followed him. His one thought was to get to his mate. Then he could see his child and die telling the woman he loved how precious she was to him.

"It's been a long time," the Great Luna told the white wolf.

Lucian phased back into his human form and stood beside Alina's body. He looked at his creator and felt the warmth and love flowing off of her and into him.

"Why did you let me live?" he asked her, thinking of the long centuries he had spent wandering the dark forest, aching for companionship and, at times, longing for death.

"Because you have a purpose still in this life and it is an important one."

He looked down at Alina and felt the sorrow from her death and remembered the pain in his brother's eyes. "Was her purpose done?" he motioned to Alina.

The Great Luna shook her head as her lips tightened into a thin line. "No, it was not." She frowned at the still body of the Alpha female and walked over to her. She knelt down and eased her arms under her and picked her up effortlessly.

"Come, Lucian. I will not leave a child of mine out in the dark."

Lucian followed her without hesitation. He heard weeping up ahead and then he and the Luna emerged into a tiny clearing where one of the girls from the circle, Jacque, he recalled her name, sat with the brunette, Sally, lying in her lap. She looked up at them and her tears fell harder and she began to rock back and forth.

"Why?" she asked the Great Luna. "Please tell me why?"

She turned and carefully handed Alina to Lucian and then went over and knelt by the two girls. She murmured something he couldn't hear and then Jacque nodded her head and then slumped forward until her forehead rested on the Luna's shoulder. He watched as the goddess caressed the female, calming her.

"Let us go," she finally said as she picked up Sally in her arms and motioned for the other to follow.

"Where are we going?" Jacque asked.

The Great Luna smiled at her as a proud parent smiles at their child. "There will be no more death today, not of my children. It is time that I interfered."

Jen felt sweat sliding down her back and matting her hair to her face. The warm air felt cool against her damp skin and she welcomed that small relief. She squeezed her eyes closed as she embraced the pain of labor, knowing that she was bringing a precious life into the world, a life she and Decebel had created. She bit her lip as she fought back the urge to scream, as the contractions became more painful and closer together. Cynthia told her to find a focal point, to grab onto a thought and hold it in her mind, and to see it with clarity. She had no problem picking a focal point because he had been her focus since the day he had growled at her in that hospital room. He had claimed her and even when there were no signs other than what he felt, he had made it clear that she was his.

She pictured his face in her mind, his amber eyes, and the secrets they held. She envisioned his high cheek bones, straight nose, and firm lips that often stayed in a permanent scowl aimed at her but could quirk up in an amused smile at a moment's notice. She pushed all of her focus into that picture of him and finally the pain subsided from the contraction. She knew she wouldn't have a respite for very long.

"Okay," Cynthia said as she pushed the blanket over Jen's knees so she could see how far dilated she was, "that was a strong one."

"No offense doc, but you stating the obvious isn't really an indication that you know what you're doing."

Cynthia chuckled. "Yes well, between the two of us, I think I'm just a tad more qualified." Cynthia felt what she was looking for as she did her exam on Jen, "Okay it's time to start pushing."

Jen went still. "What?"

"Jen, I know you didn't really get a chance to take the classes you needed to for giving birth, but surely you knew that this was the way she would come into the world."

"If I didn't need you right now, I just might knock you senseless," Jen growled as she felt another contraction coming on.

"Okay here we go, Jen," Cynthia coached. As soon as you feel it hit, I want you to bear down and push, okay?"

Jen nodded and curled her fingers into the blanket as the contraction ripped through her. She tightened her stomach and pushed just as Cynthia told her.

"Picture your focal point, Jen. Breathe...okay, good job," she patted her thigh gently.

The contraction passed and Jen was left breathless and dripping with even more sweat. She wanted to cry. She wanted her momma and she wanted her mate; hell, she just wanted someone to tell her she could do this, but there was no one and she was giving birth in a damn cave.

She felt a tear slide from her eye and she gritted her teeth to hold them back, but as another contraction built, she couldn't contain them any longer. They poured from her eyes, blurring her vision, as she heard the doc's voice once again telling her to push. She did. She pulled her legs up and pushed with all her might and when the contraction was gone, she knew it wasn't enough.

"I can't do this," she said as she panted. She reached up to wipe away the tears but her arms were so weak that she couldn't even do that. "Cynthia, I can't do this without him, I can't."

Cynthia looked up at Jen and her eyes were glowing. "You can do this and you will do this," she said firmly. "This is your child, Jennifer. A miracle that you and Decebel created out of love and you will not let your mate or your little girl down. You are going to suck it up and do what needs to be done."

Jen heard Cynthia; she felt the truth in her words and she tried to grab on to that truth. She had to do this. There was no out clause when in labor. She listened to the sound of the doctor's voice as another contraction came and she pushed hard. She felt a stabbing pain and gasped. Immediately, she stopped pushing, and when she looked down at Cynthia's face, she knew something was very wrong.

Cynthia's eyes widened at the sight of the gush of blood that flowed from Jen's body. The blood was bright red and there was so much. She flipped through her mind, quickly trying to remember all the things that could cause that much blood. She grabbed another blanket she had laid out and placed beneath Jen, attempting to soak up the fluid. Finally it hit her, an abruption, a placental abruption could cause this much blood, and it was also extremely dangerous.

"Jen we have to get her out, I need you to push as hard as you can when this next contraction comes. Do you hear me?" Cynthia looked into Jen's panicked eye. "You can do this."

Jen knew from the sound of Cynthia's voice and the fear in her eyes that something was seriously wrong. She tried to take some slow deep breaths to get herself under control. She needed to be strong and as much as she wanted to curl up in a ball and cry her eyes out, she couldn't. Her child needed her and she would not let her down.

The contraction started and Jen took a deep breath. She pulled Decebel's face up in her mind and imagined him there beside her telling her she was strong, telling her he wouldn't leave her side, and telling her everything would be alright. She pictured him so clearly that she swore she could hear his voice. Then he was saying Cynthia's name. Why on earth would he be saying Cynthia's name in her little illusion. She opened her eyes and turned her head to see him there at the entrance to the cave. She saw her mate, strong and tall, and by the look on his face, royally pissed off. He was pounding on the invisible barrier that kept him from her side and she wanted to tell him she would be okay, to somehow ease the panic in his eyes. But the contraction hit and she couldn't think about that anymore.

"PUSH JEN!" Cynthia yelled. "Come on that's it...breathe... okay, and push again! You're doing great!" Cynthia could feel the baby's head and knew they had to hurry; Jen was losing too much blood much too quickly. She heard Decebel yelling at them and asking her if Jen was okay. The anger and rage in his voice was tangible and sent chills down her spine. Another contraction followed immediately after that one ended, and she was yelling at Jen again. Her attention was divided though, and she finally answered

Decebel. "She's had a placental abruption. I don't have time to explain what it is so don't ask. The baby seems to be doing well. I hear her heart rate and it's normal. Jen, however, has lost a lot of blood. We need Sally if you can get her."

Cynthia's eyes watered as she saw the head begin to emerge and she was shaking as she maneuvered her hands into position to help ease the infant out on the final push.

"Okay, Jennifer, you can do this. One more, big, hard, long push for me."

Jen nodded and then turned to look at Decebel. Her eyes locked onto his and a tear slid from them.

"You can do it baby," he told her through the barrier. "I'm here; I'm not leaving."

Jen nodded and then took a deep breath and pushed. She pushed with all of her strength, calling on her wolf's help to give her the endurance she needed. She felt the pain as her child was born and tears streamed down her face as she looked at Cynthia who held the messy little life. She had turned her over and had her nearly hanging upside down attempting to clean out her nose and mouth and then the most glorious sound filled the cave.

Jen heard her daughter's cry and felt the tears gush from her eyes. She was alive; she was breathing. She turned again to look at Decebel and saw that he was on his knees; his eyes were wide in utter awe of what he saw. Jen tried to look down at Cynthia and her baby girl again but her vision was blurry. She tried to raise her arms to ask to hold her child but they wouldn't respond to her command. The light was fading and she felt herself drifting. She was so tired and cold, so very cold.

Cynthia let out a deep breath once the baby began to cry. She was cleaning her up as quickly as she could and once she had laid her on a clean blanket she grabbed the surgical scissors from the kit and cut the umbilical cord and then clamped it off with the clamp provided. She wrapped her up tight in the blanket and then went to hand her to Jen but froze when she saw that Jen wasn't moving and her eyes were closed.

"Shit!" Cynthia breathed. She looked over at Decebel who was on his knees and barely holding back his panic and then looked at the baby again. The baby was breathing, alive, and vibrant. Decebel was alive and on the verge of freaking out. She pushed the thoughts aside and focused on the here and now. She set Cosmina, she remembered them saying that was what they wanted to call her, down gently on more blankets and then turned to check on Jen. She was breathing, but it was labored and shallow. Her pulse was weak and slow from lack of blood to circulate through her body. She had lost too much and Cynthia had no way to give her a transfusion. She felt warmth at her back and saw a soft glow begin to fill the cave with light. She stopped her exam to turn and see what it was. The transfusion was no longer an issue, because she was also out of time.

Decebel felt as though his lungs were on fire. He couldn't get enough air as he watched his mate and his child. Jen had passed out, or at least he hoped that was all, but he didn't know for sure. He just knew there was so much blood, too much blood. He watched as Cynthia placed their baby next to her and then began to check on Jen, but before she could do more than check her pulse, there was a soft glow emitting from behind her and then three entities, the Fates, were standing behind her.

Decebel's heart began to pound as he realized that it was time. They were here to collect him as the sacrifice for Jen's death. He wished he could hold his mate and child once before he went, but then he had gotten to see Cosmina be born and had gotten to see his amazing mate give birth to their little miracle. He didn't want to die, but he could now with a small amount of peace.

His ears perked up as he heard them begin to speak—to Cynthia, not to him.

"The child is born; the debt is now due. You have proven yourself honorable and through your silence deemed yourself worthy. We accept your sacrifice in place of the child." The forms moved forward and seemed to reach out and touch Cynthia. She turned slightly and her eyes met his; she gave him a small bow of her head. Decebel watched in utter astonishment as Cynthia's body seemed to deflate and was slowly lowered to the ground. Her chest was not moving. There wasn't the slightest movement. Cynthia's life was over, and she had given it willingly.

The Fates turned and looked at him, at least he felt like they were looking at him. And then they spoke to him.

"The magic that lives here has been given what it requires, a sacrifice. It is null and void of its power."

Decebel nearly fell on his face as the barrier disappeared and the Fates along with it. He didn't hesitate as he stood up and ran to his mate. He picked up Cosmina in his arms and held her close to his body and then knelt down next to Jen. She was barely breathing and she was pale, so very pale.

"Jennifer, baby, please stay with me, stay with us. We need you," Decebel whispered as he leaned close to her, careful not to crush his daughter. He heard voices and running footsteps and looked up when the commotion grew louder. Vasile, Adam, Cypher, and the others came rushing in. They took in the scene before them and then jumped into action.

"Decebel," Vasile said as he moved quickly to his side.

"She needs a healer now, Vasile."

Vasile looked up at Adam. "Please get Rachel."

Adam didn't wait for any other instruction but immediately flashed. He was back in less than two minutes with a very frazzled looking Rachel.

She rushed to Jen's side and laid her hands on her She pushed her spirit into Jen and began to seek out the damage her body had sustained. She saw the tear in the uterus and pushed her power there and mended the tissue. She took care of the destruction the birthing had wrought on Jen's body and the aftermath of labor. She was careful to check for any other problems, but the only thing left was the blood loss. Rachel moved her spirit to Jen's heart and pulsed power deep into it. She helped her body's blood cells multiply rapidly, replacing the blood loss and sending it to her starving organs. As her heartbeat gained strength and her breathing evened out, Rachel pulled back from Jen and then pulled her hands away. She opened her eyes and stared at her waiting.

Slowly Jen's eyes began to flutter and then blink slowly. They opened and landed on Decebel.

"Dec," she whispered.

He smiled as tears welled up in his eyes. "Hey baby." He leaned down and kissed her gently and then held up their baby girl. "She's perfect."

Jen's eyes lit up at the sight of their child and her lips trembled as the tears came. "Of course she's perfect, I'm her mother." Decebel chuckled as he handed Jen their baby and then helped her sit up, propping her against him. He wrapped his arm around her waist and tucked her into his side. His face buried in her neck and he breathed deep. She was here with him and their child; it was a miracle. He looked up then and saw Rachel hovering over Cynthia's prone form. Vasile knelt next to her. Rachel looked up then and met his eyes and he nodded. He realized what she would have seen in the last of Cynthia's memories. Cynthia had asked the Fates to take her life in place of his child. She had willingly given herself so that their baby could live and have both her parents with her.

"Cynthia," Jen said realizing for the first time that the doctor was not moving. "She's... is she, Dec?" she stumbled around her words as he heard her pulse increase.

"Shh, baby," he told her. "Cynthia has gone on to the next life. She gave herself in place of our child and the Fates accepted her sacrifice."

Jen's free hand came up to cover her mouth as she suppressed the sob that was there. Her heart was divided, part of it broken over losing her friend and part of it rejoicing over the life of her little girl.

"Thia Cosmina," She looked up at him through her tears. "That's what we will name her, in memory of the one who gave her life, in memory of our friend."

Vasile looked down at the doctor and he felt pride and pain at the same time. She had been brave and loyal and given of herself until there was nothing left. He knew she felt that she could never be forgiven for her part in Jacque's kidnapping, and she had found a way that she felt she could atone for it. As he stared at her still form, his mind wandered to all the death, pain, and torment that the day had brought and his heart broke all over again.

"I hate to interrupt this joyous, and at the same time depressing, moment," Reyaz sneered as he walked into the cave, "but I have business to attend to." He pointed at Lilly and she fell to her knees grabbing at her throat. She attempted to suck in air but none would come and she began to struggle even harder.

Cypher snarled in a blind rage and charged his brother. Alston threw out his hand, just as Reyaz raised his other hand at Cypher, blocking the spell he might have tried. Cypher crashed into his brother with a force that hurled them both back and crashing into the wall. Cypher stood quickly and turned to check on Lilly. She was breathing and Crina was helping her to her feet.

Reyaz got to his feet while Cypher was distracted and, just as he turned back, Reyaz swung and landed his fist in his brother's face. Cypher stumbled back and felt his head swim from the blow. He shook it, trying to regain his bearings, but the noises around him were muffled. He heard his brother's laughter, a deep rumble that seemed to be in slow motion, fill up the cave and then he felt the shutter of the walls as Reyaz threw out his hands launching his power at them. Adam, Alston, and Cyn were throwing their own magic as balls of white light flew at his brother. Reyaz jumped, spun, and ducked as he tried to keep from being hit. He got in a few shots that knocked Fane to the ground and Sorin into the wall. But he was out numbered and the panic in his face showed that he knew it.

With a renewed fervor he tossed a ball of blazing fire at them. It crackled as it flew through the air, the oxygen fueling its heat. He hit Cyn square in the chest and she fell back with a shout, more of anger than of pain. Suddenly Reyaz's body was flung back and he crashed into the cave wall. An arrow shot through his right shoulder and pinned him to the wall. A second arrow flew through the air and pinned his left shoulder to the cave wall. Thalion stood across the room with his bow still raised. His shoulders heaved with his breathing as he tried to gain control of his rage. He looked Reyaz in the eye and smiled a menacing smile. "Be glad it is not I who will mete out your death. For what you just did to my mate, my future Queen, is punishable by death. But in my long life, I have learned there are things so much worse than death."

Cypher stepped up to his pinned brother and shook his head. "You are a disgrace to your family and to your people. You have betrayed your king and your sentence is death."

Reyaz's fought against the arrows that held him captive but it was no use, they wouldn't budge. "LORELLE!" he roared. He refused to give in, even if it meant calling out for help from the traitor fae.

Lorelle appeared at the entrance of the cave and looked in at them all. Her face showed no emotion as she looked at Reyaz. "You called?"

"Help me," he snapped at her. His face had morphed into a beast as all the evil that ran inside of him leaked out onto his flesh and features.

Lorelle laughed. "Help you, right, well since what I wanted accomplished is done, I have no more use for you. My sister is dead, and by her own hand at that. You and I are finished."

"DON'T YOU DARE LEAVE!" Reyaz yelled but was cut off when Cypher's fist collided with his face.

"Your time is coming, Lorelle," Alston suddenly said. "You will be dealt with."

Lorelle laughed again. "You'll have to find me first." She gave them all one last look and then flashed.

"Are you really going to kill me, Cypher, your own flesh and blood?" Reyaz asked.

"No, I'm not going to kill you."

Reyaz sagged in relief.

"He is." Cypher pointed to Vasile whose eyes were glowing and his canines had lengthened. He stalked towards his prey slowly, letting him feel what it was to be hunted and what it was to see your death coming for you.

"For the crimes against my people, for the death of my mate, our healer, and our friend, I sentence you to death. I would rather imprison you and let you rot, but then I would have to run the risk of you getting out. So instead I will just have to be satisfied that you will die by my hand." Vasile grasped Reyaz's head in his hands and gave a quick twist. The bones made a sick crunching noise as his neck broke. His body would have crumpled to the ground had the arrows not held him in place. Vasile stared at the broken man before him and it was then that everything flooded into him, every emotion crashing down on him, and he flung his head back and howled.

Chapter 25
"I will follow you wherever you lead. I will be your constant shadow, the voice that cheers you on, the arms that hold you up, and the heart that loves you unconditionally. Those are the promises I made to you, and I have failed you, for you have gone and I am still here. Why am I still here?" ~Costin

"What did Vasile mean when he said he took our healer, Decebel? Where is Sally?" Jen looked up at her mate's face and though she asked the questions, she already knew the answers.

"I'm sorry baby. We failed her; we failed you all," Decebel told her. Decebel pressed a kiss to her hair and stroked it gently with his hand. He hummed to her and their child as she wept over the loss of her best friend. He held her as her heart broke and her world was shattered all over again.

Vasile placed Cynthia's body close to the cave entrance and then motioned for everyone to gather around Jen and Decebel. The group moved slowly as grief poured out of them. Each of them took a place on the ground making a circle. The mated males, whose mates were still here, each had their females as close to them as possible.

Crina sat wrapped in Adam's arms and he held her, rocking her gently, whispering to her words that would bring comfort and stability.

Elle sat next to Sorin with her head on his shoulder and his arm wrapped securely around her. She too watched Jen and Decebel and their baby with a mixture of emotions passing over her face.

SACRIFICE OF LOVE

Fane sat with his knees pulled up and his arms resting over them. He stared out into the forest beyond the cave entrance, waiting.

Costin sat next to Fane, and though his body was present, his heart, soul, and mind were elsewhere.

Vasile walked over to the group and took a seat beside Jen and Decebel. He looked at each person that filled the small space. The troll king and pixie king were still with them, faithful 'til the end. Thalion, prince of the elves, sat with them, having been willing to give whatever was needed in order to help their females. Cyn sat beside Thalion her hand was securely wrapped in his larger one and her side pressed close to his. Skender sat next to the Cyn, his jaw tight and his eyes narrowed as he continually swept the room with them. He had been willing to give his life without hesitation. Cypher, the warlock king who was finally free of his past, held his mate gently as she watched Jen with a mixture of joy and pain. All of them wore that same expression, the joy of life battling with the sorrow of death.

"Our enemy has been defeated," he began. He had to reach deep for the strength to sit there and speak when all he wanted to do was return to his mate, to join her. "It cost us much, but then the cost of freedom is always great. We will mourn the loss of those we love so dearly and we will honor their memories. The mate bonds have been broken and so Costin and I have lost our mates and not our own lives. Costin may make his own decision. But after we have buried and mourned, I will join my mate as is my right and my desire." He looked over at Decebel and Jen and attempted to smile. "I hate that such a miracle as the birth of your child is tainted with death and sorrow, and I want you to know that I am overjoyed for you. We must honor Cynthia for her sacrifice."

Decebel nodded and wiped a tear from Jen's face. "We have decided to name our child Thia in honor of Cynthia. What she has done, and who she was, will not be forgotten."

Vasile didn't know what else to say. He wanted to offer them comfort, but he had none to give, not anymore.

"I need to convey my gratitude to you all," Cypher said into the silence, "You all are here because of me, and I am forever indebted to you all for your help and willingness to bring my brother to justice." Cypher bowed his head respectfully to them.

They sat in silence for a few minutes. The only sound was Jen speaking softly to Thia. She leaned into Decebel and choked back more tears as she rocked their child. She looked over at Costin and her heart broke all over as she saw the shell of a man that was left after losing his mate.

"What now?" she asked. "What do we do now Vasile?" She needed someone to tell her how to move forward, how to go on, especially now that she had a child who needed her.

Vasile stared at her, at a loss on how to answer. How do you tell someone to carry on when all you want to do is die?

"Now," a bold voice filled the space around them, "we rejoice over new life," the Great Luna said as she stepped into the cave. She walked towards the group and her heart hurt at the loss and pain she saw in them. "We mourn over sacrifice and we give thanks for second chances." There was movement behind her and she stepped aside to reveal Alina, Sally, Jacque, and Lucian, all whole and alive.

It was hard to say who moved faster, Vasile, Costin, or Fane, but regardless they were each at their mates' sides instantly.

Vasile stood so close to Alina he could feel her breath on his face. She looked up at him with eye glistening and he gently wiped away a stray drop.

"Mina," he whispered and pulled her into his arms. He shook with the emotion of a man who had just had the world ripped from him and then given back. She pressed her face into his chest and then stood on her toes to kiss his neck. When he pulled back to look down at her, the love she felt for him was radiating off of her and wrapped him in warmth. He had been so cold from the moment he lost her and now, standing before him, she chased the cold away. "I love you," he told her.

She smiled at him. "*I know and I love you.*" His eyes widened as he heard her voice in his mind and realized he felt her inside as well. Their bond was restored; her soul back where it belonged, joined with his, man and woman, wolf to wolf.

Costin fell to his knees in front of Sally and looked up into her face. He was afraid to touch her, afraid she wasn't real, and afraid this was all some crazy delusion his mind had concocted in an attempt to cope. She smiled down at him and ran her fingers through his hair.

Her scent crashed into him and the warmth from her hand drew him like a moth to a flame. He stood and took her face gently in his hands. "You're real."

She nodded her head and her smile grew. "I'm real, I'm here, and I'm yours."

Costin savored the words as a lion savors a feast after a kill. He stepped closer to her and lowered his face to hers. His lips brushed against hers as he spoke. "Sally mine, I had lost you," his voice broke on his words, bringing tears to Sally's eyes.

"You didn't. I'm here, love," she tried to reassure him.

He nodded and then pressed his lips to hers. His arms wrapped around her and pulled her tight against him and he felt their bond snap back into place. He groaned as the familiar sensation flowed through him and the light his mate brought to him flooded his heart and soul.

"Mine," he growled against her lips.

"Yours," she agreed.

Fane didn't waste time with words as he reached his mate. He wrapped his arms around her, pulling her flush against him, and kissed her hard. He poured his need, desire, pain, fear, devotion, hope, and love into the kiss. He devoured her as his hands moved up into her hair, wrapping it around his fingers, and angling her head so he could kiss her deeper.

"I missed you," he told her through their mended bond.

She sighed and gave in fully to the kiss. *"I missed you too. I love you."*

"My Luna," he whispered huskily into her mind. *"I love you and I will love you still more tomorrow."*

Vasile stepped back just a little from his mate so that he could look at his brother. He tried to process what he was seeing, but all he could think was that he couldn't believe it.

"How?" he asked.

"I survived in the dark forest," Lucian told him simply. "I have a purpose to fulfill still."

Vasile looked at the Great Luna and she smiled warmly at him.

"Thank you," Vasile told her.

She nodded to him and he saw the love shining from her eyes.

Jen stared at her best friends with wide eyes. She watched as they reunited with their mates and she tried to be patient, but then patience never was her strong suite and she never pretended it was.

"Decebel, take Thia please."

Decebel frowned at her but gently took their daughter in his arms. She pushed away from him as she stood on shaky legs. Thanks to Rachel, she was mostly healed, but she was still weak. Crina and Elle rushed to her side to help her up. There was a blanket wrapped around her waist that made moving even more difficult.

"Jennifer," Decebel growled, "you need to rest. They can come to you."

Jennifer waved him off. "My best friend was dead, my other best friend was off coping with that all alone, and now they are both here... alive. I'm not waiting."

Decebel walked beside her. He was scowling at her but still being gentle as he helped keep her upright with one arm and holding Thia in the other.

"Hmm, hmm," Jen cleared her throat from behind Costin and Fane. Jacque and Sally looked around their mates at the same time and their faces broke into huge smiles. They started to rush towards Jen, but Decebel stepped in front of her to block her.

"Slow and gentle," he said sternly, "she's just given birth."

Their gasps replaced their smiles and then their attention was immediately on Thia. Decebel held her proudly as they oohed and awed over her.

Jen stepped around Decebel and watched as her friends caressed their child and her heart swelled with love and thankfulness. Sally looked up and smiled at Jen. "She's incredible."

Jen wiped away a tear and nodded. "Yeah, I'd have to say we did good." She winked at Decebel and then held her arms open. This time Sally and Jacque moved slower as they wrapped each other in a hug. Lilly too came over and wrapped her arms around all three girls and whispered in Jacque's ear. "I love you; I'm so, so glad you are okay."

Jacque pulled back and looked at her mom. She watched as Cypher came up behind her and wrapped his arms around her protectively. It filled her with warmth inside to see her mom happy and loved.

"I'm so much better than okay, mom, and holy crap, it's good to see you," she said as she threw herself into her mom's arms. Lilly let out a small laugh as she pulled her daughter close.

"It's good to see you too," she looked at Sally and Jen then, "all of you."

Jen looked around, her brow furrowed, and she looked at the Great Luna. "Where is Peri?"

The room was immediately silent as they watched the goddess.

She smiled at them. "She is well, and she told me to tell you three that she would be by very soon to see you."

"I totally just gave birth in a cave, and she has been brought back from the dead and she can't show her undead face to tell me how awesome my kid is?" Jen asked dryly.

"She said she needed to deal with some things," the Great Luna said vaguely.

Jen didn't miss the way Lucian's jaw tensed.

"Uh uhm, I see," Jen eyed Vasile's brother and grinned when he frowned at her.

"Jennifer," Decebel warned as he caught on to her thoughts, and then he nearly lost his balance as he realized their bond was whole and strong again. Jen's eyes met his when she felt him in her mind and she let out a sigh of relief. But then, as quickly as the relief had come, it was replaced with annoyance and anger.

"You're not off the hook, you know," she narrowed her eyes at him. "We are going to be having a serious conversation, and I have a feeling it isn't going to end well for you."

Decebel flashed his devilish smile at her. "Is that a promise?"

The Great Luna stepped forward to the center of the group and looked at them all with love and hope. She bathed the cave in her light, filling them with purpose and renewed strength.

"The deaths brought on by the evil that lived inside of Reyaz were not appointed. It was not their time. Therefore, I stepped in and took back what was mine. These lives restored still have much to give in this life, much to do. Cynthia, my precious child with a heart so full of remorse over her past, chose to give her life in the place of another. It was not her time, but the Fates agreed to it, and I allowed her the free will to choose. There is no greater gift than do die for another, to sacrifice yourself so that another will not suffer. And

Cynthia gave this gift to Thia, to Jennifer, and to Decebel. This child is blessed and great things await her."

"Once again you have stepped up to defend those who needed you. You took the narrow path, one filled with danger and fear, and you didn't give into the need to run—to keep yourself safe. I'm so very proud of you and I love you all. Rest now for a time; rest in my peace and love. Rejoice in your triumph. Celebrate the lives brought back to you and live each day so that you can lie down at night with no regrets. And should you have regrets, know that forgiveness, mercy, grace and the promise of a new day are my assurance to you."

When she had gone, her peace flowed through them. There were hugs and tears of happiness and sorrow.

"I don't know about the rest of you, but I need some hot chocolate," Jen spoke over the other voices.

Jacque and Sally smiled at her.

"Make mine a double," Alina spoke up from behind them.

"You heard the woman," Jen turned to Adam. "Fairy Peri isn't here for me to abuse. I guess you will have to do until she returns. So fairy boy, you and your posse get us home."

Adam's lips quirked up as he looked at her. "I'm going to let that the whole fairy boy slide since you just gave birth and all."

"Dude, you know who my mate is? There will be a whole lot of sliding."

Adam looked over at Decebel who was cooing to his daughter in a very un-Decebel like fashion. He looked back over at Jen. "Forgive me if I'm not shaking in my boots."

Jen smacked Decebel's arm. "Hey, figure out a way to coo and look menacing at the same time please; my happiness on being able to belittle others depends on it."

Decebel rolled his eyes, "Sure baby, I'll get right on that."

He watched her as she moved slowly around their room, straightening this and that, and each time she passed the basinet she would pause and stare down at their Thia. She would wait a few heartbeats to watch her breathing and then she would move on. She had been doing this for the past eight hours since they had returned from the cave. She was exhausted and her emotions were raw and plain as day on her face.

"Jennifer, come here baby," he told her softly, not wanting to disturb Thia. He wanted his little one to get much needed rest because he knew he wouldn't be able to hold off the eager packmates and friends for long. They would want to see the first werewolf child born in a very long time.

Jen turned to glare at him. Though she was so tired and her legs threatened to give out on her at any moment, she had to talk this out. "You are so lucky that we have an infant in this room. You will have to thank your daughter later for saving you from my wrath," she wanted to say she was joking, but she wasn't, not this time. "How could you Decebel? You forfeited your life. You willingly had our bond broken; you pushed me away when I needed you most. I can't even begin to tell you how hurt and angry I am. I love you, god how I love you, and I thank the Great Luna that you are alive and safe, but that does nothing for the anger that I feel right now."

"I know, Jennifer. I knew the minute I did it that I shouldn't, but I didn't know what else to do," he fought to keep his voice calm and low as he tried to make her see, make her understand. "All I could see was you watching our child die in your arms. Over and over it played in my mind and I didn't know how to fix it. It is my job to keep you safe, to protect you from the ugly things in this life, and yet this life—our very existence—is what continually brings the ugly things straight to our doorstep."

He slumped down onto the edge of the bed as he felt the fight rush out of him. "I didn't want to leave you, baby. I was dying a little more each day and my nights were constant torment with no rest. You weren't here in our bed and that was my fault. Your voice didn't fill the empty air and that was my fault." Decebel looked up at her, his eyes locking on hers, beckoning her to come to him, to forgive him, and to accept him. "I love," he paused as he caught his breath, "I love you, and I am sorry that I deceived you. Please, love, please forgive me."

Jen looked on as her mate wilted before her. This was a man who had faced an impossible situation, with no good solution, and he had chosen what he felt was best for his family, the lesser of two evils in his mind. She couldn't say that she wouldn't have made the same decision in his place. She felt her anger seep out of her, leaving only fear. Fear was what truly fueled her rage. She was terrified of losing him, of facing life without him by her side. When she realized that his plan had been to die in place of their daughter, her life had flashed before her eyes. She saw everything. She saw what her life would be without Decebel in it, and there was a huge hole inside of her. There would still be joy because of Thia, but following that joy would always be the anguish of not having Decebel to share it with.

"There is nothing to forgive, Dec, not really. I know why you did it, and it makes me love you more." She walked over to him and closed her eyes when his arms came around her and pulled her against him. Her wolf rumbled her approval of the strong mate that belonged to them, a mate able to provide and protect them.

"Don't leave me, Dec, not ever again." She felt a tear slide down her cheek and opened her eyes to meet his amber ones.

"Never again," he agreed. He leaned forward and pressed his lips to hers and then peppered her jaw line with kisses, down her neck to the mark he had given her. He heard her breath catch and felt her body tense in expectation. "My mate, my wife, my love," he whispered against her flesh, his warm breath causing her to shiver. He chuckled, pleased by her response to him.

"Shut up and bite me already," she growled breathlessly.

"As you wish," he murmured and then sank his teeth deep into her flesh.

Jacque climbed out of the shower, exhausted but clean, which was something that she felt needed to happen immediately once Adam had flashed them back home. She needed to wash away the darkness that clung to her like a sticky film. It leached the joy from her and was a constant reminder of the things that had transpired that day.

"Feel better?" Fane asked as she came out of the bathroom wrapped in a robe.

"Cleaner at least," she told him with a small smile.

"Are you going to call your dad?"

Jacque shook her head. "Not right now. I need some time. I feel like my nerves are exposed to the elements; everything is just so raw."

Fane nodded. "I know what you mean." He ran his hand through his hair and clasped the back of his neck and with a huff of skepticism he said. "I thought I was going to lose you and all I could think about was how I would take my life so that I could be with you."

"Fane," Jacque hurried to him and grabbed his face and pressed her lips to his. He immediately responded to her and kissed her back. His hands came up and caressed her face, down her neck and shoulders, and rested on her hips. He pulled her against him with a deep growl. He took comfort in her touch; he found solace and peace in her love. "I'm here now; we're here," she told him as she tilted her head back so he could kiss her neck down to her collar bone.

Fane pushed the robe aside bearing her shoulders and then pushed it away completely. Her skin was soft under his hands and flushed under his gaze. He smiled at her and knew she felt the depth of the love that shone in his eyes. "You're here," he whispered as he picked her up in his arms and walked to their bed. "You're mine," he laid her down and covered her body with his own, protecting her, claiming her, loving her. "I am so thankful that I moved in across the street from you, Jacquelyn. I am so incredibly thankful that you took me as your mate, your husband, friend, and lover," his voice dropped and grew husky, "and I will spend the rest of our lives showing you just how thankful I am."

Jacque welcomed her mate, his passion, and his love. She soaked it up as a parched plant soaks up water, and she returned it with her own. There was still much to do, and she was sure they would be needed again to stand up to evil, but tonight they would rest. Tonight they would celebrate their victory, their survival, and new life.

"Do you need anything?" Costin asked her for the fifth time since they had gotten home. She was tired but otherwise completely okay. His mind was still having a hard time grasping on to this fact since he had watched her die, held her still body in his arms, and felt the horror of it in his soul only a few hours ago.

"Costin love, I'm alright. I feel perfect, just tired," she told him—again.

He smiled at her and pressed a kiss to her forehead. He fought the urge to pick her up and wrap her in his arms, to take her away from anything that could harm her ever again. He knew that wasn't realistic, but that didn't stop him from wishing it could be.

"How about a shower, a story, and then bed?"

Sally looked at him curiously. "A story?"

Costin grinned and his deep dimple flashed at her. "It's about this amazing gypsy who loved her people, and her mate, so much that she gave everything up for them. Now, shower," he pointed to the bathroom, "story after."

Costin pulled Sally onto his lap as they sat on the couch. Her wet hair stuck to his face. As he nuzzled her neck, his wolf let out a growl of contentment.

"Okay let's hear it," she teased him.

Costin took a deep breath and let it out before he started his tale. "Once upon a time there was a gypsy healer. She had been blessed by the Great Luna to minister to a pack of Canis lupus, healing them when they were injured or sick and protecting them when no one else could. She was brave, strong, honest, and breathtakingly beautiful."

"Okay, now you're stretching it a bit."

Costin tapped her on the nose in admonishment. "Shh, no interrupting or you don't get intermission."

"What happens at intermission?" she asked with a coy smile.

"If you will be quiet, you will get to find out," Costin kissed her quickly and then continued with his story. "She had a mate, one of the wolves had been given to her. The wolf considered her his precious gift, and he was madly in love with her. She only had to breathe and she captivated him. His life before her had been bleak, and he lived only for the next laugh. But those were becoming few and far between as the darkness crept into his soul. But she changed all that. She embraced him as her own, and he claimed her and let her know that not even death would keep them apart. He had explained that it was the nature of their mated pairs that when one died, the other followed and did so gladly.

One day, one horrible day, evil came knocking at their door. It broke their bond, ripping them apart, and then it wrapped itself around their loved ones and began to strangle them, and this precious healer could only stand by and watch," he paused and looked at her, "or could she?" his words were a whisper. "She knew of something that could save them and could keep her people and her mate safe. She pleaded with him to understand and needed him to know that she was not choosing others over him, but that she was choosing life for him and the others under her care. He watched helplessly as she sacrificed her life, giving the ultimate gift to those who needed her.

Her mate held her still body, kissed her lifeless lips, and begged for death to take him so that he could be with her. She was his light, and now all he could see was darkness."

He lifted her chin and kissed her deeply while running his fingers along her jaw. He smiled when she giggled as he nipped her skin.

"Wait," she said pushing on his chest. "Aren't you going to tell the rest? That seems like a sad place to end."

Costin shook his head. "It's intermission. We need some happiness after all that doom and gloom. Then I will be able to tell you the rest." He silenced her protest with another kiss and pushed all thoughts of the story from her mind.

"How long is intermission exactly," she asked him nearly two hours later.

Costin looked at his wrist, where there was no watch. "Well, we've gone a little over, but I got a little carried away at the snack counter."

Sally's mouth dropped open as she looked at him. "Did you just call me a snack counter?"

Costin grinned shamelessly. "Totally did."

"That's it; intermission is officially over." Sally stood from the bed grabbing the sheet to wrap around her.

Costin stood, following her shaking his head. "Nope, not quite yet, mate. Now it's time for a bathroom break."

Sally laughed as he picked her up and carried her to their bathroom.

"Costin, I don't have to go to pee, and even if I did I wouldn't do it in front of you. Put me down."

Costin laughed and smacked her lightly on her backside. "Who said anything about peeing?"

Epilogue

"There is no journey as great as the journey of life. We are brought into this world with a purpose for our lives and then given free will to make the choice to fulfill our purpose, or not. We are given the choice to love selflessly, to forgive endlessly, and to give sacrificially. Some days we will get it right and we will rejoice, and then some days we will screw it up so good that we wonder if there is any hope for us. Rest assured, my friend, there is always hope…Unless you are mated to a werewolf, then you have two choices; make yourself a nice hand bag, or run—fast and far." ~Perizada

Six weeks had passed since the showdown with Reyaz. "Are you ever going to let anyone else hold her?" Jen asked Decebel as he sat rocking Thia in their room.

Decebel looked up from his daughter and curled a lip at his mate, revealing white, sharp teeth.

Jen rolled her eyes. "Babe, you keep trying to intimidate me and all it does is turn me on; you'd think you'd learn."

Decebel grinned. "Who says I'm trying to intimidate you?"

Jen laughed as she came over and took Thia from him. He frowned at her and stood to follow her. "Relax B, I'm just laying her in her crib so she can sleep."

"She can sleep while I hold her," he argued.

Jen gently laid Thia in her crib and then turned back to her mate. She propped a hand on her hip and tilted her head at him. "Okay, so if you are holding her, then how can you be holding me?"

Decebel stared at her blankly.

Jen let out a huff. "Seriously, I have to spell this out for you? And here I thought I mated to the smart one," she grumbled as she walked away. He followed her from the small nursery they had added on to their bedroom suite and back into the main room.

His eyes narrowed as he watched her walk around their room, her hips swaying seductively. He felt his lips spreading into a smile yet again. He seemed to be doing that a lot lately. "Are you saying what I think you're saying?"

Jen stopped. Maybe the pointless straightening up she had been doing in the hopes that she would catch his eye had actually worked. "That depends, if what you think I'm saying is that I want you to hold me gently and whisper sweet nothings, then no, I'm definitely not saying that."

Decebel stalked towards her, his movements slow and deliberate. "And if what I think your saying is more along the lines of me holding you," he paused and chuckled when she shivered, "down…,"

"Looks like we have a winner," she interrupted and grabbed his hand. She pulled him to their bed and waggled her eyebrows at him. "So, you feeling up to it, or is being a daddy wearing you out too much?"

Decebel didn't dignify her question with an answer verbally, but instead pushed her onto their bed and showed her just how not worn out he was.

Jen lay sprawled across Decebel's chest as he ran his fingers through her hair. Relaxed and well-loved, she stretched like a satisfied cat waking from a long nap and then looked up at him.

"Don't ever do it again."

Decebel frowned. "Don't ever make love to you again?"

Jen snorted. "No butthead. Don't ever think of sacrificing yourself without running it by me first. I should at least be given first dibs on killing you if you want to plan something so freaking stupid without talking to me."

Decebel pulled her closer and kissed the tip of her nose. "Don't be angry with me, baby. I thought we were past this."

Jen fidgeted with the sheet, not wanting to meet his gaze. "I was…."

"What happened?" He put a finger under her chin and gently lifted it so he could see her eyes.

"I dreamt that I'd lost you and that I had to raise Thia alone."

Decebel saw the hurt and fear in them. "Baby I'm not going anywhere, and I promise if I decide I need to die for some worthy cause, I will discuss it with you first."

Jen couldn't help but smile at him. She wasn't mad, not really. She knew why he had done it. She couldn't say that she wouldn't have done the same thing and she was incredibly proud and honored to have a mate who would sacrifice so much for her and their child, but she still felt the need to remind him that he should have talked to her about it.

"Hey," he said softly.

"Hey," she smiled back. She squealed when he deftly flipped them so that he was on top of her.

"Have I told you what an incredible mother you are?"

She blushed at his compliment and nodded.

Decebel stared down into her blue eyes and took in her beautiful face. She was his and she was precious to him. She brought him joy and life when he was sure he would never have those things, and now she had given him a miracle in their little Thia. He closed his eyes briefly just to take in her scent and enjoy the feel of her against him and reminded himself to never take her for granted. He had nearly lost her more than once, and it had taught him to drench himself in the joy of being her mate.

"What are you thinking?" she asked him.

"Our bond is wide open, love. You know what I'm thinking."

"I want you to *tell* me B. Tell me what you think."

She ran her hands through his hair and down his back, drawing a deep growl from him.

He felt his canines lengthen and the urge to bite her and to mark her grew strong as his wolf perked up at the feel and smell of their mate.

"I think you are the most incredible woman I've ever met. I treasure you. Every single piece of you inside and out is precious to me. I love you, Jennifer, with a love that is so desperate, deep, and unwavering. You bring me joy and peace, and light up my dark world." He looked into her eyes and lowered his head to kiss her. She tasted like his, felt like his, and moved like his.

"I *am* yours," she told him, "and you, fur ball, are mine."

Fane paced restlessly in their bedroom as he waited for Jacque. His mind was a jumbled mess and his nerves were on edge.

"Would you calm down," she told him as she opened the bathroom door and came out.

He stepped in front of her and cupped her face, searching her eyes for any emotion that would give him a tiny clue. "Well?"

She nodded as a huge grin spread across her face and then squealed when he picked her up and swung her around as he laughed joyously. When he set her back down on the ground, he kissed her deep and long, enjoying her taste and savoring her touch.

He paused and looked at her. "I told you we'd have a child one day." He kissed her again and then pulled back to nip her bottom lip.

"Are you happy?" she asked him. "I mean, you're not…you don't think it's too soon?"

Fanes brow rose as he looked at his mate in amusement. "I'm ecstatic, love. To see you carrying my child, to see you glowing with life, and to know that we made this…" he pressed his hand to her flat stomach, "our love did this."

Jacque felt the tears starting and she fought against them, though they were happy tears. She felt she had cried quite enough in the past weeks for one lifetime. "I love you, Fane."

He pressed his forehead to hers and let out a slow breath. "Heaven help me, Jacquelyn, I love you more than you could possibly understand."

"When do you want to tell everyone?" she asked him.

"That depends on you, love,"

Jacque frowned. "Why?"

"Because you need to be ready to endure Jen's ribbing."

Jacque groaned. "Bloody hell, I'm going to have to listen to big butt jokes, comments about my boobs getting bigger and never bouncing back to where they belong, and snide remarks about me not being able to get off the couch. Crap you're right. Let's not tell them until I go into labor."

Fane laughed. "I think they will figure it out at some point."

"Okay, well then we'll have to move to plan B."

"I'm afraid to ask, but like looking at a bad wreck, I have to know. What's plan B?"

"I'm going to kidnap the Alpha female of the Serbia pack."

"That's makes no sense."

"Doesn't have to, it is what it is, Fane. Get on board or jump ship."

Fane's brow rose as he looked at his mate, his incredible mate, and he grinned.

"Fine, we'll kidnap her," he agreed dryly, playing along.

Jacque squealed. "I've always wanted to kidnap someone."

Fane shook his head at her. "Sometimes, love, you scare me."

Jacque eyes narrowed and she let her wolf out just enough for them to glow. "You should be afraid wolf-man, very afraid."

"Costin, I swear if you toss one more bottle in the air I'm going to go all Jen on you," Sally warned. He was getting the bar ready for the night and had decided to show off for her with his fancy tricks. And she would be okay with that if he hadn't dropped the last three bottles because he was checking her out. And she totally wasn't distracting him on purpose.

"Let me turn on the music so you'll have a beat you can strip to," he teased.

Sally threw her hands in the air. "I didn't mean her strip routine, you beast, and you know it."

"Maybe, but I did get a good blush out of you, so mission accomplished. Now come over here and let me teach you how to make sex on a beach," Costin's grin got even wider as Sally's blush deepened. She shook her head at him. "Okay, how about a screwdriver or a hairy virgin?"

She was laughing now but still shaking her head at him.

Costin pretended to think about it and then snapped his fingers. "I've got it, you totally have to learn how to make this one, screaming org—,"

"FINE," she cut him off, "I'll learn the first one, just quit hollering them out already." She walked over to the bar and nudged her grinning mate out of the way. "Okay 'O great bartender, please teach me your ways."

She felt his breath on the back of her neck as he stepped up close behind her. Sally froze just as she started to turn a glass over. She trembled as his warm breath tickled her skin and she nearly moaned out loud when he pressed his lips to her ear. She was expecting a flippant, flirty remark, and she wouldn't have minded it. It was one of the things she loved about him. But every now and then, he surprised her.

"You are so beautiful." His hands gripped her hips and she felt his fingers squeeze and bite into her skin. "In all my life I never imagined I would be blessed with someone like you." He paused and she held her breath, waiting for what he would do next and knowing it would be something that might just make her pass out.

His next words were punctuated with breathtaking kisses on her skin. "You honor me, Sally mine," he kissed her neck. "You amaze me," then below her ear. "You bring life and passion to my world," then on the other side of her neck. "I love you more than anything," then he kissed his bite mark. He held onto her as she gasped, and Sally gripped the bar to steady herself. She closed her eyes and leaned back into his chest. His lips still hovered over her skin and his arms wrapped around her holding her securely.

He had written those words on her heart, and she never tired of hearing him say things like that to her. She reveled in it, and she forced herself to believe him because it wasn't only by his words that she felt the truth, it was in his actions as well. Since he had watched her die, he had become even more attentive and showed her his serious side more often. But gradually his playfulness was returning and it brought her joy to see her mate healing from such a traumatic experience.

She looked over her shoulder at him and smiled. "Thank you, Costin, for loving me."

He leaned down and kissed her lips gently and stared into her big brown eyes. "You don't have to thank me for that. It's a blessing to get to love you. But if we're throwing around thank yous, then you can totally toss me one for last night."

And he's back, she thought to herself. Sally turned in his arms and gently pushed him back, giving him a playful smirk. "If that's the case, mate, then I think you owe me." She tapped her finger on her lips and looked up at the ceiling seemingly in thought, "four, wait," her eyes widened and she grinned, "no make that five; you owe me five thank yous."

Costin chuckled as he reached out to snatch her around the waist. "You've been hanging around Jen too much, Sally mine. She's rubbing off on you." He nipped her ear playfully.

Sally snorted. "You weren't complaining last n—,"

Costin whipped her around and pinned her to the bar and pressed his lips to hers before she could finish her sentence.

"Behave," he growled in her mind.

He heard her laughter through their bond and he wanted to howl with joy.

"Only if you do."

"That's going to be a problem."

Sally pulled back from the kiss and winked "That's what I'm counting on."

Perizada

"I've decided to move. To hang up my fairy magic and move to an obscure little town, buy a creepy looking house, and fill it with cats. Every day I'll walk to the mail box, talking to myself and yelling profanities at annoying neighbors. Yep, I'm going to be *that* lady. Why, you ask? Well, because right now, that is looking a whole freaking lot better than my current situation. Yeah, it's that bad."

"So kind of you to grace us with your presence," Jen said as Peri appeared in the library where Jacque, Sally, and she were drinking hot chocolate and staring at Thia like she was the best thing since sliced bread, which she was, so it was totally appropriate.

"I've been busy," Peri snapped as she walked over to where they sat on the floor, circling the little baby that was lying on a blanket. "Now quit your whining and let me see the crumb catcher."

Jen reached down and picked Thia up and handed her to Peri. Peri held her with one hand under her neck and one under her bottom, holding her up in front of her face so she could get a good look at her.

"I have to admit, she's beautiful," Peri smiled at her. She tucked her into a football hold and then leaned down and kissed her forehead. Then she whispered something the others couldn't hear. A soft glow emitted off of Peri and enveloped her and Thia for several seconds and then was gone.

The girls stared at the fae with opened mouths.

"Okay, what was that?" Jen motioned to the area around Peri where the glowing had been.

Peri waved her hand at her as if batting the question away. "Mind your own business. That was between me and Thia."

"Fine, whatevs," Jen said with a shrug, "let's talk about what's really important. Why are you hiding?"

Peri's eyes narrowed at the Alpha. "I'm not hiding."

Jen smiled knowingly. "Oh Peri fairy, I'm totally in the know, so you might as well just spill it."

Jacque frowned. "What are you in the know about? You didn't tell us you were in the know. Sally, did you know she was in the know?" she rambled quickly as she looked from Jen to Sally then Peri and then back to Jen.

Sally shook her head. "I never know jack around here so welcome to my world."

"I haven't really had time to tell you guys because I've been investigating. I wanted my facts straight first," she told them, sounding a tad defensive.

"What investigating?" Peri asked as she narrowed her eyes.

"There's been a certain wolf hanging around the Romanian, and sometimes Serbian, mansions. And I might have followed him one day to Vasile's office. And I might have heard him say that he knew who his mate was when Vasile hinted that he would have a good chance of finding a mate now that the fae were compatible. And I might have noticed that said wolf has some new art work running up his neck."

"No!?"

"Seriously!?"

Jacque and Sally spoke together as they gasped at the same time. They both looked at Peri with wide eyes.

Peri wouldn't look at either of them, but she just stared down at Thia, smiling when she grasped her finger in her tiny hand.

"Lucian?" Jacque finally spoke after several minutes of shocked silence. "You're mated to Lucian?"

"No!" Peri growled. "There has been no mating."

Jen grinned. "There's a bond though isn't there? You guys can totally talk to one another. SHUT UP!" Jen exclaimed as she clapped her hands. "Wait, do you have markings? I mean his changed so you must have them now."

Again, Peri refused to look at them.

"Peri, you can't run from this forever," Sally said gently.

"I'm not running," Peri disagreed. "Okay, so I am hiding; I know better than to run from a predator. But hiding is a fae specialty."

"So you aren't interested in him at all?" Jacque asked. "You don't find him the least bit attractive?"

"I didn't say that, but you all know that there is no way I can be mated to a wolf. It would be like setting gun powder next to an open flame."

Jen made an exploding motion with her hands as she said, "Fireworks, baby." She smiled at her, "You're telling me you're scared of a little fireworks?"

"I haven't told you anything you, brat. You keep putting words in my mouth."

"Well, I feel it's my duty as your friend and designated know-it-all to tell you that there are a few females in my pack who are totally not scared of fireworks." She shrugged. "I'm just sayin. You got this hot wolf walking around clueless about anything and everything in this new world, and these chicks are more than happy to share their knowledge, if you know what I mean."

Peri's lips tightened as she listened to Jen tell her things she didn't want to hear and didn't want to be upset about, but she was anyway. She stood stiffly and handed Jacque the sleeping child gently and then stepped back from the girls. Her emotions were all over the place and she didn't want to inadvertently hurt anyone. She looked at Jen and steeled herself for the words that she knew she didn't mean but had to say because they were true.

"He deserves a wolf mate, someone not jaded by the world or bitter from seeing too much death. He's been through much and will need someone with patience and a gentle touch and we all know I have neither of those things. He should choose someone else."

"Peri you know that's not how it works," Jacque argued. "The Great Luna has matched you two. You're missing half of your soul. You have probably always felt something was missing. Now you know, and there is only one man who can give it to you."

Peri shook her head. "Well the Great Luna got it wrong. I can't be anyone's mate. You're telling me that he has half of my soul, right?" The girls nodded. "That means I have the other half of his, and I can tell you that if that's the case, then he got screwed because what little bit of soul that was in me has been shattered. So you see, he has to have someone else."

The three girls jumped when the library door suddenly flew open and crashed into the wall. Jacque tightened her hold on Thia and looked down at her to make sure she was alright. She was still sound asleep. *Good thing she's gotten used to males who have absolutely no manners and are basically like bulls in a china shop*, she thought as she watched the wolf at the door walk coolly into the room.

He was big, he was angry, and he was looking right at Peri.

Jen grinned to herself. *"Dec you're totally missing this. Bring me some popcorn. Lucian has that look you get in your eyes when you're pissed at me, so we might see some action."*

She heard Decebel's annoyed growl through their bond which only made her smile wider.

Peri stared at Lucian as he walked into the room. He was bigger than she remembered and, as it pained her to admit, was incredibly hot. She didn't think she was too bad herself. I mean someone her age should be, well, dust, and she didn't look a day over twenty, okay twenty-five, but Lucian was in a whole other league.

His eyes glowed and his presence filled the room, making it feel incredibly crowded. He took several more steps toward her and then stopped. He was within touching distance. A couple steps closer and he would totally be in licking distance. *Stop it Peri*, she snarled at herself. She kept the bond that had opened between them the moment their eyes had met in the forest, when the Great Luna had restored her life, closed tight. That sort of intimacy freaked her out and, frankly, she was tired of being freaked out.

"There is no other for me," Lucian told her in his oddly formal way. She reminded herself that he was centuries behind them in social knowledge and that only meant that his dominance and chivalry were going to be off the stinking charts. "You are my mate; you are exactly what I need and exactly what I want. Whatever it is inside you that you feel is broken, it is my duty and my honor to mend you, and where I am broken, you will mend me. That is what it means to be mates, Perizada. You have been alone for a long time, as have I. You do not have to be alone any longer."

"Bloody hell," Jen whispered, "how do you say no to that?"

"Right?" Jacque and Sally said at the same time.

Peri just stood there looking up at Lucian, at her mate, and then finally said the only thing she could think of, "I'm so screwed."

From the author

This is the final story for the three girls and the fur balls we have grown to love. But, it's not the end of the road for all of our GWS characters. Stay tuned for Book One of my new series, Into the Fae, coming soon.

How do I even begin to express what this series has meant to me? When I wrote Prince of Wolves I never dreamed it would turn into seven books. I never imagined that others would love these characters as much as I do, and yet here we are. I am so proud of this series and I'm sad to see it end. I hope that I have ended it in such a way that you feel the girls are getting their HEAs. This book was a nightmare to write.

First, because I cried through most of it - second, because I wanted it to be freaking awesome and third, because I wanted it to be freaking awesome. I don't know if I've succeeded, but I pray that I have met your high expectations.

There are eight books in The Grey Wolves series. However, the final story belongs to Vasile and Alina. The characters will be different, since they met over two centuries ago. I'm excited and terrified about it but then that's pretty much my norm for every book I write.

So, though this is sort of the end for this series, there are exciting things to come! Thank you so much for joining me in this journey. Thank you for cheering these characters on, for yelling at them, crying with them, telling them to get a freaking clue, and for loving them. You all have blessed me beyond measure with your support and I'm humbled by it.

Sincerely,

Quinn

Printed in Great Britain
by Amazon